PINEY HILL

a novel

To Morgan
Hope you enjoy this !
Anita Foster
4-4-2023

Anita Roper Foster

Published by Yawn Publishing LLC
2555 Marietta Hwy, Ste 103
Canton, GA 30114
www.yawnspublishing.com

Library of Congress Control Number: 2022913348

ISBN: 978-1-954617-44-5

Printed in the United States

Front cover image by Gudrun Chadwick, Canton, Georgia

Dedication

For my grandsons,
The Foster Boys,
Luke, Andrew, Will, and Daniel

"Between every two pines there is a doorway to a new world."
-- John Muir

Prelude

The mountain community that I grew up in was called Piney Hill. If you blinked, you would miss it. There was no sign on the road announcing its existence at the foot of the Blue Ridge Mountains in North Georgia. The people who lived in Piney Hill had called it so since they arrived, Cherokee Land Lottery deed in hand, and turned the first red furrow at its base.

Piney Hill was more like a short mountain really, covered with loblolly and Virginia pines and lined with roads of crusty red dirt. The road curved up to the mountaintop and switch-backed down to the main dirt road below. All along this one-lane road going up the mountain were roads that veered off and led to the various farms and pastures that had been on top of the mountain for ages. These were the farms of my family.

There were barns weathered by the heat of the hot Georgia sun, their siding crackled by the winds and rains of harsh winters. You could see them peeking through the creaking boughs of the pine thickets. If you didn't know better you would think the barns had grown out of the ground with the trees, so close were their colors and textures.

Woods, pastures, family, and church were a constant for me during my childhood. I lived my young life within this small circle, that governed my being and guided my conscience. It was a different time. A man's word and his handshake were as good as money. And it was a time when, if a child knew about something bad that someone had done, that knowledge would stick in his or her throat like a piece of dry biscuit until it finally got spit out. I learned about conflicts of conscience during the summer I was ten years old. That summer brought us one of the worst heatwave our small community had ever known. Heat that even midnight didn't cool.

The grown-ups talked about how hot it was. Record-setting, they said. During that summer, mothers fussed if a child emptied the ice trays and forgot to fill them up. Oscillating fans hummed on coffee tables and linoleum floors, doing little to soothe the babies that had been left there to nap on top of pallets made from old quilts.

Daddies, uncles, grandpas, and older brothers plowed the dusty fields and baled hay, their skin as brown as a catcher's mitt. Hot and sticky, they returned home to their suppers only to find there was no ice for their sweet tea.

The heat did not bother me. School was out, and I had a lot of playing to do before it started back in the fall. My only problems were chiggers, poison ivy, and getting splinters in my bare feet. I was carefree, and my mama allowed me to roam our property, barn, and pastures from daylight until dark, as long as I came home before the sun set and made sure I closed the pasture gates behind me.

But then things happened to change all that. Events that caused mothers to rein in their kids, demanding that they stay in the yard. That summer was when the old Landers' place burned to the ground, and a convict working on the chain gang escaped. And that is the summer that *she* arrived. During chaos, calamity, and confinement, she appeared unexpectedly, like a yellow butterfly landing on top of the sunbaked clay.

That would be a summer that I would never forget, along with a year whose dramas and lessons would go with me throughout the rest of my life.

Summer, 1968
No. 1

I had a diary, of sorts. It was an old composition book that I filled with events from my daily life. I was ten years old and really wanted one like my friends had with a lock and key, but we did not get things like that except on special occasions. I remember I had been saving nickels and dimes in an old coffee can so that I could buy my own, but nickels and dimes for a ten-year-old were about as scarce as new diaries. I was also saving for a horse. A spotted Indian pony like I saw on television. My imagination had me riding like a cowgirl in a wild west show, hair flying out behind me as I spurred my pony around the arena.

Try as she may, my mother could not instill in me the more ladylike qualities of my sister. "If you are going to play wild west," she would sigh, "why can't you be like Donna and not act so wild?" But I was not that kind of child, and she knew it. Between westerns, jungle stories, and all of those old movies about Egyptian mummies, my mind was sparked with thoughts of adventure. Sometimes, the adventure presented itself in the most curious ways. Such as the mysterious fire at the Landers' place and the events of that day that sparked more adventure for me than I had bargained for.

July 2, 1968

Dear Diary,

It's my bedtime and it's hot as blue blazes! I can't hardly go to sleep. I'm sweatin so much! I'm gonna to meet Trixie at the creek in the mornin and we are gonna build a dam so we can swim.

I'm gonna make me a ape-man suit and we might even build a tree house.
Brownie

I woke up with my sweaty pajama top stuck to my back. It was eight in the morning and already the humidity hung damp and heavy in our house. The bedroom that I shared with my sister was bright with sunlight. The curtains hanging at the open window lay still, waiting for a breeze to move them. But no wind stirred. Just the hot, stifling Georgia air sliding in on a beam of bright sunlight.

I walked into the living room where my little brother, Roger, was watching cartoons. He was lying on his stomach in front of the television eating a bowl of cereal. Roger laughed, and the spoon missed his mouth, sending little red and yellow balls rolling underneath the couch. He was seven. Roger's hair, like my mother's and sister's, was white blonde. I noticed that the back of his neck was sunburned.

I was the dark one. My dark brown hair and eyes came from my grandmother's Cherokee blood. People said I looked like my Daddy; that made me proud.

Mama was in the kitchen, as she was every morning. She was wearing a yellow house dress and was barefoot. My mother, just a girl herself, was pretty with her hair in a shiny blonde ponytail and just a smear of pink lipstick adorning her face. She was talking on the telephone that was mounted to the kitchen wall. My sister Donna, an exact replica of her, was standing next to Mama.

Donna was seventeen, and all she ever thought about these days was fashion and boys. I asked my sister who was on the phone, and she mouthed that it was Aunt Janelle. Donna and our mother's sister were only four years apart, so Donna had more in common with our aunt than I did. I got a bowl and a box of cereal out of the cabinet, but when I tipped the box over my bowl, nothing came out but a cloud of cereal dust.

"Rah-geer!" I cried, "You ate all the cereal!" Donna scowled at me and told me to hush. Mama put the telephone receiver back into its cradle and turned around. My sister began flipping through the instructions that came out of a box of permanent wave. "What's going on?" I said as I smeared peanut butter on a piece of bread.

"Aunt Janelle is coming to fix Donna's hair," Mama said, looking me over. "Don't you want her to cut your hair too? Your pixie is getting a little shaggy." I shook my head and took a bite of my sandwich. "We've got revival comin' up," Mama continued, "You need your hair cut before then." I went to the sink and filled a glass with water. When I had swallowed, I said, "It'll make me itchy, all that hair stickin' to my sweat. And besides, I'm gonna meet Trixie at the creek." Mama sighed and went to the sink to wash dishes.

Donna had left the room but returned shortly with a teen magazine. She was showing Mama a picture of the hairstyle she wanted. They had forgotten about me, so I hurried to the bedroom to change out of my pajamas. After putting on a pair of cut-off blue jeans and a sleeveless shirt, I slipped out the backdoor and down the steps.

I had almost made it out of the yard with my bicycle when I heard Daddy holler, "Brownie! Go git a knife and cut the squash." He was headed to the chicken house to feed and did not even look up. I sighed and turned around to head back up the driveway. I knew there was no use to whine.

I was just pulling open the screen door to get a knife from the kitchen when a long, beige four-door sedan pulled up and parked underneath the shade tree at the side of the house. I watched as Miz Jenkins, our neighbor, heaved herself out of the passenger seat. She was wearing a red, checkered dress and a pair of clunky brown shoes. I thought she looked like a picnic table that had sat up and took off walking. Her thick, black glasses magnified the permanent scowl on her face. Miz Jenkins reached inside the car and took out a black handbag that she slung over her arm as she slammed the car door. Her husband Earl took his hat off and started fanning himself. "I'll be back in a minute, Earl", she said. "You just stay in the car." Mr. Jenkins looked sheepishly at his wife and nodded.

I had known Mr. and Miz Jenkins all my life. Miz Jenkins played the piano at Gethsemane Baptist Church, where our family attended. Her husband Earl was a disabled veteran and did not work. I had heard some people say that he was shell-shocked. It made him look nervous all the time.

Mister and Miz Jenkins lived at the bottom of Piney Hill in a little house beside Merchant's store. Miz Jenkins worked in our school lunchroom at Piney Hill Elementary. But even though they went to the same church as me and I saw her every day during school, Miz Jenkins had never said more than two words to me. Mr. Jenkins hardly talked at all. Sometimes I thought that getting his leg shot off in Korea changed his personality somehow. It made me wonder if that was why Miz Jenkins bossed him so. Mr. and Miz Jenkins had never had children.

"Hey Miz Jenkins," I said. Miz Jenkins pushed past me without saying a word. She opened the screen door and walked right into the house, letting the door go with a loud bang. I followed her onto the back porch and watched her walk into the kitchen.

"Jeanette!" she hollered. I followed Miz Jenkins into the kitchen where Mama was washing Donna's hair in the sink. Mama jumped at the sound of Miz Jenkins' voice and slung soap suds all over the floor. Looking flustered, she told Donna to finish up her hair.

"Hey, Edna," Mama said. "You scared me." Miz Jenkins walked over to the table and pulled out a chair to sit down. She grunted as she did so. "You hear 'bout Frances Landers?" Miz Jenkins asked. "'Bout that hussy that her boy Lonnie married down in Flo-ree-dur?" It was clear by Miz Jenkins' rapid-fire statements that she wanted to gossip.

Mama wrapped Donna's hair in a towel. She looked at the clock then back at Donna. "Go in the bathroom and comb your hair out. Aunt Janell will be here in a minute." Then mama saw me and said, "Tina, go outside." I went out onto the porch. And just so Mama would think I was gone, I opened the screen door and gave it a slam. Then I tip-toed back and stood just outside the kitchen door to listen. "No," Mama said, "I haven't heard a thing."

Mis Jenkins blew out her cheeks. "Well, Frances is in the hospital with a heart attack and may not live." Miz Jenkins shook her head and blew her cheeks out again, "Frances didn't know that her boy was married six months before he died. You remember Lonnie, don't ye? Skinny, bookish young 'un?" Miz Jenkins fixed her gaze on Mama waiting for a response. "Yes," Mama said, "I knew Lonnie. He moved to Miami, didn't he?"

"Yeah, he got kilt when his boat blowed up this past spring. They never fount his body. Frances was so pitiful. Henry dead and then her only child kilt like that. Just pitiful." Miz Jenkins shook her head and blew out her cheeks again.

"Frances had a bad heart and with all this trouble and her trying to keep that big ole place up well, it'uz takin' it's toll. Anyway, this woman shows up a day or two ago and tells Frances that her and Lonnie was married before he got kilt. Can you believe 'at? Well, let me tell you another

5

thing, Jeanette. That woman is as brown as a mud pie! I seed her yesterday." Miz Jenkins paused for effect. "Says her name is Lola and tells Frances that the farm that was left to Lonnie now belongs to her! Well, Frances had a heart attack and is in the hospital and that darkie woman is living in her house!" Miz Jenkins was breathing hard, and her face was red and sweaty. I wondered if Mama would offer her a glass of water.

"Well, that's awful about Miz Frances," Mama said, "but the other is none of our business." Mama was watching the driveway, expecting Aunt Janelle to pull up any minute. Miz Jenkins always made Mama nervous.

Miz Jenkins pulled herself up from the chair and prepared to leave. "Well, I consider it *my* business! Frances is my cousin. And if you ask me," she said, "the whole thang's sapicious. We will have to keep an eye on that woman, Jeanette. You mark my word. She'll cause trouble in the community." I heard heavy clomping footsteps and barely got out of the way when Miz Jenkins stormed out the kitchen. She walked right past me and out the screen door, slamming it on her way out. I walked down the steps behind her. To be such a large woman, she sure could walk fast.

Miz Jenkins found her husband sound asleep in the car with his head on the steering wheel. Miz Jenkins got into the passenger seat and slammed the door. The noise startled Mr. Jenkins and caused him to lean on the horn, blowing it loudly. "Earl!" Miz Jenkins cried. "Quit blowing the horn! You'll cause Boyd's chickens to pack up!"

I walked over to the pump house and stood there while Mr. Jenkins backed the beige sedan up and turned around to drive out of the driveway. Just in time too, because Aunt Janelle passed them coming up the driveway in her compact car.

The two vehicles had stirred up a cloud of dry, red dust. Aunt Janelle's car radio was blasting a country song through her open windows. I walked over when she got the car stopped and opened her door.

"Well, hey there, Brownie Rivers!" Aunt Janelle cried. "You can help me get my stuff out of the car." Aunt Janelle and Mama were as different as night and day. Where Mama had white blonde hair and was slim and petite with a gentle nature, Aunt Janelle was a strawberry blonde with a big bosom and a hot temper. She was wearing bright orange knee pants with a tropical tank top to match, hot pink flip-flops, and no makeup. A river of freckles streamed across her nose.

"Was that Ole Busy Body I saw leavin'?" she asked as she lifted her train case of curlers out of the backseat. "Yes ma'am," I said, heaving a brown grocery bag of stuff onto my hip and slamming the backdoor of her car.

"I can't stand that woman!" said Aunt Janelle. "She saw me in the bank the other day and told me that I had better watch myself or I was going to ruin my reputation! And she said it in front of my friends from the courthouse!" Aunt Janelle was fuming as she walked through the screen door, slamming it in my face. "Hey, Janette," she called, "let's get going! I've got a date with Dwayne at four o'clock!"

Mama was at the sink where Donna was sitting straddle of a backwards-facing kitchen chair. Mama wrapped a bath towel around her shoulders and secured it with a clothes pin. "Well, we've been waiting on *you!*" Mama had her hands on her hips. "Donna's hair has dried, so you'll have to wet it before you cut it."

Aunt Janelle gave a wave of dismissal and sat her stuff on the table. She walked over to the refrigerator and took a metal ice tray out of the freezer. Grabbing the lever on the tray with her bright orange fingernails, she popped it open and plopped some ice cubes into a glass. Then, she rummaged in her grocery sack and took out a glass bottle of diet soda. Aunt Janelle took a bottle opener out of the drawer and opened it. I watched as she poured the fizzy diet drink over ice. Aunt Janelle took a long gulp before answering Mama.

"Well, it won't take me long to do a cut and a perm" she said, waving her hand around as if it were no big deal. "You know, a Toni shouldn't be left in too long." Aunt Janelle rinsed her glass out and refilled it with water. She got a comb and walked over to Donna who was showing her the style she wanted. Since it looked like it was going to get boring in the kitchen, I turned to leave. That is when I heard Aunt Janelle begin to talk about something that caught my attention. I leaned on the doorjamb of the kitchen door to listen.

"I saw Ole Lady Jenkins pullin' out," she said, as she wet the comb in the glass of water and raked it through Donna's hair. "I'm gonna put the Toni right here in the crown," she said to Donna. "You need body at the top for that style." Donna nodded and Aunt Janelle continued talking all the while wetting, combing, and cutting.

"I bet she was telling you everything she knew about Lonnie's widow showing up, wasn't she?" Splash, comb, snip, snip, snip. "But did she tell you that he married a woman from *Cuba*? Sit up straight, Donna." Mama shook her head and said that Miz Jenkins just referred to her as dark.

"Well," Aunt Janelle continued, "Dewayne said she is dark, dark brown. And she can't speak good English." Aunt Janelle's boyfriend, Dewayne Beechum, was a deputy Sheriff and knew a lot about what was going on behind the scenes in the county.

Aunt Janelle's fury flashed each time she opened and closed the scissors. Splash, comb, snip, snip, snip. "Dewayne said she came by the Sheriff's office trying to find out how to get to the Landers' farm. Dewayne *claims* he just gave her directions and didn't pay much attention to her, but I was told by Sandra Davis, who has the insurance office next to the jail, that that woman is tall with a good figure and long legs, *and* she was wearing a halter top and short shorts with *high heels*!" Splash, comb, snip, snip, snip. "Can you imagine?" Aunt Janelle said disgustedly. "An outfit like that in Pine Crest!" Mama shook her head. No one would dare walk the streets of our county seat dressed like that. "Anyway, Sandra saw her sashaying past the picture window of her office," Aunt Janelle continued. "She watched until that woman left the jail and then she went over there to find out who she was."

"Sandra said Dwayne and Sonny, you know, the other deputy, were talking about that... Lola? Zat it? with their tongues hanging out!" I was watching Aunt Janelle and thought Donna should be worried about her so close to her neck with those sharp scissors. Aunt Janelle was mad and her scissors were flying through Donna's wet hair.

"Well," Aunt Janelle huffed. "Dewayne Beechum had better not let me catch him making eyes at her!" She stopped cutting to comb through Donna's hair, which was shorter than I had ever seen it. "Let's get that perm in," Aunt Janelle huffed.

I turned and walked out through the back screen door and almost bumped into Daddy. "I thought I told you to go cut the squash!" he bellowed. "Oh, Daddy," I wailed. "I plumb forgot!" Daddy handed me his pocketknife and told me to be careful opening it because the blade was sharp. I grabbed a bushel basket from beside the back steps and ran to the garden as fast as I could.

After I had lugged a bushel basket of yellow crook-necked squash to the back porch, I got on my bicycle and pedaled as fast as I could down to the creek. I slammed the brakes on my bicycle and skidded sideways. Trixie was walking up the road from the creek and she was mad as a hornet. She walked straight over to me, grabbed my wrist in her hands and twisted. "Hey!" I cried. "Why'd you give me an Indian sunburn?" I spit on my wrist and rubbed it.

Trixie put her hands on her hips and frowned. My cousin, Trixie, was chubby with chin length blonde hair that would never stay out of her face. She blew her hair out of her eyes. "I got up early and waited on you forever!" Trixie cried. I quit rubbing my wrist and tried to explain. "I got caught up with gossip," I said. "Miz Jenkins was tellin' Mama about Lonnie's wife and all!" Trixie started walking up the road towards the crossroads where she would go right to her house, and I would go left to mine. I walked my bike beside her.

"Yeah," she said as I walked beside her, pushing my bicycle. "I heard she was colored." I scratched my head. "No, I don't think she's colored. I think Aunt Janelle said she was *Cuban*, you know, like Ricky Ricardo." Trixie nodded. "Well, I heard she's a gold digger and ain't no more than got here than she almost killed Miz Landers."

"How can it be her fault that Miz Landers had a heart attack? Seems like folks have got it in for her without giving her a chance to tell her side," I said. Trixie fished around in her short's pocket and pulled out a piece of bubble gum. She unwrapped it and gave me half. Trixie laughed, "Ha, that Bazooka Joe walked under a ladder and got red paint all over his head!" She handed me the wrapper with the comic strip on it. I laughed and shoved it in my shorts pocket. We walked to the crossroads together where Trixie hopped on the fender of my bike and rode with me over to my house.

When we got to the house and walked up the back porch steps, we could hear Donna crying in the kitchen. I glanced over my shoulder and saw that Aunt Janelle's car was gone. Trixie looked at me, and I shrugged. We walked into the kitchen and saw Donna slumped down in a chair with her head on the table bawling like a baby.

"Now, Donna," Mama was saying. "It's a beautiful hairdo. It's just a little short is all."

Donna wailed between sobs, "No, it's not! It's too short and the perm is too tight! I look awful!" Then she laid her head back down on the table and resumed her sobbing.

"Here's your sister," Mama said, motioning me over. "Now, just look at Donna, Tina. Don't you think her hairdo is pretty?" Mama was recruiting me to boost Donna's confidence, but when my sister looked up from the table, all I could do was laugh. "She looks like Harpo Marx!" I said and Trixie and I both burst out laughing, which I soon learned was the wrong thing to do.

"Well," mama suggested to Donna, "Go wash your hair and maybe it will look better when you fix it yourself." Mama shot me an angry look, so I grabbed Trixie's hand and we went to the bedroom that I shared with my sister.

We plopped down on my bed, and I rolled over on my stomach. That is when I noticed my piggy bank. I had made a piggy bank out of an old coffee can and kept it on top of my chest of drawers. But it wasn't *on* the chest of drawers. It was on the floor beside the bed. I bolted upright and scrambled off the bed pouring the contents of the coffee can onto the floor. "Seventy-five, eighty-two, ninety-one cents." I let out a growl. "What's wrong?" Trixie asked me. "Roger! That's what!" I snapped. I got up and ran to Roger's bedroom. I was fit to be tied.

"Rah-gerr! You little thief! Get out here!" I looked under his bed, inside his toy box, and inside his closet. Then I saw him. Hiding on the shelf in the top of the closet, underneath a blanket. I reached up to grab his legs, but he took me by surprise and jumped down, knocking me to the floor. Roger broke into a run with me after him. He got out the backdoor, but Mama grabbed me as I ran by her.

"What's going on?" she cried. I pushed at mama, trying to get loose from her grip, all the while exclaiming that Roger was getting away. "What are you so mad about?" Mama asked me. I stood there breathing hard. "Roger took my money from my coffee can!" I cried. "I had six dollars and ninety-one cents! Roger took six dollars cash from me!" Mama let go of my arm. Stealing and lying were not tolerated by my parents. I could see Mama was trying to decide whether to tell Daddy about it now or wait until after supper.

"You let me handle it," she said. I nodded and went back to the bedroom where I plopped down on the bed beside Trixie. "That's just great," I sighed. "Roger took my money. Now, I'll *never* get a real diary or a horse!"

That evening, Daddy washed up at the sink and sat down at the table with our family to eat supper. After saying the blessing, he looked at Donna and grinned. Daddy was about to speak when Mama looked at him and shook her head. So, Daddy swallowed his laughter and began spooning white gravy onto his plate. After a while of pushing her food around with her fork, Donna asked to be excused and went to the bedroom.

"What happened to her hair?" Daddy snickered under his breath. Mama snickered, too. "Oh, Janelle came over to do a cut and perm for Donna and got to talkin' about how jealous she was over Dwayne. She kinda got scissor happy and cut Donna's hair too short. Then, she put the perm in too tight. Donna's been upset all day." "Well, it's no wonder," Daddy said. "She looks like Harpo Marx!"

"That's what *I* said!" I cried. I looked over at Roger and we started laughing. But Daddy was no longer smiling. "Roger, what's this I hear 'bout you stealin'?" Daddy's stare bore down on Roger. "Mama said you took some of Brownie's money. Zat right?" Roger lowered his head and mumbled.

"What'd you do with it?" Daddy asked. Roger shrugged. "Well, you'd better come up with that six dollars or you're gonna git a whoopin'." Daddy cut into his pork chop and looked directly at Roger. "I really ort to whoop you anyway. For stealing." Without looking up Roger mumbled, "Yes, sir."

Daddy placed a spoonful of mashed potatoes on his plate and said, "I'm gonna give you through tomower to give yer sister back her money. If you do, you'll only be punished for stealin'. If you can't come up with it, then I'm gonna punish you for stealin' *and* not makin' it right with Brownie. Hear me?"

"Yes, sir," Roger said. Then my brother pushed *his* food around with his fork. Now and again, he would sniff and wipe his eyes. After a while Roger asked to be excused. I put another pork chop on my plate and ate without saying a word.

July 4, 1968
Dear Diary,
Roger stole my coffee can money now I won't never get a real diary or an Indian pony! He wouldn't tell Daddy what he got the money for, so I'm gonna find out. Me and Trixie are gonna spy on him all day.
Brownie

It was hot again, but at least it was the Fourth of July. A holiday. In the evening, Daddy was going to cook weenies on the grill and make ice cream in our ice cream churn with the hand crank. My daddy's parents, Papa, and Granny Rivers, along with his brother, Uncle Gil, and Aunt

Brenda, Trixie, and the boys Eddie and Ronnie. They always came to join us. Sometimes, Daddy and Uncle Gil would light firecrackers, but not today. Daddy and Uncle Gil worked with the volunteer fire department and told us that the draught was so bad the county had put a ban on fireworks this fourth.

I was out in the yard when Aunt Brenda drove up in their station wagon. My cousin Trixie got out and walked toward me. "Hey, Brownie!" Aunt Brenda yelled from the driver's side window. "You be good Trixie. I'll be back later with your daddy and the boys." Aunt Brenda smiled her big smile as she turned the car around. "I'm going to town to check on Mama," she yelled. "She ain't feelin' well!" And waving her hand out the window, she drove off.

"Come on," I said to Trixie. "I think I saw Roger go in the barn."

Trixie and I were running toward the barn when we met Daddy coming out of it. It was ten o'clock in the morning, so that was kind of a surprise. He should have had all of his barn work finished long before now. My father was almost six feet tall and very stocky. With his jet-black hair and dark brown eyes, he was quite a handsome man. Daddy was quiet and led by example. When my daddy spoke, people listened and considered what he had to say. I loved my daddy more than words could ever express.

"Hey, Daddy," I said. "What are you doing here? I thought you were in the hay field with Uncle Gil." Daddy had his toolbox and was walking fast. "Baler's broke down," he said and kept walking.

Trixie and I went on to the barn and quietly opened the door. We were both barefoot, so we did not make much noise. I motioned her to go to one side of the barn while I went to the corncrib and eased the door open. There he was, the little sneak.

"Okay, Roger," I said, hands on hips, "What'd you do with my money? You know Daddy's gonna whoop you if you don't give it back to me." Roger was hiding something behind his back. He seemed very nervous, so I grabbed my brother and wrestled him on top of the dried corn that was stacked knee deep in the crib. I finally got his arm pulled behind his back and held it tight.

"Ow! Ow! Calf rope!" Roger hollered. I grabbed the brown paper sack from his hands and let him fall back in the corn. Trixie had heard the commotion and was standing outside the corncrib looking in.

"Well, looky here!" I said smugly. "Firecrackers!" Actually, as I rummaged through the sack, I noticed more than simple firecrackers. Roger had fireworks that I did not recognize. Danger and Extreme Caution were written in red lettering down the sides. "I'm showing these to Daddy!" I cried and ran toward the house with the sack and Roger and Trixie following close behind. Roger was pleading with me not to show Daddy.

Daddy was getting into his pickup to leave. I was out of breath and shook the sack at Daddy. When I got to the truck, I handed Daddy the paper bag. "This is what Roger spent my money on!" I exclaimed. Roger's beagle, Buster, came running when he heard me rattle the bag. He jumped up on Daddy, thinking there might be a treat in the sack. "Git down!" Daddy ordered. But Buster jumped from Roger to Daddy, barking up a storm.

"I can explain! I can explain!" Roger cried. "Roger, git hold of yore dog!" Daddy hollered. I started yelling over my brother, "Daddy he was hiding these fireworks in the barn! That's what he spent my money on!" Buster kept barking and Roger fell down, trying to get hold of his collar.

"One at a time!" Daddy ordered. "Now, will one of you tell me what's going on?" Daddy looked at me. "Brownie?" So, I told Daddy that I had caught Roger trying to hide the fireworks in the corncrib and that I was sure he didn't have any money to buy them, so he must have used my coffee can money to get them.

Daddy looked through the sack and frowned. "What's all this?" he asked Roger. Roger started to cry. "I just wanted to surprise my family with fireworks for the Fourth of July!" he wailed. Daddy was not swayed. "But you stole from Brownie. Who'd ye buy these from?"

Roger shook his head. "I promised I wouldn't tell," he said.

"Well, if ye don't tell me," Daddy said sternly, "I'm gonna give you that whoopin' I promised ye." Daddy looked at Trixie and me and said, "You girls git on in the house." We did as we were told and found Mama and Donna listening at the kitchen door.

I heard Daddy say to Roger, "I'm asking ye for the last time, Roger. Where'd ye git these fireworks?" Roger's crying broke into sobs as he blurted out, "Carl Jacobs!"

Carl Jacobs and his little brother, Tater, lived in a shack over in the woods behind the elementary school. The shack they lived in was an old chicken house with no indoor plumbing. Carl was thirteen and Tater was six. Carl smoked cigarettes and only went to school when the truant officer could catch him. He had been in and out of the juvenile home for stealing, the most recent theft being Mr. Edwards' old pickup truck. Tater, on the other hand, was just a sweet little six-year-old who was a little slow and had a lazy eye. Their mama had run off with a salesman and left the boys to fend for themselves.

"Carl said if I told, he'd beat me to a pulp!" We could hear the fear in Roger's voice. Daddy took all this in and his voice softened. Buster had given up on a treat and left. Probably to chase the rabbits in Daddy's hay field.

"Roger," Daddy sighed. "This is serious. Some of these fireworks are illegal. You're only six years old. I don't want you taking up with the wrong crowd and believe me son, that boy is *the wrong crowd*."

We heard the paper sack rumpling. All four of us that were in the kitchen moved to the window. Daddy and Roger were walking toward the chicken house. We watched Daddy tussle Roger's hair and put his arm around his shoulders. Mama smiled and said, "Well, everything worked out in the end." I looked at my mother and frowned. "Oh, yeah? What about my horse?"

Later on, Daddy and Roger came back to the house. Mama handed Daddy a sandwich and a canning jar filled with iced tea so that he could get back to the hayfield. Roger sat down at the table and fixed himself a bologna sandwich. I watched as mama walked out on the back stoop to talk to Daddy. I eased over to the door so I could hear.

"He's going to have to work off what he owes to Brownie," Daddy said. "I threw the fireworks in the chicken pit. Next time I have to burn, we'll have a show." Daddy chuckled and told Mama it was a good thing that I had brought the fireworks to him, or Roger could have gotten himself into a whole lot of trouble, maybe even burned the barn down.

"But I think he's learned his lesson," Daddy said. "Poor boy was scared to death. And I'm still going to have to re-port Carl Jacobs. Roger said he didn't know where Carl got the fireworks, but he did know that ole worthless uncle of theirs that's been in the penitentiary took them to the mountains over the weekend. I bet Carl got 'em at one of those roadside fireworks stands."

Mama asked Daddy if Carl would hurt Roger because he had told on him. Daddy told Mama it might not be a bad idea if Roger stayed close to home for the next few days.

Then Daddy walked to his truck and drove off. Mama came back into the kitchen and looked at the clock.

"Let's eat dinner and then get the table cleaned up. I've got to get the beans canned before our weenie roast tonight."

Mama had just set the canner on top of the stove when the phone rang. I was just about to head outside to throw away the bean strings but sat back down at the table when I realized that it was Miz Jenkins on the phone.

"What?" Mama gasped and covered her mouth with her hand. "I will. No. No. I won't. Thanks for calling to let me know." Mama hung up the receiver and looked at me. "Where's Roger?" she asked. Trixie and I had been helping mama can, so we looked at her and shrugged. Mama took off her apron and turned off the stove.

"Come on," she said to me. "We've got to find him and your Daddy. Where's Donna?" Mama was suddenly very nervous. "Donna is in the bedroom," I said. "Want me to fetch her?" Mama walked ahead of me to the bedroom where Donna was sitting at the dresser trying to flatten her hair. "We're going to the hay field for a minute, but I want you to stay inside and don't come out. Lock the doors!" she instructed my sister. Donna nodded and Trixie and I went outside, trailing behind Mama.

"What is it, Mama?" panic was rising up inside me.

"We've got to find Roger and your Daddy," she said. Mama looked around the yard and called out Roger's name, so Trixie and I did the same. Then Mama ran all the way to the hayfield across the road from our house. Roger was riding on the tractor with Daddy while Uncle Gil loaded square bales of hay onto the flatbed trailer. Mama waved her arms over her head until Daddy noticed her. He drove the tractor over to where we Mama waited for him and shut off the motor.

"What now?" Daddy was obviously annoyed. "There's a convict loose!" Mama explained. "He got loose from the chain gang that was working up on Highway 20. All the neighbors are warning each other." Mama looked at Uncle Gil who had joined us. "Where're the boys?" she asked him. Gill rubbed the back of his neck. "At home, I guess," he said. "I'd better go check on 'em. We done here?" Uncle Gil asked my daddy. Daddy nodded and said, "Me and Roger'll git up the last of the bales. You go on." Uncle Gil walked out of the field and down the bank to his pickup parked next to the field road.

"We'll be home in a minute," Daddy said. "Roger, help me load these last five bales onto the flatbed." Trixie and I looked to Mama for what we should do next. Without saying a word, Mama just turned around and headed back to the house.

By the time Daddy and Roger got back home, Mama's canner was hissing on the stove. Trixie and I were in the living room playing a board game. We stopped though, just as soon as we heard the screen door slam.

Mama told Daddy that the escaped man had been convicted of robbing a bank down in Macon and that he had overtaken a guard on the chain gang and gotten his gun. "They say he's armed and dangerous." Mama was timid in all her ways, but the things that scared her most were snakes, tornadoes, and bad people. Daddy looked at Mama and then looked at us kids. We were all scared. Trixie was biting her fingernails. I walked into the kitchen to stand beside Daddy.

"Well, he's not gonna bother us," Daddy said. He turned and started washing his hands in the kitchen sink. I thought about how broad Daddy's shoulders were. With his sleeves rolled up, I could see the big muscles in his arms. Daddy always wore long-sleeved shirts, that he rolled up to his elbows. His tan stopped right about mid-arm and the upper part of his arm was milky-white. It made his arms look as though they had been dipped in brown paint. Seeing daddy at home made me feel safe.

"And since I'm back early," he continued, "we can go ahead and have our weenie roast!" Daddy looked around at his family and gave us a reassuring smile. "I've gotta go to the store for ice, though. It's not the Fourth of July without ice cream." Daddy smiled as he finished drying his hands on a kitchen towel. He reached over and pecked Mama on the lips. That cheered us up. Mama turned her canner off to begin the cool down, and I walked Daddy to the door so I could lock the screen behind him.

At twilight, everybody but Mama was on the front porch getting ready to make ice cream. I was already full of weenies and potato chips, but I was going to gorge myself on ice cream, even if I got a bellyache. Granny and Papa were sitting in the porch rockers, laughing at Roger, Eddie, and Ronnie who were running around in the yard catching lightning bugs. The air still held the heat of the day and the sweet smell of the hay stubble. In the pastures, cows lowed softly as they wandered around in the high grass of summer. Every now and then I could smell the sweet scent of the blooms on the mimosa tree. I sat down at the edge of the porch and let my bare feet dangle.

Uncle Gil sat straddling a straight-backed chair and Aunt Brenda was sitting on the steps. Daddy was putting a large dishpan underneath the ice cream freezer to catch the run-off of salt brine when they began churning the ice cream. He and Uncle Gill had on their nice short-sleeved shirts and jeans. Their forearms were the color of a polished saddle, which got me to thinking about the horse I would never get.

"Daddy," I said. "When's Roger gonna give me my money back?" I squatted down beside my father and picked a chunk of ice out of the bag to suck on. Daddy stood up and looked down at me. "I don't expect he ever will, Brownie," he said. "How'd you think he's gonna git the money to pay you? I'm makin' him work it off as punishment, but I guess your money's just gone." Daddy looked at Uncle Gil and winked. I blew out my cheeks in defeat. I could save enough money to buy a diary. Maybe. But my dreams of buying a horse were as gone as my six dollars.

"But Daddy," I continued, "I won't ever git no horse now!" Daddy looked up at the night sky. The Big and Little Dippers were sparkling bright. He put a piece of chewing gum in his mouth and said, "Well, I hate to burst your bubble on the cruel rock of reality, but six dollars wadnt even close to what ye'd need to buy a horse." I was disappointed but at least I would have ice cream to console me.

We were all talking and waiting on Mama to come out with the steel cylinder that held the ice cream mixture. Then we could start taking turns turning the metal crank on the ice cream freezer. And that is when we saw it. A huge ball of fire exploding through the pine trees over at the Landers' place. Daddy and Uncle Gil jumped up from their chairs. "Look at that!" Daddy shouted. From our hill we could see much of the farmland down below. The explosion of Miz Landers' house sent fiery debris out in all directions.

Just then, Mama came outside with a dish towel in her hand. "Eudora," Mama said to Granny, "Can I borrow some vanilla. We're plumb out." Mama looked at everyone and saw that they were all looking at the sky, so she looked up too. There was a huge fire now, big enough to be seen all over Piney Hill community.

Mama dropped her dishtowel, her eyes fixed on the pine trees silhouetted by the backlighting of the fire. "Good ice cream takes lots of vanilla," she mumbled as she stared at the blaze down below.

I took my eyes off the sky just long enough to see a Sheriff's car pull into our driveway. Dwayne hung his head out of the car window and yelled to Daddy and Uncle Gil that the volunteer firemen were needed over at the Landers' place. They wanted to try and keep the fire from spreading. Then he backed up and drove out of our driveway, slinging gravel everywhere.

"I'll see you there, Boyd," Uncle Gil said to Daddy. He rushed down the steps to get in his pickup. Daddy wasted no time. He went inside, giving the screen door a loud bang, and came out carrying his firefighting gear.

"Don't know when I'll be home," he told Mama. "Remember there's a convict loose. Keep those doors locked." Then Daddy ran down the steps and got into his truck. In a matter of minutes, he was gone and the promise of ice cream with him.

Papa spit tobacco over the porch railing. "I ain't never seen setch a ball of farr. Reckin' what made it?" But his question hung in the air without one theory offered, as the blaze shot higher and higher into the trees around the Landers' farmhouse. After a while, Roger broke the silence. "Does this mean we ain't gonna git no ice cream?" Papa spit again, then stood to leave. "No, son," he said. "Don't look like we'll be makin' ice cream tonight."

No ice cream. No fireworks. Locked doors. If it wasn't for the heat, you would never know it was the Fourth of July. Papa took hold of Granny's elbow and helped her down the dark steps. "Come on, Brenda," he called to my aunt. "We'll take you and the younguns' home."

Trixie and her two brothers piled into the bed of Papa's truck while Aunt Brenda squeezed in the front seat with Granny and Papa. Mama bid everyone good night. Aunt Brenda said she'd wash the canning jars the boys used for lightning bugs and bring them back in the morning. Everybody waved goodbye and Papa drove slowly out of the yard. Mama watched the horizon. The fire seemed less now, but the acrid smell of smoke hung in the air like a fog. Mama shooed us back inside the house and locked the doors. "I sure hope that fire doesn't spread," she said softly while the sounds of sirens screamed in the air.

Mama put us in front of the television with popcorn. It was so hot! Every fan we owned was blowing on us but with all the doors closed, we were still sweating. "What are you watching?" Mama asked. It was the new comedy show. None of us cared much for the comedian. We were all waiting for the puppeteer to come on. Roger, who was laying on his stomach, suddenly sat up and knocked my soda bottle over.

"Rah-gerrr!" I shouted, "Now, look what you've done! I've got soda all over my pajama bottoms!" "I'm sorry! I'm sorry!" Roger cried. Mama came back from the kitchen with a wet dish towel and handed it to my brother. "Clean that up," she instructed. "And after you see the puppets, y'all are going to bed."

I rubbed the sticky brown spot on my pjs and fumed. "Why'd you do that, Roger!" I cried. Roger put his forefinger to his lips and waved his hands for us to get down closer to him so that we could hear. "I heerd something,'" he whispered.

Donna and I became quiet, straining to hear above the whirring fans. Mama reached over the end table and cut out the light. Then we heard a sound just off the kitchen. Someone was jiggling the backdoor knob. I swallowed hard. Roger wrapped his arms around Mama's legs, and Donna reached over to the hearth and pulled the fireplace poker out of its hanger.

The doorknob jiggled again, then silence returned. Mama rubbed the top of Roger's head while Donna and I held our breath. I eased around the wall of the room and then crawled to the backdoor. Slowly, I stood up to look out the window. Mama shouted, "Tina, stop! You might get shot!" But I was already at the door, and no one was there.

Mama came running into the kitchen and pulled me back from the window. She had glided in behind me so silently that I did not hear her. "You could have been killed!" she hissed. Then she hugged me. I could hear her heart racing through her blouse. "Mama," I said. "Can I slip out the front door? I might be able to see who it was?" By now my brother and sister had decided that it was safe enough to join us in the dark kitchen. "No!" Mama whispered, "Whoever it was has gone now."

"Maybe we should turn on all the lights," Donna reasoned. "You know, so they know the house isn't empty and people are inside." Mama nodded and we all scampered around turning on the lamps and overhead lights. Roger even turned the volume up on the television.

"Okay," Mama said. "Now, y'all should all go to bed." But sleep was the last thing on our minds. We were all hyped-up on crime, suspense and near danger. So, Donna brought out a board game, and we started setting it up on the coffee table.

The clock struck eleven. Roger had been yawning for over an hour, but I kept encouraging him to stay awake or he would miss his chance to buy Townwalk. Donna and I had an agreement that every time we played this game, we would let Roger buy Townwalk if he landed on it and if we landed on it, we would pass.

Just then, we heard a key in the lock and the front door opened. Daddy came in, and a gust of cool air blew in behind him. He left the door standing open and sat down in his chair. He smelled like a campfire.

"I bet you're hungry," Mama said. "I have some weenies and baked beans. Do you want some?" Daddy shook his head. "I'm not hungry," he said. "I just want to take a bath and go to bed." He got up from his chair just as Mama was coming back from the kitchen with a glass of iced tea. Daddy guzzled it down and told us all good night.

Donna and I cleaned up the board game while Mama helped Roger to bed. Then Donna turned off the lights, and I went to shut and lock the front door. I stood in the doorway for a moment, savoring the cool night breeze. It would be a while before the smell of smoke left the area. I latched the screen and locked the door. But I'm not sure that anyone slept well that night except Roger.

July 5, 1968
Dear Diary,
Donna can be so mean! She asked me why I was always writin in this Blue Horse notebook all the time. I told her it was my diary. She called me a moron and walked off.
My friend Patty Simpson has a pink leather diary with a gold clasp and a key that locks it. She keeps her key on a chain around her neck. Mama said I have to wait til my birthday to get a diary like that because money don't grow on trees.
I've got a Spam key on a piece of kite string just so I can pretend to lock my diary.
Outside it still smells like smoke from the fire last night. Me and Trixie are going over to the Landers' place today to see what's going on. Daddy said it was a set fire. I don't know what that means.
Brownie

After breakfast, I packed my woods bag that Granny made for me. It was out of an old pillowcase and had a long strap that I could put over my head and wear across my body. That way, my hands could be free.

I had an old pair of binoculars that I had won off of Stevie Wentworth at school. Stevie was playing basketball with some of the other boys at recess one day and hollered over to me that he bet I couldn't sink three baskets in a row. Which, of course, I did. Donna said he only bet me because he *likes* me. I told her to go bite a hog!

So, the binoculars went in the sack. Next, I put a quart jar of ice water and a bologna sandwich in, along with an old handkerchief. I put my head through the strap and headed out the backdoor. "Stay in the yard!" Mama called. "They've not caught that convict yet. I mean it, Tina Marie!" I pretended not to hear and ran off to the barn to get my bicycle. Trixie said she would wait by her mailbox for me.

I knew Mama would pitch a fit if she saw me riding out the driveway, so I rode down the chicken house road, turned right and rode off the steep, red bank onto the dirt road that led down Piney Hill to Uncle Gil's place. Trixie was waiting by the mailbox with her woods sack that our Granny had made for her. Granny always said we were like "Mutt and Jeff".

"Mama thanks I'm hepin my brothers in the chicken house," Trixie said. "I had to promise 'em my dessert to keep 'em from telling on me." Trixie was plump and very fond of dessert. I could see what a sacrifice that must have been for her. "You don't gotta come," I offered, but she climbed onto the fender of my bicycle and shrugged. So, off we went down the hill until we got to the main road that ran by the Landers' farm.

"Daddy said somebody set the house on fire *on purpose!*" Trixie shouted in my ear. I had found a deck of cards in the hall desk and had attached one with a clothes pin to the spoke of my back tire. It made a cool motorcycle sound as I pedaled, but it was awfully hard to hear over it. "I know," I shouted over my shoulder. "That's why we're gonna go over there and look for clues!"

We rode up close to the yard of the Landers' place and saw several vehicles parked near the house. A tall man in a gray suit was taking pictures of the ground at the back of the house. The house was a smoldering pile of rubble. Two other men in suits walked around scribbling on note-pads, pulling debris away from the charred ruins. I rode on past the driveway to where a field road ran up next to the Lander's property. The field road was divided from the Landers' yard by a little pine thicket. We rode up the dirt road and got off my bike, which I laid quietly on the ground. The smell of wet ashes made me feel sick.

"Come on," I said to Trixie. "We can climb up the bank and see what's going on." Trixie nodded, and we crept through the pine trees to the edge of Mrs. Landers' yard. Now we could hear what the men were saying without being seen.

"Take a picture of the burn trail, Frank." A man in a dark blue suit who seemed to be in charge was pointing to a black streak in the grass, that ran all the way to where the house used to sit. The explosion had strewn debris outward from the foundation. The man in charge pushed his hat back and took a handkerchief out of his pocket to wipe his face. He was young and handsome with dark hair that framed his face. It was so hot! I wondered why all those men had on suits and ties instead of something sensible like overalls. One worker gave in to the heat and took off his coat and loosened his tie.

A red-headed man was talking to the one in charge, "We found this box of matches over by the edge of the yard." The man in charge swung his attention our way, and I grabbed Trixie and pulled her down just in time. "We also found these cigarette butts beside the burn trail," the red-headed man continued. "It looks like someone mixed diesel fuel with gasoline to start this fire."

"So," the man in charge reasoned, "gas was mixed with diesel fuel, poured out onto the ground in a trail leading up to the house, and a cigarette was used to light the fire?"

The red-headed man said, "Yeah, Frank interviewed the owner, who was in the hospital when the fire happened. He found out that she had a wall-mount gas heater in the living room. So, whoever did it must have broken off the copper line from the heater allowing gas vapors to build up in the house. Then when the burn trail was lit, 'kaplooey'." The man in charge rubbed the back of his neck and looked thoughtful.

I tapped Trixie and motioned that we should leave. As I slid backwards off the bank my hand grazed something. A piece of dirty shoelace with a rabbit's foot tied to the end. It was laying in the pine straw next to a box of matches. I shoved them both in my pocket.

Trixie and I rode back up the road to my house where we jumped off my bicycle and ran straight to my bedroom. I put my fingers to my lips and mouthed "Roger," so that she would be quiet. After I had searched the room and was sure we were alone, I pulled the shoelace and match box from my pocket and showed them to Trixie.

Trixie looked puzzled. "That's Tater's rabbit foot!" she whispered. "Where'd you git that?" "On the bank, right next to this," I said, shaking the matchbox. "It looks like Carl and Tater are in big trouble." Trixie looked at me, concerned. "Are you gonna tell?" Trixie gasped. As all kids knew, telling on one of your peers was breaking an unspoken rule. "I *have* to," I said slumping down on the bed. "The Sheriff thinks that woman Lonnie married burnt the house down. I can't let her go to prison for something that she didn't do."

Trixie shook her head, "But you don't know she *didn't* do it! She may be a criminal, just like Miz Jenkins says. Anyways, we don't know her, and we've known Carl and Tater all our lives. I don't give a fig for Carl, but Tater, you know he's kind of slow and don't know no better than to follow his brother around."

I didn't know what to do. The whole thing made me feel guilty, as though I was somehow to blame for Miz Landers' place burning down. I shoved the rabbit's foot and match-box back into the pocket of my cut-offs.

"I don't know, Trix," I said softly. "I'm gonna have to think about this. I sure don't want to be the one that gets little Tater sent to reform school."

I was sitting on the tire swing when Granny came walk-ing up the driveway. She was wearing her bonnet and had one of Papa's long-sleeved shirts over her dress. Under her dress she had on a pair of his pants. She was carrying two buckets in one hand and one bucket and a hoe in the other. I got a whiff of kerosene, which could only mean one thing. Blackberries.

"Hey thar," Granny said. "Git yer brother. We're gonna pick burries." Granny had strips of rags that had been dipped in kerosene tied to her wrists. This was to keep chiggers away. I jumped down and gave Granny a hug. "I'll go get him," I said and ran off toward the barn. "And put ye some long pants on!" Granny hollered after me.

I hated the kerosene rags and begged Granny not to put them on me saying I would wear a long-sleeved shirt and long pants. She ignored me and tied a bracelet of soaked rag strips to mine and Roger's wrists and ankles. My eyes watered. Granny gave us each a bucket and she started walking down the road using the hoe as a walking stick. She turned off onto the first field road that we came to. Wild blackberry bushes arched in sprays over each other, the aroma of their dark, ripening fruit filled the warm summer air. Granny took her hoe and beat the weeds all around checking for snakes. When she felt like it was safe, she told us we could start picking.

While we worked, Granny told us stories. She told us folklore about coach whip snakes. "Ye don't see 'em much nowadays," she said. "They useta be ever whur 'round these parts. Did ye know they'll chase ye?" she asked spitting snuff on the ground. "They'll chase ye by bitin' thur tail and turnin' into ah wheel." Granny laughed. "They'll roll and roll like a wheel 'til they ketch ye, then they'll slap ye with their tail 'til they think yur dead and then they'll put thar tail up yer nose to see if yur still ah breathin'!" She took a glance at us to check our reaction. Roger had stopped picking and stared wide-eyed at her with a mouthful of berries drizzling down his chin. "Zat true, Granny?" he mumbled through his chewing. "Wah, shore," Granny said. "Good thang they ain't around here anymore, ain't it?" she laughed. Roger looked over his shoulder and then narrowed his eyes and looked at the weeds we were standing in.

Roger and I had eaten as many blackberries as we picked and still managed to fill our buckets. When Granny was satisfied that we had picked enough, she said we could go home. On the walk back the road was dusty, and the sun was beating down, but the smell of pasture grass and ripe berries was worth it. Granny whistled an old bluegrass song and I started singing.

Down the road, 'bout a mile or two, lives a little gal named Pearly Blue.
Not so tall, eyes of brown, prettiest gal boys in this town!

Roger refused to join in. He was too busy watching for snakes. Granny and I sang and whistled all the way back home.

When we walked up on our yard, we saw Mama taking the washing off the line. "Looks like y'all got a lot of blackberries!" she said. Mama put the basket of clothes on her hip and smiled, her blonde hair shining in the sun like spun gold. "Won't you stay a while, Eudora?" she said to my grandmother.

"Naw," Granny said. "Ah gotter go and git my burries under sugar sos I kin make mah jelly in tha mornin'." Granny took my bucket and put it with hers and pointed to Roger's bucket with her hoe. "Yun's kin keep thatern," she said. "That's yer pay fer heppin me pick." Roger clutched the bucket happily to his chest. "I'll see ye. You young'uns be sweet," she said and turned to go. I watched her walking down the driveway with her two buckets in one hand and the hoe in the other. I could hear her whistling as she passed out of sight.

That evening, Mama, Daddy, and Roger went to the store to pick up some groceries. I was sitting on my bed in the bedroom that I shared with my sister. I was watching Donna get ready for her date.

Donna had taken to wearing wide headbands to cover up her awful haircut. With hoop earrings and extra eye makeup she looked pretty good. Every day she teased and backcombed the crown of her hair and applied a cloud of hairspray. I came into the bedroom and watched as she applied black eyeliner. Donna was going out with David Burgess from church. They were going to the movie house in Pine Crest, our county seat.

"You look pretty," I said and meant it. "What picture are you gonna see?" Donna ran frosted pink lipstick across her lips and stood up. Her skirt was incredibly short!

"Donna!" I exclaimed, "Daddy'll skin you alive when he sees you!" Donna shrugged.

"Well, he aint here," she said as she pulled on a pair of white go-go boots that I had never seen before. "Besides," she continued, "David will be here any minute to get me, so you'd better not say a word if you know what's good for you!"

"I won't, but how you gonna git back in the house without them seein' how you're dressed?" Donna pulled her overnight bag off the bed and rolled her eyes.

"After the show's over, David is gonna drop me off at Aunt Janelle's so I can spend the night." Donna turned to look at herself in the mirror.

"But whacha gonna see?" I asked again.

Donna sighed, "Some ole war movie with that cowboy actor he likes" she sighed. "*The Green* something or other."

Donna was level-headed and never did anything wrong, so I knew the short skirt and boots were just her trying to be a normal teenager. I decided now might be a good time to ask her what I should do about Tater's rabbit foot. I followed my sister through the house, talking to her back.

"Donna, what would you do if you knew something about somebody that would git them into really bad trouble?"

Donna swung around and stared at me. "I told you not to say anything about my skirt, Brownie! I mean, *everybody's* wearing short skirts these days. I'm not indecent and..."

I held up my hand, "No, no, no! I'm not talking about you! I'm talking about Tater Jacobs!" Donna's face softened and she kissed my cheek.

"Well, Carl has gotten Tater into so much trouble it'd be a shame for him to get into more." Then she bounded out the front door and onto the porch just as David pulled up.

"Hey, squirt!" David hollered out the window of his sports car. "Hey, ugly!" I hollered back. David was so nice. Everybody liked him. He was almost eighteen. I heard Mama tell Daddy that he would be registering for selective service this month and that his mother was very worried about it. We all hoped the war in Vietnam would be over soon.

Donna got in and shut the car door. I waved as they drove out of the driveway. "She didn't even ask me what Tater did that might get him into trouble," I thought. It was hot and sticky, so I went back in the house to sit in front of the fan and watch tv. During commercials, I leaned over in front of the fan and talked into the blades. My voice was transformed to a robot.

It was hard to concentrate on the television shows. Mama, Daddy, and Roger would be home soon, and I needed time to think. But the more I thought about it, the more I did not know what to do. I dug the rabbit's foot and matchbox out of my short's pocket and went into the kitchen to find a brown paper lunch bag. I stuffed them in the bag and went back to my room. I went to the closet, pulled up the loose floorboard from the corner and laid the sack underneath it. The plank stuck up a little from the stuff in the bag, so I put a pair of my old Sunday shoes on top to weigh it down. There now. It would stay there until I could settle my mind on what to do.

July 6, 1968
Dear Diary,
I have to go with mama to Rosen's today to buy church shoes. Wouldn't you know it, Roger has decided to tag along and that means Mama might not take us to eat at the lunch counter inside Rex's Drugs. Roger ruins everything!
The only thing that makes me happy about goin shoppin is Mama said I can pick out my own shoes this time.
Brownie

Saturday morning, I hurried through my morning of eating breakfast, brushing my teeth, combing my hair, and dressing. The only shoes that I could get on my feet were my flip-flops. I had just pulled a shift dress over my head when Mama came in to look at me. She sighed, "Oh well, Roger doesn't look much better." Roger came into my room wearing a red, stripped polo shirt that barely tucked into his cut-off blue jeans. This was accessorized by his old, scuffed cowboy boots.

"Mr. Rosen is going to take one look at y'all and try to sell me the whole store!" she chuckled.

Once I got my mind off mama ruining my Saturday by taking me shopping, I actually began to enjoy it. Town was always so busy on Saturdays. Country farm folk came into town to shop or run by the bank. Farmers visited the co-op, while their wives went to the hardware store to get essentials like seals for their pressure cookers or can lids for their jelly making. Mama told us if we were good, she would take us to June's Department Store to look around. We never bought anything at June's because the prices were out of our range, but it was two levels and we loved to go up and down the stairs and also to watch the sales ladies send charge receipts to the office in the pressurized tubes that zoomed off in a flash.

As we entered Rosen's store, a plump lady in a green dress rushed up to greet us. "Welcome to Rosen's!" she said cheerfully, "How may I assist you today?" Her blue eyes twinkled behind black, horn-rimmed glasses. Her mouth continued to hold us with a fixed smile, which was outlined in a bright coral lipstick. I promptly smiled back at her and told her in my most polite voice that I needed some church shoes that didn't pinch my feet.

Mama cleared her throat and said, "Yes, I need shoes for both of my children." The lady in green turned and with a crooked finger, motioned for us to follow her, which we did. Roger and I were familiar with the shoe section from previous years. We were expecting to get to see the goose, where you put in a coin, and she laid a special golden egg for you. The egg was made of plastic that would split open to reveal toys and candy. But now the goose was gone, and a cardboard cut-out of a boy in an old-fashioned suit stood in its place.

Roger plopped down on one of the leather chairs and started playing with the slide on the metal shoe ruler. I followed mama and the sales lady to the girls' section. "Are we looking for sandals?" the lady in green asked. Now, I knew that mama never bought anything without planning for it to be used until its' usefulness had been worn out. Sandals were for summer and summer only. Whereas penny loafers would take me from summer through most of the winter unless my feet had a growth spurt.

"I think a nice pair of penny loafers would work best for her," mama replied. Hard as I tried not to get my hopes up for something as wasteful as summer sandals, I just could not help myself. I could see a strappy pair of white sandals on my feet. I had even dreamed of getting Aunt Janelle to paint my toenails a bubblegum pink. Now my heart sank as we walked over to the display of loafers. The penny loafers all looked the same except some had tassels on them.

I pouted. It did not matter to me what pair we got. I knew it would be either brown or black, tassel or no tassel. I walked over and sat down by Roger who was flying the metal shoe ruler around and making rat-a-tat-tat noises, blowing spit all over me. I did not care. I was not getting sandals. I was not eating lunch at the drugstore counter. And Roger would probably ruin going to June's Department Store for me, too.

"How about these, Tina?" Mama was standing in front of me with a pair of *white* penny loafers *with* tassels. *White?* I could hardly believe it. I grinned from ear to ear. The sales lady pulled one of the loafers out of the box. I dropped my flip-flops onto the floor in a so-long, see you later fashion as she slid the beautiful shoe onto my foot.

"If she had on a pair of socks, I could see how much room she had to grow" Mama said. The sales lady stepped over to the hosiery counter and returned with a two-pack of white bobbie socks. She took them out of their package and handed me one pair and gave the other pair in the package to Mama. I put the socks and the loafers on and walked over to the mirror. Perfection! I thought I looked real ladylike. The sales lady bent over and pressed down on my toe. "You know, if you get this size in a wide, she probably could wear these through Christmas," the lady in green said. Mama smiled, "We'll take them!" she said.

We went back to our car and Mama put our shoes into the trunk. She then instructed us to stand on the sidewalk while she fed the parking meter. Mama led us to June's Department Store. I always enjoyed the hustle and bustle of the sales ladies in June's. Watching them in their smart dresses made me want to get a job there one day. Mama took us over to menswear and told us to sit down and stay put because she had to get daddy a new shirt. Roger squirmed and sighed, then he started whining. "Stop it, Roger!" I said, but Mama didn't take long and as soon as she had paid for her purchase, we left the store. "Their prices are outrageous," mama sighed. "Eight, ninety-nine for a short-sleeve shirt!"

Mama handed me the bag with Daddy's expensive shirt in it and got her change purse out. After she had counted up her money, she looked at us and smiled. "Okay. Who wants a hamburger at Rex's?"

That night Mama turned on the television to watch the news and daddy settled down with the newspaper. There was a news reel playing that showed soldiers wading through a swamp with their guns held over their heads. Daddy frowned. Daddy's baby brother, Uncle Ray, had been killed in Vietnam in 1966. The news must have brought that memory back to him. News about the war always made me feel sad and sick to my stomach.

Then the news switched to protestors at the White House. Young people with long hair and strange clothing carrying signs that read *Peace, not War.* "Turn that off, Jeanette" he said, "I don't want to watch those hippies." Mama got up and turned the tv off. "The cornbread should be about done," she said as she turned and walked into the kitchen.

"Daddy, what's a hippie?" Roger asked. He was laying on the floor on his stomach propped up on his elbows. Daddy picked the newspaper back up. "They're dope users who don't work and don't take baths," he said and focused on the print in front of him.

"Eddie told me a joke about hippies," Roger continued, "Do you know how a hippy takes a bubble bath? They sit in a mudhole and..." Daddy interrupted him by saying that was enough, so Roger hushed.

I had heard about hippies too and did not understand what the word meant or anything about them because nobody would discuss it with me. Funny how secretive grown-ups were when I was young. If an adult subject came up, they did not talk about it in front of us kids. It's no wonder that I eavesdropped on the grown-ups when I was a girl.

Donna, on the other hand, was always glued to the television whenever the stories about the hippies and their communes came on. It was a culture of her generation, and I think maybe it made living in a place like Piney Hill seem dull and uninteresting to her. I had seen other teens her age around the county, and it seemed like she was not the only one who thought this.

July 7, 1968

It's Sunday and I'm gonna wear my new white shoes and my new green checkered dress. The pockets on my dress look like two big daisies. Mama did take us to June's Department Store yesterday and to the drugstore lunch counter. It was a lot of fun.

Our revival starts tonight, so I will be going to church a lot. At least I will get to see Trixie and Patty!

Brownie

Gethsemane Baptist Church stood clean and white against a backdrop of green pastures where a small herd of cows grazed. The one room structure was square and built from white marble. Its tin roof stood tall and glittering in the morning sun. A smaller version of the roof sheltered the little concrete porch out front and was supported by two strong, square posts. Boxwood hedges at the front of the church also ran down each side. The day was getting warmer, and the sun's heat pulled a sweet essence from their boughs. Bumblebees buzzed beneath the open windows of the church; their lazy drone promoting the peace and tranquility of the day.

Daddy pulled our car up to the red oak tree that stood shading the east side of the church. A small knot of cars was parked beneath it. Half a dozen more were parked next to the cemetery where two elderly ladies stood looking at a headstone. Church started at eight o'clock. We got out of the car, and I walked to the outdoor dinner table where the water bucket sat. Trixie was there, dipping a paper cup into the water. Roger followed me and hopped up onto the marble table to sit.

Trixie mopped her mouth with the back of her hand. "I'm about to burn up!" she exclaimed. Sweat rings were already developing underneath her arms. Trixie was wearing a navy A-line style sleeveless dress, which made her look even plumper than she was. Her hair was pulled up into two dog-ear ponytails. I took the paper cup from her and dipped a drink of water for myself.

"Ain't nothin' we can do about it" I said, "Maybe it'll rain." The deacons and preachers were all beginning to congregate around the table to talk before church, so Trixie and I decided to go to the womens' toilet. We were just about to go in when we came full-stop before bumping into Patty, who was coming out.

"Lord!" I exclaimed, "You're as red as a scalded beet!" Patty had a terrible sunburn that was beginning to peel. Her hair and eyelashes were blonder than usual and the freckles on her face resembled black pepper sprinkled on top of a sliced tomato. This coloring was not helped by the strawberry pink shift she was wearing.

"How in the world did you get so sunburnt?" I asked.

"Well as you both know, I spent last week camping with the scouts at the scout lodge. One day, we were laying out on beach towels trying to get a suntan. Some of the girls from Ellijay told me the best thing for redheads to use for preventing sunburn was motor oil. They said if I used motor oil instead of suntan lotion that I'd get tanned and not burnt!" She picked a thin layer of peeled skin off her arm. "So, they gave me an old cold cream jar filled with it and I slathered it all over me." Trixie looked at Patty and said sincerely, "Patty, I think they lied to you."

Patty frowned and blew out a huff in Trixie's direction, then she stomped off toward the front door of the church. We followed her and went inside where, to our surprise, it was nice and cool. The three of us took our usual seats, fourth bench down the western side, beside the window. Trixie took the window, I was in the middle, and Patty was beside me. Now that we were in church, we knew better than to talk in our regular voice, so Patty lowered hers to a whisper.

"That's not all that happened either," Patty said. "One night, some of those mean girls from Ellijay invited me to go on a snipe hunt with them. I was excited because they were older than me. So, of course I said yes. I met them outside their tent after dark and they handed me a sack and a flashlight. Then I followed them to the edge of the woods.

"'Now, you take the snipe bag, and we'll show you where to sit,' one girl said. We walked into a pine thicket and the leader of the Ellijay girls said, 'Ok. You sit down here and get ready. We are going to go find the snipe and run him this way, and all you have to do is throw the sack over him. You got that?' So, I nodded and sat down on the pine straw while they walked on into the dark with their flashlights. Well, it got really dark, and I stretched my legs out and waited. I turned my flashlight on, and I waited and waited and waited some more. After a while I realized they wasn't comin' back, so I got up and went back to their tent to look for them. I found them sittin' around the campfire. When they saw me, they started laughing fit to split! And *now*, not only am I peeling like a snake from this nasty sunburn, but I am tee-totally covered up with chiggers!" Trixie and I broke into snickering.

Patty dropped her voice until I had to strain to hear her. "*And,* I even have chiggers on my *privates!*" she whispered, pointing down at her lap. Trixie and I looked at each other. If it was sympathy that Patty was expecting, she did not get it.

"You moron!" Trixie exploded with laughter, "Ain't you never heard of a snipe hunt?" Patty frowned. "Well, no, I haven't!" she snapped. Patty stood up with her hands on her hips and glared at Trixie.

"Well, if you're that ignert, Patty Simpson, you deserve to have chiggers!" Trixie got her giggle box turned over and could not stop herself from laughing and, if I am being honest, I was snickering, too. Patty was so filled with rage that her red face looked like a tick about to pop.

"Well, that ain't very nice of you, Trixie!" Patty fumed, "Aint you ashamed for sayin' that to me in church! In front of God and everybody!"

"I'm sorry, Patty," Trixie said. "But I'm pretty sure the preacher would side with me." Patty stomped outside. I turned around to watch her go and immediately stopped laughing. There, at the front door, stood Mama, Miz Taylor, and Miz Jenkins. I did not know how much of our conversation they had heard, but I knew that our loud outburst was enough to get us fussed at. I decided to go on the offensive. I got up and walked slowly toward them.

I looked at mama and swallowed hard. "I'll just go see what's upset Patty so," I whispered. Mama gave me a stern look and said, "That's a good idea Tina Marie and y'all better hurry back. Church is fixin' to start." I said a quick yes ma'am and darted out the door, but not before I heard Miz Jenkins tell Trixie to put her knees together, that little girls did not sit like plow boys.

After I had coaxed Patty back inside to sit with us and Trixie had given her a whole pack of chewing gum as an apology, we seemed to be back on the right side. The church was full of our family, friends, and neighbors all clothed in their best. Miz Jenkins walked over to the piano and heaved herself down onto the bench while the song leader called out the page number from the song book. Singing was my absolute favorite. The rise and fall of the music, whether serious or joyous, always made me happy. I sang soprano and sang each song as loudly as I could. I was enjoying singing *I'll Fly Away* when Trixie punched me in the ribs. A wasp was walking the back of the bench in front of me like it was a tightrope. Trixie was afraid of any kind of insect that had a stinger, and Patty was also afraid because she had had an allergic reaction one time which caused her lips to swell up.

I closed my songbook, steadied my hand and whacked at it! The wasp flew out the window and Mona Lester's baby boy woke up and began to wail. I slid down in my seat, out of view of Mama's searchlight-eyes.

Patty got some paper and a pencil out of her pocketbook and the three of us started playing tic-tac-toe during the preaching. That is when I decided that a pocketbook was a good idea and that I would bring one to the next church service stuffed with supplies to keep us occupied. Soon, Patty's piece of paper was covered, and we couldn't play the game anymore. I looked up toward the altar. Miz Jenkins was sitting in the choir with her arms folded over her enormous bosoms. Her face was set in a permanent scowl, and wouldn't you know it, she was sitting with her knees apart, just like a plow boy! I pointed this out to Trixie, and we began to snicker. About that time, Patty punched me in the arm and asked me who it was that was sitting beside Miz Jenkins. The young blonde woman, in the bright yellow dress.

I shrugged, but Trixie, leaning over me so that Patty could hear her too, said that the young lady was Miz Jenkins' niece and that she went to college and was really good at playing the piano. I was glad when Trixie leaned back to her side of the bench. Her elbows were punching holes in my legs.

"Then, why didn't she play the piano tonight instead of Miz Jenkins?" Patty wondered. I shrugged, but Trixie leaned over me again and said that Miz Jenkins was jealous of her piano playing job and wouldn't share it with anybody, so she probably never asked her. Truth be told Miz Jenkins was not a bad piano player. She just played plain notes and did not put any style or twiddly bits into her playing. We sat there wondering among ourselves how the niece in the yellow dress would do if she was asked to play sometime.

It was cool on the ride home. Roger fell asleep in my lap, and I stroked his hair. In the coal-black sky white stars twinkled. I could see the Big Dipper and his Little Dipper. The North Star blinked brightly, and the moon shone with a soft halo around it.

"We're gonna git rain in three days," Daddy said. I yawned as we turned into the drive at our house and parked at the backdoor. "How'd you know?" I asked. Daddy opened my door and picked Roger up to carry him into the house. "Cause you count the stars inside the ring around the moon and that's how many days 'til it rains. There was three stars inside it tonight," Daddy said. I looked up and counted three.

Lights were turned on and bedcovers turned down. It was the peaceful routine of bedtime. I was turning out the bathroom light and heading to the room I shared with my sister when I heard Daddy and Mama in soft conversation. I stood still and listened.

"She's been arrested," Daddy said. "Her bond is high, but they say she has a lawyer from Marietta, so she's bound to make bail."

"Do you think she did it, Boyd?" Mama asked.

Daddy started to answer her when, suddenly, he boomed, "Tina, go to bed!" I jumped. Tiptoeing back to my room, I had to feel my way to my bed. I did not dare to turn on the light. "Busted again," Donna whispered. "When will you ever learn?" My guess was never. I knew our parents were talking about The Widow, as Trixie and I had started calling her, and I wanted to learn more about what they knew. For Tater's sake. The rabbit's foot and matchbox hidden in the bottom of our closet was never far from my mind.

It was Saturday night. The last service of our revival. Tomorrow Gethsemane would baptize four converts down at our baptizing site on the Etowah River. The church members were tired, and the service was slow. I looked around at the handful of people in attendance. Mr. Coker in the deacons' corner was sitting next to the wall, leaning on his hand, sound asleep. The women in the choir were listening attentively to the preacher. Miz Jenkins had her arms folded across her bosom. Once, when the preaching reached a crescendo, she hollered, "Amen" and startled Mr. Coker, who sat straight up and shouted, "Amen!" too. Trixie, Patty, and I laughed uncontrollably.

Then the song leader got up and motioned for Miz Jenkins to come and play the piano. But instead of getting up, she pointed to her niece who was wearing a hot pink, sleeveless dress and had her hair piled up on top of her head like a movie star. Shyly, the niece got up and walked to the piano. The page number was called out, and I opened my songbook to begin singing. It was an up-tempo song that I liked a lot, but I had never before in my life heard the *Land Where Living Waters Flow* played the way I was about to hear it.

The niece played a modest introduction, paused, then took off! She bounced and ran her long fingers over the keys in a frenzy. Trixie looked at me and said, "She's as good as Joanne Castle!" and I had to agree. We watched Joanne Castle on the Lawrence Welk Show every Saturday night. Our song leader was caught by surprise and was having a hard time keeping up with Miz Jenkins' niece. By the end of the song, he looked plum out of breath. I wanted to stand up and clap but knew better than to do that. It was like we had watched a show!

The song leader, jittery from all the exertion, took a handkerchief out of his pocket and mopped his forehead. Miz Jenkins sat in her seat looking proud as a peacock. The song leader composed himself and called out another page number. When I saw the title of the song, I was disappointed. The congregation took a collective breath. There was no way Miz Jenkins' niece could play *Softly and Tenderly* anyway but slow.

July 14, 1968

Dear Diary,
You won't believe this! Daddy took us up to the mountains in Towns County to see some of his people on the Rivers' side. They live way out in the boonies. Mama said we won't be going there again if she can help it.
Brownie

On Sunday morning we loaded into the car and headed three counties away to spend some time with my father's relatives. The drive was long and hot and none of us wanted to go. Mama had promised we would stop for a milk shake on the way home if we were good. She said that we were going to see Daddy's family that he had not seen in fifteen years, and it was important to him. Mama told us we should all be polite and mind our manners.

Donna slumped against the passenger side rear window, pouting, while I slumped against the other one. Roger was squirming in the middle repeating every few minutes that he was going to throw up. Daddy and Mama ignored us all as best they could.

My leg went to sleep, and I started stamping my foot on the floorboard. That's when Daddy turned off the county road that we had been traveling on for the last hour and onto a dirt road that forded a shallow creek. The little pig trail, as Mama kept calling it, went straight up a mountain. It was obvious that the road had not been scraped in some time. There were gullies and washouts that Daddy had to maneuver around and, occasionally, briars and brush that scraped against the car and flipped inside the open windows.

"Are you sure this is the way, Boyd?" Mama asked nervously. The longer we traveled, the higher we climbed. Once the trees and brush on Daddy's side cleared away, we could see a wide expanse of sky and the valley down below. "Daddy, are we at Lookout Mountain?" Roger asked.

Daddy had a job of it trying to keep our family car in the middle of the dirt track while remaining optimistic about his choice for our Sunday drive. "Well, it's been a long time since I came up here to see Able and Lo-eeshur, but I'm pretty sure this is the way." I looked off down the ravine and thought that this must be what it would look like to go visit Snuffy Smith. Mama sat there in her Sunday best looking like she was riding a roller coaster. Every time Daddy swerved the car left toward the ravine, she pushed herself hard right against the passenger door and held on to the door hanger until her knuckles were white.

Before long we reached a place where the dirt road topped the mountain. Then, we traveled on flat ground, and the road took a circuitous route through an oak grove until it came to a clearing. Daddy brought the car to an abrupt stop in front of a run-down farmhouse with a little creek running in front of it. After the long journey, we were all ready to get out of the car. But when we did, a pack of Plott hounds came running out from under the porch, baying loud enough to wake the dead. Mama got back into the car and slammed the door shut.

There was a long bridge made of rough sawmill boards that stretched across the creek. A narrow dirt path ran up to the house. Beside the bridge was a battered mailbox on a weathered pole. The baying hounds swarmed around us. "They won't bite," Daddy said. "They're huntin' dogs." I reached out and petted one of them and got a hand full of slobber in return. I wiped my hand down the backside of my Sunday dress.

Out of nowhere, a boy about my age came and scolded the dogs to get them away from us. The dogs ran back to their lookout post beneath the porch. "Mama's in the kitchen and Daddy's by the farr," the boy said. I could see the smoke snaking up from the rock and chink-mud chimney at the back of the house. I wondered why anybody needed a fire in the hot summertime. The boy motioned for us to follow him.

"Git out of the car, Jeanette," Daddy called to Mama. "The dogs won't hurt you." "How do you know that, Boyd!" Mama eased open the car door and got out, watching the dogs underneath the house closely. She flung her sweater over her shoulders and gave Daddy her hand to help her cross the bridge. Her eyes seemed to say, "Well, Boyd?"

We waited on them to get up to the house and when they did, Daddy walked up and knocked on the screen door that covered the interior door. The screen door rattled a couple of times and a gray-haired man of about fifty opened the inside door. Daddy did not give the man time to speak. "Hey there, Able!" he said grinning. The gray-haired man guffawed and grinned like a mule eating briars. "Whah, ifn it ain't Boyd Rivers! What in tarnation are yuns a doin' way up hyar?" At that time the man opened the screen door and put out his hand to shake Daddy's. Daddy answered the man back, "We'uz just out ridin' around. I wadnt sure I could find ye. It's been so long." The man stepped back, and Daddy stepped inside. All the rest of us followed, with Mama bringing up the rear.

"I hope we ain't hindering you by showing up like this," Daddy said. "Naw, naw!" the man replied, "Lo-eeshur's about got dinner ready, so yer right on time!" The man gave Daddy a friendly slap on the shoulder.

I was glad to hear we had not missed lunch and followed Mama over to the couch to sit down. Mama put Roger in her lap, much like a shield, and Donna sat down in a rocker beside the woodstove. The room was dark, I guess because the sun had already gone down behind the mountain, but it was warm and cozy. "I don't think ye've ever seen my wife and kids," Daddy said. Then one by one we were introduced. That's when I noticed the boy that we had seen earlier standing in a back doorway with a woman about the same age as Able. She had her hair in a tight bun and was wearing a faded house dress with an apron that sported the spills and splatters of untold meals. This woman was what Granny would call "stout". Rolls of fat spilled out over the ties of her apron. Then, I looked at Able and noticed that his overalls were unbuttoned on the sides, and he too had a large roll of fat pouching out over the sides. I began to think this woman was probably a good cook.

Able grinned at the woman. "Lo-eesher," he said. "I bet ye don't know who this is?" Lo-eesher came into the light and scowled at Daddy, then she began to smile. "Well, I'll swar! Ifn it ain't Boyd Rivers!" The woman walked up to Daddy and grabbed him around the neck until I thought his eyes were going to pop out. "We ain't seen ye in quite a whal!" Daddy began the introductions again and Lo-eesher motioned for the boy to come and "meet his kin".

"This here is Royce," Able said. "Say hey, Royce," he instructed. Royce said "Hey" then went back to being a ghost. Since we had all been introduced and pleasantries had been exchanged, Mama began to relax. "Can I help you with anything?" she asked Lo-eesher. Lo-eesher started walking to the back from where she came and hollered over her shoulder, "Naw. Y'all jes sit an talk. I won't be long." Then she and Royce disappeared. Somewhere in that darkness where they went, I heard a door slam.

Daddy and Able talked about the weather, farming, and the government. Able said that Royce was Lynn Dale's boy and that he and Lo-eeshur were raising him. "Caint git the gov'mint to hep us out atall," he grumbled. He got up from his chair and opened the door on the wood stove. Then he picked up a poker and punched the fire. "I keep a little farr lak this all summer. Ye see, I'm on blood thinner and I stay cold." I listened hard to the conversation but could not for the life of me figure out who Lynn Dale, Lo-eesher, and Able *were* or how they were related to Daddy. Mama sat there holding Roger and dared him to get down. Meanwhile, the men continued their discussion about the price of hay, turning sixty-five in seven years and the "gov-mint". "We don't git no cump-ny," Able said. "We did have ah insurance salesman tha other day, but I run 'im off!" There was a loud racket off in some room that caused Mama to jump.

Suddenly, a loud metal bell was ringing somewhere at the back of the house. "Now then," Able said happily. "That means dinner's ready!" We all stood up and followed Able into the darkness where Lo-eesher had gone. It turns out the darkness was a dimly lit hall. I wondered to myself why these people didn't turn their lights on, then remembered the gov-mint wouldn't help them and decided that they were saving money. We walked, single file, down the little hallway where Able opened a door and we were led outside. Mama gasped and looked at Daddy with raised eyebrows.

Able kept walking until we came to the same creek that we had seen outside only it was wider here. A bigger bridge stretched over the water, but there were no handrails, and we did not know where it led, nor could we see to figure it out because the sun had dipped below the mountain and cast everything in shadow. I do know it was humid outside and my bare legs were quickly getting eaten up by mosquitoes.

"Y'all may not be used to tha kitchen bein' outside," Able commented as he led the way over the rickety bridge. "But the cookhouse was here when we bought the place after Lo-eeshur an me got marr-eed and we laked it so good, we jes kep it as twas." I thought it was a great adventure. I smiled and looked back at Donna, who was slapping at her arms; Mama, who was holding Roger and looking like she could die; and Daddy who was looking like, "Boy, I've done it now!" We got over the bridge and went into the cookhouse where the lights were on. I was glad, because I didn't think mama would take to eating her dinner in the dark with people she did not know.

We all trouped inside, and Able sat down in a ladder-back chair at the head of the table with his back to the stove. The dining table was made of boards that seemed very old with mismatched chairs around them. Salt and pepper shakers, a stoneware sugar bowl, and a small bowl of red-eyed gravy with a cloud of grease on its top were in the middle of the table. The table had been set with plain, white stoneware plates and tarnished forks that sometime in their life had been stainless. The tines of my fork were bent, as though someone had used them to dig up potatoes. Across the room was a deep, double sink and some rough cabinets, their countertops covered with canisters, flour, and what looked like a pile of squirrel hides.

We all sat down at the table. Mama was across the table from me, wrinkling up her nose. Something smelled bad, and I soon found out what it was. Lo-eeshur waddled to the table with a black cast iron pot and took the lid off. Inside, swimming in grease were four pigs' feet. Mama's dainty hand went immediately up to her nose. Then, Royce came over with a platter of fried something and sat that down beside the pigs' feet. Lo-eeshur came again with a stewpot full of leather britches. Then she sat down at the end of the table and pronounced, "Let's eat!" At that time Royce jumped up from his seat and came back with a pan of cornbread that he sat on the table in front of Able.

"Y'all dig in!" Able said cheerily. He reached his meaty hands into the cornbread pan and broke off a hunk of the bread. Mama watched him, and I could tell she was more than a little disturbed. Nobody we knew ate cornbread without slicing it.

Donna looked at her plate and then said, "I think the plates are upside down." Lo-eeshur did not miss a beat. "Yeah," she said, while using her fork and her thumb to pry open the fried meat. "We ate breakfast offn the other side. Saves on washin'." Everyone was eating noisily but us. I flipped my plate over to find egg yolk and gravy stuck to it. Mama looked at me and shook her head no.

"Is that squirrel?" Daddy asked. "Yeah," Lo-eeshur said with a mouthful of the leather britches. "Royce jus skint 'em." Daddy got a piece of squirrel and put it on the upside-down plate and then dipped out some beans to go with it. I watched as the juice from the leather britches ran off the edge of his plate.

"Ain't chall hungry?" Able said smacking. He looked at mama, "Eat somethin'! Yore poor as a snake!" Mama mumbled that the ride up the mountain had made her stomach upset, snatching the only logical excuse from Donna's already poised lips. Realizing her mistake, Mama said, "And Donna is trying to lose weight for cheerleading." The color came back into Donna's cheeks, and she leaned back in her chair to exhale. As for Roger and me, we loved leather britches and were eating them off the backside of the plates and tearing off hunks from the pone of cornbread, just like our kinfolk.

After supper and a brief spell of after dinner talk, Daddy stood to go. "Thank ye, Able. Lo-eeshur. We've sure enjoyed it." Mama nodded and we said our goodbyes. Royce took a flashlight out of a table drawer and went with us to the car. We crossed the little creek without saying anything, hound dogs trotting along behind us. When we got to the car and started to get in, Royce went up to daddy and hugged him around the waist. Then, without saying a word, he turned and went back to the house.

Daddy backed the car up and turned on the headlights. We all sat quietly, waiting to hear what Mama was going to say. Daddy had driven only a little way down the mountain when Mama suddenly burst out laughing. She laughed hysterically, crying and trying to talk, and squealing like a schoolgirl. We had never seen Mama act that way, so we started laughing too.

Between gasps of laughter Mama said, "Saves on washin!" We laughed until we were down the mountain and back on the county road. "Thanks for hangin' in there," Daddy said to Mama. Mama scooted over next to him, and Daddy put his arm around her shoulders. "That's okay, Boyd," she said. "But if you ever do anything like that to me again, I'll skin you like those squirrels!" To which Daddy said, mocking Lo-eeshur, "Royce jus skint 'em!" And we all started laughing again.

On the way home I learned some things. I learned that Able and Lo-eeshur were second cousins to Papa Rivers. That Lo-eeshur's name was really Louisa. Able just pronounced it that way. And that Lynn Dale ran off with a refrigerator repair man right after she had Royce. She was only sixteen. Mama said that Able and Lo-eeshur's situation was pitiful and Daddy agreed. I remembered the hug that Royce gave to Daddy when we left, and I felt sorry for him.

July 23, 1968

Dear Diary,

Man! We had a big blow up around here last night! Donna broke up with David because he enlisted in the Army! She was at David's house for his eighteenth birthday party and next thing I knew, Donna came stormin' into the house with David chasin after. They were hollering at each other, and Donna was crying. Mama had to take her to her room to calm her down.

Brownie

It was so hot and humid that my shorts set was sticking to me. I was sitting on the porch in a webbed folding chair waiting on supper. Mama was making potato salad to go with the green beans, and the kitchen was so hot that I could not bear to be inside. Mama had sent me out to call Roger to supper, but I had screamed my lungs out and my brother did not come. I was just sitting there on the porch, slapping at sweat bees, when I saw David's car come flying up the driveway. He barely got stopped before Donna jumped out and ran up the steps, slamming the screen door behind her.

"What's eatin' her?" I asked David, but he just ran after Donna and the screen door slammed again.

"What's goin on?" I looked up to see Roger climbing onto the porch from the end side. Then he climbed on the porch railing and sat on it like it was a horse. "Where've *you* been?" I asked my brother. "I bellered like a cow trying to get you to come to the house!" Roger shrugged and swung his legs back and forth. "I was helpin daddy gather tomaters" he said. "What's up with Donna?" Then I told him about how she and David just got here, and I was fixing to go inside and find out. Roger bounced up and down on the porch rail. "You'd better not fall off," I warned him. "If you fall into Mama's zinnias, she'll wear you out!"

I eased inside the living room. Daddy had come in the backdoor with the tomatoes. He was standing in the kitchen with a peck basket on his hip and a hand on David's shoulder. They were talking softly. I sat down in the rocker beside the living room couch to wait.

I heard Mama shut the door to the room I shared with Donna. She came into the kitchen and told David that Donna would not come out of the bedroom. David nodded, shook Daddy's hand, and quickly walked out of the house. Daddy was rubbing the back of his neck. "Well, he's an honorable young man, that's for sure," he said to Mama. "Donna's not willin' to wait on him?" David had graduated back in May and Donna would be a senior when school started back. Everyone figured that they would get married after she graduated.

"His enlisting is only part of it," Mama replied. "It seems David saw her flirting with one of those mill boys from Northside. But to his credit, he hadn't mentioned until she started fussing about his enlisting this morning." Mama walked into the kitchen to finish supper. "To tell you the truth, Boyd," she continued. "I don't think she wants to get married, and this blow up about the Army is just an excuse to break it off with him."

I walked back to the bedroom. Without knocking, I went in and shut the door behind me. "Leave me alone," Donna said. She was lying face down on her bed with a pillow over her head. "I don't want nothin'," I lied. "I just came to get my diary." I picked up my school notebook and a pencil and sat down on the bed. Donna rolled over, hugging a pillow to her chest.

"I can't marry him, Brownie," she whispered. "There's just too much life ahead of me." Donna turned onto her side and propped herself on her elbow. "I know everybody thinks that I'm bein' selfish, but I just can't do it! I have things I want to do with my life. I want to travel. I want to *find* myself before I get married." My eyes widened and I stared at her.

"Okay, what does that even mean?" I asked. I knew what finding yourself meant. I had heard it on the news when a reporter was interviewing a hippie. There was talk about this being the Summer of Love and young people were finding themselves and a whole lot of other stuff that did not make sense to me.

Donna sat up on the edge of her bed. Her hair had grown fast. For the first time since Aunt Janelle cut it, I noticed it was now almost down to her shoulders. Donna sighed, "It means, well, I don't know what it means," she huffed. "It's just that I'm a kid, really, and not ready to be a wife with a house and a job. Lately, I have felt like the walls were closing in on me. Everybody kept asking me, "When's the weddin gonna be? Do you have a job? And tellin me that I could be a teller at the bank or a cashier at the grocery store." Donna looked at me for a response. I did not know what to say, so I just stood up and turned to leave.

"Donna," I said in my most grown-up ten-year-old voice, "I don't want to get married right now either. So, I will take up for you if you need me to." Donna gave me a half-hearted smile. "Thanks," is all she said.

The breakup of Donna and David was the latest news on the party lines in Piney Hill. Some folks said Donna just had cold feet and would come around, while others thought it was awful how she had treated David and him about to go serve our country on foreign soil. But I kept my promise to my sister. If anything was said within earshot of me regarding Donna, I stood up for her and reminded everybody that she had not even graduated high school yet. But she was not to be the topic of discussion for long. All the gossip about the breakup was soon put on the back burner when mama, Aunt Brenda, and Miz Jenkins ran into The Widow Lola Landers one hot Saturday afternoon in August.

August 10, 1968
Dear Diary,
I went with Mama and Aunt Brenda to Kringle's Pick-N-Pay to get school supplies for me and Roger.
I love when you walk into Kringle's and smell the popcorn and the chocolate smells coming from the candy counter.
We were in the school section looking at bookbags and such and that's when the bell over the door dingled and in walked the most beautiful woman I have ever seen! It was The Widow, and you should have seen the look on Miz Jenkins' face!
Brownie

Mama parked our car in the parking space in front of the store and we all got out. Sweat on the back of my legs had stuck them to the vinyl upholstery, causing red marks. While mama fed coins into the meter, I rubbed my legs and brushed the seat of my dress down. I was sorry that Trixie didn't come with us. Aunt Brenda said that Trixie's grandma was still sick, and Trixie was staying with her. So, we had dropped Trixie off at her grandma's house in town on our way to Kringle's.

Miz Passley and her husband, Ken, lived in the mill village in a little five room house. Mr. Passley was a deacon at the church. His wife had been sick a lot lately, and Aunt Brenda and her sister, Carol, had been looking after her. I knew that she couldn't keep anything on her stomach, but once I had overheard Aunt Brenda say that her mama thought she had a tumor and that seemed very serious to me.

Mama turned from the parking meter ready to go. She looked so nice in her white cotton blouse and wraparound skirt with the sailboat print. Her blonde hair was brushed and glossy. Aunt Brenda was wearing a striped, shirtwaist. Both women had on stockings and low heels. We went into the store, jingling the little bell that hung over the doorway as we went in.

"There's Miz Jenkins," Aunt Brenda said under her breath. Mama took precautions and scooted Roger and me toward the school supplies where we were partially hidden by a tall corkboard case covered with pegs of pencils, crayons, and school glue. Mama looked at me and took a piece of notebook paper out of her purse.

"Now then," she said, referring to her list. "We need two of everything. One for you and one for Roger." Mama handed me a little red basket. "Here, put what I hand you in this basket," she said. I took hold of the little metal handle and Mama started putting two of everything into the basket as she went down the aisle. Two packs of number two pencils, two packs of crayons, two bottles of white glue, and two packs of notebook paper. I imagined Mama as Noah's wife and giggled. I peeked around the pegboard just in time to see Miz Jenkins holding up an enormous pair of bloomers. I started laughing, and Aunt Brenda grabbed my arm and pulled me back.

"Brownie!" she hissed. "We don't want ole nosey comin' over here!" Since I agreed with her, I tried harder to remember and stay behind the particle board partition. We were looking at three-ring notebooks when the bell over the door jangled. In walked the most beautiful woman I had ever seen. Her skin was dark brown and shiny. She had curly black hair that hung down her back and dark eyebrows. Her eyes were lined with black Cleopatra eyeliner, and her full lips were painted a dark red.

The woman was wearing a silky, summer dress similar to what anyone else I knew would wear, but somehow it fit her differently. It was tight at her little waist and her bosom was pushed up so that you could see the curves. The beautiful woman stopped on our side of the candy counter and bought a pack of gum. Her long legs were bare. Bare! In town! Now, where we lived, you never went to town without stockings. The only time it was acceptable to be seen in public bare legged was if you were on vacation or relief. I stared at her in admiration.

"Don't look, Jeannette," Aunt Brenda whispered to Mama. "Lonnie's widow is over at the candy counter." So that is *The Widow*, I thought. Mama was about to sneak a peek herself when Aunt Brenda suddenly drew in her breath. The Widow was walking back toward the ladies' department. Back toward the brick wall that was Miz Jenkins, scowling and blocking her way. It was about to get ugly. Right there between women's underwear and men's trusses.

"Excuse, me," The Widow said, trying to get by Miz Jenkins. "Oh, *I'm* sorry," Miz Jenkins sing-songed. "Am I in yore way?" The Widow stepped around Miz Jenkins' bulky frame and replied, "No, Senora. Not at all." The Widow then gave Miz Jenkins a very pleasant smile and asked her if she could point her to the lingerie. Miz Jenkins, forgetting she was supposed to be threatening, pointed to the back corner of the store, and muttered, "Under ware is thata way."

Aunt Brenda and Mama stood mesmerized. "She looks just like one of them senoritas from a western movie!" Aunt Brenda said. Miz Jenkins got hold of herself and slapped a scowl back on her face. Then she marched up to the underwear section and tried again.

"Aint you the one that married Lonnie Landers?" she asked point blank. The Widow turned around and smiled.

"Si, I am Lola. And you are?" Miz Jenkins looked stunned by The Widow being so polite and babbled for a minute before remembering her name.

"Well, I'm Edner Jenkins," she said. "Frances Landers is my second cousin on my mama's side." The Widow broke into a happy smile and spoke to Miz Landers rapidly in another language before slowing down to speak to her in English. She grabbed hold of Miz Jenkins' meaty hands. "So sorry!" she cried. "I not speak too good English," The Widow said. "It's nice to meet you."

Miz Jenkins ripped her big mitt from the tiny hand of The Widow and frowned. "Why'd you burn down Frances' house?" Miz Jenkins glared at The Widow, who looked both astonished and confused. Her delay gave Miz Jenkins another stab at it.

"Why'd you burn that house down? Say! I know you done it. They musta had e'vdence or you wouldna been locked up in the jail!" The Widow looked embarrassed by this attack for a moment, but then she threw her shoulders back and pointed her finger right at Miz Jenkins. With her dark eyes flashing fire, The Widow proceeded to put Miz Jenkins in her place. None of us, including Miz Jenkins, could understand a word she was saying, but she had Miz Jenkins backing up while she shouted and gesticulated like a wrestler on Saturday Nite Showdown.

Miz Jenkins had backed herself up against a garment table which held men's underwear and tube socks. And she stayed backed up until The Widow finally threw her hands in the air and stormed out of Kringle's Pick-N-Pay, the little bell jingling happily as The Widow slammed the door.

Kringle's Pic-n-Pay was suddenly quiet. The only customers inside were the four of us, Miz Jenkins, and the saleslady, who was standing at the cash register with her mouth open. Miz Jenkins grabbed a handful of tube socks, walked over to the register, and paid for them. Then, without saying a word, she left the Pick-n-Pay in a huff, slamming the door and making the little bell dingle again.

"Wait til Trixie hears about this!" I exclaimed. "The Widow sure got ole nosey told, huh?" Mama looked at Aunt Brenda and then told me I should not revel in the misfortunes of others. Mama then turned my attention to the book satchel display and told me to pick one out. But I noticed that Mama and Aunt Brenda were giggling and exchanging sly looks behind the particle board.

I picked out a two-pocket book satchel that was covered with red canvas and brown buckles, and Aunt Brenda got Trixie one just like it. Then we went to the register to pay.

"Can I have some candy? Pleez!" I begged mama. Mama got out her little snap change purse and pulled out a quarter. "Twenty cents worth of candy corn, please," she said to the sales lady. "And can you divide it into two bags?" The lady did just that and rang up the candy. I took hold of one of the bags and stuck my nose inside. The smell of candy corn always made me feel happy.

We had to go to the drugstore so Aunt Brenda could pick up medicine for her mama. It was really hot and humid, so I was glad for the air conditioning inside the store. Near the counter a pedestal fan stood blowing the warm air around. While Aunt Brenda spoke to the pharmacist, Mama and I went to the toiletries section. Mama picked up a box of cream deodorant and some toothpaste. Then she asked if we needed shampoo. I was not interested in bathroom supplies, so I walked over to the little two-step entrance that led to the drugstore's grill. There, in one of the booths, sat The Widow. She was absent-mindedly stirring a cup of coffee. I don't know what made me do it, but I walked over and sat down in her booth in the seat across from her.

"Hello," I said. The Widow did not seem surprised. She laid her spoon in the saucer next to her cup and smiled.

"Hello," she said in her thick accent. "I embarrass myself, no?" She looked down and I could tell she was wearing fake eyelashes. I had never seen fake eyelashes up close before, so I stared. "Su ignorancia me enoja!" continued The Widow. "What does that woman know? I do nothing wrong. I no look like you. That why she no trust me. Senora Franchesca es good to me. She no do me like that." "You mean Miz Frances?" I asked. "Si," The Widow replied, taking a sip of her coffee.

"Aw, I wouldn't worry about Ole Busybody if I was you," I said. "She's always itchin' for a fight with somebody." The Widow smiled at me. "You mean that woman? Senora tell me about her. Senora say we 'none of her business'." I felt sorry for The Widow. She looked so beautiful, sitting there all small and helpless. "Why can't you talk English?" I asked.

The Widow shrugged. "I come from Cuba. Not been here long, but I learning." I frowned. "But where is your family?" I asked. "They in Miami. We immigrate," she said. I did not know what that word meant. "Are you going to live here now?" I asked. Mama had noticed me sitting with The Widow and was coming into the grill toward us.

"There you are, Tina," Mama said in her gaspy excuse me voice. "Miz Landers," Mama nodded to The Widow in a friendly way. I stood to go, "It was nice to talk to you," I said. The Widow smiled and looked at Mama. "You have lovely daughter," she said. Mama thanked her and we said goodbye.

"What were you two talking about?" Mama sounded curious. I shrugged my shoulders and we walked quietly out of the drugstore without so much as a "Do you want a milkshake?" or anything. I was disappointed.

Mama and I waited in the car for Aunt Brenda. Roger tagged along with our aunt, hoping to get something out of it. I was sweating like a pig by the time Aunt Brenda and Roger got back. Aunt Brenda opened the car door and got into the front passenger seat. "Everything alright?" Mama asked her.

"Roger, git in! Just drive, Jeannette!" Aunt Brenda was never snippy, so her tone made me know something was not right. I shut my eyes and pretended to be asleep.

"You know that's just for nausea," Mama said. "You're still going to have to face that she's PG." Aunt Brenda let out a soft moan.

When we pulled up to the curb at Miz Passley's house, Trixie was standing in the shade waiting for us. She got in beside me. I opened one eye and put my fingers to my lips. Trixie nodded and leaned her head back like me.

"How was mama?" Aunt Brenda asked Trixie. "Uh-kay..." Trixie mumbled. She was pretending to doze off. After a while of pretending, I began to really get sleepy. It was all I could do to stay awake with all the heat and silence. Finally, Mama and Aunt Brenda began to talk in soft whispers.

"I know this medicine will only help mama to stop throwing up, but I'm so embarrassed by the whole thing!" Trixie looked over at me and grinned.

"Well, it will soon be over, and you will just have to learn how to deal with it," Mama said. "Besides. You've got to tell you-know-who about it." We turned onto the dirt road leading up Piney Hill. Mama would soon stop at Aunt Brenda's house to let her and Trixie out. I hoped that they would say more before we got there. "I know," Aunt Brenda sighed. "But I shore am dreddin' it!" was all that was said.

About that time, we hit the big ditch in the road where water had come down the hill and eroded it. A large piece of marble had been exposed, and the bump it gave the car was fierce.

"I've told Gil he needs to scrape the road down here!" Aunt Brenda said, "That rock has already thrown the front end out of alignment on my station wagon!"

Mama pulled into the driveway, and Aunt Brenda got out and opened the door to the backseat. "Wake up, sleepy head!" she said, "You've gotta run get my washing in. Looks like it's gonna rain." Trixie yawned and got out. Mama and I did too. Roger was in the backseat opening a pack of baseball cards.

Mama and Aunt Brenda rummaged through the trunk of the car collecting the things that Aunt Brenda had bought. I reached into one sack and pulled out my book satchel. "See, Trix," I cried. "Ours are just alike!" Trixie smiled.

We said our goodbyes, and I got into the front seat of the car with Mama. Mama didn't talk and that was fine with me. I had lots to think about. Like, what in the world was PG?

If Miz Landers was kind to Lola, then why was Lola arrested for burning Miz Landers' house down? What did Carl and Tater have to do with it? And more importantly, was it time for me to tell somebody about Tater's rabbit foot?

I had just sat down at the supper table when Daddy came in for supper. He was washing up at the sink. I watched as he rolled his shirtsleeves down and buttoned them.

"I wish you'd a been here this afternoon," he said in an aggravated tone. "Edner came by and liketa have talked my ears off!" Daddy walked over and sat down at the head of the table. I looked around. All we were waiting on was the cornbread and Mama.

"What about?" Mama said, walking to the table with the hot pone of bread. "We saw her in Kringle's today and she made a spectacle of herself." Mama pulled out her chair and sat down.

"Bow your heads," Daddy said. After the blessing, Mama asked him again. "Aww, she uz just goin' on and on 'bout how Lonnie's widow burnt the house down and stole Frances' car," Daddy said. "Well, I don't know tha facts and neither does she. We'll just leave it at that."

Mama brought up the subject of Miz Passley. "Brenda says that LaWanda is getting some better with that *matter* of hers, but Brenda still won't prepare herself for what's to come."

Daddy laughed. "Well, what about Ken? Nobody seems to worry about *him*." Daddy dipped out some fresh green beans and put them on his plate. "Boy, I'm hungry!" he said. "I could eat a horse!" With this, he reached over and pulled Roger's nose. We all laughed.

Donna cleared her throat and asked, "Is it okay if I go watch a movie with Poppy tonight?" I looked at my sister sitting next to me. I noticed my sister was nervously twisting her skirt tail underneath the table.

"Who's Poppy?" Mama's brow furrowed. "I've never heard that name before." Donna fiddled with her tea glass. "She was in my junior class. She only went in April and May. This is her first full year. I doubt you've seen her."

"Who are her parents?" Mama continued. Donna took a sip of tea. "Uh, I think she lives with her aunt. She moved here from Michigan."

Mama, who always ate slowly, chewed, and chewed her food before answering.

"Are you meeting her there?" she asked. Donna nodded and asked if she could borrow the car.

"What are you going to see?" Mama asked. This is what Donna always referred to as "The Third Degree". Donna replied by saying that they were going to see that new musical set in the Bavarian Alps. Mama said she had heard that was a nice movie and gave Donna the okay to use the car so she could go. I did not realize it but, up until then, I had been holding my breath.

"I wanna go too!" I whined. "No!" Donna all but shouted. "I mean, no," she corrected herself. "She's a new friend and I want it to be just us."

"That's alright, Brownie," Roger said to me. "We can watch the spy rerun that we missed. I smiled at my brother, but I really wanted to go see this movie. I had seen the commercials and it had a lot of singing, which I loved.

"I'm sorry Tina," Mama said. "But you don't need to go this time. How about we make ice cream sundaes to have while we watch tv?" I crossed my arms and pouted, but I nodded my head. I knew I would have to settle for ice cream this time.

August 11, 1968
Dear Diary,
Today is Sunday and I'm supposed to be getting ready for church but instead we are going to a family reunion on Papa's side at my Great Aunt Beulah's house in Talking Rock.
Mama made chicken and potato salad.
Brownie

Mama made me put on a Sunday dress, even though she knew I was going to be playing outside. I sat in the backseat of the car pouting. My last year's Easter dress was too small, and the frilly skirt of the dress made my legs itch. Still, I loved this reunion so much, it seemed like a small price to pay.

Aunt Beulah and Uncle Vestal's house always seemed like a long way off to me. Up the narrow highway, across a mountain, past Talking Rock church and way back in the woods. They lived in a small house with a big screened-in front porch that went all the way across the front. It had a steep tin roof, and the house was painted gray. A wide creek ran beside their yard; its waters mummering a song. I got out as soon as the car stopped so that I could take in a lung-full of air. I looked up at the treetops where the sun-beams were playing hide-and-seek with the leaves. It was a beautiful day.

"Y'all git out and git ye a cheer!" Uncle Vestal said around a mouthful of chewing tobacco. He spat into the petunias that were planted by the steps. Chairs had been set out all around the yard. "How ye doin', Boyd!" he clasped Daddy's hand and pumped it hard. Mama got out of the car and handed me the cake she had been cradling in her lap.

"Hey, Miz Bohannon." Mama waved at Aunt Beulah who was coming down from the porch, one step at a time.

Aunt Beulah looked the same as she did on our last visit, except her hair was a little whiter. She always wore it brushed back and in a low bun. Aunt Beulah was wearing a red and white polka-dot house dress with a yellow and brown duster apron covering it and her big belly. Her brown shoes made a clunking sound as she side-stepped down to the car.

"Le me hep ye, Jennette," she called. "That's okay," Mama hollered over the trunk lid. "I will get the kids to help me with the food." Mama was busy handing a red and white tea jug to Roger, so I headed toward Aunt Beulah with the cake.

"Where'd you wont this?" I asked her. Aunt Beulah's eyes shone. "Law, co-ker-nut cake! Wha, that's my fav-o-rite!" Aunt Beulah took the cake from me and smiled. "I thank I'll jes hide it 'till ever one leaves!" she giggled. I smiled back. You just could not help but love Aunt Beulah.

I went to the trunk of the car where Mama was trying to lift a cardboard box of food by herself. Donna said that she was sick with a stomach ache and did not come with us. However, I did not believe that excuse for one minute. I took hold of one side of the box and Mama got the other. Together we got it out of the car. Thank goodness Daddy came running when he saw us with it because I did not know how we were going to get it up the three steps leading up to the porch.

"Here! Give me that before the bottom falls out," he ordered. Daddy took the box and easily went up the steps and onto the porch. Mama followed right behind him.

I walked over to the creek to join Roger in throwing rocks into the water. "Look! A snake!" Roger cried. We watched as a long, black snake crawled its way up onto a log on the other side.

"I bet it's a cottonmouth!" Roger exclaimed. Uncle Vestal walked up behind us and spat tobacco down the bank.

"Naw, that's uh water snake," he said. "I see 'im around hyur all tha time." Uncle Vestal took a red bandana handkerchief out of his overall's pocket and wiped his mouth. He was a tall, slender man with bright blue eyes. I had kissed his cheek goo-bye the last time we were visiting, and it was bristly, but today he had shaved.

"Kin ah ketch him?" Roger asked. Uncle Vestal laughed. "Jes cause he aint poison don't mean he won't bite ye."

We were standing there watching the snake when a familiar car came creeping up the drive. When the car stopped, a door opened and slammed, knocking all the quiet out of the air.

"Earl! You'd better not tear up my cake when you git it out!" Miz Jenkins was out of the car, smoothing her dress down. She stomped her way across the yard, up the steps, and onto the porch, letting the screen door go with a bang. I could hear her voice over everyone else in the house.

I walked over to the car to offer Mr. Jenkins a hand. He had the trunk lid up and was looking for something. "Can I help?" I asked. He immediately bumped his head on the trunk lid.

"You shore can, Brownie, and I thank ye," he said meekly. I looked around and found the cake box. "How 'bout I carry the cake?" I offered. Mr. Jenkins looked grateful, so off I went with Miz Jenkins' big, aluminum cake box. I was careful going up the steps and Lloyd, one of Daddy's many cousins, opened the screen door for me. I walked into the house, looking for a place to set it down. I heard Miz Jenkins let out a shock wave.

"Lord, that child's got my hummingbird cake! She's liable to drop it!" Miz Jenkins hollered, slapping her hands against her cheeks. Mama ran over to take the cake box from me. She winked at me before she turned around with it and walked into the kitchen. Miz Jenkins stood in the kitchen doorway, hands on hips, and scowled at me. "You'd better not of made my layers slide!" she shouted. I walked over and sat down by Trixie, who was eating a handful of bread-and-butter pickles.

"Just how is it we're kin to her again?" I asked Trixie, who was sitting on a little brown couch in the living room. She licked the sticky syrup from the pickles off her fingers before she replied. "Earl and Papa are first cousins. I forget how it gets down to you and me," she said. "But we aint kin to Ole Busy Body, 'cept by marriage," Trixie said, shaking her head. "No. Not related, thank goodness." She stood up and smoothed out her skirt.

We sat back down on the couch watching the house fill up with aunts, uncles, and cousins until we finally had to give up our seats for the adults. We were just about to go outside when I heard Miz Jenkins' loud voice proclaiming she had heard something "Big". Trixie and I moved closer to the kitchen door so we could listen. Miz Jenkins was stirring mayonnaise into a large bowl of coleslaw.

"You know, I saw that *woman* over to Kringle's store and I shore got her told," Miz Jenkins boasted. "Well sir, I went straight over to the Sheriff's office adder that and asked them why they had let her go. I says, 'My poor cousin Frances, layin' up at the nursing home all because she aint got no home to go back to,' and that's when the deputy, you know, my nephew, Junior Gaines, Rachel's boy? told me they had got some evidence that might help crack the case!"

I heard the other ladies murmur, and someone mentioned they should put all the meats on the counter beside the stove. Miz Jenkins, not realizing they were trying to change the subject, plowed right on ahead with her big news.

"Yes sir, Junior told me right out of his own mouth that, when they questioned that ole hussy, they also searched the car. Did y'all know she was a drivin' Frances' sedan?" Miz Jenkins scoffed. "Well, Junior said they found a gas can in the trunk *and* Frances' pickle churn that belonged to our great, great grandmaw!"

"A gas can?" one of the women said. "Yes sir, a gas can," Miz Jenkins replied. Aunt Brenda said, "Well, maybe that's somethin', but what's the pickle churn got to do with the price of eggs?" Miz Jenkins sniffed. "That pickle churn is over a hunert years old and is worth a lot of money! She must have used the gas can to set the farr and was gonna sell the pickle churn to make her getaway!" All you could hear in the kitchen was the clanging of pots and scraping of spoons. Trixie and I decided to go outside and play until they called us to eat.

Out in the yard, there was a dozen or more cousins running this way and that. The sun was overhead and shone down warmly on the yard. We counted taters and chose sides for games like Red Rover, Mother May I, and Hide-and-Seek. I stopped to catch my breath. I noticed that I had popped the seam on one side of my dress, and I had red mud on my white ankle socks.

"Brownie! You've ripped your dress!" Trixie exclaimed. I tried to pull the sides together so that my skin didn't show. I had left off my slip and I knew Mama would fuss. "Don't worry," Trixie said. "That happens to me all the time." I looked at my cousin in her sleeveless navy dress with the red sailboat applique. Her chubby belly was poking out in front.

"Come on," she said. "Let's go play on the swings." Trixie grabbed my hand, and we ran to the backyard. Uncle Vestal had an old swing set with a slide back there that he had set up for his grandchildren. His grandkids were already on the swings. Johnny was eight and Joann was five. Trixie and I felt big when we were around them. Joann was quiet and shy with a head full of curly, brown hair. Johnny looked just like her, only he could not talk plain. Trixie got behind them and started pushing them on the swings.

The cousin of Johnny and Joann came to join us. She was around four years old and adorable. Her blonde hair was cut in a pixie and she had dimples. We watched her while she climbed the ladder to make sure she did not fall off. When Little Wanda got to the top, she paused.

"Are you skeered?" I asked her. "Nope," she answered. Johnny got off the swing and said, "Ahm gon puss her!" He ran and started to climb the ladder. Trixie and I called after him to leave her alone or he would make her fall.

Johnny started up the ladder behind Little Wanda and started laughing. "She ain gah no unner ware on!" And he took off running to tell on her. Little Wanda put her finger in her mouth and just stood there.

Johnny ran toward the circle of men who were sitting in webbed lawn chairs talking. Little Wanda's daddy, Gene, was one of them. "Untle Gene! Untle Gene! Wanna ain gah no unner ware on!" Then he pointed to the slide.

Little Wanda had decided it was time for her to slide down the slide. Only, with no panties on, she just sort of *screech screeched* down the slide in short, squeaky bursts. Using her feet to pull herself, she finally made it to the bottom and waited. Her daddy was walking over to the slide with Johnny fast behind him.

"Why aint you got no panties on?" Uncle Gene asked Little Wanda, who was smiling up at him with her big dimples. "I wet the bed, Daddy," she said. "I couldn't find no panties." Uncle Gene picked Little Wanda up and went to find Aunt Linda. Johnny looked at us with a big grin on his face. He said proudly, "Ah seed her butt!"

Aunt Beulah called us to eat, and we took off running. The small kitchen had a line of men holding paper plates. They stood near the table and leaned on cabinets. Uncle Lester was called on to ask the blessing, so we bowed our heads. Uncle Lester, as we kids all knew, would say a lengthy prayer. Trixie looked up at me and whispered, "Ain't he ever gonna git done!" But after what seemed like an eternity, he did, and the line of men began to move.

The men always got served first. The women and the children, last. I was looking forward to Aunt Beulah's fried chicken, but when us kids made it up to the table all that was left of the chicken was neck bones and gizzards. So, I got ham instead. Trixie had all her food piled on top of each other in a small mountain, which was topped with more pickles. Her paper plate was on the verge of folding up in the middle.

Mama shooed us out the door and told us to go sit on the grass. So, we maneuvered through the little kitchen with our burdened down plates and plastic cups of sweet tea trying hard not to spill anything. Trixie decided to leave her tea on the porch and use both hands to carry her plate.

Anita Roper Foster

"Where's your tea?" I asked as we sat our plates on the grass under the shade of a red oak tree. Trixie licked her finger. "I'm going back for it," she said. "I'da toted it for you!" I hollered, but she jumped up and ran to the house. She was back with her cup in no time.

"Lord, it's hot!" Our cousin Velda sat down on the grass beside us. August is Dog Days, and the heat and humidity were dragging the sweat out of us. Velda slapped at a sweat bee. "When's y'all's school start back?" she asked. Velda went to elementary school in the county over from us. Trixie answered with a mouthful of potato salad, "The Monday after Labor Day. Whenever that is." She shrugged her shoulders and Velma told us that was when school started for her, too. Velma forked a deviled egg and held it high while she nibbled on it and talked.

"You know, they say sores won't heal during Dog Days *and* dogs go mad." I had heard that all of my life and wondered why Velma would bring it up out of nowhere. Cousin Velma was a little strange. She was tall and lanky and wore blue horn-rimmed glasses that looked like they came out of the fifties.

"Look, y'all!" Trixie cried. She pointed at a large, ant-like insect with black and orange stripes. "It's a cow ant!" Trixie grabbed hold of her plate and scrambled to her feet. "Git up! They'll sting ye!" she cried. Velma had already scooched her bottom away from the hole where the cow ant had emerged. I sat my plate down, picked up a rock from near the tree, and began squishing the bug. The cow ant writhed and twisted until the pressure of the rock became too much for it. I lifted the rock and the bug lay there, it's middle smashed and its legs furiously pumping.

"They'll sting ye after they're dead!" Trixie warned. I had picked up a stick and was moving it away from us. "Why'd you bring up that stuff about Dog Days for, Velma?" Velma

72

pushed her glasses back up on her nose. "Cause I heard my mama say she knew this boy in high school who had sores on his mouth, and he always said he got 'em from Dog Days, even though he had the sores at Christmastime, too." Velma looked at us for our reaction. She got one from Trixie.

"Ha! He probly had the canker. They say you git the canker from stealing somebody else's food and the only way you can git rid of it is to kiss a red-headed girl or boy right on the mouth!" Velma liked this juicy bit of information, so she added more. "I know this red-headed boy that goes to school with me. He watches out for that kinda stuff. He told me he won't git near a girl if she so much as has a papercut on her lip. The girls won't even talk to him unless they git in need of the redhead's cure." Velma made a face. "Cain't say as I blame 'em. He *is* right homely with lots of freckles and *blonde* eyelashes. But he's nice to me." Velma speared a piece of hummingbird cake with her fork. "I told him he aught to steal some of their lunch. Then he would git the canker and he could see how they liked it when he came to them for the cure!" Velma made a face and spit her cake out into her plate.

"I thought that a boy had to seek out a red-headed girl for it to work," Trixie said. Velma didn't have an answer for her. She was too busy cleaning off her tongue with a napkin.

"Yuck!" she cried. "Somebody's poisoned the hummingbird cake!" I handed Velma what was left of my sweet tea, and she gulped it down. I started laughing.

"Miz Jenkins made that cake!" I said. We sat there and laughed and dared each other to go and tell her it was ruined, but we didn't have to. Uncle Vestal did that for us.

"Edner!" he cried. "I thank ye put too much sodie in yer cake! It's bitter as quinine."

Miz Jenkins came onto the screened-in porch looking quite affronted. With her hands on her hips, she opened the screen door and bellowed, "I know it, Vestal! Why don't ye say it loud enough for the whole community to hear!" We were snickering so much that Trixie got the snorts. I noticed that Mr. Jenkins was shaking with laughter too, but not making a sound.

Miz Jenkins frowned. "I'da never doubled-up my sodie if I hadn't been so upset o'er Frances dying yesterday," she said. "Well, that hussy is gonna git her just rewards. I heard the Fire Marshall *found somethin* at the scene of the crime. I'm shore that will make their case against her!"

Suddenly, I didn't feel so good. So, Miz Landers died. That made me sad. And those men that we had seen when we were at the Landers' place were fire marshals. This was just awful! I thought of Tater's rabbit foot and the box of matches in my closet.

"Did you hear that, Brownie?" Trixie chuckled. "Ole Busybody said her nerves were all to pieces and she put in half a cup of sodie instead of half a teaspoon. Who makes that kinda mistake!"

I got up without saying anything and went to throw my trash away. "Trixie!" Aunt Brenda was standing at the top of the steps with a bunch of tablecloths in her hand. "Hee-ah!" she said shaking the bundle at us, "You and Brownie come git these tablecloths and shake 'em out!" I was closest, so I went and took the bundle from Aunt Brenda and walked back over to the oak tree.

Trixie was slowly getting up from her seat on the ground, brushing coconut from her skirt. I laid the stack of colorful tablecloths on the grass and took one off the top. It was white with a yellow trim featuring green pears. I knew it to be Mama's. "Here," I said. "Take a corner." We held our corners and stretched the tablecloth out and began to shake it. A butterbean flew up into the air and hit

Trixie on top of the head on its way down. Trixie laughed, but I didn't feel much like laughing. When the pile had been shaken out, folded, and stacked I picked them up and went back into the house to find my mother. I guess Mama noticed something was wrong with me.

"Brownie? Are you sick?" she asked while taking hold of my chin. "You look peak-ed." I mumbled and shook my head no, but Mama felt of my forehead anyway. I really wanted to talk to Mama about what I knew, but I just held it in and let it eat me up inside.

August 15, 1968
Dear Diary,
I'm trying to keep a secret to protect a friend. I hope I can keep it up.
Donna has been actin weird lately. That's not like her!
There aint much summer left and I'm trying to make the most of it.
Brownie

"But I thought they caught that man before he did anything!" Mama was on the phone, the receiver cradled beneath her chin while she washed the supper dishes. "He was seen at Frances Landers' place. Uh huh. No, I hadn't heard that." I inched my way toward the kitchen table pretending to look at the calendar that hung on the wall beside the fridge. Mama finished her conversation and hung up the phone. She dried her hands on a dish towel and went out onto the back porch to find Daddy.

Miz Landers' funeral was yesterday. The whole community turned out for it. The preacher did not preach Miz Landers' life, but instead preached on getting ready to face the same hour of death that she did. It made my chest tight to listen. I felt guilty over her death somehow, even though

I had nothing to do with causing her second heart attack. It was just my conscience eating at me. I knew that I had to do something about Tater.

I slipped over to the screen door to listen. Daddy was sitting on the stoop smoking a cigarette. Mama sat down beside him and began telling him what she had found out when she was on the phone.

Apparently, the escaped convict had been seen at Miz Landers' place. No, she only knew what Edna had told her. It appears that there was some evidence seized beside the propane gas tank, but she didn't know what. Edna seemed to think the evidence would be against Miz Lola, but you know how Edna is. Mama was saying that Edna had that poor woman convicted from the very beginning.

I moved away from the door. I still didn't know anything, but that sour feeling in my stomach was back. What if Tater had left something else at the Landers' place?

As I walked down the red dirt and white gravel road from my house, I listened to the crickets singing in the pasture beside the road. I climbed the bank and took hold of the fence post so that I could pull myself up to a standing position. The fence post was old and gray. Sage-colored lichen grew in its cracks. I fiddled with the tin cap on top of the post. It was an old metal coffee can that had been cut and beaten down, then nailed to the top of the post to keep rain out. This helped to keep the fence post from rotting.

It was not as hot as it had been. A nice breeze rolled off the pasture, and the fresh smell revived my spirits. "Sue-caver! Sue-caver! Sue, sue, sue!" I called. Two cows heard me and ambled over to the fence, green slime dripping from their mouths as they chewed their cud. I reached through the fence to scratch behind their ears. Then, I knew what I was going to have to do. I patted the cows on their heads and slid down the red bank on my backside. At the bottom I found a big piece of Eisen glass. Mama said its proper name was Mica. I put it in my pocket and started walking down the hill until I got to Papa and Granny's driveway. I saw that Papa was in the tractor shed by the barn, but he did not see me, so I headed on to see Granny without saying a word. I had slipped off, and Mama would wonder where I was.

I walked straight around to the back of the house and climbed the porch steps. Granny's cat, Barzeelia, was sunning herself in Granny's petunias. I entered the kitchen with a loud bang of the screen door. "Granny!" I yelled, "Granny?" I heard the zizz-zizz of her sewing machine in the back bedroom. I found her there, biting off a thread with her teeth. "Well, thar's Brownie!" she said cheerily. "You slipped up on me." Granny grunted as she stood up and held a red checkered jumper up to my chest. "Thisuns gonna be yorn," she said.

Granny took the dress over to the bed and spread it out. "Thank you, Granny," I said. Granny was busy pinning two pockets onto the front of the dress. "I know how ye like pockets!" she said with a smile.

"Yes, ma'am," I replied. "Like you always say, dress without pockets is like a sow without tits." Granny laughed her hee-hee and patted my head. I loved Granny so much, and I knew that if I told her my secret that she would help me with it. I swallowed hard and tried to summon my courage.

"Granny," I began softly. "If I think that somebody's done something wrong, but they're my friend, should I tell on them or just let it be?"

Granny, who had sat back down in her chair by the sewing machine, looked up at me with a still and thoughtful face. I could not see her eyes because her glasses had a glare on them from the light beaming down from the ceiling. In a minute she scooted her chair back and patted the apron that was spread across her lap. I went over and sat down. Granny wrapped her arms around me, and I could smell her smell. Soap, bleach, and snuff.

Granny spoke softly, like she was trying not to wake a sleeping baby. "Now, Brownie. Ye know right from wrong." I nodded. "Well, even if ituz a wrong as simple as taking a piece of chewing gum without permission. Well, that's still a wrong." I nodded again. "And even if ituz a friend or a relative, don't matter who, you ort to at the very least try and git that person to own up to it. 'Cause it ud hep them to own up to it and it ud hep you to encourage them to own up to it. Just tell the truth and take the lumps."

I blew out my breath. Granny was not going to ask me to tell her about my problem. She was just going to advise me what to do and let me make my own choice about how to handle it. Part of me was relieved and part of me was not. It was like she could read my mind.

"Now, I thank yur old enough to do the right thang about that," she said, looking me straight in the eye. "So, let's go in the kitchen. I thank I still have some pound cake left in the cupboard."

As I was leaving through the back porch screen door, Papa was coming in. "Whur you off to in setch a hurry?" he asked, holding the door for me. "I gotta git goin'," I said. "Me and Trixie are going to ride bikes," I said and kissed his stubbly cheek.

I went down the dirt road and walked up Uncle Gil's driveway looking for Trixie. If I was going to confront Tater about the rabbit's foot and matches, then I wanted her to come along for moral support.

There was a big pasture on the right side of the road that lead to Uncle Gil's farm. I saw Trixie sitting on the pasture gate eating plums out of the skirt of her dress. I waved at her and she waved back. Trixie had her short blonde hair pulled into two little pigtails. I could not help but laugh.

"Yont a plum?" she offered a rosy one to me. Wild plum bushes grew by the roadsides and field roads everywhere in our community. But it was not until summer that they fruited, giving us firm, juicy plums that tasted full of summer sunshine. I popped the soft, rosy fruit into my mouth and spit the pit out into the ditch beside the gate.

"I been tryin' to hit that tin can over yonder" Trixie said. A pork-n-bean can was sitting on top of a rock on the other side of the drive. I sucked on another plum and spit the seed as hard as I could in the direction of the can, missing it by a mile.

"Hey, Trix," I said climbing up to sit beside her. "Will you go with me to hunt Tater Jacobs?" Trixie looked up at me and pushed some stray hair out of her eyes. "Whadaya wanna find *him* fer?" she asked. I could hear the suspicion in her voice.

"This secret is burning a hole in me," I confessed. "I just thought if I talked to Tater about it, well, he might 'fess up." Trixie jumped down and looked up at me.

"So, yore gonna git him to 'fess up? Who to?" Trixie crossed her arms across her chest.

"Well," I stalled, "I don't know! Maybe to Preacher Parsons. Who knows, maybe he didn't have anything to do with the fire. Maybe he lost his rabbit's foot a long time before that."

After a lot of cajoling, Trixie finally gave in and said she would go. "But" Trixie warned, "if his brother Carl shows up, we need to get out of there fast!" I had already thought of that. Carl was bigger than us and good at fighting. If he got it into his head that we were snooping around his place, he would give us a thrashing that no girl should ever experience.

"Do you know where Carl is?" I asked. Trixie shook her head. "No, but Eddie told me he was stealin' agin and so he might be off doing that and not at home. Heck! Tater might not even be at home!"

"Well, that's where we have to start" I said, and we set off toward the elementary school. I sure wish I had thought to bring my bicycle.

Tater was not at the school or on the playground, so we took the trail behind the playground that led into the woods behind the school. The trail was about a foot wide and over-grown with weeds. Trixie slapped at her legs as I looked for snakes. I picked up a small, fallen limb and took the shoots off it. I held it out and began beating the weeds. If a snake ran out, we would at least have warning. I also thought it might come in handy if Carl came home unexpectedly.

I had never been on this trail before and didn't really know where Tater lived. "Whatdaya think, Trix?" I said. "Is it back here?" Trixie stopped and grabbed the back of my shirt. She put her finger to her lips and pointed. Up ahead, there was an old chicken house with a rusty screen door attached to it. A metal flu ran out the top of the roof, which was covered with moss and in terrible disrepair.

Smoke curled from the flu indicating that someone was inside. "Which one you reckin is at home?" I whispered to Trixie. She shrugged. We squatted down and watched for a while.

"Do they live there alone?" I whispered. Trixie said, "Their mama has run off agin. I thank with some man from the gas station. So, it's just Carl and Tater. But Tater's by hisself most of the time."

As we watched, the screen door opened and both boys came outside. Tater picked up a couple of logs from a pile by the door and Carl was saying something to him that we could not make out. It was pitiful to watch little Tater, with his skinny arms and overalls two sizes too big, carry those big fire logs. Carl slapped his brother on the back of the head for a reminder who was boss and then he left. Tater headed back inside with the wood. It upset me to think that a six-year-old lived like this. My heart was thumping in my chest. So, I said to Trixie, "It's now or never."

I stood up and began a slow trot toward the chicken house. Trixie tried to grab my shirt but missed. I could hear her panting trying to catch up with me. I got to the door and softly called out to Tater. In a minute, he came to the screen door and let me in. Trixie stayed outside. Afraid to come in or afraid Carl would come back, I did not know which.

"Hey, Brownie," Tater said. He grinned and his lazy eye looked away from me. "Whatchye wont?" he said. "Hey, Tater," I said. "Was that Carl I saw? Where's he goin'?"

Tater scratched his head like he was trying to think. I looked around at the pathetic place that they called home. The fire was inside an old pot-bellied stove. On top of the stove was a coffee pot and an iron skillet. A dirty ice chest sat on the dirt floor beside an old card table. Two apple crates served as chairs. Behind the stove was an old mattress covered with stains. There was a ratty blanket and no pillows on top. The windows of the chicken house were covered with torn canvas curtains. The only light that I could see beside sunlight came from the fire and the kerosene lantern that hung above it.

"Oh!" Tater said suddenly. "Him gone loafin'." Tater grinned again. "Him tole me to fend fer mysef." I had a terrible pang of sympathy for Tater. He was barefoot and had dirty rust on his feet. I began to wonder what he was going to do about supper.

"Whatcha gonna eat for supper, Tater?" I asked. Tater held a finger up like a pause and ran straight to the cooler on the floor. He reached in and pulled out a small package of hamburger. "Ah gonna eat thisun!" he brought the meat over to show me.

"That's good," I said. I was glad that he would not go hungry. I walked around the room. "Tater, let me ask you somethin'," I said. "What happened to your lucky rabbit's foot?" Tater's eyes got wide and his lazy one veered back and forth with a jerk.

"Ah loss it!" he said. "I thank Carl took it." Tater wiped saliva off his mouth and put the pack of meat on the table.

"Do you remember the last time you saw it?" I asked. Tater closed his eyes and tapped the top of his head. "I thank was when me an Carl lit firecrackers!" His eyes popped open, and he grinned.

"Okay," I said as I went toward the screen door and opened it. "Well, it was good to see you. Now, don't burn yourself on that stove," I said as I walked out. Tater moved the iron skillet across the stove and nodded.

Trixie and I waved goodbye and walked back the way we came. We didn't talk until we got back to the schoolyard. As we started up the road I said to Trixie, "I feel so sorry for him I can't stand it! That's just pitiful to live like that." Trixie nodded in agreement. "So, what ye gonna do now?" she asked.

Yeah. What was I going to do? My mind was in terrible turmoil for a ten-year-old. Being branded a snitch was not the problem. The problem for me was seeing someone as young as Tater possibly going off to the detention center. I decided I would wait and see what developed over the course of the next few weeks.

August 16, 1968
Dear Diary,
This is what I know. Lola Lopez was caught driving Miz Landers' car with a gasoline can and pickle churn in the trunk.
That convict was seen at the Landers' place and they found something else there.

Tater lost his rabbit's foot and said it was when he and Carl lit firecrackers.
What was the convict doing there? And who burned the Landers' place to the ground?
And what in the world is going on with Donna?
Brownie

I had just walked into the kitchen to get a drink of water when I saw Mama and Granny at the kitchen table. They both had untouched cups of coffee sitting before them, and Mama was twisting her fingers like she always did when she was upset.

"It just doesn't make sense!" Mama cried. "Donna has always been an obedient child. She's never lied to me before." Granny just sat there and let her talk. "Donna told me that girl named Poppy is new here and she just wanted to make her feel welcome." Mama paused. "I mean, what kind of name is Poppy Sunshine? Is that a made-up name?"

Granny took a sip of her coffee. "So, Donna told ye sheuz a going to her friend Lisa's house to work on somethin' fer school." Mama nodded. "Then ye found out she really went to a party over by the county water tank, whur the law showed up and run 'em off and arrested some of 'em fer using dope? Is 'at right?" Mama buried her face in her hands and nodded. "What did Boyd say?" Granny asked.

Suddenly I remembered what happened last night. I was asleep when Donna tip-toed into our room. She put on her gown in the dark, but she didn't get into bed. Instead, she stood at the door and listened as Daddy's voice got louder and louder. I remember Daddy saying, "her reputation will be ruined".

"The kids had built a bonfire," Mama was saying. "Some of them were drinking beer, and I know that a couple of the boys climbed the water tank and spray-painted stuff on it. But I was shocked to learn that some of them were smoking marijuana!" I went into the hall to listen at the doorway.

Granny's brow furrowed. It went silent for a while then Granny leaned back in her chair and said in a loud voice, "Miss Brownie, maybe you kin hep us understand yore sister. Come in hyar."

I winced and slinked into the kitchen. Mama grabbed me by my shoulders. "*Do* you know something?" she asked. I swallowed. The only thing that I knew was that Donna had been trying different looks this year. After the mini skirt and go-go boots, she had started wearing long skirts and puffy blouses. There were a few of the girls she ran with that had even started going braless. I sure didn't know how that was going to work when school started back. I took stock of what I knew about Donna and picked out the most harmless stuff I could think of to tell Mama and Granny.

"Like what?" I asked. "Anything at all," Mama said. "If you heard or saw something different. We all know that Donna's been different ever since David shipped off to Vietnam." I screwed my face up like I was thinking.

"Well, she's been wearing a peace necklace and talkin' about how the war is wrong and maybe she'll go to Atlanta and picket it." "Protest it," Mama corrected. "Is that all?" I looked out the window at all that end-of-summer sunshine just going to waste while I was stuck in the kitchen on the hot seat. I told myself that it was my own durned fault for eavesdropping.

"Nope," I replied. "Can I go play now?" Mama nodded and I ran out the backdoor. Roger was sitting on top of the tire swing looking at something in a coffee can. "Hey, whatcha got there?" I asked him. "A baby rat snake," he replied. "I'm gonna raise him and when he's about six feet long, I'm gonna set him loose in the barn." I liked this conversation a lot better.

That night, after going to the bathroom and putting on my gown, I went to the room that I shared with my sister. When I opened the door, Donna quickly hid some sheets of notebook paper underneath her pillow. She laid down with her back towards me and covered up. "Cut the light out!" she ordered. My sister had never been short with me, but lately she acted like I got on her nerves.

"Oh! I bet that was a letter from David!" I thought. Maybe they would patch things up and it would get back to normal around our house. Anyway, tomorrow was Saturday. Trixie and I were going over to Patty's house to play.

Patty lived on the other side of Piney Hill Elementary in a brick ranch house. She was an only child and in the same grade as Trixie and me. Patty had red hair and freckles and was a might bossy, to tell you the truth. Patty's daddy sold insurance and her mama raised chickens. For some reason, every time I smelled lemon furniture polish, I thought of Patty's house.

Aunt Brenda circled the drive and pulled up to the front door of Patty's house. "I'm goin' to check on mama," she said. "I'll be back in a couple of hours. Y'all be sweet." Aunt Brenda spit on her handkerchief and wiped at a smear on Trixie's face. We got out of the station wagon and walked up to Patty's front porch. Her house is the first house I remember having a doorbell. As soon as the bell chimed, Patty appeared and pulled us into the house. She took our arms and dragged us through the living room and down the hallway to her bedroom where she shut the door.

"What's amatter with you!" Trixie demanded. "Ain't we gonna eat? My sugar has dropped, and I've got the shakes!"

Trixie got that saying from her daddy, Uncle Gil, who has diabetes.

"After while!" Patty hissed. She motioned us to sit on the floor and be quiet. When she was sure that her mother wasn't around, she spoke softly. "Did you hear that convict was seen over at Miz Landers' place?" We both nodded. Patty blew out her breath, "Well, did you hear that Carl Jacobs was with him?" This was news to us, so we shook our heads. "I think Tater was there, too, but I'm not sure. Anyway, the law got Carl and took him to jail. Now, they're wontin to talk to Tater."

It went quiet for a minute. My stomach got queasy, and my heart ached. Then Trixie said, "Soooo...when's lunch?"

Lunch was sloppy joes and French fries. Miz Helen had also made cupcakes with chocolate frosting, which Trixie got all over the front of her dress. Miz Helen made a fuss about getting the chocolate out, but Trixie assured her that her mama was used to her getting in a mess and would get the stain out.

We went out back and played on Patty's swing set and discussed going back to school and the usual things ten-year-old girls talked about. I was glad that the Landers' fire was not mentioned again.

"Oh! I just remembered!" Patty stopped her swing and turned to us. "I heard Daddy say last night that the bank in Pine Crest was robbed!"

This was interesting to Trixie and me, so we stopped swinging and looked at Patty. "My daddy's company insures the bank and he said they didn't get all the money, but they got a lot." None of us understood what that meant. "What happened to the rest of the money?" Trixie asked. Patty shrugged. These things were part of the adult world and not meant for the likes of us to know.

Miz Helen came to the backdoor and told us to come in and wash our hands. "Brenda will be here to get y'all soon and she doesn't want to have to wait on you." So, we washed our hands, told Miz Helen thank you, and went out on the front door stoop to wait. We sat there on the steps with Patty and waited and waited. About four o'clock we saw Aunt Brenda's station wagon coming up the drive with a cloud of red dust spinning out from under her wheels. We stood up, hugged Patty goodbye, and climbed into the car.

Trixie talked non-stop, telling her mama about what we had for lunch and all, but her mama just nodded and kept driving. I thought she had a faraway look in her eyes, but Trixie did not seem to notice.

"How's your mama, Aunt Brenda?" I asked. Aunt Brenda snapped out of her daze and quickly answered, "Oh! She's fine! Just Fine!" I nodded and looked at Trixie, who just shrugged and leaned over toward me. "Can you spend the night?" she asked. I nodded. Mama never cared. Trixie and I were always at each other's houses.

When we pulled into the driveway, Aunt Janelle's car was there. I soon forgot about Aunt Brenda as I got out and ran to the house. I entered the house, slamming the screen door. "Well, hey Miss Priss!" Aunt Janelle was sitting at the kitchen table drinking a bottle of diet cola and Mama was fidgeting with the salt and pepper shakers.

"Whatchall doin'?" I asked. Aunt Janelle grinned like she was dying to tell me a secret, but Mama just looked up and asked me if I had a good time at Patty's.

"Yeah, we had fun," I replied, "but Aunt Brenda sure was actin' funny. Is her Mama gonna die?" There it was. I had been wanting to ask that question for a while. Mama got up from the table and went to the refrigerator. She took out a pitcher of sweet tea.

"Go on and play, Tina," she said. "Aunt Janelle and I are talking." Aunt Janelle winked at me and grinned. Maybe she would tell me later. I went to my room but left the door open so that I could hear their conversation.

"I don't believe that Lola woman had anything to do with the Landers' place burning down," Aunt Janelle said. "Dwayne told me that Ole Busybody is pushing the Sheriff's department to keep her as a suspect all because of her driving Miz Frances' car with the gas can and that blamed pickle churn in the trunk!"

"She gave the Sheriff an explanation for that," Aunt Janelle continued. "But of course, Miz Frances ain't alive to back her up."

I grabbed my pajamas and toothbrush and went back into the kitchen. "I'm going to spend the night with Trixie," I said. Mama called me over to her and gave me a kiss on the cheek. "Well, go on then and get there before it's dark," she said.

I bounded down the back steps and got on my bicycle to head off down the hill to Trixie's. It was a nice summer evening. Katydids were singing and the air was sweet with the smell of pasture grass. I turned into Trixie's driveway and drove around to the back porch where I parked my bicycle and went into the kitchen. Aunt Brenda was frying hamburgers on the stove. Trixie was sitting at the kitchen table spooning potato salad onto her plate.

"Hey, Aunt Brenda," I said. "Boy! I'm shore hungry!" Aunt Brenda put together two hamburgers in buns and placed them on two unbreakable plates. "Git the ketchup and mustard, will you, Brownie?" I went to the refrigerator and brought them back to the table and sat down. "Yon't some grape drink?" Trixie asked. I nodded and she came back with two cold bottles. Aunt Brenda took off her apron and went into the living room. "She and daddy have already ate," Trixie explained. "The boys, too. They left to go spend the night with Terry Mason at his house."

That night, after brushing our teeth, putting on our pajamas, and playing what seemed like the longest board game ever, we finally decided to turn off the light and go to sleep. I was deep in the middle of a dream where I had an Indian pony that could outrun a pickup truck when I felt the bed shaking. Then a light came on, and I realized that I was at Uncle Gil and Aunt Brenda's house. Trixie was sitting up rubbing her eyes.

"Git up," Aunt Brenda said with urgency. "We've gotta go!" I got out of the bed and began dressing. Aunt Brenda still had curlers in her hair and was throwing clothes at Trixie, who was still trying to get awake. "Go where?" Trixie asked through a yawn. "The hospital," Aunt Brenda said. "Now, git dressed." She left the room at a trot.

"What's goin' on?" I asked. Trixie shrugged and pulled a shirt over her head. "Yont some chewing gum?" she asked, fishing around in her pants pocket. "My mouth tastes bad." Trixie peeled off a couple of sticks of gum and popped them in her mouth, which made her response to my question a bit slobbery. "I guess my grandmaw is bad again," Trixie said. "So, why didn't Aunt Brenda say she'd take me home?" Trixie shrugged again. We left the bedroom and went into the living room where Aunt Brenda was waiting with the door open. "Hurry up!" she chided. "Your daddy is in the car already!"

The trip to the hospital was fast and silent. Uncle Gil concentrated on the road and Aunt Brenda bit her fingernails. As country children growing up in the sixties, we knew when we were expected to be quiet. We did not have to be told. However, curiosity got the best of Trixie and she blurted out, "Is Grandmaw dying!" Aunt Brenda shook her head. "No," is all she said.

When we arrived at the hospital and entered the lobby, Aunt Brenda asked the Pink Lady some questions then hurried off to stand by the elevator. Uncle Gil looked at us and pointed to the couches next to a vending machine. "Y'all stay here," he ordered. It did not surprise us that we could not go with them. We had been to the hospital before visiting the sick. Children were not allowed on the patient floors after visiting hours. We went over and sat down on a brown plastic couch and looked at each other.

"Well," I said by way of comforting Trixie. "Maybe it won't be too bad." Trixie was fishing around in her pocket. She pulled out a handful of quarters. "Yont somethin' from the vending machine? I'm starving."

Later, I looked at the clock on the wall, which read one-fifteen. We had eaten two candy bars each and shared an orange drink, read all of the magazines that interested us and were just sitting there, trying to stay awake. "I know!" I said. "How 'bout we ride the elevator?" We got up and walked over to the elevator doors, and I pressed the down button.

"Where do you think you're going?" the Pink Lady asked us. She looked over her glasses and frowned. "We waz goin' to ride the elevator." I said by way of explanation. "Oh, no you're not!" the Pink Lady said firmly, "Children are not allowed on the patient floors after visiting hours." Trixie shrugged. "But we weren't gonna git off," she said. "That doesn't matter," the Pink Lady said, shuffling papers on her desk, "Every time the elevator stops the bell dings, and that disturbs the patients." The Pink Lady wiggled her index finger to motion us back to the couch. We reluctantly obeyed.

I awoke to Trixie laying across my lap. The clock above the Pink Lady said one-forty-five. I was about to go back to sleep when the elevator dinged and I saw Uncle Gil coming toward us, grinning. I felt better about Trixie's grandmaw because of that. He walked over and shook Trixie awake. "Wake up, sleepy head," he said. "You have a new aunt." Uncle Gil chuckled as Trixie sat up and rubbed her eyes. "What?" she said. "You have a new aunt," Uncle Gil repeated with a grin.

Even I was confused. What in the world was Uncle Gil talking about? He looked at the Pink Lady and said, "I'm taking them with me." The Pink Lady nodded. So, we walked with Uncle Gil to the elevator, he punched the buttons, and we all rode up to the second floor. The Second Floor. The Baby Floor. Trixie and I had been on this floor before visiting church ladies that had had babies. Trixie looked at me and shrugged.

Uncle Gil led us over to the baby window and pointed to a baby tightly rolled in a pink blanket. "That's Rebecca," Uncle Gil explained. "That's yore new aunt." Trixie frowned as she took all of this in. I noticed that her hair was flying around her face from static electricity. Plastic couches were famous for that.

"My what?" Trixie asked dumbfounded. I quickly added two and two. "So, Miz Passley was not dying?" Uncle Gil grinned and shook his head. "No, she was just going to have a baby and here she is." Trixie frowned. "So, I have an aunt? Who's a baby?" she asked. "Yep," Uncle Gil responded. "These things happen sometimes." Uncle Gil let that sink in. "Let's go see yore grandmaw and you can tell her how proud you are." Uncle Gil took Trixie's hand and I followed as he led us to room number two-o-two.

There was Trixie's grandmother. Propped up in bed with two pillows, her hair freshly combed into its bob, a salt and pepper mix of old and new. She smiled at us and held her arms out to Trixie. Aunt Brenda, who had been crying, stepped aside and blew her nose. Trixie went to her grandmother and hugged her. When she pulled back, Trixie said, "How in the world did you have a baby, grandmaw? You're old, for heaven's sake!" Miz Passley leaned back on her cotton throne and laughed. "Since when is fifty-one old?" Trixie shrugged. And that was good, because I did not want to hear the answer to any more questions.

"I like her name. Rebecca, I mean," Trixie said. Then, the door to Miz Passley's room opened and in walked Trixie's grandfather, and Mama and Daddy. Daddy was holding a tray of paper cups filled with coffee. Trixie's grandfather took one and walked over to the bed beside his granddaughter. He patted Trixie's back in a "It's gonna be alright" manner but did not say a word.

"Well, it's late," Daddy said. "We'd better get Brownie back home. I'll have to feed the chickens soon and I want to get a little sleep." Everyone shook hands, congratulations all around, hugs for Trixie, and waves goodbye. My parents did not say a word until we were in our car and pulling out of the parking lot. Then, Mama spoke up.

"You okay back there?" she asked. I nodded. "This was quite a surprise, wasn't it?" Mama continued. I nodded again.

Daddy laughed. "You'll understand it when you are older," he said. And that is the last thing I remember because I fell asleep against the car door.

August 17, 1968
Dear Diary,
Trixie's grandmaw had a baby girl! That was a big surprise. I'm just glad she wasn't dying like I thought.
Trixie and I are going to play all afternoon tomorrow after church. School starts back soon, and we are missing out on summer!
Brownie

It was less than three weeks until summer break was over, and school started back. The main focus at this time of year for kids our age was how much playing could we get done before the rigors of school set in. I remember the days were golden with sunshine and the breezes, if we got any, were always scented with the aromas of the farmland that made up our world. One day, Roger got wind that Les Owens was tearing down an old chicken house and giving away the planks and tin to anyone who was willing to help with the demolition.

"Yeah" Roger said to me one morning at the breakfast table, "Daddy told me if I helped tote and stack material, that I could have any of the planks I wanted to build my treehouse." I jumped at these words. "A treehouse? Count me in!" I said, "I'll come help!"

Roger shook his head, "No! No girls allowed!" Roger might as well have poked me in the eye, his words made me so mad. "Roger! You know I'm a better worker than you are!" I sneered, "I'm gonna ask Daddy myself!" Mama came to the table with a wet dishrag. "Y'all don't fight" she said, "There will be plenty of work for both of you." I got up from the table to go find Daddy.

The morning was overcast and very humid as we set out to Mr. Owens' farm. "Now, y'all be careful" Daddy warned us. "Don't step on a nail or cut yoreself on the tin." We were all three riding in the cab of Daddy's pickup. He took his eyes off the road long enough to look down at our feet. Shoes had to be worn if we wanted to go. I had on some sneakers that I had outgrown. They pinched my toes. Roger was wearing his worn-out cowboy boots. "Roger," Daddy said, "your boots are on the wrong feet."

When we got to Mr. Owens' place, there were two pickups there already. I opened the door and climbed out. I pulled Roger's boots off and put them on the right feet.

We walked up to the old chicken house where Ben Little was running a tractor. He cut it off and waved when he saw Daddy. The only other person there was Mr. Jenkins. He had on overalls and a straw hat. Usually, when I saw him, he was wearing Sunday clothes, so he looked strange to me. I looked around for Ole Busy Body but did not see her.

"Hey, there," Mr. Jenkins said. I said "hey" back and Mr. Jenkins stooped down and continued to pull rusty nails out of some planks off the chicken house. "Whatcha gonna do with your planks?" I asked. Mr. Jenkins didn't say, he just smiled gently and went back to his work.

"Whatcha want me to start on, Daddy?" I asked as I walked over to where Daddy stood, talking with Ben. "Don't interrupt, Brownie," Daddy said. "Go on, Ben. You was sayin'?" Ben reached up under his co-op cap and scratched his head. "Yeah, she's out on bond, but they picked up Carl and his little brother and put them in reform school until the trial comes up."

Ben sighed. "I sure do hate it that Carl can't take no better care of his baby brother than that! If they could find his mother, then I think they would release him to her. But Carol is hard to keep up with." Daddy nodded. "Where'd you hear this?" he asked Ben. Ben nodded toward Mr. Jenkins and said, "Who do you think?" We all knew he wasn't talking about the man in overalls, struggling to get a nail out of a piece of old lumber.

About that time, we heard the screen door on Mr. Owens' house slam and a familiar voice shouted loud enough to wake the dead, "Earl! Ain't you got enough wood yet?" Mr. Jenkins dropped the hammer on his foot. He gathered up two two-by-fours and headed to an old car that was not their usual one. It looked familiar to me, but I just could not place it. They got in and Mr. Jenkins drove out of the driveway, his planks sticking out of the backseat window. I wondered why he had not put them in the trunk.

On the way home, Roger was bragging on himself and how he had worked the hardest, stacked the most planks, and picked up the most nails. I was leaned against the door letting the breeze blow my hair. "Daddy?" I asked. "Did Mr. Jenkins trade cars?" Daddy, who had been whistling a song off the radio, turned and looked at me. "Well, that's Miz Landers' car," he stated. "Why'd you ask?" I shrugged. "No reason," I replied.

August 19, 1968
Dear Diary,
Big news! Miz Jenkins has Miz Landers car! I don't know why, but Mr. Jenkins didn't put the planks in the trunk. I guess the gas can and pickle churn are still in there. And that means she didn't steal them!
But what is The Widow driving? Where is she living?
AND, I need to get Tater out of jail!
Brownie

The big news in the community was the birth of Miz Passley's baby. I heard church women refer to the newborn as a "change of life baby". I did not understand that then but soon discovered why her daughter, Aunt Brenda, was so flummoxed. In my adult life Becky, Trixie and I are good friends and laugh about the mystery of her birth. The ten-year difference in our ages is hardly worth remarking on now. But back then? Well, it was confusing and a big curi-osity.

I had been sent to wash up for supper and was coming back to the kitchen when I heard Daddy say to Mama, "Yeah. Miz Landers is going before the judge next week. The judge is going to decide what to do about her case." The knot in my stomach got tighter, and my heart was beating hard in my chest. Before I knew it, I was jumping in front of my father. "Daddy!" I said. "I've got something to tell you."

We were at the supper table and after saying the blessing, I told Daddy about finding Tater's rabbit's foot and the box of matches. I explained how Tater had told me that he lost them when he and Carl were shooting off fireworks at the Lander's place. "He wasn't shooting the firecrackers, Carl was. I just happened to find the rabbit's foot on the bank beside the house." I looked around at everyone listening and realized that Donna was not there. "Where's Donna?" I asked. Mama moved her hand like she was shooing a fly and said, "Oh, with that Poppy girl, spending the night again." I frowned. I had not seen much of my sister since that Poppy girl had become her one and only friend.

"Anyway, Daddy, I don't think that Lola, Miz Landers, had anything to do with it. It's just because she's so different from us and showed up suddenly that folks are against her. She's really very nice, ain't she Mama?" Mama had a faraway look in her eyes and snapped back in time to say a feeble "yes".

"How long have you known this?" Daddy asked. I explained that I found the rabbit's foot and matches a few days after the fire. Daddy frowned. "I see," he said. "And here it is August and yore just now tellin' me?" I could feel tears welling up in my eyes. "Yes, sir," I said and began to sob. "I just didn't want little Tater to end up in reform school!" Daddy drank the last of his iced tea and stood up. "No. Neither do I," he said. "Now, go and git me the rabbit's foot and matches and we will figure out what to do."

August 25, 1968

Dear Diary,

Daddy figured it best if we met with the Sheriff. He is taking me with him to the jail on Thursday to get this thing about Tater settled once and for all.

Me and mama saw Lola Landers in town last Saturday. We didn't get to speak to her, but I wish we had.

I'm going with Trixie today to see the new baby.

Brownie

The community gossip was mostly about Trixie's grandparents, LaWanda and Ken Passley, having a baby girl while in their fifties. It was a secret well-kept and surprised everyone. But Miz Jenkins kept the Landers' fire in the gossip circle, too. She told everyone that just because they had arrested someone other than Lola Landers for the arson, that did not mean that she was not guilty. "She just plain-out got away with it!" Miz Jenkins told everyone she met. I thought that, if it was me, I would be afraid for Miz Jenkins to hold a grudge against me.

I rode to Mr. and Miz Passley's house with Aunt Brenda and Trixie. It was so hot and steamy outside that my fresh bath had already been sweated off. Trixie and I sat in the backseat of the station wagon, heads hanging out of the open windows. Mama had fixed my hair so that the cowlick stayed down, and I knew that the wind was ruining it, but I was so hot I did not care. As soon as we stopped outside Trixie's grandmother's house and Aunt Brenda shut off the engine, I began to sweat again. I looked at Trixie and her hair was sweaty all around her pink face. We got out and walked up the walkway to the front door.

"Mama?" Aunt Brenda hollered as she opened the door and went inside with us in tow. "Shh!" Miz Passley came walking toward the door bouncing a pink bundle against her chest. "I've just got her to sleep," she said and turned to take the baby to a white bassinet that was sitting in a corner by the kitchen. Trixie and I went over to look at the baby.

"She sure is a puny thang, ain't she?" Trixie said. "Reckin she's a runt?" Miz Passley laughed. Aunt Brenda cleared her throat, and the baby wiggled in the bassinet and started pretending that she was sucking on a bottle. Trixie and I both laughed.

"Why don't y'all go in the kitchen and get a soda?" Aunt Brenda said. So, we went into the kitchen and Trixie opened the refrigerator. It was stuffed with food from church and community friends. Trixie pulled out a drawer inside the fridge and got two sodas for us. There was a bottle opener mounted to the side of the knotty pine cabinets. Trixie popped the tops off, and we sat down at the kitchen table in front of a small oscillating fan. We talked into the fan to hear our robot voices and drank our sodas.

"Daddy's taking me to meet with the Sheriff this Thursday," I whispered to Trixie. "He says it will help Tater and Miz Lola if I tell him what I know." Trixie raised her eyebrows, "Golly! Ain't you skeered?" The truth was, I was afraid. Sheriff Anderson was a big man, with an intimidating face, so that was scary enough, and I had never been to the county jail. But Daddy would be with me and if it helped my friends, I wanted to do it. I had asked Daddy if I would be where the prisoners were. He had laughed, said no, and patted me on the head.

"You could go with us," I urged Trixie. "You can ask your mama today." Trixie turned up her bottle of soda and drained it, then she let out a big burp. "Okay," she said.

August 19, 1968
Dear Diary,
Today I go to the jail with Daddy. I hope I don't throw up.
Brownie

Daddy said it was okay for Trixie to go if she sat still and was quiet. So, we rode in the cab of Daddy's pickup with me in the middle and Trixie hanging her head out the window, messing up her hair. It was another hot and sticky day. My skin prickled like the time I touched the pink insulation that Daddy was putting in the attic, even though he warned me not to. My skin felt like I had that insulation all over my arms. So, I scratched, leaving a snaky trail of red streaks.

We pulled into a parking space in front of the insurance agency next to the jail. I could see a woman inside sitting at a desk typing. She stopped to look at us and wave at Daddy. I wondered if she already knew why we were there.

Just inside the door was a small lobby. A long, tall desk ran across the room, blocking people from going down the hall toward the back. There was a half door at the end of the desk that only opened from the other side. A tall, young deputy was manning the desk and asked if he could help us. "We have a meeting with Robert," Daddy said. "Are you Boyd Rivers?" the deputy asked. Daddy nodded and the deputy opened the half door and ushered us through to the other side. "Wait right here," he said.

When the deputy came back, he led us down the hall to an office on the right. The door had *Robert Anderson, Sheriff, Keetoowah County* in gold lettering. I swallowed hard. Trixie reached over and grabbed my hand. The Sheriff was a big, big man with bright blue eyes and a headful of wavy brown hair. He walked around his desk and shook hands with Daddy, calling him by name. Then, the deputy that was seated in a chair next to the desk stood up and shook hands with Daddy. Daddy said, "Hey, Sonny," like they were old friends. I began to calm down some.

There were two empty chairs in front of the desk that I supposed were for Daddy and me, but where was Trixie going to sit? "Sonny," the Sheriff said. "Go git another chair for this young lady." Sonny left and returned with a folding chair and put it next to mine. Then, we all took our seats and waited on the Sheriff to begin.

"Sonny has done the investigation on the Landers' fire," Sheriff Anderson said. "We have the suspects in custody." The Sheriff laced his big meaty fingers together on top of the desk. "We need to hear what your daughter has to say before we continue." Daddy told the Sheriff my name, and then he remembered Trixie was there and introduced her. Deputy Sonny leaned over a yellow tablet that was lying on the frontside of the desk across from where he was sitting and wrote our names down.

"Don't be nervous," Deputy Sonny said with a smile. "Just tell us what you know." I swallowed hard again and started to talk. Sheriff Anderson asked me to speak up, and then when I talked it came out too loud and too fast, but I could not help myself. The whole story flooded out of me like a volcano erupting. About playing detective and looking for clues. Finding Tater's rabbit's foot and the box of matches. When I talked to Tater about the fire and it broke my heart that he might be involved and him only six-years-old, with no mama. About Carl selling fireworks to my little brother. What Tater said about Carl and some unknown man. Then I told them that I had hid Tater's rabbit's foot and the box of matches for two months until my conscience got the better of me and I told Daddy.

I had not realized it at the time, but Trixie said I let go of her hand and waved my arms around like a whirly gig, practically hollered my story out, and all the while shaking my right foot in the air. "You looked like a lunatic!" she later told me. "I thought they might decide you needed to go to Milledgeville!" Milledgeville was the insane asylum in South Georgia, near Macon. I remember a cousin of Daddy's had been sent down there for her "wild rants" as Daddy called it. But I could not remember telling any of my story. It was all a blur to me, and when I got through telling it, the armpits of my dress were soaked through with sweat.

The Sheriff unlaced his fingers and pushed back in his chair. He grinned at Daddy. "Did you git all that, Sonny?" he asked the deputy. Sonny blew out his breath and nodded. "You always talk that fast?" Deputy Sonny asked me. I shrugged. To kids my age, shrugging could mean "I don't know" or "I ain't saying".

"Well, Sonny is going to fill you in on the case now," the Sheriff said as he pulled his chair back up to the desk and relaced his fingers. Deputy Sonny laid his pencil on top of the yellow tablet and looked at Daddy. I thought to myself that I remember the Sheriff told us that they had the suspects in custody. I figured it was Carl and Tater that were in jail, and I began to be upset for Tater all over again.

"We have ruled out Mrs. Landers as a suspect. The suspects that are in custody are Jip Lester, Carl Jacobs, and Ernest Dobbins. Ernest Dobbins was the mastermind. He was the convict who escaped from the prison road crew," Deputy Sonny paused to let us catch up. "Dobbins had recruited Jacobs through Jacobs' uncle." Deputy Sonny lifted the pages on the yellow note pad, "Ah, Barney Driscol," he said.

"Jacobs set fire to the Landers' place as a diversion. He knew that our county resources were limited and that a big fire, during a drought, would mean all the fire and police personnel would be going to the Landers' place, leaving no one in town to protect the bank." Daddy nodded. "So, they robbed the bank," Daddy said. "Yep," Deputy Sonny replied.

Trixie forgot she was only there as a spectator and said, "But how'd you ketch 'em?" I nodded. This was getting exciting. "We had an informant," Deputy Sonny replied. "A local man ratted them out." It was clear that Deputy Sonny was not going to say more on that subject. "Anyway," he said. "The bank was an inside job." Jip Lester had been working as a janitor at the bank for six months. He had been visiting Dobbins and Carl Jacobs' uncle, Barney Driscol, in prison, and that's where they hatched the plan and got Carl Jacobs involved. Jacobs drove the getaway car.

Trixie gasped and forgot her place again, "But Carl is only thirteen!" Deputy Sonny chuckled. "Well, he drove the car anyway," he laughed. Then he looked at me, "Your finding the rabbits' foot and box of matches puts Carl and his little brother, Tater, at the scene when the fire was set. We are grateful to you for bringing that evidence in to us," Deputy Sonny said. I swallowed hard. "But Tater didn't have anything to do with it! His brother used the matches and then told Tater to leave and take it with him. Tater's just a baby!" I began to sob and so did Trixie.

"Now, now," the Sheriff said. "There's no need fer that." He opened a drawer in his desk and took out a box of tissues. "Here," he said to Trixie and me. "We know all that," the Sheriff continued. I blew my nose and looked at the Sheriff and Deputy Sonny. "But Tater's in jail!" I wailed. Deputy Sonny smiled at me and said "No he ain't. We know he didn't have anything to do with it. He was referred to Child Welfare because his mother has abandoned him. She has been absent from the home and has been declared unfit." Deputy Sonny's voice softened, and he looked directly at me. "Tater is living with a very nice family that is taking real good care of him." I started crying again, but this time it was because I was so relieved.

"Well, Boyd. That just about does it," the Sheriff said. Daddy shook hands with Sheriff Anderson and Deputy Sonny. Trixie and I were each given a bottle of ice-cold soda. Then, we were all ushered to the front door by Deputy Sonny. "How's yore mama?" Daddy asked Deputy Sonny. The deputy rubbed the back of his neck and sighed, "Holdin' her own, I guess," he said, "It's been real hard on her since daddy died." Daddy clapped his hand down on Deputy Sonny's shoulder and shook his hand again.

I do not think I took an easy breath until we were all back in the cab of the truck and Daddy started backing up. "Whew!" Trixie exclaimed. "Well, that's a relief! Huh, Brownie!" I had to agree. My chest had not felt that light in weeks. But I could not talk anymore. All the way home I listened to Trixie talk and ask questions. Daddy just grunted out "Uh-huhs and Un-ahs" in response to her chattering. While I looked out the window at the free world that Tater would be coming back to.

The next day, I rode into town again. This time with Mama. Daddy had sent her to the bank to make a deposit. We pulled into a parking lot in front of the bank and got out of the car. While Mama fed the meter I looked around. It was still hot like the blast off a heater in an enclosed room. The sun shone down relentlessly, making heat waves snake up from the asphalt. Mama had already gone into the bank, leaving me by the car. I looked at the green leaves on the oak trees that lined Main Street and wondered why they didn't turn brown and fall off during this miserable hot August. That is when I saw Miz Lola coming out of the Davis Hotel beside the bank. She was bringing a suitcase to a blue sedan parked in front of the hotel.

Miz Lola stood beside the car, opened a compact, and reapplied coral lipstick to her thick lips. She was wearing a sundress with large yellow flowers on it and very tall white, high heels. Her legs were sleek and bare. She stood

there in the shade, and I thought she was like salty peanuts poured into a hot cola. Just a little more than most
people could handle.

It was obvious that Miz Lola was waiting on someone.
She checked her watch and then pulled a pair of oversized,
dark sunglasses from her purse. I walked over to say hey
to her.

"Buenos Dias, Brownie," Miz Lola said. "Did you come
to say goodbye?" She had the richest sounding voice I had
ever heard. "I didn't know you wuz leavin'," I said. "Where
are you goin'?" Miz Lola smiled and leaned against the car.
She looked like a cat preparing to sun itself. "Home," she
said. I scratched my head and frowned. "But I thought the
Landers' place was yore home now," I said. Then I remembered that it was just a place. No house to live in. I felt
embarrassed.

"I am selling the land," Miz Lola replied. "I cannot live
here, Brownie. I do not fit in." Miz Lola took my hand and
gave it a gentle squeeze. "But you'll come back. I'm yore
friend, and Trixie and Mama. You'll come back to see us."
Miz Lola nodded, whether to assure or appease me, I could
not tell. "Si, Brownie," she said. "I will come back someday." Just then, a handsome man in a suit came bounding
down the steps of the hotel with another suitcase and some
papers in his hand. He sat the suitcase on the sidewalk
beside the other one and went around to open the trunk
with his key. "So, who's this?" he asked with a grin. His
teeth were straight and sparkling white. I wondered for a
moment if he was a movie star.

"Mi amiga, Brownie," Miz Lola said. "Brownie, huh?"
the man said. "Is that because of your chocolate drop
eyes?" He grinned at me when he said it, and I felt the heat
of a blush rush up my neck. The man loaded the suitcases
into the sedan and folded the papers that he was carrying
and put them in his inside coat pocket. "We'd better get

going. We want to get to the airport early." Miz Lola leaned down and gave me a tight hug. She smelled like fruit. Then she kissed me on the cheek and told me goodbye. I was standing on the sidewalk waving when Mama came out of the bank and called my name. "Why in the world did you stay out here in this heat when the bank lobby is air conditioned?" Mama said. "Who was that?"

On the way home I told Mama about Miz Lola and the man and how she was going home and that she said she was selling the Landers' place, but that she would come back someday to visit. Mama took all of this in. "That's nice that you talked to her," Mama said. "I do think she had a really hard time of it when she was here. Did you know you have orange lipstick on your face?" I twisted the rearview mirror around so that I could see. I liked it and did not think I would ever wash it off. I turned the knob on the radio and country music started playing. I pressed the buttons until I heard one of my favorite pop songs. Mama and I both started to sing as the cool air blew through the window, messing up our hair.

FALL, 1968
No. 2

September 9, 1968
Dear Diary,
Today was the first day of school. I am in the fifth grade.
And, wouldn't you know it? I had a problem with my teacher
right off the bat!
Brownie

The first day of school was always exciting for me. I got up earlier than was necessary to make sure I had everything. I put on my white short-sleeved shirt with the Peter Pan collar. It was a year old and a little too tight, but it would be fine when I put on the green jumper that Granny had made for me. I had new gold colored knee highs to wear with the white loafers that I got back in the summer. I got dressed beside my bed next to the open window. It may have been September, but the heat and humidity was still sticking around. I looked in the mirror over our dresser and decided I needed to brush my hair and tame my cowlick. I left the bedroom and went down the hall to the bathroom. The door was closed, so I knocked.

"I'm in here!" Donna yelled. Well, okay then. "When you gonna be out?" I hollered back. "Go on, Brownie!" my sister shouted. Mama appeared in the hallway with a dishtowel in her hand. "Tina," she said. "Come eat breakfast and leave Donna alone." I left and went into the kitchen and sat down at the table across from Roger, who was eating a jelly biscuit. His blonde hair was in a crew cut and he had butch wax slicking up the hair in the front. Roger was wearing a new red plaid shirt and jeans. "Oops!" I said as Roger dropped jelly on his shirt. My brother tried to pull his shirt up and lick it off. "Roger! Stop that!" Mama had reappeared with her dishtowel and wiped furiously at the blob of jelly. I got a biscuit and ate it plain. I didn't want to risk messing up Granny's jumper.

"After y'all finish, go on to the bathroom and brush your teeth," Mama said. "And Tina, we will have to do something with your hair." I shrugged. "But Donna won't come out," I said. Mama was putting our lunch money for the week inside our bookbags. "She will be out in a minute," Mama said.

Donna did come out of the bathroom eventually. She was wearing a long, cream-colored skirt with a long-sleeved cream-colored puffy-sleeved blouse and strappy leather sandals. Her hair had grown fast since Aunt Janelle had cut it. It was down past her shoulders and parted down the middle. Donna had a brown leather strap tied around her forehead and hanging down the back of her hair. I wondered where she had gotten those clothes.

"You'd better take that headband off before Daddy sees you," I warned. Donna sighed and walked down the hallway and out the door. She brushed past Roger and bumped him into the wall. "Hey! What's eatin' you?" he exclaimed. I had a suspicion that her attitude had something to do with that girl Poppy.

Roger and I boarded the school bus at the end of our driveway. The bus doors were opened by the bus driver, Miz Johnson, and we climbed aboard. I loved the way the bus smelled on the first day. Clean and neat, with all of the windows open. Roger sat behind Miz Johnson, and I walked back to the middle to sit with Trixie. It felt good to see all of our friends on the bus looking their best and ready for the first day of school. Trixie had on her new jumper that our Granny had made. Where mine was green plaid, hers was light blue and white vertical stripes. Trixie's short blonde hair was held back with a white headband. "You look nice, Trix," I said.

The bus pulled up in front of the school and we got off. The sun was shining brightly, and a nice breeze was blowing as we walked inside the front door. Trixie and I headed for the fifth-grade classroom and saw the name of a teacher that we did not know printed on a placard beside the door. We went inside and picked out our desks. We were both on the third row. I was second from the front and Trixie was third. We were talking and laughing with our fellow fifth graders when a slim, young woman walked in and shut the door. She had short red hair and was wearing a green A-line dress with navy hose and pumps. The woman rapped a ruler on her desk to get our attention.

"Good morning, class," she said. "My name is Miss Turner, and I will be your teacher this year." She did not smile when she said this but cleared her throat. "Now, let's get started." Miss Turner walked down each aisle and handed us a piece of manila file folder that had been cut into strips. "I want you to write your first and last names on this strip of paper and then I will help you tape it to your desk. This way, I can get to know you." I dug into my bookbag and got out a pencil. Mama had already sharpened it for me. I printed my name neatly and sat back in my desk.

Miss Turner went desk by desk, taping the paper strips in place so that they faced her desk. When she got to me, I handed her my paper and smiled. She looked at it and frowned. "Brownie," she said. "Is that your real name?" I shook my head. "No ma'am," I said. "It's what everybody calls me." Miss Turner tore up the strip of paper and went to her desk to throw it away. She came back with a new piece of paper. "I want you to write your *name* not your nickname." I frowned. "But I don't want to," I said. "I go by

Brownie." I felt myself getting upset. My Papa would say I was getting my Irish up.

Miss Turner frowned down at me. "Now, we don't want to get off on the wrong foot, do we?" she said. Trixie secretly poked me in the back with her pencil as if she were advising me to do as I was told, so I blew out a sigh and said, "No ma'am" as I turned to write Tina Rivers on the piece of manila folder. Then Miss Turner said, "And, I want you all to know that I consider heavy sighs like *that* a form of talking back, which will not be tolerated." She walked back to her desk and turned around to stare at her students. "Let that be a warning," she said and sat down in her chair. I swallowed hard. Fifth grade certainly *had* started out on the wrong foot.

Miss Turner plowed right on with arithmetic, which she called mathematics. She handed out sheets of problems and told us to figure them and show our work. She said she wanted to see what we remembered from last year. I could not look at Trixie because she was behind me and I could tell that Miss Turner would not approve. I could feel sweat prickles in my armpits.

That afternoon when the three o'clock bell rang everyone in our class jumped up and headed for the door. Miss Turner banged her ruler on her desk and yelled, "Get back in your seats!" We slowly ambled our way back to our desks and sat down. Miss Turner crossed her arms over her chest. "From now on, when the dismissal bell rings you will be dismissed from this class by rows." She pointed to the first row of five students and told them they could leave. Aisle by aisle she did this until all sixteen of us were walking down the hall toward the bus line.

"My Lord, what a crab!" Tommy Holland exclaimed and the boys walking with him added "Sour puss!" and "We got a rotten apple!" to the exclamation. Trixie looked at me and frowned. "If this is how she is on the first day, just think what she will be like all year!" I nodded and asked Trixie, "Just what's wrong with Brownie anyway?"

September 9, 1968
Dear Diary,
My first day of school was awful! I cried on the bus home. Now, I have homework to do. Ten pages to read and five problems to solve! Miss Turner is mean.
Brownie

I was in my bedroom doing homework while all of the warm September afternoon was fading into dusk. It made me want to cry all over again. That is when I heard the backdoor slam. I got up just in time to see Donna racing down the porch steps toward an idling black car called a beetle. A guy with shaggy hair sat behind the steering wheel. Donna got in and they drove off down the driveway.

I went into the living room and found my parents just sitting there, looking down at the floor. "Where'd Donna go?" I asked. Mama turned her face away from me. That told me she was crying. Daddy cleared his throat and said that she was going with a group of students to Atlanta. I asked him what for, but he just got up and walked slowly outside. "Go finish your homework, Tina," Mama said. I did as I was told but stopped in the hallway when I heard Mama pick up the telephone receiver in the kitchen. I listened while she dialed. Brrrup, brrrup, brrrup-brrup. I had memorized the sound of some of the phone numbers of people that Mama called and immediately knew she was dialing Aunt Janelle.

"Hey," Mama said. "She's gone. Left with that boy Larry just a minute ago." Mama was silent for a while, but I knew Aunt Janelle was a big talker and was probably putting in her two cents worth. Then Mama said, "I don't know.

Atlanta. Somewhere on Fourteenth Street. I don't know. I'm not that familiar with Atlanta." Then Mama broke down and sobbed into the receiver.

I walked into the kitchen and encircled my mother's waist with my arms. Something bad was going on and my heart began to ache. This quiet, timid woman who never asked for anything and gave all she had to her family had just watched her seventeen-year-old daughter walk out the door, leaving a place empty at the table and uncertainty about her well-being weighing down on the bony shoulders of her mother. Mama whispered into the receiver and asked my aunt to hold on a minute.

"Tina, I'm okay," Mama said, but she did not convince me. Mama took her free hand and unclasped one of my arms. "Really, I'm okay. Just let me talk to Aunt Janelle, please." I let go and stepped back. Mama's eyes were red and beginning to swell. I walked back to my bedroom and shut the door. Somebody knew what was going on with Donna and I just had to find out. I started back on my homework and decided that, when I was finished, I would ride over to Granny's and ask her about it.

I rode up Papa and Granny's driveway on my bicycle. The trees in the woods rattled with the breeze. The wind blew my hair over my head and into my eyes. I got off my bike and laid it on its side, while holding back my hair with my free hand. Papa was on a ladder at the side of the front porch. I walked up to speak to him. "Hey there, Miss Priss," he said through lips pinched around a couple of nails. Papa had his hat pushed back and was squinting at the window frame. He was dressed as usual, overalls and a brown work shirt. His big hammer was hanging in its holder. "Hand me that roll uh plastic," Papa said. I picked up the roll that was laying on the ground and pulled it to get it started. I handed the end to Papa and kept the roll so that I could ease it off as he needed it.

I had helped put plastic up on the outside of windows since I was five. People did this to help keep the heat inside of drafty houses. Papa pulled out his hammer and nailed the plastic down on the top right corner. Then he proceeded to nail it across the top until he got to the left corner, and it was good and tight.

"Thank 'ee," he said, climbing down the ladder. I kept on holding the plastic as he ran his scarred and scuffed hand down in a rusty coffee can full of nails. "I kin git it from here," he said. I laid the roll of plastic on the ground so that it would roll toward Papa when he pulled on it. "Whatche puttin' up plastic this early for, Papa?" I asked. Papa hammered a strip of cardboard over the plastic's right edge and secured the side. "To git it over with," he said. Papa's blue eyes twinkled, and he ran his hand back into the coffee can for more nails. I couldn't argue with that, so I laughed and walked on toward the back porch to see Granny.

I went into the kitchen just in time to see Granny push her nose against the window screen over the sink. She hollered, "Silas! Don't cover this wind-er up! I gotta have it open in case somethin' smokes up on tha stove!" I went back outside to tell Papa what Granny had said, in case he had not heard her. He chuckled.

"I heered ye, Eudora! You thank I ain't never put up plastic afore?" I knew that he was teasing Granny, so I left him and went back inside the house. Granny was shaking out a dishrag over the trash can.

"Whatchee doin', Miss Brownie?" she said as she wiped down her cabinet top. It was obvious that Granny had been chopping fall cabbage to make kraut. She already had the crock packed full of chopped cabbage and salt and went over to put a dinner plate on top of it. Then she went to get a pitcher of water to sit on top of the plate so that it weighed down the cabbage while it worked off. "Now, then," she said. "That'll be good when January rolls around." I ran water into the dipper that hung beside her sink and took several sips.

"Granny?" I began, "What's going on with my sister?" Granny went over to the kitchen table and sat down in her chair. "I figured ye'd be over hyur to ask about that," she said. I picked up the saltshaker and rolled it back and forth in my hand. It was a little Dutch girl who was puckered up to kiss the little Dutch boy, who was the pepper.

"Donna is ah goin' threw a rough patch," she said. "She's got in with thu wrong crowd and they've turned her head." I frowned. I already knew this much. "But why'd she go to Atlanta? I heard Mama say somethin' about Fourteenth Street." Granny put a dip of snuff in her mouth. "Now, Brownie, I ain't supposed to be tellin' you this, but I thank, as best I can tell, she's ah wontn to be a hippie. You know about hippies?" Granny looked at me straight in the eyes and I nodded. "But that don't sound like Donna," I said.

It always amazed me how Granny could dip snuff and never spit more than a couple of times. "Granny," I said. "This all started when David was sent to Vietnam. I been watching her and she's just tryin' to forgit him with that girl Poppy and her friends. Can't we go to Atlanta after her?" I felt my eyes stinging and before I knew it, I was crying. Granny reached in her apron pocket and handed me her handkerchief. It smelled like snuff, just like it had since the first time I remember using one of her hankies.

"I thank yer Daddy is already ah thankin' about that," Granny said with a smile. "Donna may not feel like coming home on her own, but ifn her Daddy comes to git her, whah she might be relieved and thank him fer it." Granny walked over to the stove and stirred her big pot that was bubbling on the front eye. "Donna's got some thangs to work our fer hersef and when she gits home, she'll probably feel ashamed. You need to hep her, ifn ye kin. Yore her sister." I nodded.

Granny stood at the stove and asked me if I wanted to stay and eat pinto beans with her and Papa. I loved Granny's pinto beans. She always put in a big chunk of fat back and cooked them all day. But I told her that I had to get back home and help Mama fix supper. Granny leaned down to hug and kiss me. She walked as far as the backdoor stoop to watch me leave. I waved goodbye and got on my bicycle. "Tell Papa I said 'bye'," I said, and she nodded. As I rode out of the driveway I started thinking about hippies. I really didn't know much about them.

That night, I was getting a drink of water before bed, and I heard Daddy say that he was going tomorrow to bring Donna home. Then he saw me standing in the kitchen and told me 'Good night' and to go on to bed, that he and mama were trying to talk.

It felt strange to lay in my bed in the room I shared with my sister and her not there. I felt sick in my stomach because I did not know where she was. How was Daddy even going to find her?

September 10, 1968
Dear Diary,
I'm worried sick. Daddy is going to find Donna and bring her home. I hope he finds her quick. I miss her.
Brownie

Our teacher, Miss Turner, had softened a little on our second day of school. She stood at the door smiling as we came in. The lavender dress that she had on went well with her red hair. I decided I would tell her so when I had a chance. But mainly I was nervous about Daddy finding Donna.

Trixie and I sat down in our desks, and I noticed something wonderful had happened. There, neatly printed on a new sheet of manilla folder was my name, Brownie Rivers. I looked up and saw that Miss Turner was smiling at me. I nodded at her. The day was looking better, and I took her change of heart as a sign.

That afternoon, I got off the bus and walked down the driveway. Roger saw Buster, his beagle, and stopped to scratch him. Then, he raced his dog up the driveway. As I walked, I enjoyed the clear blue sky and sweet breeze off the pasture. It had not been as hot lately and the evenings had turned off cool, so it felt like autumn was here at last. I stooped down and pulled some sweet grass to chew on. When I walked up on the yard, I saw Miz Jenkins' car with Mr. Jenkins standing beside it. I ran up the back steps, onto the porch and into the kitchen. There she sat, her large girth spilling over the sides of the kitchen chair like a runny pudding.

"I tell ye, Jeanette," Miz Jenkins was saying, "If she don't end up pragnent it'll be a wonder. Why I've heered all kinds of thangs about them hippies and I," Mama cleared her throat and put her arms around me. Miz Jenkins adjusted herself on the groaning chair.

"Hey, Miz Jenkins," I said. She ignored me and looked at Mama with a grunt. "Jeanette, thar's rat pills between yore cabinet and yore 'frigerater," she declared. Mama let out a gasp and went to look. Mice scared Mama to death. "Well," Mama said, "I will have to get that up and have Boyd put out a trap." Miz Jenkins pulled herself up and adjusted the bodice of her dress. "Well, let me know how it turns out," she said, and went out the door. I followed her to the porch and watched her sidestep slowly down each step until she reached the bottom.

"Earl!" Miz Jenkins hollered. "Go 'n tell Boyd that Jeanette needs some rat traps!" Then she waddled over to the car, got inside, and slammed the door. Mr. Jenkins didn't have to tell Daddy about the mousetraps. He and all of Keetoowah County heard Miz Jenkins loud and clear. Daddy came walking up about that time and told Mr. Jenkins that he would take care of it. I was glad when they left. I thought that Miz Jenkins had been rude to Mama, but Daddy just laughed out loud. It was the first time I'd heard him laugh in days. Then Daddy looked at me and said, "Well, Brownie? Did you see yore sister?" I looked at my Daddy in surprise and took off running.

I was grown before I knew what had happened to Donna after she left home. Yes, she went to the capitol in Atlanta and protested the Vietnam war. The guy named Larry who had picked her up was with her and so was Poppy. Sometime around midnight the group had gone to Fourteenth Street and met up with some friends of Poppy. Poppy said her friends would let them stay overnight. But Donna said that she soon found out that she did not want to be there and became afraid of the drug use and other activity that was going on. She waited for a chance to slip away to a pay phone where she called Daddy to come and get her. Donna had waited inside a twenty-four-hour convenience store until Daddy got there. But I did not know any of this when I was ten. All I knew was that she got in with the wrong crowd and realized it and then called Daddy to come and get her out of it.

September 14, 1968
Dear Diary,
Yay! It's Saturday!
Brownie

I was playing in Papa's hayloft with Trixie and Roger and Trixie's brothers, Ronnie, and Eddie. Trixie and I were building a playhouse out of the hay bales, only the boys were climbing up on them and jumping off, knocking us down.

All of us stopped suddenly and listened. We heard Granny calling for us. Granny had the high sing-song holler of the people who lived in the mountains. The sound carried a long way. I stuck my head out of the loft window. "Hey! Granny!" I shouted, "We're up here!" Granny nodded. "I'uz jus lookin' fer ye," she said. "Yuns be curfull up thar an' don't fall." I waved at her as she turned to walk toward the pasture. "Where're you goin'?" I hollered. Granny turned around. She was wearing a gray housedress covered with a red and white apron. She was wearing a pair of Papa's old work boots. "I gotta go check on Sulky," she replied.

"Wait for me!" I shouted and pulled my head back in the window. "Let's go!" I said to Trixie and the boys. Roger shook his head, "Naw. I wanna stay here and build a fort outta the hay bales." Trixie looked at me and shrugged, then followed me down the ladder and out of the barn.

With a granddaughter on each side, holding to her hands, Granny made a slow trek down the rutted field road to the pasture out behind the barn. She walked us up to a spot where the barbed wire fence ran through a patch of sunshine, then she whistled. Not a sharp whistle, but a low meaningful whistle. The kind I had been practicing all of my young life to imitate.

After a while, a big black mule came plodding up from a stand of red oak trees. She had been made invisible by the dappled shade. The closer she got to the fence the more Trixie backed up. Granny let go of our hands and reached out to stroke Sulky's black nose. "Thar's mah purty girl," Granny crooned. I wasn't too keen on being this close to the mule, but I didn't want Granny to think I was afraid like Trixie. "She's gotta bad cut on her backside," Granny advised. "An 'at makes her skittish." I looked and saw that Papa was walking up toward the fence from the *inside* of the pasture with a bottle of something in his hand.

"Keep her thar, Eudora," he said. "An' let me git this medcine on that cut. You girls git back. She don't like this, and she kicks." Trixie and I moved to the other side of the field road and sat down on the bank beneath the pine trees. Papa knew that mules did not like people to sneak up on them, so he angled around the side until Sulky could see him. The mule gave a little kick. Granny continued her baby talk.

"Easy, ole Sulky," Papa said softly. "This is fer yer own good." He took a rag out of his pocket and a poured purple liquid onto it. He held the rag where the mule could see it. I found all of this fascinating, but Trixie, who was obviously scared, was almost climbing the pine tree behind me. "Easy. Easy," Papa reassured. It looked like he just might make it and get the medicine applied to Sulky's flank. It sure did. Until it didn't.

Papa got the medicine on the cut alright, but he did not get out of the way fast enough. The big black mule kicked and thrashed like she was dancing on a snake. Her left foot grazed Papa's shoulder as he was trying to back out of the way. Granny pinched Sulky's left ear hard and she kicked and stomped away from Papa. "Silas!" Granny boomed. "Come 'ere an' let me see wha' she's done."

Papa stretched the barbed wire fence and came out of the pasture through the two top lengths of wire. He immediately grabbed his left arm, but he did not grimace or say a word. Granny went over and began unbuttoning his shirt. She took his shirt off and threw it on the ground. Sulky had gone back to the pasture and was nibbling grass. Trixie and I went over to see what had happened to our grandfather.

Between Papa's left shoulder and elbow was a bright blue knot. "Kin ye move it?" Granny asked. Papa windmilled his arm around and nodded. Granny pressed around the knot, checking the bone. Papa winced once, then corrected his face. "Ah reckin ye'll live," Granny said and patted Papa's face gently. Papa picked up his shirt and began rebuttoning it. As he did this, he looked at us girls and smiled. "Well, y'all sure did git a show, didn't ye?" Trixie and I grabbed him around the waist. "That sure was scary, Papa," Trixie said. "Don't you never do that agin!" Papa laughed. "Well, let's hope ah don't have to!"

Papa and Granny walked back to the house. At some point, Papa had retrieved the bottle of medicine, but he had missed the rag. I found it and picked it up. "Here! Smell," I said to Trixie. Trixie took a sniff of the rag. "Phew!" she said, "What is that stuff?" I shrugged and looked down at the purple stain on the white rag. "I don't know," I said. "But let's call it Sulky Poison and try to smear it on the boys!" And we took off for the barn.

The five of us played until dusky-dark. That's when Uncle Gil came out onto the back porch and called us in to supper. We were all going to eat together, and that made me happy. It had turned cool while we were playing, making the inside of the kitchen feel like Granny's oven. "Whew, it's hot in here!" Trixie grumbled. "Go wash your hands," Aunt Brenda instructed. "And if you're that hot, wash your face, too." We did as we were told and when we got back, we sat down at the sawhorse table at the end of the kitchen. Granny always put it up when we were all there to eat at the same time.

Papa asked the blessing, and then we waited for our turn to fill our plates. From our little table, we could tell what we were having for supper by what the adults dipped onto their plates. It was backbones and ribs. Granny was the only person who could make them to suit me. The pork would just slip off the bone. Then I saw fried sweet potatoes. Granny would cut sweet potatoes into discs, cover them with white sugar and a stick of butter and fry them in an iron skillet until they were soft and like candy. Next, Mama dipped some black-eyed peas onto her plate, and Papa picked up a piece of cornbread and sliced it open to smear butter inside. "I'm about to die from hunger!" Trixie groaned.

"Yuns come fix yer plate," Granny motioned for us to come to the big table. She handed each one of us a plate and patted us on the back. After getting our supper and sitting back down, Trixie dove into her food. "I'm hungry, too," Ronnie said with a mouthful of cornbread. We ate and laughed and listened to the adults talk about Papa getting kicked by the mule. "Well, it could have turned out a whole lot worse, Daddy," Uncle Gil was saying. "Thank the Lord a little knot is all you got." Papa nodded and held his cup and saucer up so that Granny could pour hot, black coffee into it. "Who wonts choclit cake?" Granny asked. Trixie stopped sopping pork broth with her cornbread and raised her hand. "Kin I have coffee?" Ronnie asked. The adults laughed. "If you take it with a lot of milk," Aunt Brenda replied.

The chocolate cake was delicious. Granny had split the two yellow cake layers into four and filled and iced the whole cake with a rich fudge frosting. Because we were ten years old, Trixie and I could have one cup of coffee with our cake. The taste was out of this world.

Then Uncle Gil started telling a story about Jay Withersby losing a mule to colic some years back. "His new bride, what was her name, Boyd?" Daddy answered, "Linda." "Yeah, Linda didn't know much about farm animals, did she?" Daddy and Gill laughed. "Linda had spent the day making kraut and had a dishpan full of cabbage leaves and stalks," Uncle Gill said. "Well, when she was cleaning up her kitchen, she looked out the window and saw Jay's little brown mule. So, she took the whole dishpan of cabbage leavings out to the pasture fence and dumped them in the mule's trough." Papa started laughing.

"Well, Jay comes home and kisses his bride then looks out the kitchen window and sees his mule rolling around in the grass." It was a story that was sad to me, but funny to the menfolk. "The mule got colic from eating all of that cabbage at one time! Linda told Jay, 'Well, who would have thought that Jim would eat it all!'" More laughing at the foolishness of new brides. Uncle Gil stopped to fill his mouth with cake and Daddy took up the story. "Yeah, Jay called me to come over so that we could take turns walking the mule all night. Needless to say, he didn't make it and Linda cried the whole time."

"Well," I thought, "that story made me feel sad for the mule *and* Linda!" I did not think it was funny at all. Granny could see my distress and changed the subject. Pretty soon they were telling tales about Papa's bluetick hound, Bonnie Blue, being the best coon dog in three counties because she was fast and true on a tree. We sat and listened until Roger pushed his plate back and laid his head on the table to go to sleep. Mama, who had been helping Aunt Brenda wash dishes, laid her hand on Daddy's shoulder and said it was time to go.

On the way home, Mama started whispering to Daddy. So, Daddy cleared his throat and said, "I'm sorry about that story about the mule. We were laughing at Linda, not the mule. Still, we should not have laughed at all and I'm sorry for that." I choked and said, "Okay."

My Daddy was like that. If he had done something wrong and understood that he did, he apologized for it.

Even to us children. His humility and kindness helped to shape me when I was growing up.

I looked out the window at the starry night sky. A big moon was shining with a halo around it. I counted the stars inside the circle. Four days until it rained.

September 27, 1968
Dear Diary,
Joe-Joe Collins hit me with the pointed end of his pencil while we stood in line for the pencil sharpener. I hollered out and Miss Turner put a mark by my name in her book. Five marks in one week meant a note home to our parents. I already have two!
Brownie

I was flying on my bike down the hill and almost slid into Granny's driveway. I straightened up and went sailing down it, coming to a stop at the back porch. Laying my bike on its side, I raced up the steps calling out for Granny. I was breathless when I went crashing into the kitchen. The house was silent except for a slight dripping of her kitchen faucet. I went outside and started walking toward the barn calling out "Graaa-ney!", "Paa-paa!" every breath. Papa came out of the barn like he was startled. "What's all tha ruckus out hyur?" He looked angry, so I lowered my voice. "I'm lookin' for Granny," I said. Papa realized he was holding a wet paintbrush and went back inside the barn to put it away. "Well, I figured that out. She ain't hyar, so ye'll have to make do with me" he said. "Yore Granny has gone to tha woods and ye ain't gonna bother her."

Oh! That was today! I had forgotten. Every year on the twenty-seventh of September Granny went to the woods. Sometimes she would stay gone over night. Daddy told me that when she first found out, she left and was gone for three days. September twenty-seventh was the anniversary of the day Uncle Ray was killed in Vietnam. Uncle Ray was in the Air Force and was killed during Operation Rolling Thunder in 1966. His airplane was shot down somewhere over the China Sea. Uncle Ray's body was never found. Daddy had explained to us that our Granny, being half Cherokee, still had a lot of the Cherokee ways in her. Her way of coping with Ray's death was to go to the woods. She would build a fire, wrap in a blanket, and grieve.

"Papa, when is Granny going to be over Uncle Ray dying?" I asked my grandfather and his face softened. "Never," he said and went back into the barn. I followed him. "Well, kin *you* help me then?" I asked. Papa wiped down his paintbrush and put it into a bucket to soak. He had been painting an old tire bright red. "What do you thank? Do you think this will make Granny a nice flower bed?" Papa had used Granny's favorite color to make something to cheer her up. "Yeah," I replied, "or it would look good with tomatoes, too." Papa smiled. "What is it ye need?" he asked. I sighed. "I forgot that I had to interview one of my grandparents for school, and my paper is due tomorrow." Papa looked at me and sat down on an overturned bucket. "Well, git on with it," he said. I fished around in my skirt pocket and pulled out a pencil stub and a folded sheet of notebook paper.

"Well, I know yore name," I said grinning. "So, tell me something about yoreself that I don't know." I stood with my pencil poised, ready for him to speak. Papa scratched his head. His overalls were baggy and hung loose on his long, lanky frame. I loved my Papa with all my heart. "Okie dokie," he said, "When I was sixteen, I was put in jail." I dropped my pencil. "Huh?" was all I could say.

Papa began to tell me about how the lean times came to his family and to be able to feed his children, my great-grandfather had built a small still and started making white liquor. He was only going to do it for a little while, just until he got on his feet, but the money he made was more than he could make raising cotton. During this time, Great-grandaddy found out that he could run the liquor he was making across the county line and sell it at the pool hall there. Papa said his Daddy told him to take the truck and make the liquor run. And he always did what his Daddy told him to do. So, on a dark moonless midnight, Papa went to the pool hall to make a delivery.

"And wouldn't ye know it. That'd be tha night tha revenuers was thar. Locked me up and took the whiskey, too." Papa looked at me grinning. "I wadn't a bad boy, Brownie," he said, "Iuz jus mindin' my daddy." Papa wiped his hands on a work cloth. "Mah daddy was always ashamed that he brung me to that. And he told me more'n once that he wuz sorry. You make sure you put that in yore paper."

"Daddy brought me home from jail that night, and we busted up the still before we went to bed. He never made a drop of whiskey adder that. That's a lesson fer ye." I wrote it all down as best I could.

"Have you ever told anyone this story before?" I asked. Papa stood up and stretched. "Naw. Ituz not somethin' ta boast about" he said. I hugged him at the waist. "Well," I said. "I'm gonna make you famous!" Papa laughed and walked me out of the barn. When we got to the back porch, he stopped to look back at the hillside covered in a pine thicket. We could see a small whisp of smoke curling its way up. Papa scratched his face. "I guess I'm eatin' cornflakes fer supper."

October 4, 1968

Dear Diary,

Mama wouldn't let me write about Papa Rivers making liquor. She told me some ole story about her mama, Grandmother

Davidson being a contestant in the Miss South Carolina beauty pageant and made me write about that instead.

Tonight we are going over to Horace and Avalon Guthrie's house so Mama and Daddy can play Rook. We are taking Papa and Granny with us and Uncle Gill and Aunt Wanda, Trixie, and the boys will be there too.

Brownie

Horace and Avalon's house was always a fun place to go. The couple had no children, so any kids that came to visit were treated like royalty. Horace was a short fellow, with a balding head, and sparkling eyes. Horace could wiggle his ears and yodel. Avalon was a petite little woman with dark hair that had a white streak from her forehead to the back. She made the best gingerbread cake that I have ever tasted. She served it with warm vanilla sauce. I have never found a recipe for it, despite years of searching.

We pulled into the Guthrie's yard just as it was getting dark. Mama had fixed a quick supper of hot dogs and told us that we had better not ask for anything to eat. That would not be a problem and we knew it. Miz Avalon would offer us so many treats that we would never have to ask for anything.

Their house was a tiny white clapboard, frame house. The small front porch had white wrought-iron railing that curlicued all around. Daddy knocked on the door and Horace opened it. For a full five minutes it was a roar and flurry of "glad to see yous" and "ain't you young uns got big" until we were ushered in where the rest of the guests were.

There was Horace and Avalon, Uncle Gil, and Aunt Brenda, the two boys, Trixie, Mama, Daddy, Donna, Roger, and me and Papa and Granny. That was a lot of people for such a small house, but Horace had made it work by pushing the furniture against the walls and setting up card tables and t.v. trays all around. We had been shown to the bedroom to lay our coats, purses, and such on the bed. I could smell coffee brewing in the kitchen.

Papa and Granny did not do anything much for amusement, but they really loved to play the card game Rook. Papa always wanted to get the widder, which was what the cards in the middle were called. If you caught the last trick the widder sometimes had points in it. Also, everyone was hoping to get the Rook because he caught everything. Granny was known to "shoot the moon", which meant she bid the full amount of five hundred so that *she* could get the cards in the middle. Papa called it playing cutthroat.

Trixie poked me. "Let's go see what's for dessert." So, we ambled off to the kitchen where Miz Avalon was slicing a frosted coconut cake. "Well, hey thar!" she exclaimed. "Wont some tea cakes?" Tea cakes in our world were big, thick sugar cookies and Miz Avalon made really good ones. "It's too early," I said modestly. I looked and Trixie had a mouthful of tea cake with two in her hand. "Aw, yore at our house and I wont ye to have whatever ye wont." Miz Avalon's smile was as sweet as her cookies. Pretty soon, Roger and Trixie's brothers were in the kitchen too. We took our paper plates loaded down with sugary treats off to a corner of the kitchen where our mothers could not see us.

There was bidding and laughing in the living room as the two teams played. It took four people with two each playing as partners to play the game of Rook. One card table team consisted of Mama, Daddy, Horace and Aunt Brenda and the other card table team consisted of Uncle Gil, Papa, Granny and Avalon. I heard Mister Horace slap his hands down on the table and say, "I caught that trick!" Then he started yodeling.

"Well, she's a looooooong, gooooone
And noooow I'm lowoooonsome bluoooes!
Yodel-laytey oh, ah-laytey oh, Yodel-laytey!"

Then, Horace stood up, snapped his suspenders, and wiggled his ears. Trixie and I laughed. We had slipped and each poured ourselves a cup of coffee to go with our coconut cake. The cake melted on your tongue leaving only the sugary seven-minute frosting and coconut. It was a puff of deliciousness, and the strong black coffee was just the partner for it.

As the night played on, Miz Avalon brought out quilts and made pallets on the floor for us. Roger and the boys laid down and were soon snoring. Trixie, me, and the coffee stayed awake. We were enjoying the evening. I heard someone yell, "No trumps!" and laughter erupted. Donna had taken Mama's place and played the last two hands. I could not wait to be old enough to play Rook like the adults.

When we got ready to leave, we told Horace and Avalon how much we enjoyed, next time it'll be our place, and we love you. Daddy had Roger lying on his shoulder as he carried him to the car. It was really hard for me to stay awake on the car ride home, but eventually I must have fallen asleep because I woke up the next morning wearing my pajamas and lying beneath my own quilt.

I walked into my classroom on Monday and saw that Miss Turner was not at her desk. A paper airplane made from notebook paper sailed across the room, and the kids were all laughing and talking. Trixie and I slid into our desks. "Did you hear the news?" Robin Watson asked us with a devilish grin. "Miss Turner got married this past Saturday! She's on her honeymoon, and we are going to have a substitute this week!" Trixie and I gasped at the same time. "Maybe that's why she's been so crabby!" Trixie offered. Just then, Robin's mother walked into the room. "And my mama is the substitute!" she said with a self-important grin. We knew Miz Watson from church and figured this week of school was going to be a piece of cake. Miz Watson called the class to attention.

She began by explaining why our teacher was not there and then said she would try to be a good stand-in for her. "Now, turn to spelling and write the words, hmm? She's got here write them twenty times, but I think five will be good enough." The whole class sighed with pleasure. Yeah, this week would definitely be a lot easier.

After school, Trixie and I were sitting together on the school bus. It drove along with its familiar rumble and lurched to a stop with a hiss when someone had to be let off. We were happy because we did not have homework. Trixie, her brothers, Roger, and I were the first ones to be let off the bus. The green pastures and rolling hills seemed to urge us on as we walked up Piney Hill. We could not wait to get home and play.

Daddy and Mama were waiting at the end of our driveway in the truck. Roger, who had run on ahead of me, was in the bed of the pickup. "Hurry!" he exclaimed, banging his open hand on the side of the truck, "We're goin' to see the Goat Man!" Mama covered her eyes with her hands and Daddy laughed. I stepped up on the running board of the truck and climbed in, throwing my book satchel in first. I looked down and swiped at the red dust on the front of my school dress.

Every year in the fall old Ches McCartney would hitch up his goats to his little Conestoga wagon with its pots and pans rattling and the bells on the goats jangling and head across country. He said he was spreading God's word. He always made a stop our little community.

We never knew where Mr. McCartney was headed, and I do not think he did either. But every year, when the days began to cool down, folks could hear the clatter of his wagon train coming for miles and would make plans to take their children to see the Goat Man when he stopped to water and feed his traveling herd.

My mother was embarrassed and never got out of the truck on these trips. However, today, Daddy had heard that he was going to stop at Merchant's store and Mama was going inside to pick up some groceries.

We drove down Piney Hill and turned right, and it was only a short drive until we turned into the little community store on the right. A crowd had already started to gather. Folks who knew the Goat Man from years of seeing him, onlookers who had never spoken to the man, and children of all ages running around, laughing, and waiting for their turn to pet the goats.

"You children wash your hands as soon as you get back to the truck," Mama said. She was holding up a damp, soapy dishcloth which she had wrapped in aluminum foil. "Is that really necessary?" Daddy asked. "They're around farm animals all the time!" Mama held up the foil packet and shook it at us. "Remember!" she said and got out of the truck to quickly dart through the parking lot and slip inside the store.

Roger and I scrambled over the tailgate of the truck. Daddy gave us each a dime for the collection plate. The Goat Man was a traveling preacher. When the crowd had gathered, he told all of the children that they could form a line and he would let them pet each goat and learn their names and at the end, he would milk the goats and they could all have a taste of goat's milk. His covered wagon had a sign that said "Repent and Be Saved" tacked to it. He then preached a short sermon about not waiting until it was too late and making it right while there was still time.

All of this went right past our ears. After all, we had come for the goats. But being brought up right we listened quietly and patiently until he was finished preaching and gently ushered the first few children over to the goats. "Hey!

Kin we ride one of 'em?" A voice shouted. This brought laughter from the crowd.

The Goat Man let Roger tug on one of the big ram's horns. The animal's beard was a nasty yellow streaked with brown, like he had been dipping snuff. I liked the bells that they wore around their necks. Some were large and sturdy, but the little bells were decorated with some kind of scroll and made a high tinkling sound when the harness was shaken. It made me think of the goats in the book about the little girl in the Alps that I had just read in school.

After all the children had their turn looking at the goats, we got out of the way while the Goat Man put his stool underneath one of the nanny goats and began milking her, the creamy milk foaming up in the galvanized pail. I noticed that he had not washed his hands or the milk sack before he began. Granny would not have liked that. When the nanny had given all the milk she had, the Goat Man stood up and turned to his young audience. He took a metal cup from the side of his caravan and said, "Who wonts tha first sup?"

Mama had warned us not to drink the milk, but we could not help ourselves. Roger and I stepped up and took a sip of milk from the cup and, drinking from the same cup, all of our friends did the same. It was really rich and left a strange taste on my tongue that I tried to wipe off with the tail of my dress. Daddy laughed at me. At the end of the little covered wagon, where the goats were hitched, stood a little table with a metal basin on top. This was for donations. A small sign that read "God bless you" was taped to the base of the table. Roger and I placed our dimes in the tray and went over to Daddy.

"It's only a dollar to have yer picture made," the Goat Man said. Daddy told him that we did not bring a camera and said thank you as he guided us away and toward the pickup. When we got in the cab of the truck, I got the wet washcloth and washed my hands thoroughly. Then I handed it to Roger, who only gave his hands a lick and a promise. It was not long before Mama was back with two sacks of groceries in her arms. Roger and I bailed out of the cab of the truck to let Mama in and got back into the bed for the ride home.

October 22, 1968
Dear Diary,
Donna has a new boyfriend! I heard her talking to him on the phone.
Patty's cat had kittens and I want one. Mama is thinking about it.
Brownie

It was finally beginning to feel like fall. The days were cool with skies of cobalt blue and sunshine so sharp that looking up to watch the crows fly made you squint. The few hardwoods that stood among the evergreens on Piney Hill were all afire in their jewel tones of ruby, topaz and amber. There were poplars, red oaks, sycamores, and maples and they held on to their colorful crowns for weeks during the month of October, until mid-November, when they were scattered like crepe paper cut-outs across the pine straw floor. This was always my favorite time of year.

Trixie and I were walking in the woods collecting leaves for our school assignment. "What kind's this 'un?" Trixie held up a big sycamore leaf shaped like a large hand spread out. "Did Miz Carlisle say we could use pine needles?" I asked her. Trixie had brought a brown paper grocery bag, and we were taking two of each leaf we found and putting them in the sack to divide later. "I reckin a leaf is a leaf," she said with a shrug. I had found a wild holly bush and pulled two leaves off of it to go into the sack.

"How come you ain't said nothin' about Donna's new boyfriend?" Trixie asked me with a frown. I walked over to her with two maple leaves and said, "I just found out about it. I ain't even seen him." Trixie stood up and showed me the inside of the bag. It looked like we had enough leaves. "Well, has she give up on David then?" Trixie and I had talked often about David being in Viet Nam. We watched the news and talked about it in class. The war was very frightening to us.

I shrugged. "She ain't got no letter in a long time," I said. "I git skeered thinkin' maybe he's dead." Trixie nodded. We took our sack and headed down the bank to the road. We were going back to Trixie's house to finish our classwork. As we walked, a cold wind began to blow. "Whew!" I said. "That's right off of ice!" We pulled our sweaters tight around us and ran down the hill and up Trixie's driveway until we reached the front door. Trixie opened it, and the wind slammed it back against the side of the house with a bang. Aunt Brenda came into the living room with a dishtowel in her hands. "Goodness!" she said. "The wind sure is stirred up!" Aunt Brenda had an apron on. Good smells were coming from her kitchen.

"Mama," Trixie said, following Aunt Brenda into the kitchen. "Kin we have a snack?" Trixie sat the bag on the kitchen table and went to the sink to wash her hands. "Yeah," I said in agreement. "We're hungry." Aunt Brenda smiled and turned around to show us a plate of peanut butter cookies that she had made. I took one and grinned at her. Aunt Brenda was just the best. She was like a second mother to me.

"Whatchall doin' with them leaves?" she asked. Trixie swallowed her cookie and began explaining that we were told to paste or tape them to notebook paper and write what kind of tree they came off of beside each one. Then, we had to decorate the outside edges of the paper with fall scenes. Trixie went over to a drawer beside the kitchen wall and came back to the table with tape, crayons, and notebook paper. We sat down at the table to begin.

Aunt Brenda came over and sat down, too. She gave us each a glass of grape drink. "What's this I hear, Brownie? About Donna having a new boyfriend?" I shrugged. Why was everybody so interested in Donna? Ever since Daddy brought her back from Atlanta it was like people thought she needed a steady boyfriend to get her life back on track. "Have you heard anything about David?" I asked her. Aunt Brenda sighed. "His mama told me that they've not heard a thing since he was reported missing in action. She sure is tore up." Trixie and I both looked up. This was the first we had heard of this.

"Does Donna know he's missin'?" Aunt Brenda asked me. I shrugged and taped a poplar leaf onto my paper. "Nobody tells me anything," I said, and I suddenly felt like crying. I looked at Trixie and she was snubbing back tears. "Oh, girls!" Aunt Brenda said. "I didn't mean to upset you." She wiped Trixie's face with her dishtowel. "This war's a bad thang," she said. "If he's missin', are they lookin' fer him?" Trixie asked. Aunt Brenda nodded and smiled, "They sure are, honey, and I bet they find him soon."

After we finished with our leaf collection, I packed mine up in the folds of an old newspaper and headed back to my house. The wind was fierce and blew my hair over my head on more than one occasion. By the time I had walked up the hill and onto our porch I was half frozen. Walking into the kitchen and feeling the electric heat made me shiver with relief. "There you are!" Mama exclaimed. "I thought I was going to have to send out a search party!" I laid my leaf collection on the kitchen counter and walked over to the heat vent to get warm. Mama was cooking supper and asked me to wash my hands and set the table. While I was getting out the forks, I decided I would ask Mama about David.

Mama's face turned solemn, and she looked at me and said softly, "Yes, he was declared missing. But I do know that Carol and Jim had a visit from an Army man today around dinnertime. But the news isn't out about that yet. I am going to talk to Donna when she gets home. She is over at Granny and Papa's right now." I frowned. "What's she doin' over there?" I asked. Mama went about the kitchen first to the stove to stir the potatoes, then to the counter to make the cornbread. Mama was a good cook and she like to do it. She had followed Granny's instructions when she married Daddy, and sometimes it was hard to tell her food from my grandmother's.

"Papa took up his sweet potatoes today and she went to help them," Mama said with a shrug. "It wouldn't hurt you to take an interest in farm work, instead of goofing off all the time. I mean, you're almost eleven." Mama looked at me and grinned. It was true that I avoided work, but what kid my age did not? I struggled to think of a way to defend myself when Donna came in. Mama used her thumb and motioned for me to leave.

October 29, 1968
Dear Diary,
I am sad. David's funeral was today. They found him somewhere in a swamp. Donna went crazy when they told her. Richie Brown said at school today that somebody had seen Carl Jacobs in town. How can that be when he's in prison?
Brownie

It was a day of golden sunshine when the Vietnam war finally made its presence known to our community. Our friend nineteen-year-old David Williams had been killed not two weeks after landing in that foreign country.

I was sitting cross-legged in the floor with my back against the wall of the Williams' living room trying to keep my dress pulled down over my knees. Trixie and Patty came in almost at the same time. They sat down beside me. "It sure is crowded, huh?" said Patty. The ladies in the community had cleaned Carol and Jim's house and brought in food for after the funeral. Mama had told Roger and me that we would not be staying long and that the food was not for us, so she had better not see us with any. So, I sat in my Sunday dress with my back pressed against the living room wall trying to figure out just how quiet a church mouse was. Trixie cupped her hand to my ear and whispered, "Reckin' we could sneak a chicken leg?" Her breath tickled my ear in an annoying way, and I pushed her back. Meanwhile, Roger and Trixie's two brothers had scooted on their bottom until they were almost to the edge of the dessert table.

A burst of crying came from the kitchen. It was Miz Carol. Her husband, who was holding her up, guided her into the living room and helped her onto the couch. I looked down at my lap and busied myself with making a church and steeple by lacing my fingers. Patty leaned over and whispered behind her hand, "Y'all! Carl Jacobs' is back!" Trixie and I nodded. Patty continued, "He's got out of prison somehow and he's saying he's gonna git Tater back and bring him home. Says, Tater is his kinfolk and ain't no county gonna say diffrent." About that time Aunt Janelle came over to where we were sitting.

"Well, ain't y'all quiet," Aunt Janelle whispered. "Y'all could be those see no evil, hear no evil, and speak no evil monkeys!" The three of us giggled. Aunt Janelle was pretty in her black, fitted dress. Her hair was up in a twist, and she had on black eyeliner and pink lipstick. "Whatchall talkin' about?" she asked squatting down.

"Is Carl Jacobs really not in prison anymore, Aunt Janelle?" I asked. My aunt worked at the courthouse in the clerk's office so if anyone knew, it would be her. She pursed her lips and considered how much to say. "Well, yes," she replied. "But he has to stay out of trouble if he don't want to go back there." Trixie stood up and said her leg was going to sleep.

"But I heard that Carl's gonna git Tater back and make him live in that ole chicken house agin," said Patty. "No, we don't want Tater going back there," Trixie said. "Me 'n Brownie's seen it. It ain't fit for fleas." Aunt Janelle laughed. "Well, Carl ain't got no say-so in that," she said. "Tater has been adopted and that's that. And, have you heard this? He is going to start school at Piney Hill soon. Yep. He will be in the first grade. Won't that be nice?" Aunt Janelle waited on us to catch up.

"Oh, no!" I exclaimed a little too loudly. Some of the adults turned around and looked our way. "Carl is sure to find him if he comes to school here!" I whispered. Aunt Janelle stood up with a little grunt. "Well, his name has been changed, so y'all might not want to be calling him Tater. And his new parents have all of that worked out with the principal." Mama walked over to where we were and motioned for me to stand up. Patty stood up, too. I noticed Mama had a hold of Roger underneath his armpit. That meant that he had better not move, or else. I knew this from experience.

Mama walked us out the living room door and straight to the car. We got in the backseat but still had to wait on Daddy and Donna. The last afternoon sunlight had just been cut off by the shadow of the mountain. "Roger, stop that!" Mama cried. Roger had been blowing his breath on the back window and writing his name in it. I leaned over the front seat. "Mama? Do you know who adopted Tater?" Mama thought for a minute, then looked toward the Williams' front door. "It's just that," I continued, "Aunt Janelle said he was going to start school with us soon and that he had a new name." Mama cleared her throat. "I'm not sure I should be the one to say, Tina," she said. "Ask Daddy." But Roger piped up and said, "I know who! It's Horace and Avalon Guthrie!" My mouth flew open. "How in the world do you know that Roger?" Mama asked. "Yay!" I said, "I caint thank of anybody better!" I clapped my hands and Mama smiled.

"There's only one problem," I said. "Carl is out of prison, and he says he's gonna git Tater back." Mama brushed the hair out of my eyes. "I think Carl had better mind his Ps and Qs, if he knows what's good for him." About that time, Daddy and Donna came to the car and it was time to head back home. Donna's face was red from crying. The pink flush only made her prettier. Her new boyfriend, Tom, was standing at her side of the car talking to her in soft tones. Daddy got in the car and began tapping his fingers on the steering wheel. Finally, Tom backed away and we all waved goodbye to him.

Today, we have wreaths on our doors for all occasions whether it's Easter, Christmas, or our favorite football team. But when I was a child, the only time you saw a wreath on the door of someone's home was when there had been a death in the family. I remember looking at that wreath of white mums as we pulled away from the Williams' house and thinking that it would be thrown out in the next day or two. The first step toward healing.

October 31, 1968
Dear Diary,
It's Halloween! We are going to the Halloween Carnival at school tonight. I'm gonna be a monster.
Brownie

It was wonderful to be a child back in the days when Halloween was fun. There was no worrying about tainted treats or stranger danger then because we knew all our neighbors and were, in fact related to most of them. We made our own costumes from things that we found around the house. Sometimes we might even have a plastic mask with the elastic string that stretched across the back of your head. It was fun coming up with an outfit that would keep your friends guessing who you were.

School Halloween carnivals, which are now a thing of the past, were looked forward to almost as much as Christmas. Bobbing for apples, getting your fortune told and the spook house were lots of fun. And then there were the cakewalks. A confectionary sort of musical chairs. Mothers and grandmothers baked cakes and donated them. The cakes were then set on display so that you could see which one you wanted to "walk" for. You paid your quarter and got a ticket, and then you waited and watched for the dad with the microphone to hold up the cake you wanted and announce that it was time to walk.

If you got there in time you stood behind a folding chair, which had been placed in a circle, and when all chairs were claimed, the music started, and you walked around behind them until it stopped. At which time you scrambled to be the first one to sit in your chair. The reward would be a three-layer frosted coconut cake, vanilla pound cake, or chocolate sheet cake. But woe be unto you if you were going through the spook house when the cake you wanted to walk for came up!

I was going to meet up with Patty and Trixie at the school where we would go to the carnival together. Daddy and Mama rode in the cab of the truck while Roger and I sat in the pickup bed. It was a cool but short ride to the school. The sun was just setting sending up long red streaks through the evening clouds. We drove into the schoolyard parting waves of colorfully clad children as we rode toward a parking place in the grass beneath the flag-pole. I guessed Trixie right off.

I do not know if she could have picked anything that made her belly look any bigger. She was dressed as a clown and someone, Aunt Brenda I guessed, had made her a one-sie out of a white sheet. She wore a white shirt underneath, and the sleeves and neck of the shirt were trimmed out in red ruffles. So were the bottoms of the legs. Trixie had red circles of lipstick on her cheeks and mouth and blue eye-shadow all around her eyes. A little polka-dot cone hat sat on top of her hair which was made into little, short pigtails.

"How're you gonna keep yer hat on, Trixie?" I asked and immediately regretted it because I had given myself away. "Mama has it pinned with bobbie pins," she replied. "Nice costume," Trixie said to me. I shushed her. "Here comes Patty! Don't let on like you know who I am. I'm gonna go over to the flagpole; then I'll come back." I slipped away as quickly as I could. I watched while Patty tried to get Trixie to guess who she was. "Well, you sound like Patty," Trixie said. "I mean, yore costume's good, but you really shouldn't talk." Patty hit Trixie in the chest with a card-board wand with a cut-out star on top. She was a fairy, I think. I made my way over and didn't say a word.

"Aughhh!" Patty cried, "Git away from me!" Trixie and I snickered. "Do you know who that is?" Patty asked Trixie. Trixie just snickered. I was dressed like Frankenstein.

Aunt Janelle had bought Roger and me rubber masks that Mama was not too happy about. I had on all black and my Daddy's black boots and black gloves. But the mask with its rubber smell and small slit eyeholes made the costume. "Rrrr!" I growled and walked stiff-armed toward a group of my classmates. Debbie and Jenny squealed, and Peter gave me a push. I pulled off my mask, laughing.

We walked out of the dark and into the brightly lit gymnasium. After my eyes adjusted, I saw the circle being set up for the cake walk. Trixie wanted to go over and pick out her cake and get a ticket before we did anything else. Two card tables had been set up with around ten cakes laid out on display. Trixie immediately picked out a sheet cake with fudge icing and the name of Mrs. Noland Butler taped to the plastic wrap. Miz Butler cooked in our lunchroom, so we knew her cake would be delicious. Still, I looked at Trixie and asked her, "But what if a cake comes in later that you like better?" Trixie looked through her little snap change purse and said, "I robbed my piggy bank, so I can always buy another ticket." So, that was settled.

Trixie, Patty, and I decided to look around. There was the toss-a-penny game where you tried to land a penny in a bowl beside some donated prize that you might want. I spent about five cents trying to win a gold bracelet with a little dangling heart charm, but I got it. Then we went over to the shoot-a-basket game. I had bought a dollar's worth of tickets and was saving two for the spook house and cake walk, so I splurged and gave one to Ricky Dobson's mother for the game. Ricky, who was helping his mama, said "Brownie's really good at shooting baskets, Mama!" which made me blush. I had always had a little crush on him. Ricky's hair was thick and curly, and he played Dizzy Dean baseball for Piney Hill. I bounced the basketball a couple of times and then made my shot. Swoosh! Right into the basket. I won a small magnifying glass. I put it in my pants pocket.

"Oh! Let's go to the funhouse mirrors!" Patty cried. Someone had curtained off a corner in the gym and placed fun house mirrors inside. Colored lights played off the curtains making it look exciting when you walked in. We bumped into our other friends from school as we all tried to trade mirrors and see what shape our bodies would become. Stretched and squeezed, our reflections made us laugh. Bobby Renfroe pulled his cheeks back and stuck out his tongue. We all laughed hysterically.

"What next?" I asked. Trixie kept a watch on the cake walk circle. "Let's go see if anymore cakes have come in," she said. So, we walked back to the circle to see. And there, at the very back of the cupcakes and pound cakes, standing tall was a red velvet cake made by Mrs. Edna Jenkins. The three of us looked at each other. Miz Jenkins also worked in the school lunchroom and was known in the community as a good cook, but Trixie and I could not forget our family reunion and the debacle with her hummingbird cake. "I thank it's worth the risk," Trixie declared. So, all three of us bought a chance on the red velvet cake and watched as the cake walk for a caramel cake had come to a stop. Old Miz Hooper had won it, but her son had to bring her a walking stick and help her up off the folding chair before she could claim it. We decided to stick around to see if the red velvet went up next. It did not, so we headed at a trot for the spook house.

We gave our tickets to Aunt Brenda, who was manning the spook house door. "Oooo! Ain't y'all skeered to go in thar?" she crooned. "Sompin's liable to git ye!" We had to wait until the spook house was empty of its occupants before we could have our turn. "That's a mighty skeery Frankenstein, Brownie," Aunt Brenda said. "And are you the tooth fairy, Patty?" Patty heaved a heavy sigh. "No. I'm a garden fairy." she said. Aunt Brenda put her hands on Trixie's shoulders and said, "Okay! In you go!" And she shoved her daughter into the doorway of the infirmary, which was decorated like a haunted house and had only Christmas lights lit up to light the way. A woman dressed like a witch was guiding us through.

We came to the hospital bed where the school children who got sick at school waited for their parent to come and take them home. There, we were told to stop. I remember laying there on that hospital bed once when I had a bad sore throat. The school nurse took my temperature and everything. But there was a body lying on it now, covered with a white sheet that looked like it was soaked with blood.

Suddenly, a man wearing a mask jumped out in front of us and revved a chain saw! Then, the body on the hospital bed sat up. We screamed and followed the witch to the next section where she offered us a bag to feel around in. There was slimy stuff like eyeballs, but which we knew from past experience to be grapes in Jello.

Still, we squealed with delight and then Trixie screamed in terror. A hand had come out from under a table covered with a cloth and grabbed her ankle. "Git him off! Git him off!" she cried, and the hand retreated back underneath the tablecloth. Through the rest of the spook house, Patty and I laughed at Trixie for being so scared. When we came out of the infirmary the gym lights made us squint. "Y'all kin go right on laughin'," Trixie said angrily. "But I think I wet myself a little!" She was frowning, so we decided to change the subject when we heard the caller announce that the red velvet cake was up for grabs in the cake walk circle. We were almost running when the principal caught our eye and we slowed down. Just in time! We gave the attendant our tickets and stood behind our chairs.

Nancy Jones' mother walked around the circle showing everyone the cake. It was a beautiful sight. Then the music started playing and the circle slowly rotated around. I noticed out of the corner of my eye that Trixie would almost get between each chair as she walked around. Then, the music suddenly stopped, and everyone sat down in their chairs. But it was obvious who the winner was, and everyone started to clap. I was clapping happily for the winner when Miz Jones came and placed the red velvet cake in my lap. "Congratulations, Brownie!" she said. My mouth dropped open. I had not realized that it was me who had won!

Trixie and Patty cheered the most because the three of us had agreed, whoever it was from our group that won the cake, that person would share with the other two. "Let's go put it in the truck and I'll ask yore parents if y'all kin spend the night with me and we will share it!" I said happily. Trixie and Patty happily agreed.

After we had placed the cake in the passenger floorboard of the truck, we hurried back to the gym where a crowd had gathered beneath the floodlights at the side of the building. "What's goin' on?" Trixie had pushed herself between two boys. "I think there's gonna' be pony rides!" Ernie Stokes said.

"Looky yonder!" Donald Stephens cried. "Thar's a shitland pony!" Donald was standing next to Ernie and pointed toward a small horse, with a long blonde mane. I was thrilled. "I'm gittin' in on this!" I exclaimed to my friends. My lifelong dream of riding a horse was about to come true. "How many tickets?" I asked. "Three," Donald said. "And I'm all outta money!" I looked through my pockets. I had two tickets and twenty-seven cents. A man that I did not know was holding the reins to the pony. I walked toward him.

"If I give you two tickets and a quarter, kin I ride that horse, please?" I asked him, holding out my hand where he could see that I really had the payment.

The man, who looked about the same age as Daddy, was wearing a western shirt and blue jeans. He had a cowboy hat set to a slant on his head. The man's eyes twinkled when he smiled.

"Whah sure, little lady!" he exclaimed. "You kin be Sultan's first rider!" With that statement he handed the reins to a teenage boy standing next to him, then the man hoisted me up onto the saddle. The next thing I knew, the man was walking the pony around in a circle while I held the reins and sat tall in the saddle. It was the greatest feeling in the world! I was so disappointed a few minutes later when the man lifted me off the horse and set me back on the ground, my daddy's boots making a big thud when they hit the hard clay.

The man was shouting, "Who's next?" when I walked over to Trixie and Patty, smiling. "Wow, Brownie! You weren't skeered?" Patty asked me. Trixie patted my back, "Nah, she wasn't skeered! She's Frankenstein!" and we all laughed.

That night after the three of us girls and Roger had ridden back in the pickup to our house, we went into the warm kitchen and Mama said if we washed our hands good, she would cut us a piece of cake.

We did and all of us sat down to eat a slice of red velvet cake. Miz Jenkins did not disappoint. The red layers practically evaporated on my tongue, leaving the sweet, creamy frosting to savor. I ate all of my cake and drained a glass of milk. Trixie asked for seconds, but Mama told her it was too late to be eating the one that we had, "Muss less, seconds!" she said. Daddy, who had been drinking a cup of coffee, lit a cigarette and said, "Bill told me his wife took pictures of every child that rode the pony tonight. He is

144

going to get them printed and give them to the principal to hand out at school." Mama gasped and pulled her hands up towards her heart, "Why, ain't that the sweetest thing!" she cried. As for me, I was thinking I would have worn a dress if I had known I was getting my picture made.

Patty, Trixie, and I went to the bedroom that I shared with Donna. Donna had decided to spend the night at Granny's, so we had one extra bed. "Okay," I said. "Whose gonna sleep on the floor?" Patty and Trixie decided to count taters. "One potato, two potato, three potato, four," they said as they bumped their closed fists together. At the end Patty lost, so we went to the hall closet to get some blankets for her to make a pallet on the floor. "Here," I said. "You can use my teddy bear for a pillow." After we were all set-tled in our beds, we decided to dump out our winnings from the carnival and look at them.

Patty had a string of carnival beads, all colors, a cello-phane wrapped candied apple, and a tube of frosted pink lipstick. Trixie had a lot of empty candy wrappers, a stick of chewing gum, an orange and silver pinwheel, a figurine of a dog, and a half-eaten bag of popcorn. In my pockets was the magnifying glass, a small wooden bowl that I was going to give to Granny for a present, and a small, pink zipper bag with a cowgirl on it. That was my favorite. I looked and Patty had pink frosted lipstick all over her lips and on the outside, too.

"Ha,ha,ha! You look like a clown!" Trixie laughed and Patty stuck out her tongue. "I sure wish that I had rode that pony, Brownie," Patty said. "I think you were the only girl that did." I would be lying if I said that did not make me feel a little bit proud. "Not me!" Trixie declared, eating stale popcorn from her bag. "It looked like you were ten feet up in the air!" she mumbled. We talked and laughed until Mama came and told us it was light's out.

That night is one of my favorite childhood memories. I lost the pink zipper bag with the cowgirl on it years ago. But I still have the photograph that was taken of me at ten years old sitting on top of that beautiful pony. Although I am dressed like Frankenstein and my hair is a mess, at least I did not have my mask on. That picture of me smiling that life-can't-get-any-better-than-this smile still brings joy to my heart after all these years.

November 1, 1968
Dear Diary,
I'm to sick to write today.
Brownie

The day after Halloween in nineteen sixty-eight was the day our whole family came down with the Hong Kong flu. By the following Monday, the whole school had been infected. Our family had stomach issues, high fever, and body aches. Stomach issues in a family of five with only one bathroom would have been enough. But the fever, headaches, and body aches meant that our parents were not well enough to care for their sick children.

On Saturday morning, Papa rapped on the back door until Daddy sluggishly got out of bed and opened it a crack to see what he wanted.

"Dr. Andrews has opened up thah clinic today 'cause of so much flu hittin' folks in thah commun'ty. You should take the famlee to him and git 'em sum med'cine," Papa said. "I'm gonna set this box of food yore mama made on the stoop and you kin git it when ah leave." I heard Daddy shut the backdoor and shuffle back to the bedroom. "If we all have the same thang," he said, "why caint I go and git medicine for all of us?" I heard him ask Mama.

I must have drifted off to sleep because the next thing I knew was Mama picking my head up off the pillow to get me to swallow some pills and drink a glass of water. My throat was dry, and the pills stuck on the way down, but the cold water was a relief and soon pushed them on through. Then Mama put a spoon to my lips full of a vile tasting liquid and told me to swallow. I did, but almost did not keep it down. I looked up and Daddy was dosing Donna with the same medications. Someone had hung a towel over the windows in our bedroom to keep the sunlight out. I heard Mama and Daddy talking in the hallway.

"Doc says he's never seen anything like it," Daddy said. "Says it's from China and is an epidemic across the state. Half of the school is sick. Doc says he thinks it was brought into the Halloween Carnival by someone who didn't know they had it." Mama gasped, then whispered, "How long before it runs its course?" There was a long pause. "I don't know, Jeanette," Daddy said. "Doc allows a week to ten days. I'm gonna lay back down." I heard footsteps softly padding down the hall before I fell back to sleep.

On November eleventh, Roger and I were well enough to go back to school. We were surprised to find only a handful of students in our classrooms. Keetoowah County's School Superintendent had closed school for the previous week due to fears of spreading the virus. I sat down at my desk and waved at Lorna Buckner and Tim Payne. "Where's our teacher?" I whispered to them and marveled at how loud my voice sounded in the empty classroom. They both shook their heads. We sat there waiting, whispering, speculating until Miz Carlisle came into the room and placed her purse inside her desk drawer. "Bus seven had a break down this morning but is now fixed. It's on its way," she announced. "Until it gets here, let's go over our spelling words." Miss Carlisle sat down at her desk. "Brownie. Spell *athlete.*"

By nine-thirty, eight more of our classmates had arrived and Miz Carlisle started arithmetic. We were learning something new called *mathematics*, which I found very confusing. But the day got better when our reading lesson came around. Miz Carlisle had been reading a book about a native girl stranded on a dessert island. The orphan girl's name was Karana. She had been surviving all on her own.

When it was almost time for school to let out and Miz Carlisle had told us our homework assignments, she rapped her ruler on her desk for quiet. I looked at the clock. It was eight minutes until three. Miz Carlisle cleared her throat. "How many of you understand this flu bug that has been going around?" There was murmuring and a soft shuffling of feet.

"Well," Miz Carlisle continued, "it started over in the country of China." She walked to the world map that hung on the wall beside the blackboard and pointed to a large country a long way from America. "In a city called Hong Kong," she continued. "It came all the way from here to here." She made a long sweep across the map with her index finger. "How do you think a virus can go from here to here?" she asked the class. Half of us shrugged. The other half said nothing.

"Human contact," Miz Carlisle said. "People spreading the virus by sneezing, coughing, shaking hands. That sounds pretty amazing, doesn't it? That a little bacteria can spread like that." We nodded. Not because we understood, but because we wanted to go home. "Well, at least now you know why I ask you to use the box of tissues on my desk when you have a cold, don't you?" More nodding. Then, the bell rang, and we headed out the door as fast as we could with Miz Carlisle shouting out, "Don't forget! Spelling test tomorrow!"

Nov. 22, 1968
Dear Diary,
It's so cold! I'm gonna bundle up in three layers when I go outside today.
Papa and Granny's gonna have a hog killin'.
Brownie

It had turned so cold that the ground spewed up. That is when wet ground freezes and pushes soil up to the surface, making ice crystals form on top. When it gets cold enough to do that the old folks start wanting to kill a hog.

Papa had consulted the almanac and found that the signs were in hips and thighs and that the moon was waning. So, it was a good time for preserving the meat. He had also kept an eye on the weather forecast for our area. It would be very cold at night and cold in the daytime for three days straight. That would keep the meat from ruining. So, Papa called his sons, and his sons told their families, and we all showed up at seven o'clock in the morning on the Saturday before Thanksgiving to help with dressing the hog and working up the meat.

I did not like hog killings. I always felt bad when I heard the rifle fire. I did not like the smell, or the sights of meat being prepared. But I did like carrying wood to the fire and punching it with a stick. Roger and I were too little to do much else. Donna, who had always been squeamish, had stayed at home to do our family's washing.

Papa and Daddy had loaded the hog into the pickup bed and shot him before Mama, Roger, and me got there. Uncle Gil had a washpot full of water coming to a soft boil over the hot coals of a fire. Granny poured in some more water stating that it didn't need to be too hot, or it would set the bristles. I watched as she put the back of her hand to the surface of the water in the washpot.

"Water's ready," she hollered to Papa, just as he rolled up with the truck. It took no time at all for Dad, Uncle Gil, and Papa to string up the big boar and slit his belly. A washpot had been placed beneath him to catch the intestines, which my people did not eat. As I watched my stomach lurched so I turned away and went to get more firewood.

Scalding and scraping the hog was a skill passed down from one generation to the other in these mountains. Even I knew how to do it, although I had learned through slitted eyes. I knew that at the end, when the grindings for sausage had been saved, the head cleaned for souse meat, and the hams and middling's had been salted down, the women would get ready to make cracklings and lard. The skin and some fat was diced into small chunks and fried until golden brown for the cracklings. These would be baked inside our cornbread. Lard was rendered down from the remaining belly fat and provided our substitute for shortening. As was our tradition, that evening for supper we would have fresh tenderloin, biscuit, and gravy to enjoy.

"How come we don't eat the chitlins?" I asked Granny. She was working at the big table made by placing a long and wide piece of plywood over several sawhorses. Chitterlings was a delicacy to some southern folks. They were made from clean pig's intestines that had been chopped up and fried in hot grease.

Granny did not take her eyes off the hog's head that she was cleaning. "Cause they's nasty and ye caint git em clean enough to suit me," she said, spitting snuff between her boots. "Why are they nasty?" I persisted. "We eat almost everything else in a pig." Granny laughed her hee-hee laugh. "Cause they's full of kahyarn!" she laughed.

Well, I knew what kahyarn was. It was the stuff dogs rolled around in and wore home smelling like the outhouse. Maybe my people had once said carrion and then reduced it down to kahyarn, I never knew. I only know that when she said that she had me convinced that I did not want to eat chitlins either.

November 24 1968
Dear Diary,
What a surprise! Tater was at school today and he's not cross eyed anymore!
But I heard that Carl is out and wantin' to get him back. I hope that don't happen.
Brownie

It was the kind of cold, rainy day that got deep into your bones and made your teeth chatter. I looked down at my knees peeking out from under my wool skirt and they were splotched with purple. The sweater that I had on was warm enough in Mama's kitchen but now that it had been soaked with rain, it felt heavy and cold on my small frame. But I was no different than any of my friends riding the bus that morning, so I endured it. When we arrived at school, we hung our dripping jackets and sweaters to dry on the clothesline that had been strung over the radiator. And oh, that radiator! The heat felt so good that it was hard to leave it when Miz Carlisle ordered us to have a seat at our desks.

I made good grades in spelling, reading, English, and even history and science. But mathematics did not come easily to me. Dennis Dixon sat next to me, his pencil flying down the page and never stopping to erase. I had thought about asking him to help me with math. But Dennis was a quiet, shy boy and I did not know how he would react. I looked back down on my paper where the equations looked like astronaut arithmetic. I took a guess and wrote it down.

At lunch, Patty, Trixie, and I sat down at our assigned table. "Did you see Tater!" Trixie asked me. "He's sittin' right over thar!" I turned to look toward the first-grade table where a crowd of kids had gathered to welcome Tater to school. Everyone knew what he had been through, and everyone knew about his brother wanting to steal him away from his adopted family and take him back to a life of poverty. What we did not know was why. Why would Carl want his little brother back in the first place?

I looked down at my plate of fried chicken, mashed potatoes, green beans, and chocolate cake. Our lunchroom ladies cooked just like they did at home, so our food was always delicious. But I left it for a minute and went over to see Tater myself. He was eating happily and talking to everyone in his cheerful manner. When he looked up, I said "hey" to him. Tater's face was sweet to behold. His lazy eye had been fixed, and he had lost two teeth in front. His hair was combed back with hair cream and his clothes were new and smart. "Hey, Brownie!" he said with a grin.

Tater told me that his new name was Gary Guthrie, but that his friends could still call him Tater. He said he loved his new Mama and Daddy, and he even had a dog that he had named George. It made my heart feel happy to hear that. I looked over my shoulder and saw Miz Carlisle looking at me, so I went back to my table to eat lunch. When I sat down, I noticed that my yeast roll was missing. I immediately looked at Trixie. "Well," she said, "it was gittin' cold!"

I began a rush to eat because I did not want lunchtime to end without at least finishing my chicken and cake. "Do y'all know how it is that Carl is not still in prison?" Patty asked. Trixie mumbled through a mouthful of my roll, "Daddy says he'uz patrolled." "Whatuz that mean?" Patty asked. Trixie shrugged. "Maybe Miz Carlisle can tell us," Patty offered and immediately held up her hand. I looked at her with wide-opened eyes. We did not need a teacher involved in our business. Miz Carlisle walked over.

"Yes," she said. Then Patty whispered to her how we could not figure out why Tater's brother was not locked up and we did not understand what it meant to be *patrolled*. "Oh. You mean paroled," she said.

Miz Carlisle explained to us that sometimes a person was paroled because their sentence changed, or some deal was struck. She said that what happened with Carl Jacobs was none of our business and that we should leave it at that. "Thanks a lot, Patty," I mouthed.

That night, I had decided to ask Daddy about it. We were sitting in the living room watching the evening news. I had to pick a current event and write a paragraph about it for school the next day. There was the usual stuff. Vietnam. Hippies protesting the war. Rhodesia raised its new flag and was not part of the British Empire anymore. I decided to write about that.

"Daddy?" I asked, "why was Carl Jacobs patrolled?" Daddy chuckled. "You mean paroled," he corrected. "That's none of your business," he said. But I pressed on with it. "But Tater's my friend," I said. "And I helped put Carl away, didn't I?" Daddy loved to work his crossword puzzles while he watched the news. He laid his book on his lap and pointed his pencil at me. "You know, you are right," he said. Then Daddy told me about how Carl's lawyer had cut a deal with the District Attorney for a reduced sentence and parole if he turned state's evidence. "That means that Carl has to testify in court against the two men he helped to set fire to the Landers' place and rob the bank. See? That's why Carl isn't in jail." I nodded. To me, it seemed like the wrong thing for the District Attorney to do. He did not know Carl like I did, or he would have thought better than to let him loose on Piney Hill again.

"But what about Tater!" I cried. "Can Carl really git to Tater and steal him away from Mr. Horace and Miz Avalon?" I felt myself getting upset. My heart was racing, and

I stood up to look at my father. "They named him Gary," I whispered. Daddy sat his crossword book down on the table beside him. Then, he reached across to me and pulled me onto his lap. "Brownie, Brownie," he said softly, "my tender little one." I leaned into him and smelled his smell. Cigarette smoke and tractor grease.

"Carl caint git to his brother. Horace has Tater's best interest at heart, and he's worked that out with the Sheriff," Daddy said. "There ain't no need fer you to worry." I laid my head deep into my daddy's shoulder. I felt better about it, but I had made my mind up to keep an eye out for Carl. I was going to tell on him if he came anywhere near Tater when I was around.

November 25, 1968
Dear Diary,
I got an A on my paragraph about the flag in Rhodesia. There's been no sign of Carl lately. But get this!
We found out today that we had lost three days of our Thanksgivin' break 'cause we were out sick a week and had to make them days up. No fair!
Brownie

The week of Thanksgiving was supposed to be a week off from school. But we had to make up some of the days we were out for the Hong Kong flu, so we had to go to school on Monday, Tuesday, and Wednesday of that week. Our teacher, Miz Carlisle, wasted no time getting in extra education for us, even though our minds were already on holiday time.

"Okay class," Miz Carlisle began on Tuesday, "now, who understands the math assignment from Friday? Did anyone study over the weekend?" We all looked at each other. What kid in their right mind studied on the weekend?

Dennis Dixon raised his hand. I noticed that he had on a new pair of black-rimmed glasses, which made him look even smarter than he was.

"Thank you, Dennis," Miz Carlisle said. "Anyone else?" Stillness. "Okay. If there's anyone who needs help with math, you can come to me or Dennis during recess, and we will be glad to assist you." Fat chance. The weather had warmed to Indian Summer and none of us non-future-mathematicians was going to miss out on going to the playground.

At ten o'clock, everyone in our class except Dennis lined up to go to recess. Miz Carlisle threw her sweater over her shoulders and ushered us down the hall and out the backdoor to the playground. Then, she turned around and went back inside to the classroom and sent Dennis out to play.

I stood at the foot of the school's back steps and breathed in the air. It was a glorious day. Bright blue sky and yellow sunshine set a lovely backdrop to the pine trees and hills beyond the swings. I felt a chill as a little breeze kicked up making dust devils around the slide. But when the breeze died down, the sun was warm again. I felt like I could taste the air, it was so clean and crisp.

I walked over to the swings where Trixie and Patty were already going up and down through the crystalline atmosphere. I squatted down beside the legs of the swings but out of the way of Trixie's flying feet. There were doodlebugs there. I took a small stick and went round and around the little hole in the sandy soil. "Doodlebug, doodlebug! Come out and git yer gravy!" I said. Soon, the small head of the ant lion peered out and I smiled.

Trixie got off the swing and offered it to me for a turn. I gladly took it. When I was at last sailing up and down, Patty turned to me and said, "Lonnie said he saw Carl, just up on that hill. Watchin' Tater." I strained my eyes to see.

Everything on the hill looked still to me. I looked around for Tater. He was playing on the slide with the other first-grade children. "Where'd Carl go?" I asked. Patty shrugged. "I don't know. I never seen him," she said. "Ituz Lonnie's account." The first-grade teacher was sitting on a bench close to the slide. I felt like little Gary must be pretty safe.

Trixie had caught a doodlebug and came over to show it to me. It wriggled to get away, but Trixie kept her palm closed around it. "Yont to go after school and see if Carl's up at the chicken house?" Trixie loved to play spies, but I shook my head no. I did not want anything to do with Carl Jacobs and as long as Tater was safe, he could do what he wanted until he was put back in jail again.

That afternoon, Miz Carlisle surprised us with an art project for Thanksgiving. We got to use the whole last hour of the day working on it. She set out pinecones, construction paper, scissors, and paste. "Now, class! You make a construction paper turkey like this" she held up an example that she had made, "And you break the spurs off the pinecone and paste them on the breast of the turkey like this." She pointed to her example.

All right! Now we could have some fun! We cut, plucked, and pasted until Miz Carlisle told us that time was up, and we needed to tidy the room for the day. Paste pots and construction paper pieces were everywhere, but in no time, we had it all picked up and put into its proper place. I looked at my turkey. Its eyes were crossed and some of the spurs from the pinecone were sliding off, otherwise, it looked pretty good. When I got home and showed it to Mama, she hugged me and proudly taped it to the refrigerator door.

November 28, 1968
Dear Diary,
My belly hurts! I ate so much at dinner today I don't think I kin eat a bite of supper.
Brownie

Thanksgiving for us was always a family affair. This year, we were the hosts and Mama went all out. Granny was roasting the turkey and Aunt Brenda was bringing ambrosia but other than that, Mama cooked all the rest and had the countertops full before anyone got to our house.

There was a big pan of cornbread dressing and a bowl of gravy. Mashed potatoes, fried okra, creamed corn, and green beans filled in the remaining spaces on the countertop. A card table was set up in the corner of the kitchen and covered with a brown and orange tablecloth. On top of this table sat Mama's Japanese fruitcake, meringue-topped banana pudding, pound cake and a bowl of peaches, and even a plate of divinity, each piece topped with a pecan half. The whole house smelled delicious.

Aunt Brenda arrived with Trixie, Eddie, Ronnie, and Granny. All of them laden down with something to tote. "Where'd ye wont the turkey?" Granny asked looking down at Eddie, who was struggling to keep hold of the roasting pan. "I'll take it," Mama said and swept the big pan over to the counter just in time to set it down before *she* lost control. "Whew! That's heavy!" she exclaimed to Granny. Granny smiled and went to the sink to wash her hands. Aunt Brenda went over to the card table and set her cut-glass bowl of ambrosia down on it. Donna was finishing up with setting the table. "Happy Thanksgiving, everybody!" she said. "Happy Thanksgiving!" the crowd replied.

"I brought some rolls," Aunt Brenda said to Mama. "Ronnie, hand Aunt Jeanette the rolls, hon." Ronnie looked up at my mother and smiled a gap-toothed grin. "Oh! You've lost a tooth!" Mama said, taking two plastic bags of rolls from him.

"Look at all the food!" Trixie exclaimed handing a sack of canned cranberry sauce to Mama. "This is better than a restaurant!" Mama took the sack from Trixie and said, "Now, you young'uns get on out of here. We've got work to do." And Mama gave Trixie and me a gentle push toward the living room.

"When will the men be back?" Aunt Brenda asked. Granny waved her hand in the air, "Oh, not 'til one o'clock or so," she said as she placed Parker House rolls in rows on a baking sheet. "Unless they don't find no quail, then they may be here afore twelve." My Daddy, Uncle Gil, and Papa always went quail hunting on Thanksgiving Day. This year, Daddy said Roger was old enough to go along. My brother was so excited to go that he could hardly sleep the night before.

I sat on the couch with Trixie to watch the parade. Her brothers were laying on their stomachs in the floor. It was fun to see all the floats. I couldn't imagine what a parade might look like in color! Suddenly, there were wavy lines across the tv. "Move the antennae!" Eddie shouted. Trixie got up and adjusted the rabbit ears on top of the tv and the wavy lines cleared up.

"Ug! My stomach's growlin'!" Trixie complained. "How much longer 'fore we kin eat?" Mama walked to the doorway, drying her hands on a towel. "I just saw them pull up," she said. "Y'all go wash." The four of us scrambled over one another to get to the bathroom sink first. Two sets of hands at a time grabbed soap and washed, splashing the floor, and making the towel wet, but we were finally washed up. And just in time too. The menfolk were coming in the screen door and Roger was talking ninety miles a minute.

"An I took 'em and put 'em in the bag and kept count of 'um!" Roger said proudly. "And Daddy says maybe next year I kin shoot!" Mama gave him a hug and watched as Daddy, Papa, and Uncle Gil laid their quail on the worktable on the porch outside the kitchen. "Not bad for a day's hunt!" Uncle Gil exclaimed and called for Ronnie and Eddie to come and see.

After everyone had washed and sat down at the table, and the blessing was asked, hand over hand bowls and pans were passed around. "No, no!" Aunt Brenda said to Ronnie and Eddie, "I'll help fill yore plates. No! Don't use yer hands to git taters!" Aunt Brenda went methodically around the table with two plates lined up on her left arm while her right-hand dipped food out onto them. Then she carefully laid them in front of her sons and smiled.

We ate and ate and listened to the men talk about the hunt. "Ole Roy was really workin' them birds today!" Uncle Gil boasted. His liver-colored pointer was known as a real good hunting dog and Uncle Gil was very proud of him. "And I thank Bonnie Blue is learning a thing or two from him 'bout quail hunting" he said. Papa grinned, "Bonnie Blue is a coon dog, Gil, and always will be best at that. But she sure did back Ole Roy today, didn't she? Who'd of imagined that?" Papa's bluetick hound, Bonnie Blue, was his pride and joy.

"Is it time fer dessert?" Trixie said. Everybody laughed. "Yes, it's time for dessert!" Mama agreed, and she and Aunt Brenda went around the table and cleared the plates. Papa pushed back from the table and burped loudly, which made the three boys laugh. "Who wonts coffee?" Aunt Brenda asked. All the men said yes, and the three boys raised their hands. "Well, okay," Aunt Brenda said. "But you young'uns 'ul have tah have lots a milk in yorn," she laughed.

Trixie and I picked up a paper plate from the counter and got our desserts. I couldn't wait to taste Mama's Japanese fruitcake and the sweet divinity candy. Trixie had a little of each thing loaded onto her plate. I decided to go back and get some of the banana pudding before it got gone. I sat back down at the table and began to eat with relish. The Japanese fruitcake was made up of tender spice cake layers topped with a cooked mixture of caramel, coconut, maraschino cherries and spices. On top, this mixture dripped down the sides of the cake. The smell and taste of this fruitcake still reminds me of my Thanksgivings growing up.

WINTER, 1968-1969
No. 3

December. Year end. This marked the beginning of winter in our little corner of the Georgia mountains. It was when the weather began to shift left and right. Autumn playing tug-of-war with Old Man Winter. Old Man Winter, who rimmed the windows with frost, made cold winds rattle the rafters, and caused power lines to break, leaving people in the dark for days.

December had set the winter stage with snow that came in the evening with its soft puffy flakes and vanished before the sunrise. This was a time of happy get-togethers, shopping, family traditions and Santa Claus. This was also the time that the strength of a little girl called Brownie would be tested beyond the bounds of any ten-year-old. I look back on my young self and wonder how I ever made it through.

December 2, 1968
Dear Diary,
It snowed last night! Me and Roger watched it snow til it got so dark we couldn't see no more.
But it melted and we still have to go to school.
Brownie

And just like that, it was December. The Christmas month. The favorite time of year for young and old alike. We had a light snow on the first day of December, and we all hoped there would be more, but we realized that snow on Christmas would probably not happen in our area.

It was so cold last night that the water in the troughs froze, and Daddy had to bust it with an ax so the pigs could drink. Sometime around Thanksgiving, Roger had started bringing his dog Buster in at night. Mama allowed this during the winter. She just could not bear for an animal to be outside if it did not have to.

The wind blew hard and sharp against my bare legs as I walked with Roger to the bus stop. Trixie was already there, and her nose was running. She rubbed it across her jacket sleeve when she saw us coming. "Boy! It's cold!" she said, shivering. Trixie had a woven shawl over her head and tucked into her jacket and tights underneath her dress. I wish I had thought to wear tights. "I don't know why they won't let girls wear britches to school!" I complained. "My legs are plumb numb!" Roger was not complaining.

Roger was looking at a rock that had a lot of mica in it. "Brownie?" he asked. "Iszat silver?" I explained to him for the hundredth time what mica was. He grinned up at me, a lock of his blonde hair peeking out of his red stocking cap. He looked like he should be in a Norman Rockwell painting. I pulled him close to me and held him tight.

At school, the toilets in the girl's bathroom had frozen up so we had to form a line and use the boy's toilet when they had finished their turn. It felt strange to be in there and to see urinals for the first time. Some of the girls vowed they could hold it until our bathroom was fixed. Trixie looked at me and shrugged and we both chose a stall and attended to our business. "I bet we don't git recess today," Trixie said from the stall next to me."

But we did get recess. It warmed up just enough that the principal deemed it would be fine if we went out. We thought he was crazy. The wind was still blowing an artic blast. Trixie and I huddled against the gymnasium wall where the sun was shining. Patty was at home sick with strep throat. "She called me the night before, her voice was just a whisper," I said to Trixie, explaining why Patty was not at school.

"Hey, Brownie and Twixie!" Tater grinned and took up a space next to the gym wall with us. "I saw y'all over here and thought I'd come say hey." "Hey, Tater," Trixie and I said in unison. The three of us stood there in the sunshine, shivering. "Why'd they make us come outside in this wever?" Tater made a good point, and I was just about to answer him when Tater hollered out "Let go!" "Got ye!" a voice said.

Trixie and I were caught off guard. There, holding onto Tater's coat was his brother Carl. "Now yore goin' home with me!" Carl said as he tried to drag his little brother away from us. Trixie grabbed hold of Tater's free hand and dug her heels into the dirt. "Leave him alone, you big bully!" she cried. Meanwhile, I had grabbed hold of the back of Carl's jacket and was pulling from the other side. "Yeah!" I cried. "I'll call the law!" Carl took a hand loose from Tater and backhanded me in the face. I let go of his jacket and fell backwards onto the ground. Trixie kept on pulling on Tater trying to get him loose.

"You got me sent to prison!" Carl yelled at me. "I otta kill you!" And when he looked at me, I believed at that moment he just might. Someone had told Mr. Wilkins, the basketball coach, that there was a fight going on, and he was running toward us. Carl let go of Tater and looked at me hard before he ran off toward the pine thicket behind the school.

"Y'all alright?" he asked. "Anybody hurt? Brownie?" He gave me a hand and pulled me up. "That's gonna leave a bruise." Mr. Wilkins ran his forefinger across my swollen cheek. I could taste blood. It was running from my nose into my mouth.

Mr. Wilkins took Tater, Trixie, and me to the principal's office where we waited for our parents to come for a consultation. "We're really gonna git it." Trixie said. Tater was swinging his legs and looking around the principal's office.

Mr. Dawson was an old man who reminded me a lot of my papa. His desk was neat with a pen set on one side of his name plate and a telephone on the other side. There was a picture frame too, but since it was facing toward his chair, I could not see who it was. A big bookcase was against the wall with various books and a green plant. I heaved a sigh and touched my sore face.

The door opened and in walked Mr. Dawson, Horace and Avalon, Mama, and Aunt Brenda. Suddenly, the room was very crowded. Mr. Dawson busied himself pulling out and unfolding chairs for everyone. Avalon pulled Tater into her lap and held him tightly. "It's a good thing that Tina and Trixie were with Gary when this happened," Mr. Dawson said. "Why, Tina even took a lick for little Gary!" I was surprised. Mr. Dawson seemed quite proud of us. Mama examined my face and gave me a pat on the back. "Well, ain't somebody gonna call the law?" I asked at last. Everyone chuckled softly. "They already have," Mr. Horace said. "Reckin they'll be here any minute to talk to y'all." Trixie and I looked at each other. "Not agin!" Trixie said.

When Deputy Sonny got there, he talked to us like he did before when we were at the jail. We explained about Carl grabbing Tater and hitting me in the face. "Well, he assaulted you," Deputy Sonny said to me, "and that is a violation of his parole." I looked at Trixie. "He also threatened you. That's another violation of parole." I did not understand, so I looked down at my feet. "What he means is," Mama said. "He will be sent back to prison and not be let out again." Trixie, who was always thinking ahead, said, "But you'll have to catch him first!"

Deputy Sonny looked like catching Carl would be a piece of cake. "Oh, don't you worry, honey. We will catch him before the sun goes down." And with that, he stood up and said his goodbyes. Mama stood up too. "Y'all go get your coats," Mama said. "Brenda and I are taking y'all home."

On the drive home we saw two Sheriff's cars parked on the side of the road by the Landers' pasture. "They've already started lookin' fer him," Aunt Brenda said happily from the front seat. Mama slowed our car down to look for herself. "Well, that's that," she said. But was it? I knew that Carl had places he could hide from the law. Places only a skinny, thirteen-year-old boy could fit into. I thought of what he had said to me and felt very afraid. I looked over at Trixie who had put a piece of bubble gum in her mouth and was blowing a big bubble. She did not look worried at all.

As we turned to go up Piney Hill toward home, I looked all through the woods to see if I could spot him. What would happen when it got dark? I began to bite my fingernails.

I spent a restless night dreaming that I was running through the pine thickets being shot at by a wild looking Carl Jacobs wielding a twenty-two rifle. When I woke up the next morning, my nose was closed up with dried blood and my jaw was swollen and painful. I stared in the bathroom mirror looking at my bright, blue shiner.

I was groggy when I met Trixie at the bus stop. We did not talk. Trixie, me and the three boys walked up the bus steps. Suddenly, there was an eruption of applause. Trixie and I walked down the aisle to cheers and pats on the back. "Le'me see that pump knot, champ!" Benny Walters cried. The backhanded slap on the face that I had received yesterday from Carl had become a badge of honor for me as far as my school mates were concerned.

"Brownie and Trixie had Ole Carl headin' fer the hills!" Scotty Wainwright shouted. "Look at Brownie's shiner!" someone else cried. I smiled and Trixie laughed out loud as we took our usual seat. Our brothers just grinned. They liked getting pats on the back because they were related to us. "That Brownie's a Champ!" shouted someone else. I touched the lump on my bruised face and sighed. I did not feel like a champ. My face hurt and I was afraid. Where was Carl?

December 6, 1968
Dear Diary,
I have weekend homework- WE ARE HAVING A CHRISMAS PAGINT!
I have five songs to learn and Mama has to find me a costume! I'm gonna be a ole timey caroler.
Brownie

It had turned cold again. The temperature registering on the big co-op thermometer on our back porch read twenty-eight degrees when we came home from school that afternoon. My teeth were chattering, so I ran straight to the heat vent when I got home. Roger sat down in the floor and pulled off his sneakers and socks. "My feet are cold!" he cried. "I stepped in a mud hole and got 'em wet!" He moved over to the heat vent and pushed his cold feet up next to my bare legs. I squealed, "Roh-ger!" Mama came into the living room with two cups of hot cocoa. "Move over Tina and let him have some heat," she said, handing us the steaming mugs. Mama then walked to the hall closet and came back with a blanket, which she used to make a tent over Roger's feet, my legs, and the heat vent. She bent down and took my face in her hand. "Does it hurt?" Mama asked me. Roger answered for me. "She's a champ!" he declared. "You shoulda heard 'em on the bus, Mama!" he said smiling. I smiled, too.

Just then, Donna came in with Aunt Janelle. "I swear! If Dewayne don't stay away from that hussy, I'm gonna smack him into next week!" Donna walked into the living room and sat her books down on the couch while Aunt Janelle went to the fridge to get a bottle of soda. "Hey, Donna. How was school?" Mama asked my sister while she ignored her own sister's comments.

"It was great!" Donna beamed. "Greg Jefferies asked me out tomorrow night!" Donna had broken up with Tom only last Sunday. It seemed that she just did not want to get too involved with one person for too long. Mama went over and rubbed her back. "That's nice, Donna," she said. Aunt Janelle had kicked off the high heels she had been wearing and sat down on the couch.

"What's for supper, Jeanette?" she said, "I got tied up in the courtroom and missed lunch." I was always fascinated by Aunt Janelle's world but her life in the Keetoowah County's Clerk of Court's office was my favorite. "What's going on in court?" I asked my aunt. "Oh, it was plea day. Eee-very body wanted to plea," she groaned. I watched Mama leave the room. Aunt Janelle turned on the tv and began watching a late soap opera. I walked over and sat down on the couch between her and Donna.

"So, you like this new feller?" Aunt Janelle asked. Donna was back to being her old self. Her blonde hair was long and shiny. "Yes! Oh! He's such a hunk!" Donna slumped back into the couch with a delighted sigh. "I mean, Cindy Watson was after him big time, and then..." I interrupted my sister with something more pressing for Aunt Janelle. "Why ain't they caught Carl yet?" I demanded a little bit louder than I meant to. Mama came out of the kitchen, wiping her hands on a towel.

Aunt Janelle sat up straight and took a sip of her soda. "Dewayne says they have looked everywhere for him. Says he believes Carl mustuv hitched a ride outta Keetoowah County. There is a BOLO out on him. Don't you worry. He will be caught." I knew that a BOLO or be-on-the-lookout went out across county to county and that was good. But I had my doubts that Carl had left.

"Has anybody checked the Indian gold mine?" I asked. Carl used to brag that he had been down the tunnel all the way to the water entrance of the mine. Aunt Janelle gave me a dismissive pat on the leg. "Now, that's the Sheriff's business. I'm sure they thought to check that out."

Mama had been drawn into the soap opera playing on the television and suddenly snapped awake. "We're having pot roast," she said. "I just heard Boyd come up on the back porch." She turned and went back to the kitchen. Aunt Janelle and Donna stood up. "Aunt Janelle and me are gonna help Mama," Donna said. "You and Roger should go wash your hands." I got off the couch and went over to the heat vent to wake Roger up. He had gotten warm and fallen asleep on the blanket.

At supper, Daddy asked the blessing and Mama passed the mashed potatoes around. "You been puttin' the n'er-do-wells in jail, Janelle?" He grinned as he said it. "That's not my job, Boyd," she responded. "I'm just a grunt." Daddy laughed.

"Well, Brownie's a champ!" Roger exclaimed. Everybody laughed. "I know she is, son," Daddy said. "I heard all about it from Ronnie and Eddie when I dropped Gil off at home. 'Bout how Trixie and Brownie really gave Ole Carl a what-for!" Daddy grinned at me, and I blushed with self-satisfaction.

"I'm gonna be in the school Christmas pageant," I said cheerfully. "Me too! Me too!" Roger cried, "I'm gonna be a lamp!" Mama laughed and went to the counter to get the assignments. "I think you mean lamppost," she said. "And Tina, you're going to be a Victorian Christmas caroler. Oh, my! It says here that both of you need a costume!" Mama took school assignments seriously, and the costume request seemed to spark panic in her.

"And I've gotta learn five Christmas songs. One of 'em I ain't never heard before," I said. The list had *Silent Night, Away, in a Manger, Jingle Bells,* and *The First Noel* but I had never heard of *Christmas is a Comin.* Miz Carlisle said she would work with our class on this song during what would have been our reading circle, my favorite subject of the day.

"Why were you so mad at Dewayne when you came in?" Mama asked Aunt Janelle. Mama's sister went over to the counter to bring bowls of food to the table. "Did you know the Landers Widow is back in town?" she asked. "Seems she made some friends in here who told her to come back and visit sometime." Aunt Janelle huffed. "She was at the jail. Apparently, Millie is her biggest pal up here, and they are going to the Sheriff's Christmas party over at the Moose Lodge next Saturday night." Millie was the receptionist at the jail. She was slim and outgoing. I could see how Miz Landers and her got along. Aunt Janelle turned around and said in a low meek voice, "How can I compete with someone like her, Jeanette? I mean look at me! I'm a husky girl!" For a minute, I thought Aunt Janelle might cry.

"Gracious, Janelle!" Mama declared. "You're getting yourself all worked up for nothing. Dewayne loves *you!* He may be nice to her, but he's loyal to *you!*" Aunt Janelle smiled and wiped her eyes. "And besides," Mama continued. "She already has a beau. It's that lawyer from Marietta."

"Well, I'm going all out for that Christmas party!" Aunt Janelle said, "Can you go with me to Rich's to get a new outfit? Maybe we could go tomorrow?" Mama sat a bowl of gravy on the table and looked at her wristwatch. "Sure. I will go with you!" Mama smiled at Aunt Janelle, and they sat down to eat.

December 13, 1968
Dear Diary,
I saw Miz Landers at Kringle's Department Store today. That's weird 'cause that's where I first saw her.
I was skeered to be in town. 'Fraid I might see Carl or he might see me.
We are getting' our tree today.
Brownie

There was a lot of activity in Piney Hill during the weeks leading up to Christmas. Families were sneaking around buying surprise presents for each other and getting their Toyland lay-aways picked up for their kids. Children were writing their letters to Santa and practicing for the school Christmas pageant. Mothers and grandmothers were baking up everything they had ingredients for, and fathers and grandfathers were fattening up turkeys and cutting down trees. Our Daddy even shot mistletoe out of an oak tree with his twenty-two and brought it inside the house to hang over the doors. "Whatzat for?" I asked him. "You'll see," he said with a wink.

I had learned all the songs for the pageant and found that I really liked singing *Christmas is a Comin.* Especially when Miz Carlisle explained what "the egg is in the nog" meant. Then she told us how eggnog was made, and I said, "No, thank you!" in my mind.

Our writing assignment today was writing a letter to Santa. Miz Carlisle said that there would be a mailbox to the North Pole set up outside the principal's office, and we could drop them off before we left school for the day. "Keep your margins neat and limit your requests," Miz Carlisle said sternly. "Also today, we will be drawing names for our class Christmas party. Keep the name you receive a secret, boys and girls, and the gift that you buy *or make* for that person cannot cost more than one dollar."

Miz Carlisle walked around the room with special paper that had snowflakes printed on it and a little woven basket full of folded paper slips. She gave each student a sheet of paper and let them draw a slip from the basket. I counted heads and discovered the drawing would not come out even. Just as I was about to raise my hand, Miz Carlisle said, "Since we have fifteen students and it needs to be an even number, I have added myself to the drawing." Miz Carlisle smiled, but none of her students did. What kind of gift did you get a teacher that cost a dollar? This was suddenly on everybody's mind.

I took my pencil and began my letter to Santa Claus. Mama says I write like I talk, but I pushed grammar aside and wrote anyway:

Dear Santa,

Hey. This is Brownie. I hope you and Miz Claws and all the elfs are good. I have been tryin to save money to buy a diary and a indianpony, but my brother stole my coffee can and so I caint git eithur one. I was tryin to save you the truble of packin' up a pony on yore slay.
But if you don't mind, that's the two things I wont most.
Love,
Brownie Rivers

Mama picked Roger and me up after school to take us into Pine Crest for our Christmas shopping. We got out at Kringle's Pic-n-Pay and showed Mama the names we had drawn for our gift exchange. "And Miss Roberts says we ain't to spend moren a dollar," Roger exclaimed. "Who'd you git?" I asked him. "Johnny Samples," Roger beamed. Johnny was his best friend. "Well, I got Miss Priss," I said sourly. "I don't know what in the world to git Patty. She's got everything!" Mama laughed. "We'll figure it out," she said opening the door.

The warm air that flooded our faces was filled with the aromas of Christmas! Hot buttered popcorn, chocolate covered peanuts, and peppermint sticks to name a few. Mama took us over to look at the displays. Dolls and tea sets, baseballs and gloves, and everything in between were set out in neat rows. I was busy looking at a toy makeup set when I heard Mama greeting someone. I looked up and she was talking to Miz Landers! I walked over and they stopped talking. Miz Landers had on a red coat with a black fur collar. She was wearing shiny black plastic boots that came up to her knees. Her eyes were outlined in black, and her lips were a dark crimson.

"Buenas tardes, mi amiga!" she said, leaning down to give me a kiss on the cheek. "How have you been?" The Widow asked me. The three of us stood there and talked while Mama watched Roger out of the corner of her eye. He was slowly getting farther and farther away from her. "I heard you were staying here this Christmas," Mama said. "Do you have plans?" Miz Landers lowered her eyes and told my mother that she had plans with a certain lawyer and would not be going back until after the New Year."

Mama smiled and clutched The Widow's hands. "That's wonderful, Lola," she beamed. "But you know you are welcome at our house, anytime." Well, this was strange. Since when was Mama on a first name basis with Miz Landers? "Excuse me a minute," Mama said and went over to the gun display to take a BB gun away from my brother.

"You sure look purty," I said. Miz Landers smiled. "Iz at lawyer the man I saw puttin' yore bags in that car?" I felt bold now because Mama was her friend. "Si," Miz Landers replied. "His name is Dave Holland." I remembered Dave

Holland's blue eyes and smile and I was happy for her. Then, The Widow patted my hand and said she had to go.

Miz Landers went over to give Mama a big hug and they parted, waving, and smiling at each other. Something about seeing The Widow so happy and wanting to be here in our area during Christmastime made me feel warm all over.

"Are you ready?" Mama asked me. Roger was carrying two rolls of caps for a cap pistol. "Got mine!" he said, grinning. I picked up a bottle of peach toilet water and Mama took them to the register and paid for them. "Brownie! That toilet water costs a dollar twenty-five!" I opened up my change purse and fished out two dimes and a nickel. I handed them to my mother. "I will pay the extra," I said. "She's hard to buy for." Mama could not argue with that.

I was tired and hungry by the time we got home. Mama had to pick up her layaway, go to the hardware store, and then the grocery store while Roger and I waited in the car. I flopped down on the couch without taking my coat off. "Brownie!" Mama scolded, "Go hang your coat up and wash your hands!" I got up slowly, feeling the warm drowsiness of fatigue pulling on me. When I got to the bathroom, I washed my face with cold water to wake myself up. Donna came in while I was there and washed her hands while I was drying my face. "Hey, Brownie!" she said lively. "I haven't seen much of you lately. How've you been?" I handed my sister the towel like she was an alien that had just landed in our bathroom.

"Okay," I said. Donna smiled and went out of the bathroom. I wondered what had gotten into her, so I followed her to the kitchen. Mama had made sloppy joes and tater tots. My favorite! I quickly sat down at the table. Roger was already sneaking some tater tots off the plate. "No eating until Daddy says the blessing," Mama scolded. Roger closed his fist tightly around the potatoes and nodded.

"Mama, my counselor told me today that she has got it all arranged!" Mama gasped and went over to hug Donna. I thought, "Okay? That's weird." I knew that Donna had been staying after school with some of her friends to meet with the high school guidance counselor, but I did not know what for. "When did they say you can start?" Mama asked. "August fourth!" Donna squealed and did the Watusi. Daddy came in and put his hands on his hips and grinned. "What's all this?" he asked.

"Donna has been accepted to the women's college in Atlanta!" Mama cried. "She starts next August!" Daddy hugged Donna and went to wash his hands. "Well, that *is* good news," he said.

"Aunt Janelle has a friend that works at Rich's Department Store. She has an apartment near the college, so I can live with her and walk to school," Donna said excitedly. "I may even be able to get a job at Rich's, too!" The three of them came to the table and sat down. Daddy looked at Roger and grinned at his mouth outlined with ketchup where he had been eating tater tots while they were talking.

After supper, I called Trixie to tell her Donna's good news and to ask her who she drew for her Christmas gift at school. "Yeah, I drew ole Dennis Dixon," Trixie grouched. "For Pete's sake! Whadaya git a science freak?" I had to agree with her. "Well, I got Patty!" I countered. "I spent a whole quarter of my own money, *extra*, just to git her somethin' she might like."

We discussed things that Dennis might like. I suggested a ruler and a magnifying glass. Trixie was about to respond when we heard a clicking sound in the earpiece of the phone. It was Miz Davis. She was our elderly neighbor who lived near the county line. Miz Davis was on our party line.

"Gir-uls," she cooed in her tiny little, sweet voice. "Now, I've got to call the preacher, so y'all need to git off the phone. Y'all have talked long enough." "Yes, ma'am," Trixie and I said in unison. "And Trixie?" Miz Davis continued, "I thank Dennis would like a toy, not something for school. A magnifying glass is just not a good Christmas present. Now, y'all hang up sos I kin call the preacher." We did as we were told because that is what you did when you shared a telephone line.

I walked into the living room where Mama was making neat work of wrapping the two presents that Roger and I were to take to school on Monday. Then she started to wrap two more. I had forgotten the teachers' presents. "Which one am I givin' Miz Carlisle?" I asked her. "This pretty pink handkerchief," Mama said, holding it up. I nodded. "And Roger is giving this one to his teacher," Mama said pointing to a yellow handkerchief. Mama always knew the right thing to do.

"Mama?" I asked, "Are you and Miz Landers friends?" Mama smiled, "Yes. She, Aunt Janelle, and Aunt Brenda are friends with her, too." Since when was my Aunt Janelle friends with the woman who made her so jealous!

"We want her to feel welcome in Piney Hill. I mean, look how she was treated when she was here and falsely accused by most everybody around. I've invited her to come to church Sunday." Mama smiled at Daddy who looked at her over his newspaper and smiled back.

Daddy folded his newspaper and lit a cigarette. "Y'all wont to go git a tree tomorrow?" he asked. All of us cried with joy and Mama started talking about getting the decorations down and what did she do with the star for the top?

As I lay in bed that night, listening at the wind rustle the trees, I pulled the covers up tight under my chin and thought about all that had happened that day. Donna was already asleep, but I was too excited. Decorating the tree was one of my favorite things to do at Christmas. It was

175

while I was pondering this that I saw a shadow pass across our bedroom window.

I became terribly afraid. Then, the shadow came to the window and just hovered there, behind the heavy curtains that Mama always hung in winter. I wanted to cry out, but I could not make a sound. I wanted to get up, but I could not move. Then, I heard the back doorknob rattle. Daddy heard it too and was at the door with his shotgun in no time. He jerked open the door to look outside.

The next thing I knew, lights were being turned on, Daddy and Mama were in the kitchen talking loudly, and Daddy had picked up the telephone receiver to begin dialing.

"Dewayne, Carl Jacobs has been over here," Daddy said to the deputy who was dating my Aunt Janelle. "You need to come as quick as you can." Mama was clutching her throat and Daddy rubbed the back of his neck. "What're you kids doin' up?" Daddy asked.

"Well, you made a racket!" Roger said, rubbing his eyes. "What's going on?" Donna asked, getting her long, blonde hair out of the collar of her housecoat. "Carl Jacobs was here messin' around," Daddy said. "I saw him run past the chicken house when I opened the back door." Daddy left us to get dressed. "I'm going to look for him," Daddy said over his shoulder.

Mama looked at the clock on the kitchen wall. "It's nearly eleven," she said and went over to fill the coffee pot. "Might as well watch the news until your daddy gets back. You kids go on back to bed now." Mama lit the fire underneath the coffee pot and walked us back down the hall to our bedrooms. When she passed back by the door to our room, I whispered, "Mama?" My mother stopped at the door. "I seen him," I said. "He was standing in front of our bedroom window. I seen his shadow." Mama walked over to my bed and smoothed the covers. "Don't worry, Tina," she said softly. "They will catch him. I bet he's more interested in getting food than in hurting you." Then, she kissed me and walked into the living room where I heard the click of the tv knob, and the soft sounds of the weatherman fill the room.

I had a nightmare that woke me up. My mind returned to Carl, and I got out of the bed to see if Daddy was back. He was not in bed, so I walked to the backdoor and opened it. In the distance, I saw something blinking. I reckoned it was Daddy using a flashlight to find his way in the dark. I decided to step out onto the doorstep and wait for him. The night was cold as iron, and the ground was already spewing up again. I wanted to wait on Daddy, but I only had on my flannel gown and panties, and I was beginning to shiver.

All of the sudden, everything went pitch black and I felt someone grab me and drag me off the steps. Whatever had been shoved over my head had also been shoved into my mouth so that I gagged and choked but could not scream.

I was carried for a while, then pushed down on the ground. My hands were yanked behind me and tied with what felt like baling twine. The sack over my head was scratchy like burlap. This made me think that these things had been stolen from our barn. Carl! It had to be Carl.

I was pulled up off the ground and given a push forward. If I strained my eyes, I could see just the tiniest bit through the weave of the burlap sack. I kept working my tongue until I finally got the part of the bag that had been shoved into my mouth free and I screamed.

"Go ahead. Scream all you wont" Carl said. "With this wind, ain't nobody gonna hear ye." My teeth began to chatter, and I stubbed my big toe on a rock. "Mmmyyy Dddadddy wwwwill fffind you!" I cried.

Carl started laughing. "Naw, I got him chasin' a rabbit in tha other d'rection. Yore mah hosteeg now. I'm gonna use you to git Tater back and me 'n him are gonna hop a train outta Keetoowah County!"

My hands behind my back were beginning to get numb and itch from the baling twine. "Why caint ye take this rope off my hands, Carl. It's itchin' me to death!"

But he did not answer. He just kept poking me in the back to guide me in the direction that he wanted me to go. I tried to think which direction we had started out and remember all the turns we had made but, after a while, it all ran together so I did not know where we were at any given time.

After walking what seemed to have been an hour or so, I told Carl that I had to pee. "Pee yore pants for all I keer!" he sneered. I thought for a minute. "Oh, yeah. Ifn they git after us with the dogs, they'll smell it and find you for shore!" I said. Carl was silent for a minute. Then he half drug me through some scrub brush and pushed me down. "Cover it up with dirt and leaves," he ordered.

I watched him through the weave of the bag, and he turned his back. With my hands tied behind me it was a job to get my panties down, but I managed. When I was finished, I hollered out to Carl, "Well! I need help gittin up, you moron! My hands are tied!" Carl came over and yanked me up and pushed me again to get me walking.

After we had walked about ten or fifteen more minutes, I unbaled my fist and, when Carl got spooked by an animal in the brush, he looked away from me. I dropped my panties in the leaves and covered them up with my foot. Carl, assured that no one was following us, pushed me forward and we began walking again. But I knew that there was a chance that anyone who might be looking for us might find my panties and if they did, my mama could identify them as being mine because of all the horses on them.

I was tired and the cold wind blew icy through my little gown. My big toe was throbbing, and I was wondering to myself if the nail might come off when I heard the sound of water. Suddenly, I was plunged into a shallow creek where I tripped and fell, getting my flannel gown soaked clean through.

"Git up!" Carl hissed, "You tryin' to slow me down?" I got up, without his help, and he pushed and hauled me to the other side. "Yore ggggonna be iiin bbbig ttttrouble ifn I dddie of nnnnewmonie!" I wailed. And at that moment, I began to be afraid that this could actually happen.

"Hush yer whining,'" Carl said. "I'm gonna build a farr when we git to tha hide-out." I still could not see much because of the bag, but I could tell by feeling with my feet that we had moved out of the water onto packed dirt.

"Where are we?" I asked. Carl answered me with a hard push on the shoulders, and I fell to the ground. After rolling around for a minute, I was finally able to sit up Indian style and try to figure out where we were. I was colder than a marble headstone and did not feel like any kind of fire was going to make me warm again.

I heard a scraping sound from a short distance away. It was the sound of wood rubbing against wood. Then I heard the thud of wood being dropped. Then I was pulled up and shoved to start walking again. I felt along with my feet on the packed dirt. "Duck," Carl warned, but too late. I felt the sting as my head butted into what felt like a two-by-four. Carl pushed my head down and told me to get down and crawl. I did as I was told hoping that by doing so Carl would get to making the fire quicker. I was wrong.

As soon as I had crawled by walking on my knees with my hands behind my back, I heard the sound of wood-on-wood again and now I was in pitch black. Fear, truc fear, began rising up in my throat. "Carl?" I called out tentatively. "Carl! Carl! Where are you?" My voice echoed. I got no reply, and I began to cry. I sat back on my legs and sobbed like I had never sobbed in my life. He had shut me in this place to die, and my people would never find me.

After I had cried myself out and gotten snot all over the inside of the burlap bag, I decided I had better see if I could get loose from the ropes around my hands. I messed with them for a while and found that they had loosened during our trip to wherever we had ended up. I pulled my hands free and brought them around to rub my sore wrists. Then I took off the sack that was over my head. I could see better, but it was still very dark wherever I was. And very cold.

As my eyes adjusted, I could make out lighter gray shapes in the distance and I could hear water running somewhere. I decided to move toward the gray area. I crawled slowly, feeling with my hands all the way. I was crawling through some sort of tunnel. After a while, the tunnel opened up into a larger area big enough for me to stand up in. I looked up and could see stars twinkling through a small hole somewhere up above. That starlight made me giggle and gave to me a sense of hope. I felt better about things. I sat down on the floor and watched those stars twinkling until I laid down and went to sleep.

When I woke up, I almost did not remember that I was kidnapped. It took me a moment to realize that I was not at home about to eat breakfast and go get our Christmas tree. I blinked my eyes and sat up. My gown had dried to a damp-dry and my hair was sticking out in a mass of tangles. My big toe throbbed. But there was light in the little space from the hole and I could see better.

The room looked like a cave and the water that I had heard was a tiny stream that ran down the back side of the room and disappeared somewhere in the dark recesses of the cave. The hole that was letting the sunlight in was high up and small. The place made me think of an old mine I had once seen in a western movie. "Oh, no!" I thought. "He's locked me in the Indian gold mine!"

Daddy had brought us here before. He always liked to take us on trips to different places and share their history with us. This mine had been used long ago by a family that won the land in the Cherokee Land Lottery. It was a productive gold mine for years until it had to be shut down because a tunnel collapsed and caused the shafts to flood.

I remember distinctly Daddy showing us the cover to one of the mine shafts. It was drilled into the side of a hill at the worksite. The mouth was framed in with wooden two-by-fours and a wooden door was made that slid down into the casing like a lock. When Daddy pulled it up, we could see a dark tunnel going into the side of the mountain. Of course, Daddy told us how dangerous it was and that nobody should ever go in it. We lived a long way from the mine, so I never thought anymore about it after that day. Now here I was, trapped inside where no one could find me!

While I had light to see by, I walked as far as I could to see how big the room was. It was about the size of my bedroom. Okay. And the water? It ran just at the back of the room. I bent down and drank four or five handfuls. It was icy cold. Okay. The hole in the top was too high and there were no rocks that I could hold on to or climb. Okay. But there were some sticks laying around and I could have a fire, if only I had a match. Okay.

I sat down on the floor. No food, no fire, no way out. I was defeated. I took a stick and drew one hash mark on the floor next to the wall. "Might as well start marking how many days I'm here before I die," I thought. But wait! Maybe Carl would come back! After all, hadn't he said I was going to be his hostage? And if Carl did come back, maybe I could jump him. Knock him out or something. I began to look around for a rock that was big enough for the job and that I could still hold onto to. With my little hands there were not too many rocks that fit the bill, but I did find one. Okay. Then I looked for a sturdy stick that I could sharpen.

I found one and began rubbing a point on it with a rock. It broke. So, I found another one and finally had two weapons that I thought might work. Now, all I could do was wait.

While there was still daylight, I played tic-tac-toe and hopscotch. But the darkness came quicker than I thought it would, and before long all I could think about was being cold and the gnawing pains of hunger in my belly. After a while, I gave up and fell into a fitful sleep. I dreamed that an Indian chief had found me in his gold mine and was telling the braves that were with him to cut off my head. "No! No!" I pleaded and my head was pounding from all the drums that they were beating on.

I woke up drenched in sweat with a terrible headache and sore throat. I was shivering again. Did I have a fever? I thought I did. And every time I swallowed it felt like I swallowed razor blades. I lay back down on the packed floor and shivered and cried. I never felt so bad in all my life.

When I next opened my eyes, I saw a small fire glowing nearby. I tried to sit up, but my head hurt so bad that I lay back down. I looked toward the fire and saw Carl squatted beside it. He was toasting loaf bread on a stick. He took the toast off the stick, walked over to me and shoved it toward my face.

"Bread," he said. "It's all I got." I grabbed it out of Carl's hand and began munching like some half-starved mouse. But two bites down and the bread stuck to my dry, sore throat. I began to choke. Carl shoved a cup of water toward me with his foot. I gulped it down.

"Ain't seen nobody lookin' fer us," he said. "Sos I been out lookin' fer Tater." I ate while holding my head in my hand. "Fount him, too," Carl smirked. "Livin' tha fancy life with that Guthrie bunch. Well, me 'n yous gonna go pay 'em a visit." At the mention of getting out of the mine, I perked up.

"Soon as ahm shore they ain't thought to look fer us here, we're gonna go to tha Guthries an make a trade. You fer Tater." I thought Carl was pretty dumb to think that the Guthries would make any kind of trade at all with a skinny thirteen-year-old that did not even have a weapon. But I did not tell him that.

I was about to ask him some questions about it when Carl up and left me. Just like that. He had crawled through the tunnel, and I heard the door to the opening slide shut. I sank back down in my sickened state. I had missed my chance to ambush him.

I was sick all day. I put all the sticks I could find on the puny fire and lay down close to it. The heat felt good. I slept in agitated spells, dreaming of having that bag over my head and walking through briars that scraped the flesh from my legs.

Sweat poured off me, and I developed a deep, congested cough. I kept marking the days off with my finger, but that was all I had energy for. The fire went out, and I had not eaten anything but one piece of bread since suppertime the night that Carl kidnapped me. I was so weak and feverish that it hurt to open my eyes and roll them around in their sockets. "This is the end for me," I thought. And then I lost consciousness.

I remember a racket and loud voices in the mine, all around me. I remember being hauled up and put on something that slid me through the tunnel and out of the shaft. I remember a man wrapping me in a warm blanket. Then, I heard Daddy's voice and felt him take my hand.

It was my first ambulance ride and I missed it. I fell asleep and stayed asleep during the whole ride. Our family doctor, Dr. Nichols, was waiting for me in the emergency room. He talked to me and listened to my chest. Dr. Nichols said that I had pneumonia and strep throat, but that I would be better in a few days. I was given two shots and Daddy was given a fistful of prescriptions. Then, Dr. Nichols sent me home with instructions that I was to be confined to my bed.

I felt some better when Daddy sat me down in the passenger seat of his pickup. He already had the heater going, so it was nice and warm. "You okay over there?" he asked. I nodded because talking made my throat hurt. "You were smart to leave these on the trail," Daddy said. He handed me my horse panties, all washed and folded. I shook them out and put them on my head. Daddy laughed.

"Did they ketch 'im?" I asked through a coughing fit. Daddy rubbed my back. "Yep. They caught him yesterday evening at Horace's. Now, you just lean back, and I will tell you all about it on the way home." Daddy eased the truck out of the parking lot and started down the road from Pine Crest to Piney Hill.

It turns out that Carl had gone over to Mr. Horace's house to spy and saw Tater and his dog George playing in the yard. Carl went over and grabbed Tater, who started yelling. Then, his dog George grabbed Carl by the leg and bit down. Tater seeing his dog being brave bit down on Carl's arm. Carl was in front of the house hollering with a boy biting his arm and a collie biting his leg. Well, that brought Miz Avalon out with a broom and she commenced beating Carl's head with the broom handle. Mr. Horace was coming from the tractor shed to see what was going on, and he pulled Carl loose and held him while Miz Avalon went inside to call the Sheriff.

"The Sheriff got Carl to tell him that you were in the vicinity of the gold mine, but he wouldn't say exactly where. I guess he did that for meanness," Daddy said. "So, I decided we should start the search from *our* house towards the mine. That's when we found your underwear on the trail. Like I said, that was pretty smart of you." Daddy grinned at me, and I smiled.

"What time is it?" I whispered to Daddy. "It is exactly three o'clock in the afternoon" he replied. I nodded. It was a cold day, but the sun was shining through the window, and it felt good on my face. I leaned next to the window and fell asleep.

"What in the world!" I heard Daddy exclaim as the truck lurched to a stop in our driveway. I sat up. There was a crowd of cars and trucks parked all over our yard. A man in a business suit was standing with a man holding a camera with a big flash bulb on top. "Don't open the door, Brownie," Daddy warned. "I'll come around and git you." I did as I was told while the man with the camera flashed his camera toward me.

Daddy took me in his arms and carried me toward our backdoor. There were cheers and pats on the back from our friends and neighbors. There was another flash from the camera and the man in the suit asked Daddy if he could come inside and interview me for the newspaper. Daddy nodded and carried me up the back steps, onto the porch, and into our kitchen. Mama ran to me and held me so tight that I thought my ribs were going to break. She was crying and kissing my face. Donna came and encircled us both with a hug, and Roger joined in by grabbing my legs and holding on.

"Now, now. Let's let her be for a minute," Daddy said as he carried me into the living room and sat me down on the couch. Aunt Janelle was there, and she started laughing. "Brownie! Do you know you have panties on your head?" Everyone laughed as I reached up and took them off. "Those panties saved your life!" Mama said as she sat down beside me and hugged me close.

Granny and Papa came over to give me kisses. Granny looked at my sore toe but did not say anything. Papa said

I looked just like the champ my brother said I was. About that time the newspaper reporter and camera man came into the living room. Roger said to them, "Yeah! She's a champ!"

I answered a few of the reporter's questions while eating a hot dog and drinking cola. Then, Miz Jenkins, who seemed to come out of nowhere, came over to me and handed me a big piece of her hummingbird cake. I took a big bite. Mmm! This time there was no baking soda overload. "It's good!" I mumbled to her. Miz Jenkins smiled then sniffed. "That toenail's gonna fall off," she said and walked back into the kitchen without another word.

"That old biddy!" Aunt Janelle said and Mama laughed. I finished the cake and for the first time in a few days, I felt full. I began to feel sleepy again. "Don't you think a good hot bath will make you feel better, Tina?" Mama asked me. "Your feet are filthy!" Granny looked at Mama for a minute and then Mama said, "But if you are ready to go to bed, you can take a bath later. It will be alright." I nodded and Mama went with me to the bedroom where she helped me into bed and gently covered me up. I felt so warm and safe that I immediately went to sleep.

When I woke up the next day clouds had drifted in, making the house look dark and shaded. I walked slowly on my wobbly legs. It felt like every bone in my body hurt. Daddy met me at the kitchen door and picked me up. "Say! Whur you goin?" he grinned. "I'm hungry," I said. Daddy put me down in my chair at the table. Roger was eating pancakes and Donna was helping Mama. Donna brought me three, small pancakes and kissed my cheek as she sat them down. "You're famous, you know!" she said with a smile.

"I was gone four days, right?" I looked around for confirmation. "No. You were gone six," Daddy said. He was looking straight at me. Checking to see if I was okay. "I mustuv slept through some of it. I don't remember," I whispered.

"It's a wonder we didn't lose you, Tina!" Mama said, offering me scrambled eggs. I shook my head no. "I mean, you were sick and starving! What if we'd never found you," her voice trailed off and her eyes welled up with tears. "Well, Jeanette, we didn't lose her!" Daddy said cheerily.

"Anyway, today's the day she gets a bath and her hair washed, right Mama?" Donna pointed her fork at me while she said this. I stuck out my tongue and she laughed.

"Wuz thar iny gold in tha mine?" Roger asked. I shook my head. "None that I could see. Anyway, if I'da found it I couldn't eat it and it wouldn't ah kept me warm, so what good would it do?"

Daddy took a swallow of coffee and said, "I've heard my daddy say many a time that a bale of cotton and a million dollars would be worth the same on judgment day." I finally felt like I understood the meaning of that. My head began to pound, and I asked to be excused. Mama walked me into the bathroom where I immediately threw up my breakfast.

Mama was right. That hot bath and clean pajamas did make me feel better. Mama had put fresh sheets on the bed. She said my feet were so dirty that they left muddy prints at the bottom of the sheets. I sat in bed surrounded by pillows and blankets while Mama tried to comb the tangles out of my hair.

"What if I cut it a little, Tina? That would make the tangles easier to comb out." Mama did not wait for me to answer and was back with the scissors. "You can always grow it out again" she said. I was too tired to care.

Mama cut and combed my hair and finally let me lay down and sleep. I dreamed of an Indian pony who rode me on his back to safety. We rode and rode and rode.

December 20, 1968
Dear Diary,
I ain't wrote to you since I was kidnapped by Carl Jacobs. I was gone 6 days and missed the school pagent. But Mama is taking me to school for our Christmas party today.
Tomorrow we are putting up a tree.
Brownie

Today was the last day of school and then we were off for Christmas break. It felt strange to put on my school clothes and walk into school after being gone. When Mama and I walked into my classroom everyone clapped and cheered.

A folding table had been set up and covered with a Christmas tablecloth. On top of the table were cupcakes, Christmas cookies shaped like trees and Santas, and a cut-glass bowl full of potato chips. A punch bowl full of red punch was posted at the end ready for refreshments at the end of the gift exchange.

Miz Carlisle praised me for being so brave during my "ordeal" and asked me if I felt like some punch. Mama gave me my cup, and I sat down at our party table between Trixie and Patty.

Someone had put up a little tree in the corner and dozens of small gifts wrapped in Christmas paper lay beneath it. Trixie, Patty, and I sat chatting about the gifts that we had brought.

"Whadid you git Dennis?" I whispered to Trixie. She walked over to the tree and came back with a small, square package. On it was a tag from her to him and a note that read:

Now you can go around the world!

Patty and I looked at Trixie for an explanation.

"It's a yo-yo," Trixie said matter-of-factly. "You know. The yo-yo trick *around the world*?" Trixie began to show us by waving her arm around and around.

I looked at Trixie. Her blonde hair was longer, and it showed off her blue eyes. She had on a red corduroy jumper and white blouse. She looked very nice. "But what if that makes him think you like him?" Patty asked her. "Git outta here!" Trixie pshawed. "It will make him think about space!" she said. Patty shrugged her shoulders as if that did not make a bit of sense to her. Trixie went back to the tree and laid her present down.

"Who'd you git anyway?" Trixie asked us when she came back. Patty looked at both of us and mouthed, "I got the teacher!" Trixie and I gasped. "Whad you git her?" Trixie asked. Patty sat up straight and smiled, "Mama took me all the way to Marietta to a store that sells *novelties*" she said. "Most of their things cost a dollar, but *I* spent two!" In my mind, Patty was coming really close to being boastful. "I got her a box of *Moonlight Gardenia* Eu de Toilet spray" Patty said. "You can smell it through the box."

Miz Carlisle rapped a ruler on the top of her desk to get everyone's attention. Mama and two other mothers stood behind the refreshment table to help us with punch. We stopped talking and looked at our teacher.

Miz Carlisle called on Johnny Dobson to pass out the gifts, and we were all instructed to wait until everyone had a gift before opening them. I got my gift and admired the sweet snowman scenes on it. Then, Miz Carlisle shouted, "Go!" and there was a frenzy of fingers and flurry of papers as we opened our presents.

Patty said she *adored* the toilet water that I gave to her. Trixie got modeling clay from Cindy Brooks. She was saying how she could not wait to get home and make something with it when she was tapped on the shoulder. Trixie turned around to see Dennis Dixon grinning at her.

"Thanks for the yo-yo, Trixie!" he said. "And I like your note about doing the *around the world*. That's cool! Not many girls know about things like that." Then he turned and walked away. "See! He likes you!" Patty said. Trixie gave a shrug. "So, what if he does?" And Trixie looked at Patty in a way that caused her to drop the subject.

I began to feel really tired, so I opened my gift from Lynn Watson so that I could thank her and go home. I was thrilled! It was a little silver bracelet with a horse charm. I walked over to Lynn and gave her a hug.

Mama came over with my coat. "We'd better get you home, Tina. Before you tire yourself out." She helped me into my coat, and I waved goodbye to my classmates. We left just in time, too. My legs were beginning to feel like jelly.

When we pulled into our driveway, there sat Ole Busy Body's car with Mr. Earl sitting behind the steering wheel. Mama and I got out of the car and quietly walked up to the back porch where Mama eased the screen door open. We walked up to the back door.

"Yey-ah, caught him in tha chicken house tryin' to steal one of the chickens! Guess he-uz gonna eat it!" Miz Jenkins gave a sniff. Aunt Janelle was sitting at the kitchen table drinking coffee. "Well, that's not what the Sheriff told De-wayne!" she retorted. Miz Jenkins sniffed again. "All I know is that little gal o' Jeanette's is gonna have to testy-fi agin him at his patrol hearin'. I mean, that boy's a meanness to society!"

Mama walked in and laid her purse on the kitchen counter. "What's all this?" she asked as she rolled her eyes at her sister. I went into the living room and took off my coat. I laid down on the couch, too tired to walk to my bed.

Miz Jenkins looked at Mama. "I heered that oldest girl of yorn is offta college in sprang," she said. "Well, yes!" Mama said cheerfully. "We are very proud of her!" Miz

Jenkins looked at Mama, her thick glasses reflecting the kitchen light. "Well, you'd better be careful, Jeanette. Some girls go offta college and go boy crazy!"

My head hurt and I just wanted Miz Jenkins to leave. "Mama!" I called out, "Mama!" My mother and Aunt Janelle both came running. "I'ma leavin' Jeanette," I heard Miz Jenkins holler as she stomped out of the kitchen and slammed the back door behind her.

Mama sat beside me with her hand on my forehead. "Your fever's back," she said softly. "Mama, why can't I git better?" I asked. Mama looked at me with tears in her eyes. "I don't know, Tina, but I'm calling Dr. Nichols right now."

Mama got up and Aunt Janelle took her place. "Hey, kiddo. You feelin' puny?" I nodded. Mama came back from the kitchen and touched my forehead again.

"Dr. Nichols wants to run a test," she told me. "He thinks you have an uncommon virus." Aunt Janelle looked up and said, "What kind of virus?" Mama shrugged, "He called it mono-something and said it took a long time to get over it. She will have to take more medicine if she has it," Mama said. "I'm supposed to bring her in right now, so he can check her." Mama and Aunt Janelle looked worried.

We got to the doctor's office at closing time. Dr. Nichols took us back, and his nurse drew some blood while he swabbed my throat. That was it. He said he would call Mama when the results were back.

After supper, Daddy told me that the District Attorney would indeed need my testimony again, once at the parole hearing, and again at trial. But I could rest assured that Carl would go to prison and not be able to bother his brother or me again. That gave me the courage I needed to testify against him. Daddy said they would send a subpoena to him with the date and time I was to appear. But that would not be until the March term.

Right before bedtime, Trixie called me. Mama let me lay on their bed so that I could use the phone on their nightstand. Trixie told me all about the Christmas pageant that I missed. The gymnasium was packed for it.

Donnie Bryson got nervous and threw up on the stage next to the manager scene. Miz Garland, the fifth-grade teacher, had to step him around the mess and off stage. Meanwhile, all of the villagers who were supposed to pretend to listen to the carolers were watching Donnie instead and started bumping into the singers and knocking them down. "We all got tickled and started laughin' out of control! You shoulda seen it, Brownie!" Trixie was snorting with laughter. "My daddy said he ain't never seen anything like it!"

I was glad we were talking normal stuff instead of the kidnapping and my sickness. "And" Trixie continued, "you won't believe who called me!" I said "Who?" "Dennis!" Trixie said and I gasped. "Really? What'd he wont?" I asked her. Trixie gave a disappointed sigh and said, "Patty's phone number!"

Dec. 21, 1968
Dear Diary,
It's Saturday and Daddy is gettin' our tree. I'm not goin' cause I'm still sick.
Dr. Nichols said I have mono-something. I'm taking medicine.
Sure hope I feel better by Christmas.
Brownie

After breakfast, Daddy said he had to go feed but would be back soon. He looked at me and winked. I was still very weak, and my throat was sore every morning when I woke up. I lay cuddled up on the couch watching cartoons.

Mama was bringing down boxes of Christmas ornaments from the attic when Aunt Janelle came bursting through the backdoor. Her arms were draped with newspapers. "Extra! Extra! Read all about it!" she shouted gleefully and handed Mama, Donna, and me a paper.

I sat up. The headlines read: *She's a Champ!* And there I was in black and white. Daddy carrying me in his arms. Me. Wearing a flannel nightgown, barefoot, and with a pair of panties on my head! On the front page of the newspaper! Aunt Janelle, Mama and Donna were laughing hysterically. I smiled.

"Don't you think that's cute?" Donna asked me. "It's a real good story," Aunt Janelle agreed. "Why, you're a hero, Brownie!" I started reading the story and smiled. It was about what I had been through even though it was nothing like what I had been through. I laid the paper neatly on the floor and laid back down.

When he got back with the tree, Daddy had to stop at the backdoor steps and clean off all the leaves and pine needles that had collected while Roger was dragging it from the woods. Then Daddy sawed off the bad limbs and made it level on the bottom so that it would fit into the stand properly. Buster kept jumping up and down on the tree and generally getting in the way. "Roger! Take your dog and put him in the pen!" Daddy demanded. Roger did as he was told, telling Buster on the way that he would be back to get him out.

After supper, Daddy put the strings of lights on the tree. Then, he sat down in his chair and said, "Well, I've done my part. Y'all can do the rest." Mama gave each of us kids a box of ornaments and told us to make sure we didn't bunch them all up around the bottom. I noticed that the box she gave to Roger had all plastic or handmade ornaments in it. Roger worked around the bottom of the tree with his tongue stuck out of the side of his mouth in concentration.

The next thing was the tinsel. Our family called them icicles and we placed, draped, and sometimes threw them at the tree. We laughed and laughed.

Mama stood on a kitchen chair to put the star on top and then she told us to turn out all of the lights. When the living room was dark, Mama plugged in the Christmas tree lights. We all exclaimed how beautiful it was and that it was the prettiest tree we had ever had. As the lights warmed up the sap in the tree, our whole living room was filled with the scent of cedar. Roger began to yawn.

"Okay! Who wants hot chocolate!" Mama exclaimed and we all raised our hands excitedly. My mother could make the best hot cocoa in the world. She melted chocolate bars and sugar. Then added milk and vanilla. I have never tasted it's equal.

"Daddy, look!" cried Roger and he went over to our father with his hand open and dripping hot chocolate all over the living room floor. "What a mess!" Mama cried and went to the kitchen to get a wet cloth to clean it up.

Daddy looked in Roger's hand and saw a little white tooth. "Well, looky yonder! You've lost a tooth!" Daddy said, "Now, if you don't stick yore tongue in the hole, you'll grow a gold one in its place!" Roger drooled hot chocolate all down his shirt and onto the floor in an attempt to resist sticking his tongue into the hole left by the tooth. "Don't you do it!" Daddy said laughing.

Mama wiped Roger's hands and face and then stooped to clean up the floor. "Will I really grow a gold tooth?" Roger asked her. "Well, I don't know," Mama said. "I've never known anyone who could resist sticking their tongue in the hole." Roger swallowed. "Will I git a dollar if I put this under my piller?" he continued.

"Well, that's mighty steep for the tooth fairy," Daddy said. "More like a dime, I think." Roger smiled. "That's okay. I'll have all the dollars I need when I grow my gold tooth." Daddy pulled him onto his lap and gave him a hug. Soon, we were sent to bed. Roger went without a struggle because he wanted the tooth fairy to come as quickly as possible.

December 24, 1968
Dear Diary,
Christmas Eve is finally here! I put my old cowgirl boots by my bed sos I'll be ready when morning comes.
I wish I had asked for boots to. These hurt my feet
Brownie
ps- Roger didn't grow a gold tooth! Ha,ha

Christmas Eve was always spent at Granny and Papa's house. We had what Granny called party snacks and punch. Then we opened our gifts from our grandparents. Granny and Papa made a lot of the gifts that they gave. When I opened mine, it was a rag doll that Granny had made to look like me. I loved that doll and still have it today.

As we drove back home from the party, I asked Daddy what time it was. "Oh, it's late," he said. "I've got eleven-thirty!" I suddenly remembered the old saying that if you went to the barn at midnight on Christmas Eve, you could hear the animals talk.

"Daddy, can me and Roger go to the barn and see if Ole Bessy talks?" Daddy knew exactly what I was referring to. "I am sure our cow will have ah lively talk with our sow, but y'all've gotta git in bed so Santy Claus kin come!" I agreed. Even the magic of talking animals could not compete with Santa.

On Christmas morning, Roger and I woke up before dawn and sneaked into the living room. The tree was lit, and Santa had been. We immediately ran squealing into our parents' bedroom. "Git up, git up!" Roger repeated. He was shaking Daddy's shoulder. Mama was already up, putting on her housecoat. "Oh! The floor's like ice!" she said. "Where is Donna?" I flew down the hall into our room and found my sister putting on a pair of socks. "I'm comin'," she said.

Roger, who had been obsessed with space ever since the Apollo mission went up that week, found a plastic likeness of the spacecraft under the tree and was flying it all around the room. I ran to all the windows in the house, expecting to see my Indian pony just outside. But it was not there, and my heart sank.

"Christmas Gift!" Daddy cried to me. "Aww, you got me agin!" I said. It was a tradition with my people to see who could be the first to say Christmas Gift to someone on Christmas Day. If you were the first, the person who was too slow owed you a present. I already owed Daddy nine.

"What'd you get, Brownie?" Donna asked. She was trying on a pair of knee-high boots in that shiny material like Miz Landers was wearing, only hers were white. Since I could remember, I had had a section under the tree where my Christmas would be. It was always Donna on the left, me on the right, and Roger in the middle. Santa was very organized. I sat down cross-legged in front of my spot and began looking under the tree.

I had a science kit with experiments, a gold pullover sweater and a red and gold plaid skirt to match, and a new pair of red cowgirl boots. Some games, fashion dolls and clothes were under there, too. Then I spied a *wrapped* present. Santa Claus never wrapped our gifts, so I was curious. I reached way back and pulled the small gift out. It was wrapped in red paper with a tag that said *To Brownie from Donna.* I unwrapped the paper and opened the lid on the box. There inside was a white diary with a golden clasp, lock, and key! I ran over to my sister and hugged her tightly.

"Aunt Janelle and me went to Rich's," Donna said. "I hope you like it." I was speechless and, for the first time, remembered all of the heartbreaking things that my sister had gone through over the course of the year. This gesture of love made me hug her again. "I love it," I said and meant it.

January 1, 1969
Dear Diary,
Happy New Year!
I forgot one time and left my key on the dresser and Roger got it and almost broke it off in the lock. ROGER!
Now I wear it around my neck on a piece of kite string.
Brownie

At dinner, that is what we always called lunch, we ate the traditional turnip greens and turnips, black-eyed peas, and cornbread. Mama also made two sweet potato pies. Granny, Mama, Donna, and me watched the parades with their floats and marching bands and the men and Roger went quail hunting again. After the men came home and we had all eaten our dinner, we sat in the living room and made our New Year's resolutions.

"I thank I'm gonna vow to stop eatin' so much before my belly starts lookin' like a watermelon," Papa said. All of us laughed. "My New Year's resolution is to lose five pounds!" Mama said. "How about you, Donna?"

Donna said her resolution was to finish in the top of her class at graduation. Roger's resolution was to grow tall like Daddy. I said mine was to save enough money to buy an Indian pony. Daddy said he would pass on making a resolution.

"How 'bout you, Granny?" I asked. Granny was rocking in the rocking chair. She stopped her crocheting and said, "The scriptures say it's better not to make a vow, than to make a vow and not pay." "So, you don't think you can keep yore resolution, Mama?" Daddy was stretched back in his recliner. Granny chuckled, "My memry is so bad, I might fergit I made it, then I'd be in a mess!" We all laughed.

"Is Aunt Janelle coming to play cards?" Donna asked Mama. We always played Rook on New Year's Day after supper. "I haven't heard from her," Mama replied, "but I think she was planning on coming."

I pulled out the new game I got for Christmas and started setting it up. "Donna, will you play with me?" I asked. My sister, in a rare agreeable moment, sat down in the floor across from me. We put the game on the coffee table and began to play. But halfway through the game I had to lay my head down on the coffee table to rest.

It was almost suppertime and Aunt Janelle had not arrived. Mama said we were going to finish the leftovers from dinner and then have cake and coffee when we played cards. She had also made a new snack mix recipe that used three kinds of cereal and peanuts. The snack mix was in the oven, and it smelled so good!

"Is Trixie comin'?" I asked my mother. Mama said that Uncle Gil and Aunt Brenda's family were all coming. She said that she had bought a new deck of cards and that we could practice playing with the oldest deck. I smiled. Mama jumped up from her chair at the sound of a car door slamming. "Oh! They just pulled up. Come help me, Donna!" Mama shouted.

Trixie, Eddie, Ronnie, and my aunt and uncle all came in the house laughing. Coats were thrown on beds and hands were washed.

"Come fix your plates!" Mama called out. She grabbed the ice trays out of the freezer and began filling glasses. The kitchen was full of people and happy noises when Aunt Janelle came in the back door. But she was not alone.

"Hey, everybody!" she cried out, "I brought some free-loaders with me!" Holding her hand was Dewayne and behind her, also holding hands, were Miz Landers and the lawyer, Dave Holland. Mama told them to put their coats on the bed in the back room. She got Aunt Janelle to help her get sweet tea in the glasses and get plates filled.

Papa said the blessing and folks were picking up their forks to begin eating when Aunt Janelle jumped up and said, "I have a big announcement!" With that, she pulled Miz Landers up with one hand and Dewayne up with her other. Miz Landers used her free hand to pull Dave up from his seat.

"We're engaged!" she cried. Everyone sat dumb-founded. "I mean, me and Dewayne are engaged, and Lola and Dave are engaged! It happened last night!" All four of them were beaming and Aunt Janelle held out her engagement ring for all to admire.

Needless to say, we set our plates aside and ran over to congratulate the couples and to see Aunt Janelle's ring. Lola did not have a ring and Dave was quick to explain why. "We are going to exchange rings at the wedding," Dave said. "Lola wanted to forego an engagement ring."

We also found out that Dave and Lola were going to live in Pine Crest. They were getting married at the Justice of the Peace's office, and Aunt Janelle and Dewayne were going to be their witnesses. But Aunt Janelle's wedding was a whole other matter.

"When are you gettin' married?" Donna asked our aunt. "We are shooting for April," Aunt Janelle replied. "And I wont you and Brownie to be my bridesmaids!" I felt all grown up to be asked to do something so important. Then, Aunt Janelle turned to Mama. "Oh, Jeanette!" she exclaimed. "You've just got to help me! Mother says she's comin' down from Charlotte to arrange everything! And we both know that that just means she's gonna take over!" Mama frowned.

I had not seen Grandmother Davidson in two years, but I knew that my mother and her sister did not like her controlling ways. "Now, now," Mama said. "We will handle this like adults. Mother will understand that you have your own ideas about your wedding." But even as she said it, I knew that Mama was doubting herself.

There were so many people in the house that Trixie and I went to my bedroom to get out of the way. This also gave me a chance to lie on my bed. "Patty said Dennis called her, and she told her mama to tell him she weren't home," Trixie laughed. I showed Trixie my new diary and she looked through it. "Hey," Trixie said. "You ain't wrote in it since Christmas day! How come?"

I shrugged my shoulders. I did not want to tell Trixie that I was scared I would start writing about the kidnapping. That someone might read it and know I really was not brave at all. That I was not a champ. Also, there was something that happened during my ordeal that I vowed never to reveal. So, I closed and locked the diary and put it away without answering my cousin.

Trixie did not seem to notice. "I got a portable record player for Christmas!" she said. "I have been wanting one. I wrote Santy Claus to brang me some of that cute English band's records, too. And would you believe it? I got a whole album by *The Bugs*!" That made me laugh. "Gee whiz!" she continued, "Who gets those two mixed up! I ain't never even heered of The Bugs!" Trixie was beginning to see how funny this was and began laughing, too. But I ruined it by having a coughing fit.

Trixie was pounding on my back. "Say! When you gonna git over that virus anyway?" she asked. I shook my head and shrugged my shoulders, which was all I could manage. I had been wondering the very same thing.

January 6, 1969
Dear Diary,
It's back to school for yours truly.
I'm feeling lots better since I started takin that pinasilin.
Brownie

That new musical about the flying car was all that Patty wanted to talk about. She had spent the night with her cousin in Roswell, and they had gone to the movie matinee to see it. She waltzed around the swing set during recess singing the theme song at the top of her lungs until it got on mine and Trixie's nerves.

"Why don't you hush!" Trixie griped. "That song is making me madder than a hornet!" Patty put her hands on her hips and shot back, "Well, yore just mad cause you ain't seen it!" Trixie and I both knew this was true, but while I decided to change the subject, Trixie decided to hit back, guns a blazin'.

I began, "I think Mama's gonna..." but I did not get to finish the sentence. "Oh, yeah!" Trixie said, red-faced. Well, yore just a spoiled only child that don't know the meanin' of doin' without!" Oh, my, I thought.

Patty walked over to Trixie and pointed her finger at her and snarled, "Well, yore nothin' but a porky pig who caint even git a boyfriend!" That remark wounded Trixie who got off the swing and went stomping off. Patty cupped her hands around her lips and shouted, "Dennis and me are goin' steady! Ha, ha."

I watched as Trixie walked past the merry-go-round, straight into the pine thicket where we built playhouses. I looked at Patty. "Whyd y'all haveta git mad over some ole movie?" I asked. Patty went "Hmmph" and stomped off in the opposite direction.

After the encounter with Patty during recess, Trixie set in to pestering Aunt Brenda to take her to see the movie. She made offers to do extra house and yard work. She offered to wax the living room floor and wash and iron all of the curtains. Trixie's desire to get to do something that Patty had done was becoming an obsession.

Not too long ago, she employed these same tactics in an effort to go to Rich's Department Store during Christmas and ride *The Pink Pig*. Trixie had never set foot in Rich's, and the way Patty described the store and the thrill of riding *Priscilla the Pig* just set her on fire. But it did not appear that Aunt Brenda was going to budge.

One day, Trixie and I were going with Aunt Brenda to see Baby Becky, Trixie's new aunt who was only five months old. I could see the wheels turning in her head.

"Mah-muh," she said sweetly, "Brownie has mentioned that she would like to go see that new movie too." Trixie winked at me. I gave Trixie a "don't be dragging me into this" look, but she plowed on ahead. "Why don't you take us into Pine Crest sometime and we can git Mee-Maw to pick us up after the movie is over. We kin spend the night with her and Pawpaw." Aunt Brenda turned on her blinker to make the turn into her parents' driveway. "Now, Trixie," she said, "We've talked about this. We ain't made of money, you know!" And with that, the subject was closed.

I got back home that night just before supper. Aunt Janelle was sitting at the kitchen table with copies of magazines spread out. She was rapping a pencil on top of a spiral notebook, waiting for Mama to get off of the telephone. Ever since she had announced her engagement, Aunt Janelle had been coming over to get Mama to help her plan the wedding.

"Well, I know, Edna, but life is too short to play it safe all of the time," Mama said. "I mean, just think of what poor little Brownie has been through!" There was some loud squawking on the receiver, and I knew that Miz Jenkins was angry at being contradicted. "I know, I know. Mmm hmm. Okay, bye-bye." Mama hung up the receiver and sighed wearily.

"Whatuz that all about?" I asked. Aunt Janelle answered me with a huff, "It was *abow-ut* that old heifer interrupting us plannin' my weddin'! Come on, Jeanette! Let's finish before Boyd comes home for supper!" Mama went to the stove to stir a pot of homemade vegetable soup. "Okay, where were we?" Mama asked her sister.

I sat down at the table, too. "Oh, good! We need your opinion, Brownie!" Aunt Janelle said cheerfully. She licked her finger and flipped the pages of a magazine until she came to a page with the corner turned down. "Whadaya thank about this for your flower girl dress?"

I pulled the magazine closer to me and looked at the picture. There were lots of little girls on the page all dressed up in the finest party dresses that I had ever seen. Soft pink dresses with tulle overlays, sweet yellow dresses with matching capes, lilac dresses that went down to the floor with long, see-through sleeves. And all of them had masses of crinolines underneath them to make them stand out. But there was one little girl, way in the back of that crowd of dresses that had been circled in pen. I looked more closely at her dress. It was lime green with an enormous yellow bow tied at the neck. The sleeves were dotted with yellow polka dots, and it came down to the girl's calves where a ruffled hem went all the way around the dress. I thought it was the most beautiful dress I had ever seen.

I looked at Mama who was shaking her head and using her hand to hide it from Aunt Janelle. "I really like it, Aunt Janelle," I stammered. Aunt Janelle squealed. "I knew it! I knew you would!" she cried happily. Mama closed her eyes and sighed. "And ain't you gonna be the prettiest flower girl in the world, Miss Tina Marie!" I could not help but grin. Aunt Janelle never called me by my real name.

"I picked green and yellow 'cause the weddin's in April and its springtime, you see. Annnd, my bridesmaids and Matron of Honor are all gonna have dresses in that lime green taffeta! Wooo! I'm so excited!" she squealed.

Mama looked at her watch and got back up from the table. "I've got to get the cornbread on," she said. "Okay," Aunt Janelle said, "I will go over the list and you can listen." Aunt Janelle cleared her throat.

"Brownie's dress, bridesmaid dresses for Lola and Donna, your Matron of Honor dress, tuxedos for Roger, Boyd, and of course, Dewayne. Did I tell you, Brownie? The guys are going to have lime green bow ties and cummerbunds. Miz Hadley over at the men's store is gonna order 'em special!"

Mama came back to the table rolling her eyes. "But we've got to remember that Mama may nix everything you have planned, Janelle. I mean, she is the one paying for it." Mama reached over to rub her sister's hand. Aunt Janelle yanked her hand away.

"Well, if she starts changing too much, I will just go to the bank and take out a loan! I want my wedding my way!" she cried. About that time, Donna came in and sat a load of books down on the end of the table. "Hey, Aunt Janelle," she said. "Makin' any progress?" That made Aunt Janelle perk up.

"Say, what's Roger wearin' a suit for?" I asked. Aunt Janelle explained that he was going to be her ring bearer and carry the ring down the aisle after I had dropped the rose petals down.

"Ain't you skeered he'll drop it?" I asked. Aunt Janelle was rummaging through her bags for something. "Naw. The ring will be clasped to the pillow sos it won't fall off. Found it!" she cried and laid a piece of very shiny, lime green material on the table. "This is the swatch of fabric yore bridesmaid dress is gonna be made out of, Donna. Don't you just love it!" I rubbed my finger over the material. "That's nice!" I said. But the look on Donna's face said something different. My sister looked to Mama for help. Mama nodded. "That's, um, very bright," Donna said. "Well, yeah!" Aunt Janelle, "Like green grass in spring-time!"

Mama looked at Donna and me. "Go wash up," she said and pointed to the load of books on the table. Donna scooped them up and followed along behind me to our room. She sat her books down on her bed. "That is gonna make the ugliest dress in the history of weddin's!" she exclaimed. "How come?" I asked, puzzled.

"Have you seen the dress pattern?" Donna asked me. I shook my head. "It has poofy sleeves and a big 1950s look-ing full skirt. Plus, it will take yards and yards of that awful fabric to make it." Donna collapsed back on her bed. "I mean, who uses *lime green* in a weddin'?"

I went to the bathroom to wash my hands and found Daddy in there washing up. He left the water on and moved over to dry his hands. "It's all yores," he said and started whistling. I got the Lux and lathered my hands up. "Daddy," I said, "I don't know anythang about gittin mar-ried." Daddy laughed. "And I hope you don't fer a long time," he said and popped my backside with the towel as he walked by. I squealed but laughed, too.

Aunt Janelle would not stay for supper. She said she had too many things to do before the wedding; so, she left. Mama had already dipped mine and Roger's soup so that it could cool down some. We had the blessing, and the first thing Roger did was sneeze all over his soup bowl. "I couldn't hep it," he cried. "Daddy shook pepper and it made me sneeze!" Daddy laughed at him and began crumbling up cornbread into his soup.

"Here," Mama said taking my soup bowl from in front of me. "You can have half of Tina's, and I will set another bowl out to cool while y'all eat this." Mama always had a way of fixing problems.

"Well, Miss Brownie," Daddy said to me, "I hear yore gonna be turning elemum soon. Zat right?"

I beamed a big smile. Nobody had mentioned my eleventh birthday was coming up. I thought they had forgotten. "Yes, sir! It's Saturday!" I replied. "Oh, neat!" Donna said. "You're turning eleven on the eleventh!" I had not thought of that, so I nodded and laughed.

"So, whatz a girl of elemum wont fer her birthday, anyway?" Daddy teased. I shrugged my shoulders. "I guess I could use a new bike," I said. Daddy shook his head. "Naw, alls 'at bike needs is a coat of spray paint and two new tires. No call fer a new one," he said. "Well, maybe a dollhouse?" I suggested. Daddy nodded like this request was much more agreeable.

"Tina, you know you get to pick what we have for supper on your birthday and what kind of birthday cake," Mama said. This happened every year that I can remember. It was a family tradition. "Can we have pork bar-be-que? And a chocolate cake?" I asked. Mama nodded and got up to get the bowl of soup that had been cooling for Roger and me. I crumbled cornbread in my soup, just like Daddy had done. The thought of my birthday being celebrated made me happy all over.

Piney Hill

January 11, 1969
Dear Diary,
Today I am eleven years old!
We are having chocolate cake.
Brownie

The day of my birthday dawned bright and sunny. The temperature was supposed to be in the mid-sixties, almost like springtime. I walked into the kitchen where my Mama was. "Happy Birthday, baby!" she said with a kiss. "Yeah, Happy Birthday, Brownie!" my sister and brother chimed in. Daddy had already gone to the barn.

I went to the counter and poured myself a bowl of cereal, then sat down at the table with my brother and sister. Mama brought a cup of coffee to the table and joined us.

"How are you feeling this morning?" Mama asked me. I told her I was better. At the time, I did not understand mononucleosis. It had made me so sick for so long. But I did feel good and thought that maybe the worst of it was over.

Talk soon turned to the wedding. Aunt Janelle had chosen April nineteenth for the date. She was working on getting invitations printed and all of the sizes to the seamstress who was making the dresses. Donna made it known that she hated the dress that Aunt Janelle had picked out for the bridesmaids. Mama encouraged her by saying that it was only for one day and that we would get through it for Aunt Janelle's sake. As for me, I couldn't wait to wear that beautiful green dress.

That night at suppertime, Granny and Papa, Aunt Brenda and Uncle Gil and their kids all showed up to eat and have cake with me for my birthday. Mama had made delicious barbeque out of a pork loin that she had roasted in the oven all day until it melted in your mouth. There was a big bowl of potato salad, baked beans, and slaw to go with it.

Mama had also made a beautiful chocolate layer cake for me and had placed a plastic horse on top surrounded by candles. We all ate our fill, and everyone sang Happy Birthday. Then, Aunt Brenda said Trixie had a gift from their family for me.

"Here you go, Brownie!" Trixie beamed. It was a small, scrunchy package with a bow on it. I opened it to find a white envelope that Trixie had decorated with her own art-work. It was almost too pretty to open. I carefully peeled back the seal on the envelope and removed its contents. Inside was a ten-dollar bill tied with ribbon. "This is too much!" I protested. But Trixie just laughed and said, "Mama says that's enough for both of us to go to the movies and then get a hamburger after!" I smiled at my cousin. "It's all settled!" Trixie continued, "We are going to spend the night with Maw-Maw and Pawpaw after the show!" It was a very generous gift. I thanked everyone and told Trixie that she did a good job pulling it off.

I gave the money to Mama to hold for me. Then I walked over to get a second helping of cake. "Wait, Brownie!" Mama said, "You haven't got the present from us yet." I looked around, "But where's Daddy?" I asked. Mama smiled. "He's outside with your present!" she replied. Mama took my hand, and everyone followed us out the backdoor. When we rounded the corner of the house there stood Daddy, holding the reins of a beautiful black and white pony. I stood there with my mouth hanging open. I just could not believe my eyes.

I walked over and stroked the pony's nose. Daddy smiled. "We thought that, with the year you've had, you deserved that pony you've been asking for." The pony had a shiny saddle, and I walked up and put my foot in the stirrup. Daddy helped me up into the saddle. I was beaming. Mama took a picture of me on top of my Indian pony. I was glad that I was wearing my new cowgirl boots. "Can I ride him?" I asked. Daddy said that I could, but he was going to hold to the reins until the horse and I got use to each other.

"I want a turn! I want a turn!" Roger kept whining. "You'll get a turn when Tina's through with hers," Mama said. "What are you going to name him?" Mama asked. Now I had been going over names for a horse for the past year, but none of them suited this fellow. So, I thought for a minute and then said, "I'm gonna call him Tom-Tom. Like the Indian drum." Everyone seemed to like that name.

"You kin let go, Daddy. I kin do it," I said. Daddy handed me the reins and told me to just walk him around the yard. I walked him for a minute but when I got to the driveway, I kicked him in the sides, and he started galloping. We were off!

Tom-Tom ran down the driveway and I leaned into him. We ran down the hill to the main road. I pulled him over to the right side where Mr. and Miz Jenkins' pasture was. I got him a little too close to her pasture gate and felt the sting of metal as it cut into my skin. When we got to Merchant's store, I pulled Tom-Tom up and he stopped. Miz Jenkins was standing by her car with the door open and a paper bag of groceries cradled in her gelatinous arms.

"They, law! Yore ah bleedin'!" she said. "I told Jeanette that hoss would git you kilt!" Miz Jenkins was bellowing. "But yore mama wouldn't hear it! Now, you gotta gash in yore laig thatsa gushin' blood ever whur!" Mr. and Miz Merchant heard Miz Jenkins' fussing and rushed outside to see what was going on.

"Oh, Lord!" Miz Merchant gasped. "Her laig is tore up! Hubert, git tha kit!" Mr. Merchant went into the store and came back with an emergency first-aid kit. "I called yore daddy, Brownie. He'll be here in a minute," he said.

Miz Merchant cleaned my wound and started applying some kind of white powder on it. "Yore gonna need stitchin' up and maybe need a shot." Miz Jenkins chimed in. "Yeah! You don't wont to git no titinuss!"

"Well, the cut on my leg is yore fault!" I cried. "That gate o' yorn has a rusty piece stickin' out on it!" I started crying, although I don't know why. And little did I realize that Daddy had just driven up and had heard me arguing with an adult.

"Boyd! Did you hear how that young'un of yorn sassed me!" Miz Jenkins said, pointing her finger at me. "Wha, I orta snatch her offen that hoss and put her acrost my lap and wear her out!"

Daddy walked around her and pulled me down off of Tom-Tom. "Now, Edna," he said. "We will take care of that at home." He carried me over to the truck and sat me down on the seat. "I'd better git on to the doctor with her. Thank you Miz Merchant," Daddy said. "Do you mind tying her pony up here 'til I git back?" Mr. Merchant said he would do that, and Daddy put the truck in drive. We took off for Pine Crest to see Dr. Nichols, again.

After a while Daddy looked at me and said, "That was some fast ridin' you were doin'." Well, I was not even sure if I was riding Tom-Tom or just staying in the saddle until he decided what to do next. "You shouldn't ah fussed at Edna, Brownie. She's yore elder." I nodded and tried to look like I was sorry.

"How'd you git so close to Earl's gate?" Daddy continued. I thought for a while and remembered. "I thought rubbing the gate would slow him down and it woulda too, if that old piece of rusty metal had'nt got me!" Daddy laughed. "Well, we will git you stitched up and yore probably gonna have to have a shot." I winced. "I guess so," I said grudgingly. "I shore don't wont to git no titinuss!"

After that first ride, Tom-Tom and I had come to understand one another. By that I mean he understood he could gallop with me, and I understood that he would not let me fall off. He became my obsession.

Every morning, I ran to the barn to turn him out to pasture. I fed him sweet feed and hay and curried his coat until it shone. Tom-Tom became my good friend and would follow me around the yard like a dog.

My leg healed up leaving a nice scar to show for bragging. Granny said she would sew me some britches out of canvas for riding in the woods. And Trixie said she would ride behind me, even though she was scared to death of Tom-Tom.

My life as an eleven-year-old had changed for the better after being given that horse. I did not think about the kidnapping as much anymore. But I did worry about Carl's upcoming trial in March.

January 12, 1969
Dear Diary,
After church Daddy and Uncle Gil are takin' over the livin' room.
It's some kind of special football game. Mama made snacks.
Brownie

Sunday morning in Piney Hill was cool and sunny. We were on our way back home from church, and I was looking out the window at the pine thickets that ran alongside of our rutted, dirt road. Mama had finally given in and let me wear my cowgirl boots to church. I had cleaned them and rubbed them down with a biscuit. The red leather was shining like new money.

"I'm going to need some sheets and blankets to take with me," Donna was talking to Mama about moving to Atlanta after she graduated from high school in May. "I know," Mama said. "We will have to start making a list. Boyd! Look out!" Mama shouted and pointed to the road in front of us. There, stood Tom-Tom. "Now, how'd he git out?" Daddy wondered. He put the truck in park, and I was out my door before he was.

I walked over to my pony and held his mane and stroked him. "Who's a good buckeroo?" I cooed. "Well, I swear," Daddy said rubbing the back of his neck. "I thought you put him in the pasture this morning." Tom-Tom snorted and pawed the ground. I kept rubbing him and he settled down. "I reckin he come lookin' for me," I said.

Daddy laughed and went to the car and opened the trunk. He came back with a rope halter and put it on my horse. "Whur'd you git that?" I asked. Daddy patted Tom-Tom's neck. "I bought it at the mercantile. Thought we might need it sometime." "Can I ride him home?" I asked. Daddy heaved me up onto the horse's back. "Go slow!" he ordered. "You ain't never rode bareback. I will be right behind you in the car." Daddy showed me how to hold the mane. I nudged Tom-Tom in the side and turned him toward home.

I rode my horse all the way to the barn. Daddy stopped the car and helped me to get down. "Put him up, Brownie. I'm gonna figure out how he got out." I rubbed my horse's neck and fed him. Then, I went to the house to help Mama get dinner on the table.

At dinner, Daddy told Uncle Gil that something had mashed down the barbed wire fence at the back of the barn. Aunt Brenda asked Daddy to pass the beef roast. "What ye thank mashed it?" Uncle Gil asked, sopping gravy with a biscuit. Daddy looked around the table and lowered his voice. "I saw tracks," he said. Nobody else seemed to be listening to this but me. "What kinda tracks, Daddy?" I asked. Daddy waved his hand in the air to get me to hush. But that did not keep me from thinking about it.

After we had eaten, Donna and I helped with the dishes. Mama laid out potato chips and dip and a platter of sausage balls, then she put on a pot of coffee to have with the pound cake that she had made. Mama was a very good cook.

Aunt Janelle and Dewayne showed up with Miz Lola and Dave. The women sat at the kitchen table and talked about the refreshments Aunt Janelle wanted for the wedding. I did not realize that getting married was such a fuss.

The football game on television did not interest me, so I went out to the barn to see what tracks Daddy was talking about. I walked around to the back of the barn. Daddy had mended the fence well enough to keep Tom-Tom inside. I knew he did not like to work on Sunday and would do a better job on it tomorrow. I was walking around with my head down, looking for any sign of what might have brought the fence down in the first place when Roger jumped out from behind the henhouse and scared me.

"Ha, ha! You shoulda seen yore face!" he laughed. I returned to my examination of the ground. "Come and help me look for tracks" I said. We looked for the better part of an hour and then gave up. "Reckin what took down the fence, Roger?" I asked. My brother shrugged, "How 'bout a tree?" I looked at my little tow-headed brother and smiled. "Maybe," I said. But not likely, I thought.

Roger and I stayed outside until we got so cold that we could not take it. We were walking back to the house when we saw Mr. Jenkins driving up the driveway. He had barely got stopped before the door opened and Miz Jenkins hauled herself out. She slammed the door and made a beeline for the back porch. Roger and I went in the house after her.

"Boyd! Boyd!" she was hollering. "Thar's a barr been around here!" Miz Jenkins stopped to catch her breath as Daddy walked toward the kitchen. "Hit's done knocked over Earl's beehives and tore 'em all to pieces!" Daddy told her that he knew because it had torn down our fence, and he saw its tracks out behind the barn.

So, that was the tracks that Daddy had seen. But where had they gone? Edna said she could not stay because she was warning the neighbors to be on the lookout for it. Mama asked her why she did not just call the neighbors. "Caint git nobody to antswer!" she said. "I guess they's all watchin' that *soup bowl* or whatever it's called on tv." Then she waved goodbye and stormed out of the house, slamming the door behind her.

I asked Daddy if the bear would get our chickens or pigs. "Well, they've been known to eat pigs. But I think it's just passin' through. Thought it might git some honey over at Earl's and as it came through here, our fence was just in its way." Daddy smiled at me.

"Can it get Tom-Tom?" I asked. "Naw," Daddy said. "Tom-Tom would put his lights out if he came adder him. He's gotta mean kick!" We both laughed and that lightened my load some. "Besides, I bolted the barn door."

The Big Game in nineteen sixty-nine was more famous than I thought it was. On Monday, it was all the boys at school could talk about. The news about the bear in Piney Hill community was forgotten.

January 14, 1969

Dear Diary,

We caught the bear! Daddy called Game and Fish and they caught him. Boy was he fat!

Brownie

Daddy had been more concerned about the bear than he let on. He called the state game wardens, and they came out with a bear trap. It looked like a big oil drum on wheels. They baited it with donuts and when the bear went in to eat, the door fell shut. Roger and I had run out to the barn to see the bear and watch the game wardens haul him off.

"You were right, Boyd" one warden said to Daddy. "That bear was just passing through. We'll git him back up to the mountains where he belongs." Roger and I cupped our hands around our eyes and peered in through the grated window. The bear was laying down with a donut between his paws, eating away.

Later on, I asked Daddy why Roger and I could not find the bear's paw prints on the ground behind the barn. He told me that he had taken the rake and scraped them off the ground. Daddy said he did not want us to be afraid. Our Daddy was always thinking ahead like that.

February 10, 1969
Dear Diary,
I hate to say it but Patty was right. Me and Trix went to see the new flying car movie on Saturday and it was great! But I don't need no flyin' car. I got Tom-Tom.
We spent the night with Trixie's grandmaw. Little Becky kept us up all night cryin'!
Brownie

When Trixie and I got to our classroom on Monday morning, all the girls were chattering excitedly about a new boy that had started at our school.

"Oh! He's so cute!" one girl shivered. "He's from Florida!" another girl sighed. Trixie looked at me and shrugged her shoulders. We went to our desks and unpacked our books. Then, in through the door with several boys following behind, came the new boy. He was blonde haired and blue eyed and very tan. His teeth were as white as adhesive tape. He caught me staring at him and I blushed. I do not believe I had ever blushed like that before in my life.

Miz Carlisle came in and shut the door. "Class!" she said, rapping her ruler on the desk. "We have a new student today. His family just moved here from Panama City. I want everyone to welcome Charles Adams. But he wants to be called Chuck." Then she led the class in a round of applause.

Patty was sitting in her desk in the aisle next to me. "Isn't he a dreamboat?" she cooed. I looked down at my English book and turned the page when Miz Carlisle called out the page number. I felt strangely upset that this new boy was in our class, so I focused on the lesson on adverbs instead.

At recess the girls were all discussing Chuck. His daddy was a pilot and was beginning a new job at the Air Force base in Marietta. They had bought George Donaldson's split level out on the state highway going toward Pine Crest. He had three brothers who were older than him. It was interesting to hear about him, so I listened to the girls talk. Hard to believe, but Trixie was hanging on their every word. "He looks like a movie star!" Cindy said. "I bet he surfs!" Patty replied. I looked at Chuck and he caught me looking again. I flushed and told myself to stop.

We were packing up to go home when Miz Carlisle made an announcement. "Class! The PTA has decided to host a Valentine's Day sock-hop for the fifth and sixth grades!" Trixie and I looked at each other. "It will be this Friday evening at seven o'clock in the gymnasium. Please stop at my desk and pick up a permission form for your parents to sign."

Trixie hurried onto the bus and pulled me into the seat beside her. Patty sat behind us. "What the devil is a sock-hop?" Trixie asked me. Patty gave Trixie a look of sympathy. "It's a dance," Patty replied. "They call it a sock-hop because you dance without your shoes on. I heard all about 'em from my cousin in Marietta. We'll have to get a new dress!" I looked at Trixie. "Why in the world would we wear a new dress if we're gonna dance barefooted?" Trixie exploded.

"I don't know how to dance," I said. Trixie shrugged. "Me neither," she replied. So, Patty insisted we come over to her house on Wednesday to listen to records and practice dancing. "Chuck has been living around sophisticated girls. You don't wont him to think y'all are a bunch of rednecks, do you?"

Trixie and I got off the bus and started up Piney Hill. Roger and Trixie's brothers ran on ahead. "What are we gonna wear?" Trixie's face looked anxious. "I guess we'll have to ask our mamas that," I said. It had turned cold again, and the sky had iron-gray clouds gathering over Piney Hill. Before I got to the back porch it began to rain.

We were just sitting down to supper when Papa and Granny came in the backdoor. They were dripping wet. "Hits a rainin' cats and dawgs out thar!" Granny said. Papa wiped his feet on the mat and hung up his coat. "Aw, Eudora. A little rain wont hurt ye." "But sugar melts," Granny snickered. "Yeah, and salt lumps up!" Papa said with a mischievous grin. Granny waved her hand at him in dismissal and went to the sink to wash her hands. Papa did the same thing and then they came to sit at the table where a place had been laid for them.

"Whut's a goin' on?" Papa said as he helped himself to chicken and dumplings. "Well, Tina's class is having a Valentine's dance this Friday," Mama said. Papa whistled low. "Dain-cin? At yore age? Shorely not!" I shrugged. "She and

217

Trixie are both going to need a dress or jumper. Tina doesn't have anything nice that fits her."

Granny swallowed a drink of iced tea. "Ah got some reddish corduroy if ye thank a jumper from that'll do." Mama thanked Granny but told her no, we would not need her to sew. "Brenda and I are going to take the girls to Kringle's to see about fixing us up." I was not involved in the conversation but for some reason, I felt a rush of relief. I guess I did not realize how much I was looking forward to going to this dance. Granny smiled patiently. I could not tell if she was relieved too, or just a little bit hurt that her offer to make dresses for us was declined.

February 11, 1969
Dear Diary,
After school today, Mama and Aunt Brenda are pickin' me and Trix up at school and takin' us to Kringle's.
Then, they are gonna visit with Patty's mama while me and Trix learn to dance.
Brownie

The four of us walked through the door of Kringle's and the bell tinkled cheerfully. It was Tuesday Madness. Kringle's stayed open until eight o'clock once a month for their Tuesday Madness sale. Trixie and I walked over to look at the dresses. There were a several in red but none in my size. Trixie took a red dress off the rack and went to try it on. Mama looked at me sympathetically and then went to fetch the sales lady over.

"What size is that dress on the mannequin?" she asked. The sales lady took the mannequin down and pulled out the tag to show my mother. "How about this one, Tina? It's your size." The dress was not red. It was white with a white lace overlay. There were tiny pink roses on the bodice. I thought it was beautiful.

February 14, 1969
Dear Diary,
I went to my first ever dance. It wasn't too bad.
I think Dennis likes Trixie.
Brownie

Donna took the rollers out of my dark hair and it fell to my shoulders in soft curls. "Hold still," my sister ordered. "I want to spray it." I closed my eyes as a cloud of sticky mist encircled my head. "Now, don't pull your dress down over your head. Step into it, so it don't ruin your hair," she said.

I did like she said, and Donna zipped me. Mama had bought me a new pair of white tights and I had polished my white loafers. "Shoot! That cowlick!" Donna complained. She grabbed some hair gel and slicked down the corner of my bangs.

Mama was watching and declared that I was absolutely beautiful. Donna went to the dresser and came back with a tube of frosted pink lipstick that she smeared over my lips. I felt like Cinderella.

Aunt Brenda and Mama dropped Trixie and me off at the door of the gymnasium. I was glad to have my cousin to walk in with. Inside, the gym was dimly lit with strobe lights and pop music playing over a speaker. Neither one of us knew what we were supposed to do at a sock-hop, so we looked around to see what everyone else was doing.

"Hello, girls! Take off your shoes and leave them against the gym wall" Miz. O'Neil said. "Then go stand with the girls over there on the right." Okay. Strange as it was, we took off our shoes and went to stand with the other girls on the right. Trixie looked at Miz O'Neil. "Then what happens?" she asked. Miz O'Neil pointed at a group of boys on the left side wall. "When a boy wants to dance, he will come over to where y'all are and ask one of you to dance with him." She smiled and walked away.

Trixie said, "Ug! You mean we gotta dance with boys? I thought we'd just dance. You know. By oursefs." I felt sweat prickling under my arms. "How do you dance with a boy?" I asked Trixie. She shrugged. "Guess we're 'bout to find out. Here comes Dennis." All of the girls immediately looked down at their stockinged feet.

"Hey, Brownie! Hey, Trixie!" Dennis said in his cheerful way. "This is cool, huh?" We nodded. Yes, this was cool. No, we'd never danced in public in our bare feet. "How 'bout we dance to this one, Trix?" Dennis said with a smile. Trixie looked dumbfounded. "Nooo, you git somebody else," she said. "Aw, come on! You ain't chicken, are you?" Dennis asked. I looked at Trixie. Aunt Brenda had put her blonde hair up in a twist, and the red dress really complimented her coloring. But pretty or not, I could see that her temper was up. After all, nobody called Trixie Rivers a chicken. She grabbed Dennis by the hand and hauled him onto the gym floor. Then, she commenced to flinging her arms and swinging her hips so violently that Dennis could not keep up. I started laughing.

Patty, who was standing close by, came over to laugh too. "Boy, she shore didn't learn nothin' I taught her, did she?" We were laughing, and Patty was even snorting laughter when the new boy, Chuck Adams, walked over to our little knot of girls. I felt a tap on my shoulder and suddenly became afraid to turn around.

"Hey, Brownie," Chuck said, with all his white teeth shining. "Let's go," he said and tilted his head toward the gym floor. Chuck reached up and took my hand and we walked out into the dimness of the dance floor as a slow song started playing. "Oh, great," I thought. "We're gonna have to touch." But Chuck just held both my hands and sorted of swayed back and forth.

"So, you're The Champ," Chuck said. I cringed. Chuck smiled. "I read the story in the paper. You were really smart and brave." I looked at the floor. "Yeah. I guess so." I muttered. Chuck kept talking. He talked about the first test of the Boeing 747 aircraft recently. He told me his daddy had worked at the Air Force base, and he had been on a tour of the base. He asked me about the bear that the game wardens caught, and then he asked me if I liked horses.

"Horses? Yeah," I said. "I have an Indian pony named Tom-Tom that I got for my birthday." "Oh, yeah?" Chuck said, "Well, I have an appaloosa. We should go riding sometime." I nodded. Then, the music stopped, we clapped, and I walked back to the wall as fast as I could.

Suddenly, I was encircled by a group of girls. "Brownie! You're so lucky!" one girl cried. "What'd y'all talk about?" Patty wanted to know. But I just mumbled "guess so" and "nothin' much". I was eleven and the feeling of being shown attention by a boy was new to me. I needed time to process it.

When we left the dance at eight o'clock that night, sleet was pelting the school parking lot and everything in it. The cold air wrapped around my small frame and seeped through my new dress. Mama and Aunt Brenda pulled the car up to the gymnasium door and Trixie and I hurried to get in. Thankfully, the heater was on full force and had warmed the car up nicely.

"Did y'all have fun?" Aunt Brenda wanted to know all about it as Mama inched our car up the road from the school and turned up Piney Hill. I could hear the tires trying to get traction on the rutted, dirt road. "The road's already icing up!" Mama said. "Do you think we can make it up your driveway, Brenda?" Aunt Brenda clucked her tongue. "Git out, Jeanette and let me drive," she answered. Mama stopped at the bottom of Aunt Brenda's driveway, and they switched seats. While treacherous driving made Mama nervous, Aunt Brenda took it on like a bull rider.

Aunt Brenda put the car in gear and gave it the gas. We surged and skidded and even made it over the big rock at the top of the hill. Aunt Brenda did not let her foot off the gas until she coasted into their yard. She looked over at Mama and grinned. "Now, you've gotta drive it home," Aunt Brenda told her.

Mama was wearing a flowered headscarf knotted at her throat. Her fingers immediately began to finger the knot. "Well, I ah, I think Tina and I will take the trail through the woods. It's safer," she said. "Here, Tina. Put your coat on." Mama did not have to tell me twice. It hurt to get your exposed skin pelted by sleet.

We half walked, half ran, over the trail to our house. I was so happy to see the lights on in the kitchen and to know that we would soon be safe and warm inside. Daddy met us at the door.

"Whur's the car, Jeanette?" he asked. "Oh, I left it at Brenda's. You know me and driving on ice." Mama took off her scarf and coat and hung them on the pegs that lined the wall by the backdoor. "It's supposed to be the worst ice storm we've seen," Daddy said. "I've brought jugs in the house to ketch up water. The power's liable to go off." Mama went to the stove to make a pot of chili. "I cooked a whole chicken and a beef roast today just in case that happens," she said.

I went to the bedroom to put on my warmest pajamas and a pair of socks. Donna was sitting on her bed studying. "Hey! How'd it go?" she asked. "Okay, I guess," I replied. "Well, did you mash potato? Did you do the twist?" Donna was singing a popular song from the radio. I grinned. "I don't think what Patty taught us was real dances," I said. "Well? Did a boy ask you to dance or not?" Donna persisted. So, I told her all about Chuck Adams and his invitation to go riding together. "He's just nice. You know. A friend," I said. "Sure, he is," Donna said. And I must admit, the way she said it made me feel nice.

SPRING, 1969
No. 4

March 1, 1969
Dear Diary,
March came in like a lamb.
I dread Monday. Daddy's taking me to see the District Attorney about Carl's trial.
Brownie

I walked out of the school on Monday with my stomach in a knot. Daddy was waiting in the truck and waved at me. I climbed in and slammed the door shut. I blew out my cheeks.

"Nervous?" Daddy asked. I nodded. Daddy had already told me that Carl would not be there. That it would be just us and the D.A. in his office. "Just tell him what ye know. He'll probably have questions ready to ask ye, but if you think of anything that he don't ask, just speak up. We don't wanna leave nothin' out." I nodded again.

I had never been in the Keetoowah County courthouse before. It was massive. The polished marble columns and steps were beautiful, and inside there were long staircases on either end of the entrance, their bannisters polished to a sheen by the sliding of many hands over many years. I had seen the clock tower from outside, but inside I could not figure how you might get to it.

We walked up the stairs on the left, and when we got to the landing, Daddy walked over and pushed open a door and motioned for me to come and see. It was the courtroom. It was empty, so I could really see how it was laid out. Spectator seats sat in rows on the left and on the right with a wide aisle down the middle. At the end of the aisle was a wooden banister that ran the length of the courtroom. A swinging gate was in the middle. Long tables with padded chairs were in front of the banister. An area was laid open in front of the tables right up to the judge's bench. The jurors seating was on the right and the defendant and deputies were allocated to the left. Tall arching windows let in sunshine. I began to sweat.

Daddy said we should go. We walked out of the courtroom and went down the hall to a door that had *District Attorney* in gold lettering on its front. Daddy opened the door and walked in. A woman about my mother's age sat behind a desk. She was typing so fast that I was mesmerized. Daddy cleared his throat. "Oh, I'm sorry! Didn't hear you come in," she said cheerfully. Daddy told her who we were and what we were doing there, and she got up and went through a different door and then came back.

"Mr. Coldwater will see you now. Please follow me," the secretary led us into a modest office filled with official looking books bound in leather. An old man was sitting behind an oak desk, and he stood to greet us. He shook hands with Daddy and introduced himself as Walter Coldwater then motioned for us to sit down in the chairs opposite his desk.

Mr. Coldwater had a shock of thick white hair with an unruly cowlick that I could identify with. He was heavy set and emitted a little wheeze when he exhaled. But it was his icy blue eyes that were the most interesting. He talked with Daddy about rabbit hunting and the price of corn, but I never could tell whether he was interested in what he had to say or whether he was sizing my Daddy up. I felt myself get a little uneasy.

"And this, I take it, is The Champ that I've heard so much about." Mr. Coldwater turned his blue eyes on me, and I looked down at my lap. "You know, Miss Tina," the D.A. continued, "that pair of drawers quite possible saved your life." I nodded. Mr. Coldwater stared at me for what felt like an eternity before he cleared his throat and began his interview.

"First of all, Boyd, do you think your eleven-year-old daughter is up to all this?" The D.A. looked at Daddy for my answer. "Yes, sir. She aims to tell you everything she kin remember." The D.A. looked down at his notes and cleared his throat again. "Okay then. Let's get started."

For over an hour I went through how Carl had thrown a burlap sack over my head and drug me off the back porch step. I searched my memory and tried not to leave anything out. When I thought we were about to wrap things up, Mr. Coldwater asked me something that nobody else had asked me before.

"Now, Miss Tina," the D.A. began, "you've done mighty good thus far and I don't mean to embarrass you in any way, but there is one more question that I simply must ask you before you leave." I took a deep breath and looked at Daddy. I nodded.

"Did that boy take liberties with you?" Mr. Coldwater looked at me hard with those ice blue eyes. "Did he touch you in any way that made you feel uncomfortable?" Daddy made a move to get out of his chair and the D.A. motioned him to sit back down. I started to cry. Daddy put his arms around my shoulders. "He kissed me!" I blurted out. And there it was. The part about my ordeal that I had kept hidden all this time. I sat there and sobbed like a baby.

Mr. Coldwater looked at me. "He kissed you. That's all?" he asked. I nodded and Daddy handed me his handkerchief to blow my nose on. "Well," Mr. Coldwater smiled, "I think I've got all I need. Now you don't worry none, Miss Tina. I ain't going to ask you about that last part when you testify. So, don't you worry none about that." Then, Mr. Coldwater smiled a sweet grandfatherly smile at me and buzzed for his secretary to come in. We were escorted out and that was that. At least until March tenth, which was the beginning of March term.

On our way home, Daddy took me to get a banana split. I was drained and the fruit and ice cream seemed to perk me up. Daddy did not ask me any questions. He was thoughtful that way.

To this day, I never eat a banana split without thinking of that day.

March 3, 1969
Dear Diary,
Today in school we made kites. Miz Carlisle said we were going to fly them tomorrow.
I have my dime collecting can. I have to get my money collected to turn in to Miz Carlisle. I want to help the babys.
Brownie

The March sunshine was sharp and clear, like cut glass. Green pasture grass flowed in billows as the wind rippled over it. Daffodils or as we called them March Flowers shone in clusters of butter yellow. Songbirds sang their mating tunes from every tree and bush. When I was a girl, this thrilled me even more than it does now. I could not bear to be inside with spring just beyond the door.

I was walking through the pasture with my kite in my hand. Trixie came running out of the woods from the trail with hers and met me in the ankle-high grass. "Let's go!" I shouted and Trixie and I ran holding our kites out for the wind to catch. My kite was pink and yellow. We made them with balsam wood and tissue paper. It was so beautiful with the sunlight shining through it.

The wind caught our kites soon enough but only to swirl them around and send them crashing back down to the ground. Trixie picked her kite up and gave a discouraged huff. "What'd are we doin' wrong?" she asked. I looked my kite over for damage and, finding none, looked at my cousin whose fine, blonde hair had blown into her mouth. She had her tongue out trying to disengage it from her teeth.

"I dunno," I mumbled. "Maybe the wind ain't right today." So, we walked through the pasture, dragging our kites behind us. "Reckin we aughta collect our money?" I asked Trixie. Trixie frowned. "Who we gonna ask?" she said. "We know the same people and, even if they give both of us a donation, that ain't much." I nodded. "Reckin we could ask at church Sunday?" I asked. Trixie pulled her hair out of her face again. "Maybe," she said.

"For goodness sake!" I cried, "Why didn't you put yore hair in a ponytail!" Trixie was holding her hair with one hand and her kite with the other. She stepped in a hole and fell down. "Dad blame it!" she said. "Now, I've got cow manure on my dress!" Trixie rubbed at the green and brown stain on the hem of her play dress. Then she rubbed her hands off in the wet grass.

"I know!" I said. "Let's go build a playhouse!" Trixie agreed and we ran through the grass over to the pine thicket behind Papa's barn to play. We raked the pine straw into little walls and built rooms for our house. "Ain't we worried 'bout chiggers?" Trixie asked. If there was an insect, bee, or bug around, Trixie was always sure to get bit. "Naw," I said. "It ain't time fer chiggers."

"Did you git yore permission slip signed for the field trip?" I asked. Trixie was busy sweeping the floor of the thicket with her hands to make sure that no pine straw was left inside the walls of her house. "Yeah. Did you?" she asked me. "Thatuz the first thang I did when I got home yesterday," I said.

Friday, after we came back inside from flying our home-made kites, Miz Carlisle passed out the permission sheets for our field trip. We were going to the Atlanta Science Center and I was so excited! "Is Dennis excited about goin'?" I asked Trixie. She stood up; her play dress was filthy from raking the dirt. Trixie had lost weight and gotten taller, and the boys in class had noticed. "How should I know!" she bellowed. "He ain't my boyfriend, you know." I snickered. "He sure thinks he is!" Trixie put her hands on her hips and turned her back to me. I knew she was blushing and did not want me to see.

Our fifth-grade class boarded the school bus at nine o'clock sharp. Right after roll call, Miz Carlisle had lined us up with our sack lunches and marched us outside to the bus lane. Trixie and I sat together, and Patty sat with Cindy on the seat in front of us. We all chatted happily as the bus headed out of the schoolyard and forward to our destination of the Atlanta Science Center. Mr. Greer was driving the bus and was playfully giving us a tour of the pastures we passed and what kind of cows were in them. Mr. Greer was wearing a white long-sleeved dress shirt and khaki pants with his steel-toed boots. He had an Atlanta baseball cap shoved down over his big ears.

On our way through the big city, we stopped at a traffic light. Right before the light turned green, Mr. Greer sneezed, and his false teeth flew out of his mouth and hit the bus's windshield. Miz Carlisle and her helper, Miz Jones, scrambled around the floorboard of the now moving bus looking for Mr. Greer's teeth. Miz Jones came up victoriously with the upper dentures which had a long strand of grass attached to them. The students were all laughing hysterically.

Miz Jones pulled the strand of grass off and handed the teeth back to Mr. Greer who wiped them down the front of his white shirt and popped them back into his mouth. And he did all of this while laughing and driving through down-town Atlanta!

Miz Carlisle rapped her ruler on the stand-up pole at the front of the bus in an effort to restore order, but she was laughing just as much as we were. Thankfully, we were all laughed out by the time we parked at the Science Center.

"Now, class," Miz Carlisle said sternly, "The Atlanta Science Center is a *museum,* and we must walk quietly with no talking *and* keep our hands to ourselves at all times."

That trip to Atlanta is one that really stands out in my memory. Partly because of Mr. Greer's teeth, but mostly because of the space exhibit where we got to see the actual moon rocks brought back to earth by the astronauts. I was fascinated and picked up several brochures for myself and Roger. Then, we went to the planetarium and watched a cool thing that reflected on the roof. Suddenly we were transported into space.

The ride home on the bus was not nearly as lively as the ride to Atlanta. All the students were tired and either sat quietly or slept for the duration of the ride. We pulled in at the school and I saw Mama and Aunt Brenda waving at us. It was not time for school to be out, but our parents had checked Trixie and me out of school. We were going to Pine Crest to Trixie's grandmother's house to work on Aunt Janelle's wedding. "Oh, great," Trixie mumbled. "More ridin'! My hind end is already sore!"

We walked in the door at Miz Passley's house only to find Miz Jenkins, of all people, sitting at the kitchen table. She had pattern pieces pinned to the lime green fabric that Aunt Janelle had picked out for our dresses. I had not been told that *she* would be the one doing the sewing. Before Trixie and I had time to say anything, Aunt Janelle came like a whirlwind into the house and slammed the door.

That woke up little Becky, who immediately began crying. Miz Passley excused herself to go get her daughter.

"I thought I never was gonna git to leave the courthouse!" Aunt Janelle said. "Okay! Where'd you git to?" She put her hands on her hips and looked at Miz Jenkins. Miz Jenkins heaved herself out of the kitchen chair and picked up a measuring tape from the table.

"Well, I got Jeanette an' Brenda's cut an' pinned. Now, I gotta do tha' girls." Trixie and I cringed. "Hyur!" Miz Jenkins said pushing my arms out like a scarecrow. "I gotta measure yore bosom." It felt strange having Miz Jenkins *helping* my Aunt Janelle. But it felt even stranger having her big sausage fingers touching my chest and tugging the measuring tape across my *bosom*. I was happy when she told me I could put my arms down. Then she waddled over and did the same thing to Trixie, who looked like she wanted to swat her.

Miz Jenkins wrote the measurements on a piece of notebook paper. "Well, that big girl of yorn will have to have darts in her dress. Why ain't she wah'rin a brassiere?" Miz Jenkins's thick black glasses swung around to peer at Aunt Brenda, who shifted her feet. "Well, I thank she's too young for a bra, Edna!" Aunt Brenda said. Trixie was beet red and looked mad as a hornet. She stomped off to the living room where her grandmother sat with little Becky on her lap. I went in there, too. Becky would soon be seven months old. She looked at us and squealed. Bubbles of spit ran down her chin as she grinned.

"Well, she'll need one fer that dress or she'll be indecent," Miz Jenkins continued. "But that little 'un won't need darts. Her bosoms are like two fried eggs with the middle busted." Miz Jenkins laughed at my expense and began gathering up the material and patterns to make her way out.

Aunt Janelle, in compliance with decorum, got up to walk her to the door. "Thank you for helping us," she said as she opened the door. "Ah!" Miz Jenkins said, "Hits ah good thang yore gittin' yorn ready-made. I'd ah hated to make yorn, with all that extry material to go around that belly." And out she went. Like always, with the last word.

Aunt Janelle slammed the door and clenched her fists. "Arrg! That ole biddy makes me so mad!" she said and walked into the kitchen to cut herself a large piece of chocolate cake. Mama got up from the kitchen table and poured herself a cup of coffee. "I know, Janelle," she said to her sister. "But she *is* a good seamstress and she's close by. We'll just have to put up with her ways a little while longer." Aunt Janelle nodded and shoved a forkful of cake in her mouth.

"I ain't heard a peep outta Mama since she said she was gonna help me 'keep from making my weddin' a disaster.'" Aunt Janelle made air quotes when she said this. "Well, maybe Mama thought about what you said and has decided to let you have your way. I mean, all she has to do is show up and enjoy herself." Mama smiled, and Aunt Janelle smiled, too.

Mama and Aunt Janelle came into the living room to sit with Miz Passley and to ooo-and-ahh over little Becky. Trixie went to the kitchen and came back with cake for her and me. "You know what Edna said before you got here?" Miz Passley said. Aunt Janelle shook her head. "She said that she is going to sue Lola for that old pickle churn." Mama and Aunt Janelle started to laugh. "I said, 'Edna, they will laugh you otta the courthouse if you do something like that,'" Miz Passley said. "And then Edna said that pickle churn was made from clay that was over one hundred years old and made it worth a hundred dollars," Miz Passley explained. "Edna said that's big enough money to file suit in magistrate court. So, I would not be surprised if she don't do it." I thought to myself, "I sure hope I did not run into her next week when I had to go testify."

March 10, 1969
Dear Diary,
Court today. I threw up my breakfast.
Daddy says it will be okay.
Brownie

The courthouse steps outside, and the stairway inside, were lined with people. Some were dressed in overalls and work clothes, while others had on their Sunday best. Sweat mingled with after-shave and cheap perfume. A thick cloud of gray cigarette smoke hung in the air, illuminated by the sunlight coming through the long, paned windows. I heard my name called and turned just in time for a photographer to take my picture. Daddy said the man was from the newspaper. Carl's trial was the big case that week.

The hallway smelled awful to me, so I held my breath as long as I could stand to. When Daddy and I reached the landing at the top, we turned left and headed for the District Attorney's office. His secretary was typing away. I watched her fingers fly across the typewriter's keyboard. Then she pulled a sheath of paper from the roller and stood up.

"Mr. Coldwater is waiting for you in the courtroom," she said. "You can go through this door with me." The secretary walked around her desk and opened a door that was hidden behind the one that led into the hallway. We entered the courtroom and walked down the left aisle to the front, then turned and walked toward the right side and up to the big table where the District Attorney was sitting. Mr. Coldwater saw us and stood up to shake Daddy's hand.

"You and the little lady will have to wait in my office until she is called. She has to be sequestered until she gives evidence. But the defendant's attorney wants to interview her before trial begins. I just wanted to see how she was feeling and ask her if she has any questions for me." Mr. Coldwater looked at me with his icy blue eyes. "I'm fine," I said, and "No," I did not have any questions.

"Ah! Here comes Miss Harper now," Mr. Coldwater said. A short, stocky lady with a boyish haircut came towards the table. She was wearing a gray suit and white blouse with navy loafers. She was not wearing makeup.

"Miss Dodie Harper," Mr. Coldwater said, "this is Tina Marie Rivers." Miss Harper smiled at me. "Ah, the heroine," she said. I felt myself blush. "Do you want to take a walk?" Miss Harper asked. She tilted her head in indication that I should follow her. We walked through a door located between the floor-length windows of the courtroom and went out onto the balcony. There was a round concrete table with little concrete benches around it. We sat down.

"Now, I just want you to tell me your side of the story. Just like you remember it." Miss Harper looked at me with her dark brown eyes and smiled. I swallowed hard.

"Miss Harper, I'm nervous," I said. She reached over and patted my hand. "Call me Dodie," she said. "And there's no need to be nervous. Just tell the truth." I nodded and began to run through that night's ordeal for what felt like the hundredth time. I even told Miss Dodie that Carl had kissed me, although I don't know why I did.

"That's probably how you got mono," Miss Harper said. "Anyway, I have all I need now. Let's go back inside where your daddy is." She opened the door for me, and I walked into the courtroom and over to the table where Mr. Coldwater sat writing on a yellow notepad. He stood up when we came in and walked toward the judge's bench with Miss

Harper. There, they spoke in soft whispers. Then, Miss Harper left, giving me a little wave on her way out.

Mr. Coldwater sat back down at the table, and his secretary escorted us back to his office to wait.

It seemed like we had been waiting for hours. The secretary had given me a pencil and some paper to doodle on. After playing tic-tac-toe and drawing houses and pictures of Tom-Tom, I got sleepy and began to yawn. The big clock on the wall read 11:45. I was just about to ask where the restroom was when a bailiff came into the District Attorney's office and called out my name. Daddy stood up and identified me.

"You're excused," the bailiff said bluntly. I looked at Daddy, and he smiled at me. "The defendant pled guilty to all charges," the bailiff explained. Then, he turned and went back into the courtroom.

"Well, well! That means we can go home!" Daddy said. I stood up, and Daddy thanked the secretary for her kindness. We walked back down the staircase crowded with people and smoke and walked out of the courthouse into the bright sunshine. As we got into the truck, Daddy began to whistle a tune.

"I don't understand," I said. Daddy explained to me that Miss Harper had considered what I had told her and worked out a plea. "Carl decided to take his punishment like a man, so they did not need you to go over what had happened when he kidnapped you," Daddy said. I breathed a sigh of relief. "But what about Tater? What about what Carl did to his brother?" Daddy said that was all included in the indictment and that Tater and I did not have to worry about Carl anymore. Carl would be sent to reform school and then he would go into the Child Welfare System.

I smiled as Daddy backed out of the parking space and headed the truck out onto the highway. "Whew!" I said with much relief. "Banana split?" I grinned over at Daddy. He laughed. "Well, you did throw up yore breakfast," he said.

The Keetoowah Smoke Signal came out on Saturday, and my picture was on the front page again, this time with my eyes wide open and holding to Daddy's hand. "The Champ Faces Her Kidnapper," the headlines read.

"Wow, Brownie!" Roger gasped, "You really are famous!" His sweet little freckled face burst into a grin. I mussed his hair. "May I have your autograph?" Donna teased, handing me a pencil. We all had a good laugh. "Well, at least I didn't have panties on my head this time!" I said. I was basking in the adoration of my family when the backdoor was flung open, and Aunt Janelle and Miz Lola came in carrying garment bags over each of their arms.

"Help! Help! This un's falling off!" Mama made it to Aunt Janelle just in time for her to catch the dress on top of her left arm. "Whew! That was just in time!" Aunt Janelle waddled over to the kitchen table and laid the other dresses she was holding with the one that Mama had caught. Lola, ever so elegant, walked calmly over and added the two bags that she was carrying. "Now, let's take 'em out and hang 'em somewhere sos they don't git wrinkled," Aunt Janelle instructed. "Come 'ere, Brownie!" she called, "This un's yorn, and you need to try it on!" Aunt Janelle motioned with her hands going like a whirlybird. I walked over, and she pulled out my beautiful flower girl dress. I gasped at its beauty.

"Ain't you gonna be the purtiest flower girl ev-eeer!" Aunt Janelle squealed as she held the dress up to me. "Now, run, try it on!" I grabbed the dress and went to the bedroom.

I stood there for a minute, staring down at the sea of lime green dress laying on my bed. I detached the little cape and laid it to the side. Then I unzipped the dress that I had worn to court and let it fall to the ground and unzipped the flower girl dress and slid it over my head. I stepped over to the full-length mirror that was attached to the back of our closet door and looked at myself. I was beautiful. The zipper was a little hard to do by myself, but I managed it. Then, I put the cape over my shoulders and tied the large, yellow ribbon into a bow. I had never felt so grown up in my life. When I walked into the kitchen for everyone to see, Aunt Janelle cried with joy, Mama groaned, and Miz Lola turned away from me. Donna hid her laughter behind her hand.

"Ohhh! Ain't she the purtiest thang! Look, Jeanette! Won't Mother just have a fit!" Mama let out another soft groan as she walked to stand beside her sister. "Oh, she'll have a fit alright," Mama said and rubbed her sister's shoulders. "Oh, twirl around for us, honey!" Aunt Janelle cooed.

I was twirling and curtseying when the backdoor banged open again, and Miz Jenkins stomped in. "Well, thar's mah handiwork," she said. "I thank I done a right smart job o' it." Miz Jenkins clomped over and pulled out a kitchen chair to sit down. I walked over and looked out the window. Mr. Jenkins was standing beside the driver's side door, peeling an apple with his pocketknife.

"I told you that we did not need you to come look at the dresses, Edna," Aunt Janelle said, a bit miffed. Miz Jenkins ignored her. "Come o'er here, girl, and lemme see," Miz Jenkins said. I timidly walked over, and Miz Jenkins ran her forefinger inside the bosom of the dress to make sure the bodice was tight. "Yep. Seems 'bout right," she said.

"That too-lee nettin' that went o'er tha top wuz tricky," Miz Jenkins stated. "I'd a charged twicet as much if I'd a knowed how hard it uz ah gonna be ta sew." I might be wrong, but I thought Miz Jenkins was hinting to Aunt Janelle for a little extra pay.

Aunt Janelle rolled her eyes. "Well, you did a good job, and now you've checked Brownie's dress, so you can leave if you need to." Aunt Janelle walked over to Miz Jenkins and made like she was about to help her up. Miz Jenkins shooed Aunt Janelle's hands away. "Naw, I wont to see that heavy set 'un try hers on." Aunt Janelle sighed. "You mean Trixie? Trixie ain't here, Edna. So, you don't have to stay." Miz Jenkins blinked behind her black-rimmed glasses and heaved herself up. "Well, ifn yore shore," she said and reluctantly started for the door.

Miz Jenkins stopped at the sink, and a look came over her face like she finally realized that Miz Lola was in the room because she immediately scowled. "So, it's you, is it?" Miz Jenkins said. "You gonna give me back Frances' hunert-year-old pickle churn, or am ah gonna havta sue ye ta git it?" Miz Lola, cool as a cucumber, walked over to her and smiled her rich, red Latina smile. "Like I have told you before, Miss Edna, I left it on your back porch last month. Mr. Earl said to leave it there, and so I did." Then Miz Lola swept out of the room with as graceful a sashay as you have ever seen. In a minute, I heard the bathroom door lock. Miz Jenkins stood there and blinked.

Mama took hold of Miz Jenkins' elbow and started her toward the back steps. "Have you asked Earl about it?" Mama asked her. "I mean, he could have moved it off the porch to somewhere safe," she said. Miz Jenkins was mumbling and holding onto her purse like somebody was going to snatch it. Mama walked her to the bottom of the steps and gave her a hug and warm goodbye. Before Mama could make it back up the porch steps, we heard Miz Jenkins hollering at her husband.

"Earl! Is it true? Did that hussy give ye mah pickle churn?" Then, we heard the car doors slam and the car leaving the driveway. Donna and I were laughing. Mama was standing at the sink feeling sorry for Mr. Jenkins, and

Aunt Janelle was fuming. "Ooo! I'll be so glad when I git married and don't havta deal with her fer a while! I may just not come back from Florida!" she said. Miz Lola appeared in the doorway and smiled.

"Mujer odiosa!" she said, "You forget you have to be my maid of honor in June?" Mama looked at both of them and tied her apron on. "Well, April or June, whatever! I've got to get supper on!" she said and pulled out her pressure cooker. "Tina, go lay those dresses on my bed. Brenda and Trixie are coming after supper." Mama poured a can of green beans into the pressure and quickly peeled potatoes to go on top of them. Soon, the hiss-hiss of the cooker was going, and Mama started grating cabbage for slaw. "Are y'all gonna stay and eat?" Mama said cheerfully.

"No, gracias," Lola said. "I am meeting Dave for supper." Aunt Janelle came back from helping me put the bags on Mama's bed. "I caint stay, neither," she said. "Dewayne is comin' over." So, within a matter of minutes, Aunt Janelle and Lola were gone, and it was just our family again. "Who wants fried okra?" Mama asked.

April 1, 1969
Dear Diary,
March went out like a lion. It thundered and lightninged last night.
It's April Fool's Day, and I'm gonna play a prank on Mama.
Brownie

I walked into the kitchen like nothing was wrong and sat down at my place. Donna stopped eating and looked at her watch. "Good gracious!" she said, "Tad will be here any minute!" She jumped up from the table and dashed to the bathroom. "She sure likes Tad!" Roger said with a grin. I did not say anything because I was waiting for Mama to ask me what was wrong with me. I usually talk a lot at breakfast. She had her back turned away from me and was busy at the stove.

"What's the matter, Tina? Are you getting sick?" Mama asked me over her shoulder. Roger studied me as he spooned cereal into his mouth. "Naw, she jus...." I shooshed him before he could give me away. I had bought a pair of *Bubba Teeth* at Merchant's store and had saved them for my prank. Bubba Teeth are fake teeth that buck-out and even had some teeth that look rotten. Roger and I snickered.

"Well, you're not talking," Mama said as she turned around. "What's wrong?" But just as I opened my mouth to show her my teeth, I noticed that she was wearing a pair of black glasses with googly eyes that popped out on springs. All three of us started laughing. "I think I got you this year, Tina!" Mama laughed.

At school that morning, we were given a lecture by Miz Carlisle that April Fool's pranks would not be tolerated and that any student that tried to pull one would be sent to the principal's office. "After all," our teacher said, "you *are* in fifth grade." Then she told us to turn to page fifty-seven in our math books, and that was that. A chapter in our childhood suddenly slammed shut.

Our class assignment was to write a paragraph about how the assassination of Martin Luther King had affected us. April fourth would be the first anniversary of his death.

I knew what I would write. I would say that it made me feel horrible that somebody would do that to him. I would say how awful I would feel if it was my daddy. I would say that Jesus did not like it. When our paragraphs were turned in, Miz Carlisle said she would pick two out and read them when we came back in from the playground.

During recess, several of my classmates wanted to know what it was like being in a trial at the courthouse.

"Were you scared?" one asked. "Did you see Carl?" asked another. I told them that I did not want to talk about it anymore and that I just wanted to forget it ever happened. Then I saw Tater playing in the dirt with some other first-grade boys. I walked over to where he was crouched down.

"Hey, Gary," I said. Lately, I had taken to calling him by his name instead of Tater. It just seemed like that would help me forget Carl and the terrible matter that held us together. "Hey, Brownie!" Gary said cheerfully. He really was a cute little boy. He had two teeth missing now, and when he talked, he made a slight whistle.

"You doin' okay?" I asked Gary. He looked up at me and squinched one eye shut. "Yep," was all he said. I leaned over and kissed his cheek, and the other boys laughed and made fun of him. But Gary just grinned and stood up and hugged me around the waist. "Thank you, Brownie," was all he said.

When we got back to our room, Miz Carlisle fussed at us for our spelling and grammar mistakes on our paragraph about Martin Luther King. Then, she picked up two papers and read Cindy's and mine out loud.

That evening, Aunt Janelle was going over wedding plans with Mama again. The closer the wedding got, the more nervous she became. She had her notebook and receipts scattered all over the kitchen table. Daddy was in his armchair working a crossword puzzle, and Donna, Roger, and me were watching television. Buster was lying next to Roger in the floor, snoring. Then, there was a knock at the front door.

No one but salesmen ever came to the front door, so we all sat up in alarm. Mama said, "Janelle, run get that, will you?" while she flipped through a flower arranging book. Aunt Janelle stepped over to the door in her stockinged feet and pulled it open.

"Hello, Mother," she said dryly.

Aunt Janelle's hackles were up the moment she stepped back to let Grandmother Davidson into the house. I could see her fists clenching and unclenching.

"Mother!" Mama cried. "You didn't say you were coming!" Mama walked over to give her mother a peck on the cheek. "Well, I thought since the wedding is so close, I would come early and spend some time with my grandchildren." Upon hearing this, we all got up and went over to greet our grandmother.

Roger pulled down his lip to show Grandmother that he had a new tooth growing in. "That's nice," she said and moved to hug Donna. Roger persisted. "But it ain't no gold tooth," he said. "Isn't a gold tooth," Grandmother corrected.

"Donna!" Grandmother exclaimed. "So, you're off to college in Atlanta. I am so proud of you." Donna beamed. "Yes, ma'am! Will you be here for my high school graduation in May?" Aunt Janelle winced. "I am afraid not, dear," Grandmother said. "I am going on a cruise of the Caribbean," she smiled, but I don't think Grandmother was sorry she could not be there.

Roger tried again. "This is Buster," he said, pointing to his dog, who upon hearing his name, began to jump up on Grandmother who was dressed in an expensive traveling suit. Grandmother held her purse high above her head and looked appalled. "Git on, Buster!" Roger cried. It finally took Daddy intervening to get the jumping dog pulled back and calmed down. Daddy took Buster to Roger's room and shut the door. Buster immediately began to howl.

"Where are you staying, mother?" Mama asked. It was well known that Grandmother Davidson did not stay with family when she came to visit. "I'm at the hotel in Pine Crest," she said. "It's perfectly fine." And by that, she meant she could endure it. Grandmother Davidson suddenly realized that I was standing there.

"And Miss Tina," she said, "I hear you have been making quite a name for yourself." I blushed and secretly hoped she would not ask me to repeat the ordeal I had been through. She did not. In fact, she never mentioned it again during her whole stay.

"You had any thang to eat, Maureen?" Daddy asked Grandmother. "Yes, thank you," she said curtly. "Well, we have some squirrel dumplins' left if ye want Janette to heat ye up some." Daddy was trying not to grin, and I knew that he was teasing our grandmother. Grandmother wrinkled her nose and ignored him.

"Let's hear your plans for the wedding, Janelle," Grandmother turned her attention to my aunt. Aunt Janelle and Mama motioned for her to come to the kitchen table to look at the pictures of the dresses. Grandmother made a face when she saw the shocking lime green material that Aunt Janelle was going to use.

"And the Matron of Honor, bridesmaids, and flower girl are all going to wear crowns of daisies!" Aunt Janelle said nervously. Grandmother's sour expression never changed. I could see the wheels turning in Mama's head. She was going to try to calm the situation if she could.

"Who wants cake and coffee?" she asked and quickly went to the sink to fill the coffee pot. "None for me, thank you," my grandmother said. "I am slimming for the cruise." Then she looked at the pudgy frame of Aunt Janelle.

"What size is your wedding dress, Janelle? You probably should not be eating cake either." Aunt Janelle was trying to ignore her comment and flipped the pages of the flower arranging book back and forth.

I could tell that if Grandmother was going to be here until the wedding, which was over two weeks away, that there was going to be stormy seas around our house.

At eight o'clock I decided to call Trixie. "Well, you knowed sheuz gonna make trouble the minute she showed up!" Trixie said. I agreed. "Yeah, she and Aunt Janelle have never gee-hawed," I replied. "For some reason, she don't like our beautiful lime green dresses," I said. "Oh! And Aunt Janelle is gonna have us crowns made outta daisies!" I exclaimed. Trixie agreed that would make the outfit even more beautiful.

Suddenly, we heard breathing on our line and the familiar click-click of the receiver button being pressed. "Hon, y'all need to git off now. I need to call Edna, and y'all have been on the phone long enough." Miz Davis, who shared our party line, was a sweet old woman, but she never let kids talk more than two minutes if she wanted use of the telephone.

"Yes, ma'am," Trixie and I said in unison. "And" Miz Davis continued, "I thank those dresses that Edna made you are purty as kin be no matter what yore grandmaw from Charlotte says!" "Yes, ma'am," Trixie and I said again. Trixie and I told each other goodbye and let Miz Davis have the phone line. I hung up and walked to my bedroom, where Donna was sitting cross-legged on her bed studying.

"I have a test in algebra tomorrow, Brownie," she said. "So, if you're gonna be in here, you will have to be quiet." I decided to go into the living room. I crawled up into Daddy's lap, and he moved his crossword to the end table and wrapped his arms around me. We watched a new country music show with the volume turned way down.

April 5, 1969
Dear Diary,
Yikes! Grandmother Davidson is here from Charlotte, N.C.
Trixie and I have been avoiding her. We are going to ride Tom-Tom down to the school to meet Chuck and go riding.
Brownie

Saturday morning was overcast and windy. Trixie was in the barn with me, watching me saddle Tom-Tom. She was sneezing wildly. "Ah got me ah cold ur somethin'," she said and blew her nose on a brown-plaid man's handkerchief. "Ah gotta take this ole snot rag with me today, or mama said she'd tan mah hide." Trixie looked for a place to put her handkerchief, but her dress did not have pockets. "Here," I said. "I will put it in my britches pocket." I was careful to avoid the damp area as I shoved the handkerchief into the canvas pants that Granny had made for me.

I climbed up on Tom-Tom and held my hand out for Trixie to get up behind me. "Don't you let 'im buck me off!" she warned. "He ain't a gonna buck ye off, Trix! He's gentle as a lamb." I pulled Trixie up, and Tom-Tom snorted. Trixie grabbed me so tight around the waist she almost cut my breath off. I gently eased Tom-Tom forward, and he walked out of the barn and down the driveway to the road.

"Kin I at least trot?" I asked Trixie. "If we keep walking like this, we ain't never gonna git there!" "Don't you let 'im buck me off, Brownie!" Trixie said, gripping my waist tighter. I gently nudged my pony in the side, and he began to trot down the road from Piney Hill.

When we got to the schoolyard, Chuck was already there. He was sitting on the most beautiful white horse with brown speckles. "Hey," I said to Chuck. "Hey, Brownie. Trixie," Chuck replied. "How do ya like my appaloosa?" Chuck was beaming as he patted his horse's neck. "His name is Sand Piper, but I just call him Sandy." I could tell that Chuck was really proud of that horse.

"This is Tom-Tom," I said, "you know, like the drums Indians play." Chuck nodded and said, "That name's far out. But it's not an Indian pony, Brownie. It's called a Pinto." I looked at him funny. No one had ever told me that. Chuck could see my confusion. "An Indian pony would be a Cayuse," he said by way of explanation. I shrugged. "Well, he's an Indian pony to me," I said, and Chuck nodded.

Trixie spoke up. "Hey! Why don't we git some picnic stuff over at tha store. My daddy has an account thar. We kin put it on tha tab." We all agreed that was a good idea and walked our horses over to Merchant's store to pick up some snacks.

Trixie and I climbed back on Tom-Tom, and the appaloosa let out a whinny. We trotted to the empty field beside the school and began to ride its length back and forth. "Hey! Let's race!" Chuck cried. "Nuuuu, not me! I'm gittin off!" Trixie cried and slid clumsily down the side of my horse. She walked over to the edge of the field and sat down in the grass.

"Tell us when we're even!" I hollered over to Trixie. Chuck and I walked our horses back and forth until Trixie was satisfied. Then she shouted, "On yer mark! Git set! Go!" and we were off!

Chuck could ride better than me, but I was not to be outdone. I nudged Tom-Tom in the sides to get him to go faster. I quit looking over at Chuck and tried to concentrate on the edge of the field up ahead. Suddenly, we were there, and Tom-Tom stopped, and the momentum flung me over his head. The landing on the ground knocked the breath out of me. I struggled to take in air. I felt Trixie beating my back. Then, with relish, I sucked in air and started breathing normally again.

I stood up and brushed myself off. "Wow, Brownie!" Chuck exclaimed. "That was some good riding! You beat me and Sandy by about a foot!" Chuck was smiling big, and his white teeth shone in the sun. "Well, it's a wonder you weren't kilt!" Trixie groused. "You liketa have skeered me ta death!" I looked at my cousin. Her face was pale. "Well," I said, "how 'bout we eat lunch?" I grinned at her, and she grinned back.

We had our picnic of pork-n-beans, potted meat and saltine crackers, candy bars, and bottles of grape drink. The sun was warming up, and the breeze was blowing gently across the field. Every now and then, a brown butterfly would fly out of the field and toward us, then back again. Our horses were grazing and making a pleasant chomping sound. I laid back to let the sunshine on my face.

"It doesn't get any better than this," Chuck said and laid back beside me. Trixie was going through the grocery sack to see if we had missed anything.

"What mountain is that over there?" Chuck asked. I raised up on my elbows and squinted in the direction that he was pointing. "That's Sharp Top," I said. "I like topography," Chuck replied. I looked at him. "What's zat?" Trixie asked. She was sporting a grape drink moustache. I wiped my mouth and wondered if I was, too.

"Topography is map making. I like to go home and draw the mountains around here into a map. Like that little one that y'all live on. Don't they call it Piney Hill?" Trixie and I nodded. "Why?" Chuck wondered. "I don't know," I said. "It's been called that all my life. Our family has always owned the land there." Chuck broke off a piece of grass and started chewing it. "How'd they get it?" he pondered.

Trixie spoke up. "Daddy told me tha Rivers famlee got it in a lottery." Chuck perked up. "Oh! You mean like the Cherokee Land Lottery?" Trixie shrugged and scratched a bug bite on her leg. "I've read about that," Chuck continued. "The whites took the Cherokees land when they were rounded up and sent on the Trail of Tears. Then they sold it off to each other in a land lottery." We did not know this but pretended that we did.

"Yeah," I said, not wanting to appear ignorant of our own history. "That was sad. But we caint hep what our people did back yonder." I suddenly felt defensive of the Rivers' name. Trixie joined in. "Besides, it's ah nice hill, an' we've kep it in tha famlee all these years." Chuck studied this. "I'd like to see it," he said. So, we got on our horses and took Chuck up Piney Hill to show him around.

When we got to our driveway, we saw Roger, Ronnie, and Eddie playing in the woods. They were taking turns riding a green sapling. In the spring, young trees were limber, and you could bend them over to the ground, climb on, and ride them as they tried to straighten themselves back up. They stopped when they saw us and came running to the barn where we were dismounting.

"Hey, guys!" Chuck said. We introduced him, and the boys all started begging to ride his beautiful appaloosa. Chuck was very nice to our brothers and said that he would like to come back and explore some more, but it was getting late, and he needed to head back home. As Chuck rode off down our driveway, Trixie sighed. "He's a real dreamboat."

Easter Sunday dawned bright and beautiful. We were all in the car, ready for church, when Daddy got behind the wheel. "Well, don't my famlee look nice!" he said, smiling. Mama was wearing a yellow skirt suit with pearl buttons. She had bought it last year, and it still looked nice on her. I was wearing the white dress that I wore to the Valentine's dance, and Roger had on a white shirt with a polka-dot bow tie and his blue pants, which I noticed were up to his ankles. Donna was the only one with something new. She was wearing a white sleeveless dress that she had bought to wear underneath her graduation gown.

We parked in our usual spot beneath the oak tree and in front of the cemetery. I got out to meet Trixie and Patty at the water bucket. Trixie had on a new dress that actually fit her. It was a sleeveless pink drop-waist that barely grazed the top of her knee. Her blonde hair was straight and down to her shoulders. It had been rolled and was bouncy and shiny. Trixie had a slip of frosted pink lipstick on. She looked all grown up.

"Wow, Trix!" I exclaimed, "you look so purty!" Patty, who was wearing a purple dress with a white Peter Pan collar, joined in. "Yeah, I've never seen you with lipstick on before!" Trixie took the backside of her hand and wiped her mouth. "Well, it's gone now!" she mumbled.

We decided to go to the ladies' room before church. Even before we opened the door, we could hear Miz Jenkins talking. She was leaned against one of the stall doors talking to Miz Davis. Miz Jenkins stopped talking when we came in. I tried to avoid her gaze as I went into a stall and locked the door. It did not matter.

"Little Miss," Miz Jenkins hollered at me through the door, "if yore grandmaw from *Charlotte* don't like mah dressmakin', she kin come kiss mah foot!" I sighed, but Trixie went into defender mode. "*She* caint hep it! Her grandmaw is jus a hoity-toity!" Miz Davis spoke up, "Now, now. This is the Lord's Day. Let's all remember that!" I finished my business and flushed. "Let's go," I said as I hurriedly washed my hands to leave, Trixie and Patty trailing behind me.

After listening to the preaching about the empty tomb and the real meaning of Easter, we went to Granny and Papa's house to eat dinner and hide eggs. In the car on the way to their house, Mama told us that the preacher and his wife would be there to eat and that we had better be on our best behavior. Roger and I knew that she was not talking to Donna.

We parked down by the barn and went up the back porch and into the kitchen. Granny and Miz Parsons, the preacher's wife, had aprons on and were working quickly back and forth from the countertop to the stove where they were warming up the dinner. We followed Mama and Daddy into the living where they shook hands with Preacher Parsons. I walked over and sat on Papa's knee.

"That's some mighty fine grandkids you've got, Silas," the preacher said. "Wha, these knot heads?" Papa teased. "You wont 'em? I'll sell 'em to ye fer a nickel a piece." Then he laughed really big, which caused him to have a coughing fit. I got down and walked over to the back of the living room, where the big table was set for company.

There was the white tablecloth that Granny used on special occasions. It was set with her best stoneware and the stainless cutlery that we gave her for Christmas a few years back. Mama and Miz Parsons came in with bowls and pans, followed by Granny with a large platter. The women went to and fro until they had all the warmed dinner on the table. Then, Preacher Parsons was asked to say the blessing.

The five of us kids had to stay in the kitchen until everyone at the table was served, including Donna. Trixie's little brothers and Roger began to whine. "Mah stomach thanks my throat's been cut!" said Ronnie, the eight-year-old. Eddie and Roger were both six, and they just faked crying until Mama brought a basket of rolls and told us to eat them and be quiet.

As soon as we were allowed back into the living/dining room, our parents helped us with our plates, and we went back into the kitchen to eat. The three boys gobbled noisily. "Y'all sound like pigs!" Trixie grouched. I ignored them all and enjoyed a good meal of baked ham, cornbread dressing and gravy, green beans, mashed potatoes, and hot rolls.

The desserts had been left on the kitchen counter. When the ladies came in to get dessert for the adults at the table, they made sure to give us ours first. Granny had made a stack of fried dried apple pies, chocolate cake, and a blackberry cobbler. I had some of all of it!

After we had helped to do the dishes, shake out the tablecloth, and put the leftovers in the refrigerator, it was time to hide the eggs. Donna hid them while we stayed in the kitchen and tried to watch her out the window. Finally, she hollered out, "Okay!"

The five of us burst out the kitchen door and off the porch to start hunting the eggs. Everyone was laughing. The adults were sitting in yard chairs underneath the shade trees, watching us. Aunt Brenda had her new camera that she got for Christmas from Uncle Gil. She took pictures of us and of the adults sitting under the trees. My favorite one is of Trixie and me standing beneath Granny's flowering peach tree. That picture always makes me laugh because in it, Trixie looks thirteen, and I look eight!

April 22, 1969
Dear Diary,
We got school pictures back today. My cowlick is sticking up! Grandmother said she wants to take me to get my hair fixed. Ug!
Brownie

Roger and I ran up the driveway. We were going to help Daddy and Papa ditch out the creek where it had been blocked by a beaver dam. I ran as quickly as I could up the back steps and through the house to my bedroom.

"Tina Marie!" Grandmother snapped. "Young ladies do not bolt through the house like a stallion!" Grandmother Davidson had taken to visiting us every afternoon until suppertime. The only time she acknowledged that I existed was when I did something *inappropriate.* I carefully shut the bedroom door and changed into my play clothes.

"Is it warm enough to go barefoot?" I asked Mama when I went back to the kitchen. Grandmother frowned. "Well, it says seventy-eight on the thermometer, but that water will be cold. Where are those old rain boots of yours?" I told Mama that those boots were about two sizes too small. Our family wore our clothing until it was worn out.

"Well, okay then," Mama sighed, "but don't be in that water unless it's absolutely necessary." I heard Grandmother about to protest, so I ran out the backdoor as fast as I could. Daddy was putting a shovel in the bed of the pickup.

"Kin I brang Buster?" Roger asked Daddy. My brother's beagle was jumping around his legs. "No, he'd better stay here. He'll just be in the water carrying on." Daddy opened the driver's side door to get in. Roger leaned down to tell his dog to stay. "We'll be back afore ye know it, Buster. Now, stay!" he said.

Roger and I climbed in the bed of the truck, and that was the first time that I noticed Papa was sitting in the cab. I leaned over the side of the truck bed and hollered into the window at him. "Hey, Papa!" I said.

"Hey, Brownie," Papa replied, "Now, git yer head in and set 'own." I sat down in the bed of the truck beside my brother. We left the driveway with Buster barking and following along behind. There were some mud clods in the bed, and Roger began chucking them at his dog. "Go home, Buster!" Roger commanded, and the dog stopped in the road and laid down, watching his family drive away without him.

When we got to the creek, I took my ratty sneakers off and laid them on the bank so they would not get wet. Whew! Was that water cold! Roger never seemed to notice. He was belly deep, determined to be a big helper to Daddy and Papa.

"Yont me ta yank this un out?" Roger asked, pulling on a pine limb that was sticking out of the little dam. "No, I don't!" Daddy said. "Yore here to haul out whatever needs hauling. Now, here's one ye kin git. Move it over thar and thow it on tha bank." Daddy handed a Roger-sized limb to my brother, and it made him happy. Roger hauled the little limb to the bank and gave it a sling. It landed back in the water, and he had to do it again and again before he actually got it on the bank.

"Whurs Brownie?" Papa asked. "Here I am," I said. "Git this un fer me." Papa handed me a large piece of pine trunk, and I waddled through the creek to the bank and heaved it onto the dry ground. Roger and I did this over and over until the water started to run free again.

"You young 'uns git outta tha water. It's risin'," Daddy said. Roger and I were happy to comply. I walked to the bank with my brother, my arms folded tightly across my chest and my teeth chattering.

"Yore Granny put some ole blankets in the truck fer ye," Papa said. "Ye can dry off with 'em." I walked to the truck and got two blankets out for Roger and me. They were old ones that I had seen throughout my lifetime. They smelled slightly of moth balls.

"Rah-ger!" I shouted. "Come git yer blain-kit!" Roger was busy down at the curve of the creek. I guessed he was playing and did not want to be bothered. I climbed into the truck, put on my sneakers. Then, I wrapped myself in one of the old blankets. After a while, my teeth stopped chattering. It was not long before Papa and Daddy came back to the truck. Daddy put his shovel in the bed and called out to Roger, who came running with something that was dripping mud.

"Looky here!" Roger hollered. "I caught me the biggest terrapin I ever seed!" Roger was covered in mud and smiling big. He was carrying a big turtle.

"Roger! Put that down!" Daddy hollered, "That's not a terrapin! That's a snappin' turtle!" Roger frowned and grumbled, "But I worked real hard to git him! He kept tryin' to crawl into tha bank!" "Hit don't matter!" Papa joined in, "Ifn he bites ye, he'll hold on and won't let go until it thunders!"

Roger's eyes grew wide. "Golly!" he said and immediately dropped the turtle and ran away from it. Papa was bent double laughing. "Yore Mama's gonna pitch a fit when she sees you!" Daddy said to my brother.

We all climbed into the truck and headed home. I pulled my brother close and put my arm around him. He was wet and smelled bad, but I held him anyway. He was shivering, so I tried to get him warm. Roger leaned into me and said, "I could 'a had a snappy turtle, Brownie. Reckin I coulda got my picture in the paper with sumpin like that?"

April 26, 1969
Dear Diary,
Today my Aunt Janelle is getting married. It's about time. My grandmother is makin everybody nervous.
Brownie

You could almost hear our family's collective sigh of relief on the day of Aunt Janelle's wedding. The weeks leading up to the big day were filled with tension and arguments between Grandmother and her youngest daughter. All of us were ready to get it over with.

Grandmother made suggestions for the wedding, which quickly escalated into demands. But Aunt Janelle held her ground. The only concessions she made were to allow her mother to be in charge of the flowers and the photographer. I was relieved. My green dress was saved.

Mama made breakfast and hurried us along so that she could get the dishes done. Linda Brown was going to come over and do Mama, Donna, and my hair. I hated getting my hair cut and had never in my life had it *done*, so I was not looking forward to it.

We arrive at the church by one o'clock. I got out of our family's car feeling like a princess. My hair was cut into a new pixie with the crown of daisies perched on top of my head. Donna had slicked pink lip gloss over my lips. My lime green dress shone electric in the bright spring sunshine. I was met by Aunt Brenda, who was managing Aunt Janelle's wedding.

"They, Lord! You look like a girl in a picture book!" Aunt Brenda gushed as she handed me a basket full of rose petals and daisies. "Trixie is already in the church. I didn't wont her to git sweaty." It was a typical spring day. Warm and humid, with the temperature reaching eighty degrees by afternoon. Off in the distance, clouds were beginning to gather as though the heat of the day might bring in a thunderstorm.

Aunt Brenda had on a new yellow dress with a matching jacket. She looked really nice. "Now, I'll set y'all in yore places when the bride gits here. Lord, I'm so nervous!" Aunt Brenda began to fan herself with half of a paper plate. I left and went to find Trixie.

If you had told me that the girl that I saw sitting on the back pew was my cousin Trixie, I would not have believed you. Trixie looked like a model! Her hair was up in a French twist, and the crown of daisies looked like a halo around her blonde hair. Whisps of hair at the side of her face had been curled, and she was wearing makeup! Her eye shadow was a soft blue, and a smear of mascara set her blue eyes off well. Her skin was flawless with cheek powder and pink frosted lipstick. I have to admit that I was a little jealous.

"Gee, Trix," I said, "you look great!" Trixie had the other half of that paper plate that Aunt Brenda had been fanning with. She held her arm up and fanned her arm pit. "Well, git a good look," she grumped. "Cause when I git home, this frou-frou stuff is a comin' off!" Trixie stood up to straighten the tail of her dress, and I noticed that the darts that Miz Jenkins had put into her bodice really showed off her developing figure.

"And that durned cape is making me hot as blue blazes!" she said. I looked and saw the cape was slung onto the bench and was half hanging off. "If Dennis Dixon could only see you now," I grinned. Trixie grinned back at me. "You shut up," she said jokingly.

The church was full of our family and friends. Preacher Parsons had already come in to speak with the groom and his best man. Dewayne had chosen Deputy Sonny Carson to stand up with him. They both looked very nice.

The altar of the church was filled with baskets of yellow jonquils and daisies. You might have thought it was a funeral if not for the happy banter being volleyed about. A cool breeze was blowing gently through the open windows, and a box fan sat on the floor in the altar to add its coolness for the bride and groom to enjoy. Even so, Trixie complained of being hot.

"Quit grippin'," I scowled. "It'll be over soon, and we can go ride Tom-Tom." That seemed to make Trixie happy. Just then, Aunt Brenda and Mama came up and motioned us off the bench and out the door. "The weddin's about to start," Mama said. I looked at a car that had just driven up and saw Daddy run around to the passenger side to help my beautiful Aunt Janelle out.

"Whoa! She's so pretty!" I said softly. Aunt Janelle had on a full bridal gown with many petticoats beneath it. The lace of the dress went all the way to her throat, and the sleeves came all the way down to her wrists, where they were fastened with pearl buttons. She had on a crown of white roses with a lace and netting train that stretched out in the back two feet past her gown. "Good grief! She's gonna be cooked alive!" Trixie cried.

I looked down to see my little brother standing there in his new blue suit with the green and yellow polka-dot bow tie. He was grinning and trying to get me to see the ring pillow that he had to carry. "My job is impor'nt. Ah gotta carry tha rang!" I smiled at him and nodded.

Aunt Brenda was using the half paper plate to fan Aunt Janelle. "We'd better git started afore the bride faints!" she declared. Mama lined us up in our positions. Trixie and I were first so we could scatter the flower petals. Roger was next with the ring on a pillow. Mama, who was Matron of Honor, followed Roger, then Donna, who was bridesmaid. Aunt Janelle was last with Daddy walking her down the aisle to give her away to Dewayne. It had been planned and practiced for a month.

"Now, where's Maureen?" Aunt Brenda asked. Grandmother Davidson had not been seen since yesterday when she and Aunt Janelle had had a big fight in front of the courthouse. But there she was coming up into the church-yard in a big black sedan. A driver in a smart-looking uniform came around to the passenger side and opened the door for her. Grandmother exited the car like a celebrity.

"That's just like her," Aunt Janelle hissed from beneath her veil. "Always makin' a show!" Mama rubbed her sister's back and said that we should get started as soon as Grandmother was seated.

My grandmother from Charlotte. First Runner-Up in the Miss North Carolina pageant. Member of a bridge club. Going on a *cruise* at the end of the month. My Grandmother Davidson sashayed up to her daughter in a pale lemon-yellow ladies' day suit with matching pill box hat. Grandmother lifted Aunt Janelle's veil and kissed her cheek. "You look beautiful," she said and walked into the church and took her seat.

"Well, I guess she's repented over telling me that my dress made me look like a beached whale!" Aunt Janelle laughed. She took my Daddy's arm, and Trixie and I started up the aisle, tossing petals to the tune of *Oh, Promise Me* played on the church piano by Miz Jenkins. When we got to the altar, Trixie and I sat down on the front row of the left side.

Then came Roger. He was grinning from ear to ear and walking slowly so he would not drop the ring. Then, when my brother got almost up to Dewayne, where he would stand, he saw Granny and tried to wave. The wave jostled the pillow, and the ring flew off, hit the wooden planks of the floor in the altar, and rolled between Dewayne's feet until it fell into the grates of the floor furnace. It made a little tinkling sound beneath the grates before coming to a stop.

We all burst into laughing. Two elderly deacons came running, and both got down on their hands and knees and commenced to trying to get the floor furnace cover off. Finally, a pocketknife was produced, the screws removed, and the lid pulled away and given to the groom to hold. Mr. Stephens was the youngest of the two deacons, so he ran his hand down in the rectangle opening of the floor furnace and tried to find the ring. Meanwhile, Mr. Cross, the elder, leaned over with a flashlight that someone had handed him and was shining a light for Mr. Stephens to see by.

The whole congregation was entranced by this spectacle, and Aunt Janelle, stalled at the church door, was sweating, and getting nervous. You could feel tensions rising. And that is when Mr. Cross, the elder deacon, let it be known that he had eaten his fill of pinto beans and cooked cabbage the night before because he passed gas in such a loud manner that some might have thought that Gabriel had blown his trumpet!

Laughter broke out afresh, and this time the delirium could not be contained. Everyone was laughing, even the pastor. After a while, Mr. Stephens emerged triumphant with the ring safely inside his clenched fist. The grate was restored to its place in the floor, and the wedding could at last commence. Mr. Stephens gave the ring to the groom for safekeeping and told Roger that he could *pretend* that he was giving Dewayne the ring.

"Well, durn!" Roger said loudly. "That thang just sprouted wings and flew away!" This started the people laughing all over again. The preacher was looking at his watch, trying to stop laughing. Dewayne was looking at his bride and snorting with suppressed laughter, and Grandmother Davidson looked like she had just witnessed a hillbilly circus!

After the wedding, which took less than ten minutes, pictures were made, the catered food was eaten, and rice was thrown. Roger, Eddie, and Ronnie, with the help of Deputy Sonny, had tied empty tin cans to the bumper of Dewayne's car and hung streamers all over it. Aunt Janelle and Uncle Dewayne were off on their way to Florida for their honeymoon. All that was left to do was the clean-up.

Trixie and I helped Granny load the last of the catered food into our car. Trixie and I had changed into our play dresses because we were not allowed to wear britches in the meeting house. Granny worked steadily like she would have done at home. Granny closed the trunk of the car and pulled Trixie and me in for a hug. "You girls shore were purty today," she said. "I'uz shore proud of you." It was nice to be held by Granny, so I lingered a little longer than Trixie did. It struck me, and not for the first time, that Granny was so much more different than Grandmother. Not just in her ways and speech, but in her aura. Granny just made you feel comfortable in your own skin.

I walked over to Mama and hugged her around the waist. "Oh, here, Tina, don't you want me to take your daisy crown off?" Mama began pulling out bobbie pins, and finally my hair was freed. I gave my head a good scratching.

"You have an Uncle Dewayne," Mama said to me as she put her arm around my shoulder. I nodded, "Yeah, I have an Uncle Dewayne."

SUMMER, 1969
No. 6

May was how we marked the beginning of summer when I was growing up. Farmers waited until the whip-poorwills started calling to plant their corn. Kids could go barefoot as soon as the butterflies began to appear. Schools let out for summer vacation before the Memorial Day holiday.

The pastures stood ankle-deep in lush green Easter grass. It was a beautiful month in the foothills of the Blue Ridge Mountains. May could also be a tumultuous time when warm fronts hit cold fronts and caused terrible storms. But us kids just looked forward to the end of school so that our wonderful three months of summer could begin.

May 1, 1969
Dear Diary,
Today is our May Day party. I aint never done this before. We spent all day yesterday making May baskets to give away. I got tired just making three!
Brownie

May Day arrived hot and humid. Our teacher had told us the day before that since we would be outside all day for the celebration, girls would be permitted to wear shorts sets to school. Mama and Aunt Brenda were helping at May Day by providing the refreshment table. They had even bought Trixie and me matching shorts sets to wear that were red, white, and blue.

The playground was transformed into a carnival. Miz Carlisle called our class over and had us to join hands and circle around the May Pole. The May Pole. The first one I had ever seen was adorned with pastel crepe paper streamers, which had been attached at the top. Next, some kind of fancy music with violins was played on a record player, and we were shown how to hold the crepe paper streamer and weave in and out to the music.

Johnny got tangled up with Leslie and caused everyone to laugh. Miz Carlisle tried to help us by counting "One, two! One, two!" When we were finished weaving, the May Pole looked like a pink, green, and yellow candy cane. Next were the relay races and three-legged races for prizes. It was so hot that everyone was wringing wet with sweat by the time school was let out. The day had ended up being a very fun day and an event that I would not ever forget. On the way home, the dark clouds had become so thick that it was like midnight outside.

That evening, Trixie and I walked down the hill to give Granny her May Day basket. The baskets were woven out of green and yellow construction paper and lined with pink tissue. Small, wrapped candies and paper flowers filled them. According to tradition, we were supposed to place the baskets on the doorstep, knock on the door, and run, so that the recipient of the baskets would be surprised. But the black clouds were now boiling like in a cauldron of sky. Soon it started to rain, so we ran into Granny's kitchen without thinking of following the May Basket tradition.

Trixie and I ran into Papa and Granny's house and slammed the back screen door. Granny jumped up from her rocker in the living room with a start. "Well, yuns jus beat tha rain," she said and walked back into the living room to sit down. She and Papa had the local news on. The weatherman was talking about bad storms moving in that would spawn tornadoes. Trixie and I never paid bad weather any attention. We had never seen a tornado in our lives, so it was like a myth to us. No big deal.

"Hits fixin to git real bad out thar," Papa said. "I'd better call yer mamas and let 'em know yur hyar." Papa got up and went to the hallway, where his black telephone hung on the wall.

Just then, the wind began to blow really fierce, and I heard a bang against the side of the house. Lightening was cracking, and thunder was booming. "Whada we do!" Trixie asked Granny. "I guess thatuz mah dishpan that hit the house," she said. In summer, she kept her dishpan on a nail to use when she canned. "Let's wait fer Papa." Granny went to the front door and opened it to look out. The wind blew fiercely, and I heard another crash outside against the front porch railing.

"Silas!" Granny hollered over the wailing wind. Papa came running into their little living room. "Hits a tornader!" Papa looked out the front door to confirm what Granny had seen. "Down in tha celler with ye!" he said and pushed Trixie and me by our shoulders to the hallway. Papa pulled the trapdoor up, and Granny handed him a flashlight. He helped us all to scramble down the little ladder that led down into the cellar.

Trixie and I hated the cellar. Sometimes Granny would send us down for a head of cabbage or some turnips, but we never volunteered to go. Papa had seen a black snake down there once.

Papa made sure Granny was seated on the cane-backed chair that he kept down there before he turned off the flashlight. It was pitch black in that cramped space. Just then, we heard a mighty crash and a whirring of wind that sounded like the trains that occasionally passed through Pine Crest.

"Are we gonna git kilt? I'm skeered!" Trixie panicked. I was too scared to say anything. Then there was a thudding crash so loud it sounded like a mountain had fallen on top of the house. After that, it was suddenly quiet. Like the storm had been on tv and someone had turned it off.

"Listen," Papa said. Then he turned the flashlight back on and handed it to Granny. Papa climbed back up the ladder. We waited for him to come back, straining our ears with the effort to hear something. We heard a door slam, and then we heard it again. After that, Papa appeared in the hole above the ladder. "Hit's over," he said. "Yuns kin come up now." "It's over? Are you sure?" Trixie asked. "Yeah" Papa said.

When we were all out of the cellar and back in the living room, we saw what had caused all of the noise. A large pine tree had fallen, taking the front porch with it. A big limb from the pine had crashed through the living room window and tore the window frame all to pieces. I stretched around Papa to see outside. The porch looked like a pile of splinters, and the pine tree had been twisted around and around like a wrung-out wash cloth.

Granny went to the hall and picked up the telephone receiver. "We ain't got no phone," she said. "We ain't got no 'lectricity neither," Papa replied. Papa was putting on his rubber boots. "I'm gonna check it out. You young 'uns stay inside with yer grandmaw," he instructed. Trixie and I sat down on the couch, and Granny sat in her rocker. She did not get excited or go around looking out windows. Granny just sat in her rocking chair and prayed softly. Trixie and I could hear her thanking God for sparing us and praying that the rest of her family and the community were safe.

Clean up around Piney Hill went on for two weeks. Our house and Trixie's were spared, but Daddy's barn had the roof ripped off. Everyone in the community had some form of damage, and all the neighbors pitched in to help one another. A couple of weeks later, when Daddy, Uncle Gil, and Papa had worked to get the damage to Papa and

Granny's house repaired, Granny decided she was going to have the preacher and his wife back over for dinner after church. "Hits ah time to be thankful," she said.

On a hot and humid Sunday in May, we all gathered in at Papa and Granny's house for Sunday dinner. The house was roasting hot, so Granny decided to leave the doors open and let the breeze blow in through the screen doors. She bustled about getting the food on the table, and after the blessing was asked, we all sat down to eat. Papa made a talk about the Lord protecting us during the storms, and everyone said how grateful they were.

That's when Granny's female cat, Barzeelia, being chased by an old tom, came crashing through a hole that was in the kitchen's screen door. The cats raced around the dinner table growling and hissing. Then, Barzeelia decided to jump up on the buffet cabinet and landed right in the middle of Granny's banana pudding! Granny got her broom and beat and shoved the tom cat back out into the yard. In the meantime, Papa was lifting Barzeelia out of the yellow pudding and laughing while he was doing it.

Everyone had a good laugh out of the cat fiasco. Of course, the pudding had to be thrown out, leaving Granny with no dessert to serve, so she put peanut butter and graham crackers on the buffet cabinet for our something sweet.

Preacher Parsons still talks about that to this day. He will say, "Silas. You remember when those cats fell in love and took a bath in Eudora's banana puddin'?"

May 23, 1969
Dear Diary,
Donna graduates tomorrow night. Aunt Janelle and Uncle Dewayne don't come around as often. And I never see Lola anymore!

But good news! TODAY IS THE LAST DAY OF FIFTH GRADE!
Brownie

The last day of school is always a lot of fun. By two-thirty p.m., paper airplanes were zooming through the air, and the racket made by the children's squeals and laughter was deafening. Finally, Miz Carlisle had had enough and told us to pack up our things and stand beside our desks. The bell rang, and off we went into the hallway and onto the bus toward freedom!

I got off the bus and ran straight to the barn to get Tom-Tom. I rode down the road to pick up Trixie at her house, but Trixie was not outside waiting. So, I had to get off Tom-Tom and go inside to get her. I found Trixie sitting in front of the tv with little Becky on her lap. Trixie was frowning.

"Mama says I gotta take care of Becky while she and Grandmaw go to the doctor," she complained. I squatted down in the floor where Becky was playing with blocks. I stacked them up, and she knocked them over with a squeal of delight.

"Well, I gotta go tie Tom-Tom out in the grass then," I said. I patted Becky's head and left to go tie up my horse. But when I got outside, Tom-Tom was not there. I called his name as I ran down Trixie's driveway. He was nowhere to be seen. I ran back inside to tell Trixie and then called Mama.

"Hey!" I said when Mama answered the phone. "I'm at Trixie's! Tom-Tom got loose, and I caint find him!" I thought I was going to start crying. "Well, your Daddy went with Uncle Gil to the co-op. Let me turn my oven down, and I will come help you look." After Mama hung up the phone, I ran back outside to look for my pony.

"Tahm-Tahm!" I cried. I ran to Uncle Gil's pasture to look. Nothing. I ran to Uncle Gil's barn and called out again. That's when I saw Mama coming up the driveway in our car. I hopped in, and we rode all the way down our hill to the main road. Now, where could my horse be?

"Tahm-Tahm!" I hung out of the window while Mama slowly drove past Miz Jenkins' house, Merchant's store, and to the intersection with the main highway. No Tom-Tom. I started to cry. "There now, Tina," Mama said. "He's bound to be *somewhere.*" But all I could imagine was that he was gone from me forever.

Mama and I rode all around Piney Hill looking for Tom-Tom. We road as far as the county line, turned around, and rode all the way to the next community of Walnut Flat. Mama thought it might be a good idea to tell Mr. and Miz. Merchant that my horse was gone, so we stopped at the store. Miz Merchant saw how sad I was and gave me a small bag full of penny candy. But no amount of sweets was going to make me feel better or bring my friend back.

I cried off and on all evening. Mama cajoled me out of my room and into the living room with the family by making chocolate chip cookies. "You'd better hurry, or I'm gonna eat 'em all!" Donna teased. Then, there was a knock at the back door. Daddy went to open it.

"Well, hey there, Boyd!" a cheerful man said. "I've just come to bring your horse back." I jumped up and ran to the door. There at the back screen door, stood Mr. Woods. He lived down at the county line. "Whur'd ye find him?" Daddy asked him. I was straining my eyes to see Tom-Tom. It was already dark, and I could barely see him in the horse trailer behind Mr. Woods' truck.

"Oh, I never found him," Mr. Woods replied. "I stopped in to see Earl Jenkins, and he had him tied up to a fence-post in the yard. Their telephone's out, you know." Daddy said, "No. I didn't know that." Mr. Woods continued. "Yeah.

Anyway, I went to see Earl about picking up my trailer that he'd borrowed. Miz Jenkins was pitchin' one of her hissy fits. Told me your horse had busted a fence and got in with their Shetland pony. You would have already heard about it if her telephone wasn't out." Mr. Woods starting snickering. Daddy laughed, too.

"Well, I appreciate your bringin' him back," Daddy said. "I will make it right with Earl about the fence. Here, let me walk out here with you and take Brownie's pony off your hands. How much do I owe ye?" I went right out the door with Daddy. If anybody was going to see Tom-Tom, it was going to be me. "Aw, you don't owe me a thing," Mr. Woods said. "I was at Earl's to pick up that trailer anyway."

Tom-Tom saw me and whinnied. Mr. Woods let the trailer gate down, and Daddy backed my pony out into the yard. I ran over and grabbed Tom-Tom around the neck and kissed him. "Who's a good buckaroo?" I said. Daddy sat me on top of Tom-Tom, and we waited for Mr. Woods to back out of the driveway.

As I slowly walked Tom-Tom back to his barn and secured him in his stall, I asked Daddy if I could sleep in the stall with my pony. "No. He might step on you," Daddy said. "But he's been excited!" I whined. Daddy shook his head no. I rubbed Tom-Tom and kissed him again before walking back to the house with Daddy. That night, I had sweet dreams about riding Tom-Tom in a giant pasture with the golden sun shining down.

We had just finished breakfast when the back door flung open, and Miz Jenkins came storming in. "Mornin', Edna," Daddy said and calmly took another sip of his coffee. Miz Jenkins stomped over to the table where Daddy was reading the newspaper. She was scowling, and her bottom lip was pouched out.

"What ye gonna do 'bout mah fence?" she demanded. Daddy took another sip of coffee. "What do ye mean?" Daddy asked, looking up at her. Miz Jenkins blew her cheeks out. "That wild hoss of yorn done busted down four feet of mah fence an took two fence posts with it!" Daddy turned around where he could see Miz Jenkins. "Why ye reckin he did that?" Daddy asked innocently.

Miz Jenkins' face began to turn red. "A cause mah Shetland pony is a mare, and she's in season!" Miz Jenkins blurted out. "Earl like ta have never caught that crazy hoss of yorn. I finally had ta put Minnie in tha barn sos Earl could git a halter on 'im." Daddy looked at Miz Jenkins and grinned. "Well, I thank ye fer ketchin' him up. I'll be down to mend yer fence in a little whahl."

Miz Jenkins seemed satisfied and turned around to start for the door. Then she turned back around before she got there. "Earl got that Shetland to plow his garden. We don't need her to git PG," she sniffed. "And one more thang. You really ort ta scrape yore drive. Gittin' up hyhar almost tore Earl's muffler off." Then she stomped out the door and down the backsteps.

"Nice of her to point out the state of our driveway, wasn't it?" Mama said with a grin. Daddy laughed. Roger was yanking on Daddy's shirt sleeve. "Daddy," Roger said. "Yes, son?" Daddy replied. "What's *in season* mean?" Mama and Daddy both laughed. "Oh, it just means that Minnie the Shetland pony is friendly." Mama started laughing and tried to hide it with her hand. Roger just nodded and walked away.

June 1, 1969
Dear Diary,
Tom-Tom ran away, and I thought I was going to die. But we got him back.

Donna graduated high school. She was the Sallytorian.
Brownie

Donna graduated from high school second in her class.
We were all so proud of her. Next week she would be leaving
home to go and live in Atlanta with Miz Glenda Giles. It was
all arranged that Donna would go to work at Rich's Department Store. Donna was registered to start college in the
fall. It would all be a new experience for her.

It was Sunday. Aunt Janelle and Uncle Dewayne came
to church and then back home with us for dinner. Mama
had fried two chickens and made a strawberry shortcake.
I liked seeing how happy my Aunt Janelle was these days.
Marriage seemed to agree with her.

Soon, the conversation turned to Tom-Tom running
away and the cost to repair Mr. Earl's fence. "Aw. That's
just what happens with animals sometimes," Daddy said.
Uncle Dewayne helped himself to gravy. "Well, they should
have had that mare put up," he said. Roger put his drum-
stick down. "Why? Miss Minnie is just friendly," he said.
Daddy burst out laughing and promised to fill Dewayne in
on it later.

After eating our fill, we were all sitting around getting
sleepy. Donna said to Aunt Janelle, "Hey! Let's go down
and see where they have done the grading at the Landers'
place. We can put our feet in the creek!" Aunt Janelle was
all for it and pulled Mama out of her chair to come join us.

It was very hot and humid, and the walk down Piney
Hill made us eager to get to the creek. "They sure have done
a lot," Aunt Janelle said, surveying the place where the
house had burned down. "You'd never know a house had
been there," she said.

Mama nodded. "The plan is to sow a hay field here,"
she said. I nodded, too. I could not wait for hay to come up

on the property that Daddy and Uncle Gil had bought from Miz Lola. I loved to run and jump in the young, green grasses.

Mama continued, "Boyd said he was going to lease the upper pasture to a Mr. Adams for his son's horse." Mama looked at me. "That was his son, Chuck, that you went horseback riding with, wasn't it?" I blushed and sweat prickled underneath my arms. "Whoo-hoo! Who's this Chuck, Brownie? I ain't heard nothin' about you havin' a boyfriend!" I turned away and walked down to the creek. I heard Mama and Aunt Janelle laughing as I walked away.

The weeks passed swiftly, and soon it was the middle of June. Chuck and I had been riding almost every day since his daddy started leasing my daddy's pasture. I got teased a lot by my family, but Chuck and I were just good friends. He was very smart, a lot of which he attributed to reading. His knowledge about things that I did not know made me more interested in books, so I decided to ask Mama if our county had a library. I caught her walking back from the mailbox one day and asked her about it.

"Well, yes," Mama said. "The county library is in Pine Crest. Why?" I explained that I just wanted to read more, and I figured that summer was a good time to start. Mama smiled and said she was proud of me for wanting to read. We made a plan to go to the library on Saturday. "Meanwhile," she said, "we've got a letter from Donna!"

June 17, 1969
Dear Diary,
Mama's takin me to the library Sat.
Got a letter from Donna today. She loves Atlanter. I ain't never been.
Brownie

In letters from Donna, we heard all about her room at Miz Glenda Giles' house. *It's on the second floor! The view out the window is beautiful. I get breakfast and supper, but I have to be on time, or I miss it! Working at Rich's is great. Miz Liebowitz has already assigned me to a register with a counter all my own! I sell lingerie and hosiery.*

Donna also told us about her tour of the all-women's college and how she had been approached by some girls from the upcoming sophomore class to join a sorority when classes begin in September. "Well," Mama beamed. "It sounds like she's found her way." I reminded her that I wanted to find my way too, and that's why I wanted to go to the library. "Brenda and I are going to take all of you kids on Saturday! What a good idea you had, Tina!"

I frowned. I had envisioned only me and my mother going. But if it took all us kids going for me to get some books, I would endure it.

Saturday's trip into Pine Crest was a disaster. When we arrived at Trixie's, we all piled into Aunt Brenda's station wagon for the trip. Trixie, Ronnie, Eddie, Roger, and me. All the way to town, the boys fussed and scuffled in the way-back seat. Trixie and I sat in the backseat and occasionally got our hair pulled or a Wet Willy because we were girls, and "Girls got cooties!" Trixie hauled off and slapped Ronnie, who hollered out to Aunt Brenda, who then shouted, "Don't you make me turn this car around!" But eventually, we got there and parked outside the little square building made of red bricks. The library had maple trees and hedge bushes in front. We were scolded about behaving and keeping our voices at a whisper. Then, we went in.

The building was new and had a faint smell of plaster. "Now, the first thing we need to do is get library cards for everybody," Mama said. Mama and Aunt Janelle were dressed in their Sunday best. They walked up to the counter and told them what we were there for.

"How, sweet!" the lady at the counter said. "I'll get them ready while you choose your books. The elementary school level books are over to the right." We followed the woman's hand gesture, reading the signs taped to the outside of the bookshelves.

"Brenda? Why don't you help the boys, and I'll help the girls," Mama said. Aunt Brenda smacked Eddie on the bottom and nodded to my mother in response. Mama ushered Trixie and me to a long row of books neatly displayed. "Now, y'all just look around and pull out any books you think might interest you." Mama was so happy today. You would think that we had never seen a book before.

I ran my fingers down the spines reading the titles, until I came to one that piqued my interest. Then, I looked into the book to decide if I might want to take it home. The trouble for me was, I wanted *all* of them! I walked over to Mama, who was sitting in an armchair looking at a magazine.

"Well! I've got mine!" I declared and sat twenty-two books on the coffee table in front of Mama. Her eyes widened. "Good gracious! Tina, you can only check-out three books at a time!" I did not know that. Now, how was I going to choose!

"But Mama!" I protested, "It's too hard to pick just three!" Mama smiled and rummaged around in her purse. "I have an idea," she said. "How about you pick three for today, and I will make a list of the others that you found? We will strike them off the list as you return them!" That sounded like a good idea to me, so I chose a book about training your horse, one about wilderness survival for kids, and a book about the space mission.

273

Mama frowned. "Don't you think those last two are, well, more for boys?" I thought for a minute. "No. Chuck talks about those things, and I want to understand him," I said with a shrug. Mama smiled.

When everyone had gathered back together, we walked up to the counter. The nice lady checked out our books and gave each of us our very own laminated library card. Eddie immediately folded his in half and shoved it into the band of his shorts. "No, no!" Aunt Brenda scolded. "Here! Y'all give your library cards to me, and I will keep up with them!" Her children did as they were told, and I handed mine to Mama.

Trixie had a little, thin book about kittens. Ronnie had a book about pirates, Eddie had a book about a little boy with a purple crayon, and Roger had a book about airplanes. I felt proud carrying my three books to the car. I could not wait until we got home so that I could begin reading.

June 25, 1969
Me and Chuck talk about books all the time! I'm so glad Mama got me a library card!
Donna's letter said she will be home for the 4th of July.
Today I strung and broke so many beans that I can hardly hold my pencil.
Brownie

I rode Tom-Tom into the yard to stable him. We had been riding for most of the afternoon. Granny, Papa, Mama, and Aunt Janelle were all sitting underneath the mimosa trees stringing beans. There were two bushel baskets full, and everyone had lined their laps with newspaper stacked with fresh green beans. Mama had an old sheet stretched out on the grass, and the corners weighted down with bricks. The plan was to string the beans and break them into pieces, then put the broken green beans into a dishpan. When the dishpan got full, it would be dumped onto the sheet so that the beans would stay cool.

"We're havin' a party!" Papa cried. "Come join tha fun!" The crowd snickered as I rode to the barn with my horse. After I got Tom-Tom settled, I ran as fast as I could to where my family sat working. I loved to string and break beans! We would laugh, and Papa would tell stories. Tonight, they were listening to the baseball game out of Atlanta on Donna's transistor radio. "Two swings and a miss!" the baseball announcer said.

"Did ye wash the hoss offin yer hands?" Granny asked. I ran to the water hydrant beside the porch steps and washed. When I came back, I got a piece of newspaper and piled beans on top of it. I sat down cross-legged on the grass. "Arg!" Papa grunted, "He allus stracks out! I don' know wha they don' trade 'im!" Granny laughed, "An' ifn he'd a hit it out, ye'd say he-uz the best thang ever!" Mama and Aunt Brenda laughed.

At some time, Mama brought out hot dogs, potato chips, and colas. We ate the salty food with relish and washed it down with the crisp sodas in their icy bottles.

Papa got up and stretched his legs. "Well, I've gotta visit the necessary room," he said and went inside the house to the bathroom. That's when I saw my chance to ask Mama a question that had been bothering me.

"Mama?" I whispered, "What does PG mean?" All eyes turned on me at once. "Where'd you hear that, Tina?" I blushed. "Well, I heard Miz Jenkins say it. She said she didn't want her Shetland pony to be PG!" Granny and Aunt Brenda bent over laughing.

Mama grinned, "That's just short for pregnant," she explained. People in our community were modest. A woman's pregnancy was treated with discretion. *In the family way* or *expecting* were commonly used to explain this female condition. "It is not a nice way to refer to being in the family way, so I don't want you to ever use it. It sounds vulgar." Mama went about breaking beans, all the while trying to stifle laughter.

By the time we had all of the beans strung and broken, lightening bugs were out, and the sad sound of the whip-poorwill was resonating over the pastures. Daddy had even made it home in time to string a few. Now, it was dark, and the air was scented with the perfume of the mimosa trees.

"Thank y'all for helping me. I would still be stringing if it wasn't for y'all!" Mama picked up dirty newspaper and collected up dishpans. Papa walked over to take a brick off the corner of the bedsheet, which was now covered in broken green beans. Tomorrow, Mama would wash the beans and can them.

"Leave that, Dad," my Daddy said. "I'll take it in." Papa straightened up and yawned. "Well, if we're done, we'd better git home, Eudora. I thank I heard mah piller callin' me!" We told everyone good night, and as we started walking into the house, I suddenly missed my brother.

"Where's Roger?" I asked. Mama told me he had gone to spend the night with Ronnie and Eddie. I looked at her. "You mean, Trixie's had to watch her two brothers and mine!" Mama laughed. "Yeah, ain't she lucky!"

July 4, 1969
Dear Diary,
Donna came home last night! We are having Uncle Gil's family, Papa and Granny, Aunt Janelle and Uncle Dewayne, and Miz Lola and Mr. Dave for a cook-out.
Brownie

As always, the Fourth of July was a working day. Daddy and Uncle Gil stayed in the hayfield until five o'clock. By the time Uncle Gil got back to our house with Aunt Brenda, Trixie, and the boys, he and Daddy had both had a bath.

Daddy stood beside the charcoal grill taking up weenies. Mama took the plate and put it on the table made from two sawhorses and a plank. A bowl of baked beans, one of potato salad, and one of slaw sat on the table. Homemade lemonade and sweet tea stood beside Styrofoam cups on the end.

We heard a car honking and looked up to see Dave's fine sedan pull up into the yard. Miz Lola got out and raised the seat for Aunt Janelle to get out of the seat behind her. Dave and Uncle Dewayne were already out and headed for the food. Aunt Janelle ambled over in a pink polka-dot shorts set. Miz Lola wore very short cut-off jeans and a red sleeveless top. She didn't walk so much as glide.

"Hey, y'all!" Aunt Janelle hollered, her hand flapping up and down in a wave. "Have you made the ice cream yet?" Aunt Janelle loved homemade ice cream and did not want to be left out. "No, we've been waiting on you!" Mama chided. There was lots of laughing and folks talking. The boys were playing hide-and-seek in the yard. I looked, and Trixie was sitting in a lounge chair with her plate on her lap. I went over to sit with her.

"Trix! Yore not eatin' enough to keep a bird alive!" I said. Trixie had one plain hot dog and a spoonful of baked beans. She only had water in her cup. "Hey," she said grumpily. "Mama said if I wonted ice cream, I had to eat light." I looked at my cousin. She had become tall and thin since spring. I did not see that she needed to fast like this.

"Well, I don't think she meant fer you ta starve!" I cried. "I'm gonna git you some more!" I sat down my plate and went over to the table. I piled plain weenies, potato salad, and potato chips on a plate and took it to Trixie. She ate it all.

While the men and boys took turns cranking the ice cream freezer, Miz Lola told us that Dave had accepted a job at a law firm in Miami. She was ecstatic.

"Si! We will be near my family! I will be home!" she said happily.

Soon, the ice cream was passed around, and the boys started lighting firecrackers. Spizzz, crack! A burst of color and a whiff of gunpowder. What a happy night!

"You know Trixie," I said to my cousin, "this Fourth of July is definitely different than last year." Trixie nodded. I thought back to all that had happened. How Miz Lola was subjected to prejudice that almost landed her in prison. Now, she was like family to us. How Tater had lived six years of his life, never knowing the love of good parents until Mr. Horace and Miz Avalon had adopted him. Donna had almost become a hippie. Aunt Janelle found love and marriage with Deputy Dewayne Beechum. And I had been kidnapped. It had been quite a year.

I was brought out of my daydream by the sound of a siren blaring. My family had all stood up as a Sheriff's car and an unmarked, black sedan pulled into the driveway. Sheriff Anderson and Deputy Sonny got out and stood beside the car. Two men in black suits got out of the sedan and walked over to our group. The eldest man walked over and stood in front of Lola.

"Lola Lopez Landers Holland?" the man asked our friend. "Si," she replied coolly. "I am Agent Lloyd Velazquez of the FBI," he explained. Then the man pulled out a folded document and handed it to Lola. "I am here to arrest you for the murder of Lonnie Landers on September 2, 1967. You have the right to remain silent..." The rest of what Agent Velazquez had to say did not register with me after he said the word *murder.*

Lola was handcuffed and walked to the black sedan. Her husband, Dave Holland, was telling Lola not to say anything and that he would be following right behind them. Daddy and Uncle Gil had gone over to speak with Sheriff Anderson and Deputy Sonny. Within a matter of minutes, Lola was placed in the sedan, and the men got back inside and drove her away from us.

Mama and Donna were crying and Aunt Janelle, though tearful, had her hands balled up into fists and her jaw set. Trixie and I stood there, dumbfounded. The smell of lit charcoal still clung to the air. For some reason, I made a comparison of the air last year being filled with hateful smoke from the arson and the air this year being filled with the aromas of a cheerful gathering.

The Sheriff held up his hands to request quiet. "Now, I know all y'all believe in Miz Holland and want to support her. But the best way y'all kin do that is to let the law take its full course and stay out of it. I mean, that happened all the way down in Miami, Florida." The Sheriff's remarks brought on a clamoring of voices, all talking at once.

"What evidence do they have?" Daddy shouted above the din. "I don't know, Boyd," Sheriff Anderson replied. "They didn't tell us a thang. Just stormed into the jail and said they needed county assistance in serving a warrant." The Sheriff looked us over and, satisfied that we would not take matters into our own hands, walked to his patrol car to leave.

"Y'all must have known this day would come." Sheriff Anderson said. "I mean, haven't y'all wondered how Lonnie's boat blowed up under mysterious circumstances, just four months after he married her?" The Sheriff let this sink in and then motioned for Deputy Sonny to get in the car. They drove away, leaving the Sheriff's remarks hovering over us like an angry swarm of mosquitoes.

"What are we going to do, Boyd?" Mama sniffled. Daddy was just about to speak when Aunt Janelle said, "Well, I don't know about y'all, but *I'm* goin' to Miami."

We watched as my hot-tempered aunt stomped off and got into her car. Then she was gone in a cloud of red dust, while we were left there to think about another Fourth of July that did not turn out as planned.

Epilogue

It is funny when I think back, all these years later, on this time in my life. I am reminded that you can make plans and see them cancelled or even ruined. The future is not held in your hands. I am reminded that you can be given challenges that test your mettle, teaching you that you are stronger than you ever dreamed. And it is how you handle these challenges that show you just how much you have changed year-by-year.

Reminiscing over life events and the people that were with you through it all is one of the best parts about growing older.

Appreciation

I would like to thank the following people for giving their time and talents to help me make my book what I imagined it could be.

Thank you Farris, Stacy, and Nadine Yawn of Yawn's Publishing for editing and publishing my book. I could never find better friends and colleagues to work with me, answer my never-ending stream of phone calls and emails, and help me produce a book that I am proud of. Y'all are the best!

Thank you to Gudrun Chadwick for all the hard work that you put into creating the beautiful watercolor map that became the cover of my book. You truly made Brownie's world come to life! You are a talented woman and I love and appreciate you so very much.

Acknowledgements

For the author photograph on the book:
The Louis Tonsmeire Studio
Cartersville, Georgia

For the original watercolor map/book cover:
Gudrun Chadwick
Canton, Georgia